# THE COLLECTED STORIES

ALSO BY FRANK TUOHY

NOVELS

*The Animal Game*
*The Warm Nights of January*
*The Ice Saints*

STORIES

*The Admiral and the Nuns*
*Fingers in the Door*
*Live Bait*

BIOGRAPHY

*Yeats*

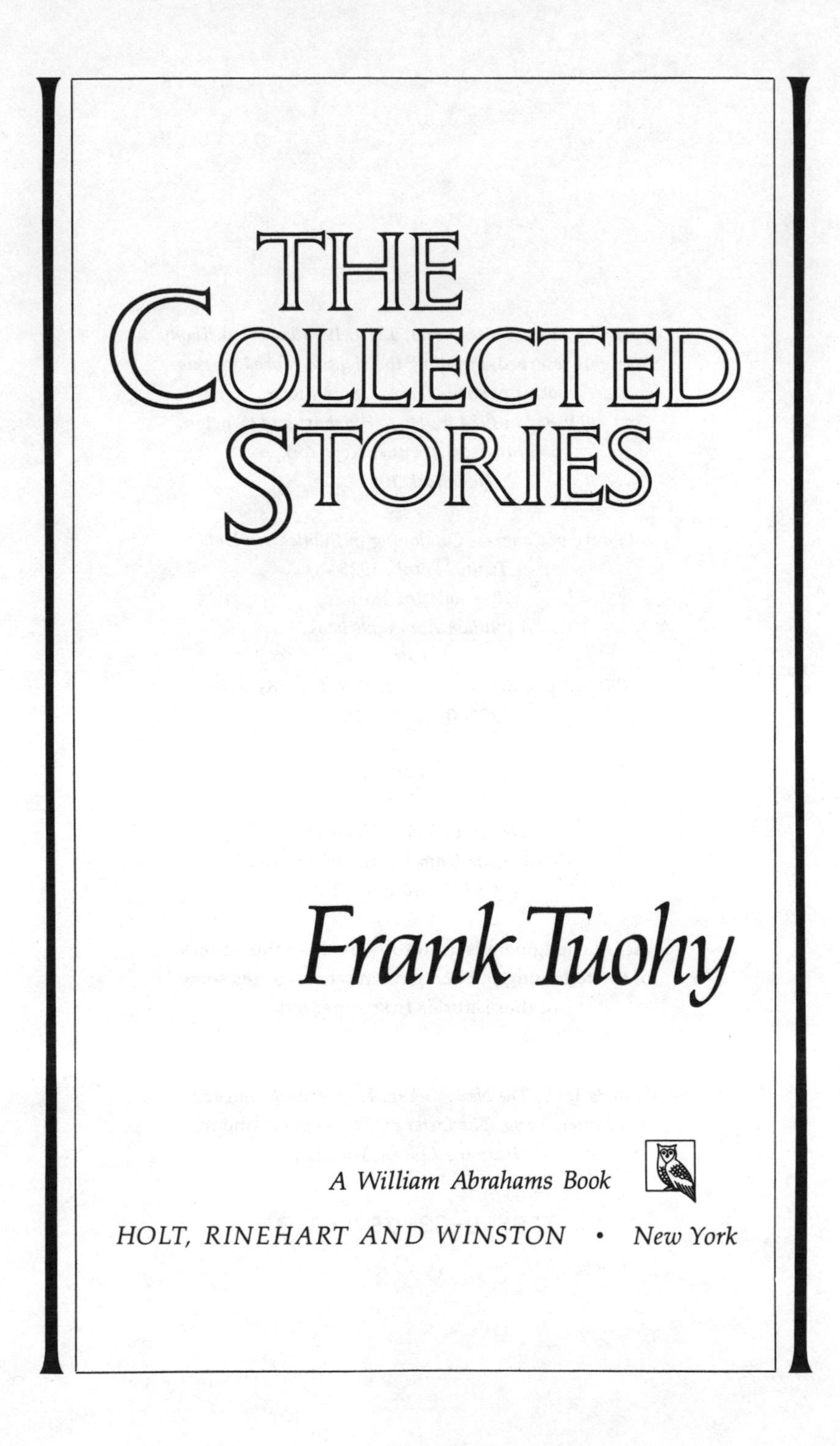

# THE COLLECTED STORIES

## Frank Tuohy

*A William Abrahams Book*

HOLT, RINEHART AND WINSTON • *New York*

*First published in 1984 by Holt, Rinehart and Winston,*
*383 Madison Avenue, New York,*
*New York 10017.*

*Library of Congress Cataloging in Publication Data*
*Tuohy, Frank, 1925–*
*The collected stories.*
*"A William Abrahams book."*
*I. Title.*
*PR6070.U5S87 1984 823'.914 84-3769*
*ISBN 0-03-057648-2*

*First Edition*

*Design by Lucy Albanese*
*Printed in the United States of America*
*1 3 5 7 9 10 8 6 4 2*

Acknowledgment is gratefully made to the editors of the following publications in whose pages some of these stories first appeared:

*Chance, The London Magazine, The Transatlantic Review, Winter's Tales, The New Yorker, The Cornhill Magazine, Encounter, Nova, The Listener, The Times* (London), *Harper's-Queen, Voices.*

ISBN 0-03-057648-2

# Contents

THE
ADMIRAL AND
THE NUNS

# The Admiral and the Nuns

Sitting opposite me, Mrs. Woroszylski broke the string of her necklace. Together the pearls slid down her dress and then raced away in all directions across the floor. I went down after them. Under my shoe, one of them cracked into powder.

"Oh, please don't worry. You are an angel, really. That seems to be nearly the lot. Could you take them back to the man again?"

It was the second occasion she had broken her pearls since I had known her. "They're artificial, you know," she had said the first time. "But good artificial, if you see what I mean. Anyway, not cheap ones. They have great sentimental value for me."

This time, I thought down on the floor, I'll give them to Fernando Ferreira to return to her, together with the bill. Mrs. Woroszylski lived a hundred miles away, in the interior of this South American State. If she needed an excuse to visit me the next time she came to the city, it would be to fetch her pearls.

I did not dislike her but she had problems, and up to now they had always been insoluble. Talking to me she was merely giving them an airing, teasing herself with the idea that she would one day come to a decision about her life.

I had met her first two months ago on an expedition to the industrial settlement where she lived. I had made several journeys like this before: you drove for hours and hours, with the car windows closed, until the red dust began to come up through the floorboards. This had been a country of coffee plantations, but the land was exhausted. Eucalyptus had taken over, the deadest of all living things, whose pharmaceutical smell drives away insects, birds and animals.

Fernando Ferreira, whose car I was traveling in, had been brought up in one of the little yellow-ochre towns that we passed through from time to time. Earlier on, we had stopped for coffee; we stepped out of the car into a fierce pungent stink of mules, and were at once surrounded by beggars, old men in rags, cripples and insect-like children.

Perhaps it was his childhood in a place like this that had given Fernando his taste for formal international friendships. He had attended post-graduate seminars in the United States; he had been, before his marriage, the secretary to a couple of Inter-American congresses; he was an organizer of lectures and study groups, the traveling salesman of a progressive North-Americanized civilization. He was taking me to see the new area of his efforts; he thought the contact would be fruitful, whatever that meant. Fernando was a boring admirable man. He spoke American fluently; whenever he was with me he professed admiration for England, but his heart was not really in it.

He had many redeeming qualities. In conversation, he had shyness and gentleness, and he looked naturally pleasant. He was solid and strong, like a little bull, his eyes were very bright, with the meltingness that comes from Italian blood; his skin was olive and his lips deep carmine. Everything about him was vivid except his mind; he was quite humorless and had no imagination. He was full of Latin prejudices, without having any idea they made nonsense of his smart Americanism.

Fernando was taking me to Santa Ifigenia, an Industrial Development Project (he treasured the words) situated in the barren heart of the State. Its object was to restore life and prosperity to an area devastated by bad husbandry and economic switchbacks. The project differed from others here—such as those of Dunlop,

Volkswagen, Ford—in that it was financed by a group of national businessmen who had made their fortunes under the last dictatorship. Nevertheless, a number of the technicians were foreigners.

Fernando avoided the squalid town of Santa Ifigenia and drove straight out to the colony of houses that had been built for executives and technicians. The houses, designed by a famous architect, were aquarium-like, with glass walls and slanted roofs; they lay in rows under the eucalyptus trees.

Doralice Ferreira, a pretty woman of about twenty-three, was waiting with lunch when we arrived. She was restless and busy, gliding to and fro across the polished floors of the beautifully kept house. During lunch she rarely succeeded in joining us for more than five minutes at a time, and even then she would only sit on the edge of her chair before returning to the kitchen or to help with the children. She took no part in our conversation, and yet it seemed to take place only with her acquiescence, as a part of the whole setting which was under her control.

Afterwards a little Negro girl, wearing a white smock, brought in the two eldest children. In this country you asked about a child "Is it a man or a woman?" To Fernando's enormous pride, these were both men. He took them into his strong arms and began to play with them. The black girl grinned with a strange mature irony, and her eyes slid round in my direction; being forgotten, we could both comfortably watch. Fernando felt the children's shaven heads and their fawn-colored limbs. He kissed the napes of their necks, tickling them with his breath to make them laugh. His own face was beyond laughing. He was so full of delighted pride that he could not adequately contain it; small, half-controlled noises came out of him.

When finally he tore his attention away, his eyes were quite moist. The black girl led the two little boys back to the kitchen.

"Come on," he said, much too loud. "Let's go to the factory."

He was chuckling to himself with pleasure along the way. I watched him respectfully, not wanting to disturb his ecstasy.

While Fernando was escorting me around the factory, I found it difficult, as always, to be adequately responsive: one is always moving off in the wrong direction or taking an interest in things that have not yet been brought up to standard. Besides this, though, I was worried by something that Fernando himself would never have observed: the obvious humiliation in the eyes of the work people as he passed them. We were in a country that had known slavery, almost within living memory; manual labor, even involving the management of complicated machinery, was still an indignity. It was a relief to get to the laboratories, where the atmosphere was easier. Groups of assistants in white coats came up to shake hands and try out their English.

Among them was Stefan Woroszylski. The Ferreiras had already spoken about him; I only remembered this, now that Fernando suggested leaving me with him. Woroszylski was short, with colorless hair and a snouty face. He reminded you of an otter or a pine marten—a benevolent, comic, European animal.

Woroszylski led us on a tour of inspection around his department. Again I did my best, but Fernando was obviously bored, even a little contemptuous. It was a help when he took leave of us.

Woroszylski and I, the two Europeans, were left looking at one another. His eyes were whitish gray, deeply sunken, and friendly in a mad sort of way.

"One moment, please. I go and spend penny."

This somewhat surprising remark showed that he had learned his English from his wife. When he returned he had put away his overall and was wearing a square blue suit and light-brown shoes. For some reason he already seemed twice as real to me as Fernando.

We walked back to the technicians' houses. The air was glassy clear in the evening, and there was a spring feeling as the dew fell onto clumps of sagebrush along the path. The bark of wild dogs came everywhere from the low scrub that covered the surrounding country.

"Later I show you how I shoot."

"Shoot?"

"The wild dogs."

The Woroszylskis' house was a replica of the Ferreiras'. Inside, an attempt had been made to divide the main room into two, with olive-green curtains on runners—in the same way that, in London, people divide up and let off the drawing rooms of gloomy Victorian houses. The curtains were apart, revealing a large drab space of floor on which two children were crawling about, howling.

Mrs. Woroszylski came out of the kitchen. She was a massive young woman, given to large gestures, such as pushing away her hair, which at this time was black, from her forehead with the back of her hand. (During the months I knew her, her hair became streaked with gray, but in retrospect I can see no reason why this should have happened at this time rather than earlier.)

"Oh, hullo," she said. She had gray eyes and a charming smile. Her voice was pure Kensington. "I'm so glad you could come." She gave me a big rough hand. "Do sit down. It's an awful mess, I'm afraid."

Woroszylski had picked up the children and was trying to calm them. They were twins and their personal crises occurred simultaneously. There was also a baby, but it was asleep somewhere else.

Mrs. Woroszylski turned accusingly to her husband. "Darling, that girl has been out since three. I sent her to the store and she never came back. It's the girl we have to look after the children," she said to me rather grandly. "Unfortunately she's in love with one of the factory police. She goes away for hours sometimes," she added in a wondering voice, as though this in itself was extraordinary and mysterious.

Thus in her first remarks to me, Mrs. Woroszylski displayed some of the emotional confusion by which I was afterwards to know her.

The glass door opened to let in a plump sullen girl, with the musky look that comes from Amerindian blood. There was a moment's silence while she inspected myself and Woroszylski. When this was over, she took charge of the children. Woroszylski followed her out of the room.

"Do please sit down. I'm sure Stefan's getting something to drink." She settled herself opposite me and we smiled at each other.

While her husband was outside, she told me how long it was since she had spoken to an Englishman. She had been here two years now; they had arrived just before the twins were born.

"I still get lonely sometimes, not having anyone to talk to. I mean"—she flushed a little—"Stefan's English is not too grand. Besides, he's lucky, there are several Poles here. One of them was married to a Scots girl, but she went back, nearly a year ago now."

The thought of this made us suddenly silent.

"Perhaps I'm just not the pioneering type," she went on. "I was always one for social life, parties and so on. I mean, I was in the Wrens, Daddy was an Admiral—he died five years ago—and so I had lots of fun. I went practically straight from the convent to the Wrens, never a dull moment."

She frowned at the tip of her cigarette, held in an unsteady hand.

"Us girls, we got sort of used to the life—Alex, Malta, Gib—you know. Makes you think, sometimes."

Stefan returned with a bottle of cheap local rum. While he was slicing lemons, he said: "We have one drink and then go to shoot."

"Isn't it cruel!" his wife said. "He tries to get one every night. But of course these pi-dogs they have here are past praying for, aren't they? It's kinder to put them out of their misery."

He handed me the drink, which was deep brown and very strong. "We must go quick or it is too dark."

Woroszylski was carrying a service revolver. We walked into the twilight for about two hundred yards. There was already one star at the top of the sky. The night smell of the "mato" was rank and powerful, and the whole air resounded with the whine of insects: it was like wearing headphones that have gone wrong.

Then a small group of dogs emerged on a path parallel to our own, about forty yards away. They seemed to be following a bitch, but without giving her their entire attention; they stopped to look at us. You can judge your distance from civilization by the state of the dogs: tonight we were very far away.

Woroszylski whistled softly. Two or three of them responded—they still had dim memories of a human world that had rejected them. They advanced a few steps in our direction, then paused, staring at us and licking their lips. Woroszylski brought the revolver up and fired.

He was a good shot. One of the dogs was knocked over stiffly, like a small table upsetting. Then it suddenly became frantically supple, twisting and tearing at itself, and screaming.

"Go on. Finish it off."

Woroszylski shook his head. "Other shot costing too much. Every night one shot and one dog. His friends will kill him for us."

We walked back, until the dog's dying screams became distant and monotonous, like an owl hunting in a far-off valley.

"Did you get one?" Mrs. Woroszylski asked. "Isn't it horrid!" She laughed shyly.

We drank more rum. It made your cheeks burn, and the brains seemed to swell out into the corners of your head.

During our absence Mrs. Woroszylski had brought out her collection of photographs for me to see. I would only be there this evening; consequently she had decided that there was no time to waste. I had to be made aware of her identity, to understand what she was and had been, to admire and perhaps, later, commiserate with her for her present circumstances.

"That's my favorite one of Daddy, taken a year before he died."

"That's brother Mark." The first fifteen at Ampleforth.

"Those are our lot at Gib." Another Admiral, in the middle of a group of younger officers. On the back were signatures, with the nicknames carefuly inserted in brackets and inverted commas. Where were "Bonzo" and "The Twerp" now? Had she loved any of them or had it all gone too quickly and been too jolly for that? She was an Admiral's daughter. What had gone wrong?

"There's Mark again." Ensign, Irish Guards. A waxen, priggish face.

"That's our wedding. Weren't those hats we poor Third Officers had to wear simply dreadful?" Woroszylski was in his Polish Air Force uniform. Perhaps her parents were also present, in another photograph of the wedding. If so, it was not among those shown to me. Indeed, her mother appeared only once, standing in front of the charabanc on a Lourdes pilgrimage. She was short and stout, with fluffy hair; she had that beady Irish look which Anglo-Saxons sometimes mistake for intelligence.

Woroszylski refilled my glass.

"Where you live now?" he asked me. "You have good house?" He sat down on a stool near my chair, staring up with his crazy white eyes. The slight repulsion I had felt after the shooting expedition had by now worn off. Looking at the photographs I had developed a grudging admiration for him—the sort one feels for a favorite cat with a thrush fluttering in its jaws. I imagined him a talented destroyer, in his comic way.

Mrs. Woroszylski said: "Those are the Hendersons, old friends of Mummy's. Miranda Henderson was at the convent with me."

"Oh yes."

"That's taken at Miranda's wedding. She married an Irish peer. She was my best convent friend. I was at the Holy Child, they were evacuated during the War. The nuns were so sweet, some of them still write to me. Of course they hear all about me from Mummy."

"Perhaps I am coming to city next week," Woroszylski said.

"That's fine."

"I show many places to you. You know Bar Metro?"

"No."

"Very good place. I take you there. Very good girls there."

His wife broke in forcefully: "Now I come to think of it, the Hendersons live in Sussex too. Near Horsham. Perhaps you know them?"

"I don't think so." I was getting confused; they were like two children competing for one's attention.

"I go to Bar Metro two times with other Polish fellow."

"Let me think. There are our cousins the Braithwaites who live at Crawley. Perhaps—"

"I'm afraid not."

I very much wanted to help her. To find a mutual acquaintance would be a proof that her world had existed, that it was not a mere illusion which Woroszylski had destroyed.

"We meet very nice girl there. Very clean."

I looked deeply into my glass and then out of the window. The night had come down quickly, and we were terribly far away from anywhere. I remembered the wounded dog and wondered if it had stopped screaming, out there in the darkness.

I turned back to the room.

"All these girls not clean. You must be careful."

Mrs. Woroszylski's evidence had been given, her point was made, and now she began briskly to collect the photographs together. To a certain extent they were both behaving in a way typical of many married couples: they had used the truce provided by a stranger's presence for shock tactics, for outrageous raids into the other's emotional territory. They were both desperately lonely, and neither was capable of helping the other.

I was leaving when she made her request. "You see, I broke the string of my pearls the other day, and there's simply nowhere here to have them restrung." Then she explained about the pearls. As she went on talking about them, I grasped that I was to know that their value was sentimental, and this was not connected with her husband. She must have got some emotional relief out of my possession of this knowledge.

She handed me the little packet. "I'll come and call for them, then, may I?"

"Of course." I had already given them my address.

They both came out on the roadway to say goodbye. I took her rough hand again and saw that her eyes were gleaming with tears. Woroszylski slapped me on the back.

Behind us, the big glass window was lit like a stage. The Woroszylskis went into the house together. Once beyond the door, they walked off in different directions, without looking at one another.

It was only about a hundred yards to the Ferreiras', but on the dark road I felt as though I was walking off the world into emptiness. Then another lit window appeared and I could see Fernando and Doralice sitting inside, like specimens of an entirely different form of life.

Being slightly drunk when I went in, I was perhaps too much aware of tensions. Fernando was not talkative. Doralice was gliding around restlessly, moving with that detached lightness and airiness by which young women sometimes express extreme anger.

"Did you enjoy yourself?" she asked.

"Yes, I did."

She smiled incredulously and padded away, humming a little.

After dinner I found out that I had become contaminated by my visit to the Woroszylskis'; they were an obsession with her.

Doralice giggled. "She is not very intelligent, is she, your friend?"

"Why?"

"She says such foolish things. She talks about her family in England the whole time. Her house is in a terrible state and she does not know how to look after her children. We all laugh at her."

It appeared that the other wives in the settlement, too, had turned against Mrs. Woroszylski. From the way Doralice Ferreira spoke of them, they seemed abnormally united as a group: they were like Arab women combining against a newcomer to the harem—except that here there was no jealousy, only contempt at what they considered to be human failure.

"Her children have no one to play with. We do not allow ours to go there because of the dirt. Also, there is that girl who works there. Did you see her?"

Fernando looked up warningly.

"She's famous. She's been in nearly every house here. Nobody will keep her. Now, of course, everyone says that—"

"No!"

Fernando said nothing more: there was no sign now that a word had left his mouth. But Doralice stopped short, like a radio cut off on a crescendo. She flushed, moving her head from side to side and blinking.

This moment, embarrassing enough to an unwilling spectator, was suddenly made much worse. There was a tapping sound behind me. Fernando opened the glass door, and Barbara Woroszylski came in.

Doralice could not carry it off; she retreated, frankly and immediately, to the kitchen, like a child running away.

Fernando offered Mrs. Woroszylski a cup of coffee. When he went to see about it I guessed that he too was making his escape. Now that we were alone, Barbara looked inquisitively around her. There was something of a district visitor about her, who considered it her right to intrude into the houses of her inferiors.

At last she sat down, smiling. She seemed unconscious of the disturbance she caused.

"I remembered something that I had to tell you."

But what she had remembered was of no immediate importance. I realized that I had become someone she wanted at all costs to involve in her life.

This was at the period of the Queen's Coronation, and a ball was to take place at the British Club in the city. "The Watsons—they're an English family who've a farm up on the Serra beyond Santa Ifigenia—have offered us a lift in their station wagon. I told Stefan we simply mustn't refuse. It's ages and ages since we had such a chance and heaven knows when we'll get it again. Have you got your ticket yet?"

"I'm not going to the ball," I said.

"Oh, you are a spoilsport! Why on earth not? Do come with us, it'll be such fun."

Barbara's naïve excitement was understandable. She had absolutely no idea of what the British Club was like. She assumed it to be a sort of smaller version of Gib or Alex, where there would be people who would understand about Daddy and the Wrens—who would, in fact, accept her in the way she wanted to be accepted as a person.

I did not disillusion her. Fernando had not come back, and her presence here was increasingly awkward. In an effort to end our conversation I invited Stefan and her to dine with me on the night of the ball. I stood up, to show that there was nothing more to say.

"Lovely. How heavenly it is to have something to look forward to." Barbara lay back in her chair, and showed no sign of wanting to leave. She went on, in a different voice: "Anyway, after this I am going to have to live quietly for a long time because I am going to have another baby."

"Congratulations."

Her face saddened. "Oh, I don't know. Stefan doesn't seem to take much interest. Gets you down a bit sometimes, ducks." She lapsed into Kensington cockney.

I sat down again.

"I haven't told Mummy yet," she went on, after puffing at her cigarette for a few moments in an unconvincing manner. "As a matter of fact, Stefan doesn't know this, but Mummy wants to come out here. She longs to see her grandchildren. They're the only ones she's got, as Mark's wife doesn't seem to be going to have any."

"When is she coming?"

"That's just it. Does it sound dreadful?—I don't want her here. Of course I'd love to see Mummy, but somehow, you know, I don't want her to see me like this. If only she'd wait until we get a bit more settled and straightened out. Perhaps they'll give Stefan a wonderful raise or something." Barbara laughed incredulously at herself saying this.

"What are you going to do?"

"I've written to a great friend of the family, Father Beddoes, asking him to discourage her. I felt awful about it, but it was the only thing to do. Her letter came at a bad moment, anyway, because I was being sick all the time with this new baby."

She certainly did not look sick now. The thing she could rely on, I thought, was not her confused childish mind, but the placid strength of her body.

"I haven't mentioned the new baby in my letters, even to the nuns at the convent. Mummy's always going there, and one of them would be bound to ask after me, and then it'd all come out."

She sighed heavily, heartbreakingly. "What a life! Well, up the Navy! Everything'll turn out right in the end. Don't forget about me pearls, ducks, will you?"

Fernando and Doralice came back into the room. A few minutes later we had to use force to break down the silence that had arisen.

Fernando drove me back to the city on the following day. The last part of my visit had not been easy. They were an admirable couple but limited and untransfigured in any way. The risks of savagery in their immediate surroundings had only increased their respectability.

Fernando was much the less spirited of the two. His conventionality was so deeply rooted that he imagined everyone else to be conventional. He accepted every remark one made as a representative national judgment.

Remembering his explosion at dinner the night before, I asked suddenly: "Did your wife mean that Woroszylski had an affair with that girl?"

"You know how women say these things. It is such a small place here, there is a lot of gossip."

But, when dealing with personalities, he was terribly unsure of himself. He hurried back to the subjects he was used to speaking about in English: industrial progress and the raising of the overall economic and cultural levels.

Fernando left me at my house in the city. That afternoon I took Mrs. Woroszylski's necklace to a jeweler. On the day I received it back Stefan Woroszylski himself appeared at my front door, early in the evening.

He came in grinning, delighted at having found me.

"If you are free tonight we go to the town. I show you Bar Metro."

We sat on the balcony and I gave him a gin and tonic. He told me how glad his wife was to have met me. I felt a slight lowering of spirits.

"It is great thing for her. My friends are always speaking with me Polish. She have not friends among the womans in the settlement."

I went to get myself a drink. On returning I saw that Woroszylski's face had altered; he had the expression of someone tackling a serious problem.

"You see, is difficult for Barbara out here. She not used to such peoples. Barbara is from very good English family. Her father was Admiral, very high up. Her mother is of old Irish stock." The way he spoke showed a lingering sense of triumph at the victory of capturing such a woman.

The German restaurant where we had dinner was crowded and hot, and everyone was in their shirt-sleeves. Parties of Central European businessmen, of a tusked, wild-boar-like appearance, were drinking schnapps and beer, and devouring food which, in the tropical climate, was in itself a threat of apoplexy.

"Here is good," Woroszylski said. "At home, is horrible. Barbara is not interested to cook. The servant girl cook very badly."

During dinner he told me his life story, but I can recall only my conception of him gathered from the evening as a whole. In this, he was perpetually the peasant arriving in the great cities of the world and staring uninvolved at the palaces or the skyscrapers. In the same way at the age of eighteen, a representative of innocent bucolic riot, reeking of black soil and thawing snow and dwarf willow, he had first arrived in Cracow, to study at the Technological Institute. In his adventures he transformed the low bars and their bored inhabitants, because he accepted with gratitude what was offered and hankered after nothing better.

Throughout all this we were eating quantities of cabbage, warm ham and pale tightly boiled sausages which, when you cut into them, exploded all over the plate. We dug out knifefuls of mustard, drank beer and talked and stoked food into ourselves until we were as hot as stoves. Then we went out into the neon-burnt darkness and had coffee at a sidewalk café.

An hour later we had worked ourselves down to the level of the Bar Metro. Leda, his previous acquaintance, was on hand. He introduced us, then went to talk to the proprietress, who was a Polish Jewess. Leda and I sat at the table, looking at each other shyly; she was kind, puddingish and almost middle-aged. She said to me in English: "Later my girl friend come. You like her."

"Good."

One of the other women, wearing a dirty apron over transparent black gauze, came up to the table. Leda asked for whisky and I ordered beer for myself and Stefan. She took my hand, laid it on the table and began to tell my fortune. She did the same for Stefan when he came back. We spoke in elementary English. It was very dull and domestic, but Stefan was obviously enjoying himself. He listened to Leda and answered her questions with the greatest attention, although at the same time and in the same voice he was commenting to me on her physical characteristics.

The tone of the conversation could have had no novelty for him. Leda had built herself a little refuge of distinctions, just as Barbara and Doralice Ferreira had. She was not, she kept saying, like some of these girls. She wouldn't have anything to do with some of the customers who came in here. She preferred to talk to foreigners, she said, and funnily enough it was always the foreigners who chose to talk to her.

Fortunately her girl friend did not appear. I wanted to leave, but the two of them refused to let me go, even though it was obvious I had said all I could in the limited vocabulary at our disposal. (This wasn't even basic English, since nearly all the verbs meant the same thing.)

"Look, listen," Stefan said, catching my arm. "I am drunk now. I not say good-bye. How I find truck in the morning?" He looked scared; the city was revenging itself on the lost peasant who had tried to take it too easily. Having accompanied him thus far down the line, I had to answer for his return.

"I'll come and look for you on my way to work," I said.

Leda wrote down the address and room number of her hotel. She returned her white flabby arm to Woroszylski's shoulder. He didn't look riotous any more, but like an animal that has gone off its feed and is ready for hibernation. She would have a hard time keeping him awake.

The following morning I knocked at the door of the hotel bedroom, and she appeared, puffy-eyed but cheerful, in brassiere and pants. At the basin, Stefan was shaving, with a sinister little razor she'd lent him.

She was as chatty as on the evening before. "I like you," she said. "You come see me. Next time you not need stay in bar. I give key, you come back and can sleep till I finish work."

"Thank you."

Stefan was ready. I said good-bye and turned tactfully into the corridor while he settled accounts.

The truck for Santa Ifigenia, loaded up with iron barrels, was waiting at the depot. The air was still misty with early morning and without the dreadful cheap smell of day. Looking at the truck you could think of it as a way of escape, even though you knew that it was moving farther off into the dusty jail of this continent. The drivers got down and shook hands with Stefan and myself.

Suddenly Stefan slapped his pockets. "My lord! Barbara's necklace! I forget, in your house. She have kittens!"

Wren officer's slang was the strongest English at his command. He was appalled, conscience-stricken. I told him not to worry, to say that the necklace was not yet ready. He calmed down but still looked rueful. We all shook hands again, Stefan and the drivers got up into the truck and I was left alone.

I thought that Barbara would now have an excuse to visit me—to fetch her necklace. Two weeks passed and she did not appear; perhaps she was angry with me about my evening with Stefan.

On the night of the Coronation Ball, however, when she arrived at my house, she had decided on a humorous tone.

"You boys seem to have had a whale of a time together. Thank you for looking after Stefan."

By now she must be adult, resigned. Or if she was not, I hoped that a saving heartiness, a cushioning stupidity, kept her safe.

The Woroszylskis had been to their hotel, and Barbara had already changed into a matronly dress of dark-red taffeta. Stefan was wearing a shabby brown suit.

"He hasn't got a dinner jacket. Do you think it matters?"

I gave them both a drink, and delivered her pearls to Barbara.

"It's wonderful to have them back. Have you such a thing as a mirror anywhere?"

"In the bedroom. I'll show you."

Once out in the corridor, she gripped my arm with her strong fingers. "Do watch out for Stefan, will you? He's well away, I'm afraid. The Watsons were really quite nasty about him in the car. Those sort of people make me livid—imagine attacking my own husband in front of me!"

Unobservant, I had already given Stefan an ice-breaking load of gin. I left Barbara and returned to the other room. He seemed all right, but his eyes were glittering and unsteady, like a dog's when it is looking out of a car window.

A few minutes later Barbara came rustling into the room. She spoke in a bright, social voice: "I've got a surprise for you."

Ever since I can remember, these words have possessed a more sudden and violent power to depress than almost any others. I waited for her to go on.

"One of the Watson boys couldn't make it tonight, so I've got his ticket. For you."

"But—"

"Oh, please come. He simply must come, mustn't he, Stefan?" She did not look at her husband when she said this. She stood in front of me, with her fine eyes passionately, almost crazily, imploring.

Under this treatment my resistance crumbled. I went into the bedroom to change.

Barbara was triumphant. We dined at a restaurant—unwisely, for in public there was no way of putting a brake on Stefan. I tried to drink as much of the wine as possible, but he merely called for a second bottle. He insisted on paying for everything and, when I protested, threatened to become violent. Barbara looked in sudden despair at the notes fanned out on the plate.

Later, in the taxi to the club, she appeared to be cheerful. She squeezed my arm tightly. "It's such fun to be going to one of these 'do's' again."

Now that I was wedged beside her, however, it seemed to me that I could feel all her anxieties and desperation fluttering through her body. More and more, she was pushing me into alliance with her.

The British Club was a large, chalet-styled building in the suburbs, encircled by tamarisk hedges and hard tennis courts. The manager of the club, an Austrian called Schneidermann, was standing at the door. I paid off the taxi, while the Woroszylskis went on ahead. When I joined them a sharp altercation was going on in German. A member of the Club Committee came up to see what was happening.

"He hasn't a smoking, Mr. Blackham."

"But it's on the card. In writing. I don't see how—"

"You must let him in," Barbara said. "He's got a ticket. He's paid."

Blackham, a young businessman with a greenish face and social ambitions, was impressed and resentful at Barbara's upper-middle-class voice.

"We are under no obligation," he muttered. "Only British subjects—" Then he caught sight of me in the background. Although he knew me only by sight, he turned with relief. "Who is this lady, old boy?" he whispered.

"She is his wife. They are friends of mine." I introduced him to the Woroszylskis.

There was nothing he could do now. He assumed a jocular patronizing expression. "Well, just this once, Mrs.—er—, I suppose we must waive the rules."

Inside the club there were baize notice boards and the noise and smell of plumbing; its everyday atmosphere reminded you of a cheap private school. Tonight, red, white and blue decorations had been pinned all over the place, and the ballroom itself was decorated with innumerable portraits of the Queen and the Duke of Edinburgh. It was like being inside a stamp album.

Barbara's smiles grew brighter and more desperate. After all the trouble with the Watsons, the strain at dinner and the final indignity of Stefan's entrance, she was suffering from a desolate sense of anti-climax. It was early and only the regular habitués of the Club had arrived, somewhat transformed by the occasion: clusters of wives in long flowered dresses, and works managers wearing shawl-collared white dinner jackets. They would not do for Barbara.

We danced and then went to the bar. There seemed to be nothing that it was not perilous to talk about. Stefan had disappeared but we both felt continually conscious of him, as one senses a wasp buzzing around the room behind the back of one's head.

We danced again. Then fortunately I caught sight of the wife of the British Consul. With her I left Barbara, who was already talking about the Wrens. I returned to the bar. Some time later, I wasn't surprised to see Barbara again alone. She looked completely dejected, though she brightened when I approached her. Stefan had emerged from somewhere and was dancing with an English girl, a child of about seventeen, with blonde fluffy hair.

"Hold me tight," Barbara whispered. "Hold me very tight." She leaned her cheek on mine and her body was pushed against me. I knew she wanted Stefan to see her. We moved near to him but it wasn't any good at all. By the time we had come around the floor again, he and the blonde girl had disappeared.

Barbara let her arms drop. "Oh God, God," she said.

"Are you all right?"

"Yes, it's nothing. I'm sorry." She began striding towards the chairs along the wall. I called after her: "Let's go and have a drink."

"Yes, of course. I want to drink lots and lots. I don't care if I get quite blotto. Up the Navy!"

And so we secured a table in a corner of the bar and sat there trying to blunt our melancholy.

"I say, old boy, your friend seems to have got himself into trouble."

Blackham only brushed past the back of my chair. When he saw that Barbara was sitting with me, he turned scarlet and went away.

"What did he say?" she asked.

"Just a moment. Stay there, will you?"

Blackham had disappeared. I went through dingy lounges and game rooms and corridors. At the end of the glassed-in veranda, among the bamboo chairs, I discovered them. The situation was there waiting, not needing explanation.

The child herself excited pity: colorless, lymphatic, with poor features and fuzzy hair, she had a momentary tropical prettiness. She was sobbing quietly. It was her father, an elderly Welshman working for the State Railways, who had hunted them out.

Woroszylski looked convincingly incredulous and perplexed. He had behaved as he had expected to behave, the peasant who comes to the big city to get drunk and chase women. Blackham and another member of the committee were standing in front of him.

"We must ask you to leave."

"I not go. What for do they have party? She's not so stupid. She know quite well what she is doing." Now that he had been attacked, he hit where it hurt, as he had always done. He had more standards than they had.

"Come on, Stefan. We're on our way." Without my knowing it, Barbara had followed me.

"Who is this lady?" the committee member asked.

"She's his wife," Blackham said.

"Poor girl."

"If you leave us, he'll come," Barbara said. Perhaps she had to speak like this, but I suddenly began to hate her for it. When they had gone we didn't look at each other.

"What dreadful common little people!" Barbara said fiercely. "Really, who on earth do they think they are? I never heard of such a thing. Come on, Stefan, old chap."

Up to now I had seen no legitimate way of dodging what was inevitable: I would be there the day the dam broke. It broke now.

In the Woroszylskis' hotel room Stefan lay asleep. His shoes had been removed and his collar loosened. He smelled of drink and he looked happy.

Since we left the Club Barbara had scarcely spoken. The bossy competence had disappeared: she had remembered that she was dealing, not with a tipsy young midshipman, but her own husband. With each minute her silence had grown in meaning and tension; it was like a load that shifts and settles, increasingly difficult to bear. In the bedroom now she began to shake in a subterranean, earthquaking way.

When she finally broke out it was with the voice of an aggrieved schoolgirl: "It isn't fair! It isn't fair! I've borne so much, so much." She wept into her handkerchief. "You'd think, wouldn't you, that just this once when there was something *I* wanted to do . . ." She returned to her heaving silence.

I waited, looking at the peaceful figure on the bed.

A little later she emerged again. "I've reached the end now. The very end. I'm fed up."

"Let's go down to the bar. We can leave him here."

"Leave him! I should just think we will."

In the hotel bar the air-conditioning hummed faintly. The waiters whispered and yawned.

Barbara calmed down a little. Her social voice reappeared: "I am so sorry to involve you in all this. Poor you, I must say." But she could not keep this up: self-pity was too strong. Her eyes opened wide with drama. "It just so happens I'm desperate. I simply haven't a clue. Most of the time I think I'll leave him, just like that, and go to England with the brats."

I was tired and I was finding Barbara insupportable. It wasn't that she was in the wrong, but she was hopelessly, slothfully inadequate. Her upbringing had provided her with too many retreats into the cozinesses of class and religion. She was far too stupid to realize what a bad wife she was. She was responsible for the squalor of their lives. In her own eyes, however, she was still the best thing that could ever have happened to Stefan; she bemused him with all her chatter of admirals and old stock.

Tonight he had had to endure Barbara's propaganda for the Coronation Ball, then the Watsons, and finally the chill misery of an English official celebration. He had protested, with a certain riotous geniality, and got drunk. And now I had to listen to Barbara saying that she would leave him.

"Why don't you, then?"

"How can I? I haven't a penny. All the money that Daddy left me we spent on the fares coming out here, and in those awful first months when I was pregnant and Stefan hadn't got a job. Now he's got some money he doesn't give me a penny for myself. Did you see what he spent tonight? That happens every time. Just think what it means to me. We'll be starving by the end of the month."

"Your mother might help you."

"No."

"Why not?"

"I could never ask Mummy. Besides, I'd feel I was letting everyone down, Mummy, Mark, the convent, Father Beddoes, everyone. I feel kind of responsible to them all. I'm sure they've all been praying for me such a lot."

She drank some of her whisky and began to look calmer. The worst was over. Indeed, when she spoke again, it seemed that she had completely forgotten the dionysiac peasant who was asleep upstairs.

"Just before I left England I went to see the Mother Superior. She was so sweet. She asked me what language I'd be speaking and so I said 'Portuguese, I suppose,' and she said, 'You are going among people who are especially dear to Our Lady's heart.' She was thinking of Fatima, of course."

"I see."

I got a whisky for myself but Barbara refused a second one. Already the events of the evening were retreating into the past. I knew that Barbara would go on in the same way, and that this was the best thing.

She confirmed this when we were separating that night. "I'm all right, don't you worry about me. I don't know why I'm telling you this but, you see, Mummy never wanted me to marry Stefan. She had great dreams for me, Mummy had. But I married him and I must stay."

"I think you must." After all, she was strong and she would not break down.

"Besides, it is my business to keep him from sin."

Did she believe that she did this, or had she returned to her usual game of lying to herself again?

A few days afterwards a car stopped outside my gate. When I went out Fernando Ferreira was standing on the sidewalk in the sunshine. He had lost his self-contained look. He seemed fluffy, riled, subtly disarranged.

"I have brought you a visitor." He sounded uncomfortable about it. When I saw who was in the car I knew the reason at once. Barbara was thick-skinned. She had the characteristic, perhaps inherited from her Irish mother, of making use of people without considering whether they liked her or not. For her, it had been the most obvious thing in the world to cadge a lift from Fernando.

But he was gravely embarrassed, poor man. The mere idea of driving for three hours alone with somebody's wife must have shaken him by its imprudence. Depositing her at another man's house made it even worse. I guessed he had not known how to refuse. Or he had attempted to refuse in so complicated a fashion that Barbara had grabbed it as an acceptance.

Barbara got out of the car and started towards the house without speaking. I softened a little; she looked desperate.

As usual, Fernando avoided saying anything that might imply comment on the behavior of the English. He kept a dubious look that you see only on the faces of very simple people: preserving the formalities on the edge of civilization required all his concentration. With the Woroszylskis, he wasn't sure on which side civilization lay. We shook hands again, and he drove off, without telling me whether he would fetch Barbara or not.

I had left the front door open. In the sitting room she was already in an armchair. Her head was bowed and her face hidden. She was completely silent. I waited, my heart sinking.

Finally she looked up. Her face was tired but she had not been crying.

"This is it," she said.

My mind raced with speculations. If she had deserted him, what had become of the children? I felt on the defensive. My desire was to be helpful, but at all costs uninvolved. Barbara emotionally on the loose was too ungainly, almost too absurd to be thought about. Yet, several times, I had been afraid that I might somehow be landed with her.

She came to the surface again a few moments later. "It's the end," she said.

"You've left him?"

Barbara stared at me, shocked and horrified. "I could never do that, I'm married to him. Oh, please, please forget everything I said that night. I must have been squiffy."

"Oh." For some reason I was disappointed, and annoyed at myself for having taken her seriously.

"We're going to Poland."

I felt for her now, more deeply than she had previously made it possible for me to do. At this time, in the Coronation year, going to Poland seemed like walking off the edge of the world. For Barbara, tied up in her background and beliefs, it would be even worse.

She drank some of the whisky. "You see I thought it was a sort of threat. I didn't think he would do it. But the other day two men from their Embassy arrived and now—it's all fixed up. In a month's time."

Later, when we were able to talk easily, I tried to believe that Barbara had changed—that she had been punished for her triviality, her insensitivity, her sluttishness. Today she was grave and dignified, as though external powers were forcing her to live seriously. Woroszylski was only an agent to bring this about.

She laughed ruefully. "Mummy'll be able to see her grandchildren, when we're passing through. For the first and last time. Poor Mummy! I hope in a way the ship doesn't stop long in England. I want to go on, right to the end."

Sitting opposite me, Barbara was beginning to show signs of the child she would bear. She looked massively healthy, and only the clumsy movements of her hands showed the strain she felt. Suddenly the string of her necklace snapped, and the pearls went racing all over the floor.

When I had finished looking for them, I realized that in any case she would be visiting me for the last time. She had no more problems to air: they had been solved for her.

"I'll take them to the same place. It's on the street where I work."

"Wonderful. Now I simply must go. I have to go to confession. You see, there isn't an English-speaking priest out there in Santa Ifigenia. Well, thank you for everything. I'll be all right now, don't worry. Up the Navy!"

I accompanied her to the gate and hailed a taxi. We shook hands and suddenly we smiled at each other. I wished her well. She had not changed at all; she was one of those people whom experience leaves untouched. But she was durable. After all, she was an Admiral's daughter.

As for the nuns, I cannot decide whether they had given her the worst, or the best, education in the world.

# *Two Private Lives*

I

When he arrived in San Jaime, the new English Consul revealed himself as a small man with an unnaturally blanched face, and hooded eyes that rarely met yours. The Consul had charm and intelligence, but he also had a habit—it may have been conscious—of making the people he spoke to subtly uncomfortable. However amusing he had been, the discomfort remained. You explained it by saying that he had been too long away from England—he had served in several other countries in this part of the world—and had become "South Americanized." But none of the natives of the country produced this effect.

Andrew Tripp, who had been out here as Press Officer since the war, felt this initial aversion. It was not until later, however, that he really began to hate the Consul. Tripp himself was a big, lethargic man. His Spanish was excellent, but he was only reasonably conscientious at his job.

One morning the Consul and Tripp met by chance at the door of the building. Across the marble vestibule they walked, for some reason in perfect step, to the elevator. When the Consul entered it, the elevator started at once. Had Tripp been alone, three other people would have arrived before Jose pressed the button. Jose was an obstinate old Negro whose hair seemed to have been pushed violently back on his skull, leaving his forehead ridged and corrugated. Tripp and the Consul stood face to face at the back of the lift.

"Buenas dias, señores." Jose was half drunk, and bowed uncertainly.

The Consul muttered something. Tripp smiled, but the Consul avoided his look. Tripp, a whole head and more taller, was wearing a shabby tropical suit; his hair was black, his glasses heavy-rimmed. His dull moon face stared down on to the Consul's circle of scalp and thin sandy hair, and detected an aura of tension and disquiet arising from it.

The lift stopped at the eighth floor. Without looking at either of the secretaries, the Consul muttered "Good morning" and hurried through into the office. The women exchanged significant glances. Nora Blackeby made a wry face and Candida giggled. The two women, however, did not like each other, and their relationship was stagey and false.

Later Candida had to go into Tripp's office. She stood with one hand on the doorjamb.

"Hullo."

"My dear Candida." He shifted his pipe in his mouth and smiled. "How is your lovely self this day?"

Candida stood on one foot for a moment and watched him. She was innocently charmed by his laborious flirtation, which he wisely carried on in English, thus not inviting comparison with the limp young men who pursued her. But today she let her face, which had the vivid animation of a monkey or a parrot, fall into dull seriousness.

"The Consul is wanting to see you, if you are not so busy." The Press Officer spent these hot mornings looking at the ceiling. Perhaps there had been a childish sarcasm in the Consul's message, but Candida served it up stone dead, while staring over Tripp's left shoulder.

The Press Officer put his pipe down on the desk. "OK, sweetie," he said in a fake American voice. "I'll be right along."

He leered at her, and though her face was still dull, she pranced ahead of him with her small bottom swinging.

Going through to the Consul's office, Tripp glanced at Nora

Blackeby. Nora, who was leafing through some files, looked steadily back at him. Poor Nora was perspiring painfully, almost shamefully, through her blouse, and always seemed unhappy. Nora was Rosemary Tripp's greatest friend out here. The hatred she felt for him gave Tripp no sense of discomfort; he was incapable of thinking about a plain woman for any longer than was necessary.

When Tripp entered, the consul immediately dropped his eyes and stared into the blotting paper in front of him. His smooth, well-manicured hands pushed against the edge of the desk, and Tripp knew that, if the Consul released them, they would start trembling violently.

"You were seen with Miss de Paula"—he pronounced the name with an exaggerated English intonation—"in the Boîte of the Hotel Eldorado, last Saturday evening."

"I was there, yes."

The Consul twisted his head nervously without looking up. Tripp waited.

The Consul hoped to get away with saying nothing more. Indeed, there was nothing he need say: the social laws of the country were boringly familiar. They both knew that Candida Marcondes de Paula had been allowed to take the Consulate job because, for middle-class girls, employment with Englishmen was believed to be "safe" in a way that employment with their own countrymen was not. Further, you did not go to a night club with a girl of this class unless you were engaged to her, and then with a chaperon. When, like Tripp, you were publicly known to be married with two children, your pleasures must be private.

But Tripp remembered how the Consul and himself had discussed the possibility of "making" Candida. The Consul, whose pleasures were perforce private by nature, enjoyed such discussions, but for him they were purely academic. Tripp, however, had speculated further. The warmth of the girl's voice, her eyes, the movements of her body, gave signals of a curious intensity; it seemed impossible that these were unconscious or that she could be unaware of their meaning. One day,at a charity dance given by the British community, Tripp had danced with her. It had been a surprising experience.

The Consul began again. "You realize, I suppose, what the consequences of doing such a thing are likely to be?"

One of his hands had twisted free and was quivering on the blotting paper. In the Consul's defense, it must be said that his experience of nonprofessional love was limited. He assumed that the Press Officer had slept with Candida and was prepared to run risks in order to do so again. He was wrong.

"Naturally," Tripp answered. "But in this case—"

"Her father's Secretary to the University—a political appointment."

"I know."

"I don't want to have to get rid of this girl," added the Consul, showing that his courage had finally failed him.

Tripp went back to his desk. In his absence the post, including the weekly magazines from England, had arrived. He ripped off the buff wrappers and unfolded the tender leaves of the Air Editions. Later some journalists would come to question him about England and oil. But the leading articles in the *Economist* danced in front of his eyes. He was not well, his blood was impure and there were some unpleasant spots on the back of his neck.

He threw down the newspapers and looked out of the window, at a view that usually pleased him. Le Corbusier had contributed to the building opposite. Its rows of vanes slanted against the violent sun, and between it and another white wall stood a shining panel of the sea. Posters and cloth streamers for the forthcoming General Election hung limply from the palm trees. Tripp's eyes began to ache and so he clipped dark lenses on to the front of his glasses. Now the world outside was lurid and thunderous; the trees dangled leaves of copper into the dark swamp of the street. Candida, a green girl, swam into sight in front of his desk. "Have you any aspirin?" he asked.

He swallowed two of the pills and she gave him a glass of water, watching him in a motherly way. She was in a better humor now. The Press Officer belched and Candida broke into peals of laughter at the face he made. "Mr. Tripp is so funny, he is so kind and so funny," she used to say. Nora Blackeby seemed not to agree. But there is no doubt that Tripp was kind, to young girls, to his children, even to his wife. The son of a vicar in the Midlands, he had read Romance Languages at Liverpool University and had been prominent in the Union there; the war had brought him a temporary appointment in the Foreign Service, where he had survived till now.

The journalists arrived—small men in white suits, with eyes like oiled black olives. They embraced him, patting him fraternally with both hands on the small of the back. They told him dirty stories about the forthcoming General Election, and in return he informed them, in his good Spanish, of what the British government was doing about Persian oil, and what the London newspapers had commented. He was dogmatic, humorless and extremely dull. Nobody minded at all; they expected mediocrity in government offices, where one owed one's position to a brother or father-in-law. They would never have criticized the incompetent holder of an important job, but rather have admired his cleverness at having obtained it. They all shook hands with Tripp, patted him once more, and then they left.

Just as the Press Officer went out to lunch, he noticed the Consul lurking near the door of his office. He turned his back and waited for the lift, but the Consul came sidling up to him.

"My wife's playing canasta tonight." His dead eyes were alive again. "There's a new place opened near the Calle San Martin. I thought we might give it a try?"

Tripp's house was out in the suburbs, and he did not go home. The Consul reappeared at nightfall, brisk, wearing a fresh suit and carrying a small camera. They dined at an Italian restaurant, with hams and straw-colored bottles of Chianti hanging from the ceiling. The tramline turned a corner outside; the trams were always overloaded at this time of day, with men and boys hanging on to the sides, straddling the buffers or crowded around the driver. But in spite of the turmoil in the streets, the restaurant was a good one. The two Englishmen ate melon with raw ham, and a risotto of oysters and the giant shrimps from the bay; with this they drank a bottle of dry white Chilean wine. An atmosphere of truce hung over them. Neither of them spoke much, and their thoughts also were detached and unemotional. At the end of the meal they divided the bill and the tip precisely in two. The Consul had no change and Tripp said he could wait; but the other called the waiter and procured the exact amount. Then they left, and walked through the twilight towards the Calle San Martin.

Somewhat later, the Press Officer was standing in the upstairs passage of an old house. "The bedroom's not ready yet," the girl said. She wore a curious whore's costume of jacket and knickers, made of blue and crimson silk, something like a pantomime principal boy's. Downstairs the place had been clean-looking, almost smart, but here the walls were leprous, the floor covered with unanalyzable filth. At length a door at the end of the passage was unlocked, and a small old man came out, followed by a woman who was tucking the money between her breasts, while pulling a tight dress down over her hips with her other hand. The passage was silent, save for the rustle of feet on the dirty floor, as the two couples passed one another in the doorway.

Tripp waited while his girl was getting ready. Though he had never been here before, he seemed to know the room already—the low flat bed, the colored photographs of girls on the wall, a sickly plant sprouting in a painted tin. A small lamp was lit on one of the tables, and into its light the mulatto girl skipped. Her skin was greenish-brown and a gold cross dangled between her breasts. Her thick lips, mauve in this light with a pale rim surrounding them, had a submarine softness. He heard the breath sawing in her throat, the counterfeit of passion.

"Well?" the Consul asked, when the two men met once more in the cool air outside.

Tripp nodded. As he always did, he felt an enormous release, a burst of happiness inside him. Latterday moralists—who indicate that lechery is not so much wicked as unsatisfying—ignore the existence of such men as Tripp. For him the experience was always entirely what he wanted, and he was grateful.

"And yours?"

The tired lids hooded the Consul's eyes again. His face was white as paper.

"Attractive," the Consul replied, "but not completely adequate to my purposes."

Tripp hailed a taxi. "El Alhambra," he said. This was a part of their ritual on these evenings.

Two policemen, belted and holstered, stood by the doors of the dance hall; the red glare from inside shone on their white truncheons. Above the *guichet* was a notice: "Men 3 pesos, Couples 50 pesos." The Consul and Tripp bought tickets.

The girls were sitting on sofas around the dance floor. Behind them were the tables crowded with men. From time to time a man would rise, button his coat and go out on to the floor, where he held out a limp hand to one of the girls and pulled her to her feet.

Tripp sat quiet, drinking the thin beer they were obliged to buy, waiting for the touch of desire again. The Consul danced.

Left alone at the table, the Press Officer felt himself disloyal to the truce between them. He watched the little Englishman appearing and disappearing around his blonde partner. All the time the music went on thudding, straining loosely and wetly, like an exposed heart—a chicken's heart hanging on a hook. Thud thud, boom boom, thud thud. All the time, too, a light flickered on and off: the girls were counting the minutes their partners must pay for. Tripp watched the Consul moving neatly around the floor, talking to the girl. He was getting what he wanted. Late middle age found the Consul untrustworthy and without imagination, but he had a rat's pugnacity. He had once been Minister in a small republic farther up the coast; but now Tripp could count among the Consul's merits that he was modest, unambitious, and not nearly a gentleman.

He returned to the table with the girl's telephone number. "She says she will be responsive to anything I suggest. I think that should be quite an interesting contact."

It was after midnight when Tripp took a bus to one of the far suburbs along the bay, where his house was. He got out at the corner of an avenue which was wet and greasy with mist from the sea. Many Germans lived in this quarter, and their dogs—pointers, boxers, and Great Danes with clipped ears—hurled themselves savagely out of the darkness at the wrought-iron gates as he passed.

At the door of his house, tiredness struck the Press Officer suddenly; his bones ached, his body felt dirty and overused. Contributing to his exhaustion was the whole ambiguity of the situation: this morning the Consul had, as it were, declared war on him. From this evening they seemed to know as much about each other as two men are ever likely to know.

He undressed in the bathroom and took a shower. When he went into the bedroom, his wife stirred in half-sleep. The bedside lamp clicked on.

"Oh, Andrew," she yawned. "Wha's time?"

"It's after midnight," he said. The room was hot and there was a smell of the fumigator used to kill vermin.

"I thought you—"

"It was those Americans," he said quickly. "You know what an American party is like." (She could not have known, for he had always pleaded the children as an excuse against taking her anywhere.) "I couldn't get away. I'm fairly tight," he added with a little laugh. "Anything been happening?"

"Nora looked in. I asked her to stay to supper, as you weren't coming back."

A suspicion crossed the Press Officer's mind, as he stood gaunt and naked between the two beds. "What's up with Nora?"

"You see her every day. You ought to know."

"I mean, did anything special bring her here?"

Rosemary Tripp yawned again. She was four months pregnant, and through the thin night gown her breasts were already heavy and maternal.

"Nora's all right," she answered, with the louder voice of one who has just yawned successfully. "Dominic had a temperature."

"Dominic *what*?"

"I said he had a temperature," she replied, glad to have made him worried. "It's all right though."

"How do you mean, all right? You know one can't tell out here." Her job was to look after his children, and he was accusing her of neglecting them.

"It's nothing, I tell you. Dr. Souza Lima came in on his way home and said it was nothing. Now get to bed and don't worry."

But even when she had switched off the light, the Press Officer stood still, holding his pajama top.

## II

Tripp had little work to do, for foreign news had been swept out of the papers by the General Election. He was looking out of the window, when the Consul came quietly into his office one morning.

"Have one of my matches." The Consul watched him, flushed and excited.

The Press Officer took the small silver box suspiciously. He disliked, more than his enmity, the morning friendliness of the other.

As he slid open the matchbox, a whirring sound came from inside. He saw the metal figures of a recumbent man and woman; that of the man was kept in motion by clockwork.

The Consul still watched him. "I thought it might appeal to you."

Tripp felt a whirl of anger and disgust inside him, but it was more at the face across his desk than the box he still held in his hand. "I think it's perfectly revolting," he said.

The other's face darkened. He picked up his offering, pocketed it and left the room.

It was then, perhaps, more than at any other time, that Tripp made an enemy of the Consul. The next time the latter was writing confidentially to his ambassador, he included a recommendation that the Press Officer's contract be terminated at the end of his present tour of duty.

In the outside office Nora was very busy; at this time of year there was always a crowd waiting for visas. Candida was not being helpful. Today she had told them all that she was engaged to her first cousin; she had spent most of the morning telephoning friends.

Candida herself went to Tripp with the news.

"Cor strike me pink," the Press Officer said jovially. She laughed, mystified. He couldn't help looking her up and down with his old look, but she was laughing far away from him now, in a world he had probably never entered. Once he had thought of himself as taking charge of her "éducation sentimentale," but now even he knew that they were not after the same thing. The touch of sensuality in her eyes was transformed. Candida belonged to the aristocracy of desire, a world into which Tripp had never been received.

When Candida had gone, he thought of the approaching evening and what it would bring. For Tripp there were no problems there. He shifted, uncomfortably lecherous, in his chair.

These afternoons Tripp left the Consulate early, diving down into the still-light streets. At twilight there was usually a thunderstorm. Until then, cars with megaphones slowly circled the blocks, shouting political slogans. Leaflets which had been scattered from rooftops and from airplanes collected in drifts in the gutters. As the sky grew darker, squibs were dropped on the pavements; fireworks shot up from the cruising cars to join the blue sparks from the tramwires; loudspeakers began spouting dance tunes, with words adapted to the Christian names of the rival demagogues. Then clouds appeared over the mountains and the sense of tension, of unbearable oppression, increased. Working late on one of these evenings, Nora opened the Consulate windows. A sudden gust blew papers all over the room; banging against the portrait of the Queen and the Duke of Edinburgh, it smashed the glass.

The storm broke. The streets were soon a sea of churning yellow water. Running for shelter, young men bought newspapers which they held up like little roofs to protect their elaborately greased hair. Silent huddled crowds, suddenly shivering with cold, waited in the doorways of bars or under the awnings of cafés.

By the time of the storm, Tripp was usually far from the office. He had found a girl who rented a flat on her own. He could stay there for as long as he wished, have a bath afterwards, look out of the window for the end of the storm, or start again if the rain didn't look like stopping. Curiously enough, the girl was the same responsive one that the Consul had found in El Alhambra. Neither of the two thought it distasteful that she should be passed from one to another like this.

But in spite of this satisfactory situation, Tripp was obsessed by a feeling of impermanence. Things couldn't continue much longer, and Candida's departure, though he believed it made him safer, seemed to lead on to a prospect of continuous change.

Now that she had brought him to the point, Candida's fiancé was in a hurry. He had booked passages to Europe; he wanted her to leave her job and get married at once. The girl, who was dazed with desire, went in to tell the Consul.

He listened to her in silence. His face shone dully; it was as though the effort of thought made him sweat. Looking away from her, he muttered: "We require your services until the end of the month."

Candida, who did not understand him, stood smiling.

"A month's notice before leaving." His voice seemed to slide away from the words.

Then Candida understood, but she lost what English she had. Enraged, she turned from him and hurried out. When Tripp found her later, she was crying into her typewriter. They spoke for once in Spanish. The Press Officer went slowly through into the Consul's office.

"I don't think you have a right to treat your staff like that."

Tripp was as angry as it was possible for him to be, but it made little difference to his appearance. The Consul, however, was shaking. He pulled open a drawer and produced a printed copy of the local labor decrees. He began to read a paragraph aloud in a heavy English accent. The Press Officer waited. They were animals not bred for fighting—one slothful and unenterprising, the other cowardly.

"It's merely a matter of common decency."

"You obviously have a personal interest in the case," the Consul said, staring at the In tray. "The law here entirely justifies me."

"It would be better if you could look at people when you are acting like this." The Press Officer went out.

A day or two later he learnt that his own appointment was to end when he went on leave in three months' time. There was no question of a transfer.

This news, however, happened to find Tripp in a state of inanition, of sensual fatigue. He knew that Nora was watching him, and he was slow to react. Later he would express his detestation of the Consul's conduct; later, too, he would get into contact with his important friends in England, who would arrange a new job for him; later he would tell his wife. For the moment, he did nothing. The General Election took place, the State Governor assumed office amid the whine of motorcycle sirens, the blare of trumpets from Negro cavalry regiments. The girl Tripp visited went away to the capital with one of the new politicians, and his evenings with the Consul began again. They split the bill exactly between them; they were still tersely appreciative after each new adventure.

Then, one evening when his son was running a temperature, the Press Officer went home early. He met Nora Blackeby leaving the house. Indoors he found his wife in tears.

From old experience Tripp was careful not to speak to his wife until she had revealed what it was all about.

"Why didn't you tell me? Everyone knew but me. When Nora mentioned it and I didn't know, I felt such a fool."

"I didn't want to worry you," he said; he glanced down at her—"at this time especially."

"But you knew long ago, Nora said the letter came weeks ago."

"Still, that was why. I didn't want you to worry." He began to believe it himself.

"Worry! What'll happen to me when we do go? The ship in all that hot weather will kill me."

Tripp ignored this. "I'm writing to all the old contacts in London. I'll soon get something fixed up. You know I've never liked working with this Consul, and that makes all the difference in a place like this."

But the next day he confronted Nora in the Consulate: "I particularly didn't want Rosemary to know about this at this time. You know how apt she is to worry."

"Rosemary's been kept in the dark too long. There's a lot of things she ought to know." The effort to be dramatic made Nora flush down to her neck.

The Press Officer did not bother with denials. He felt on bad ground, for a fear had suddenly come to him that he might be in danger of losing, not only his job, but also the custody of his children. He had a vision of Dominic ill, somewhere where he himself could not give orders. When, later that day, the Consul invited him to come to a "special" film show in the garage of a private house, Tripp refused. He went home early and sat silent and gloomy. Rosemary was turning out cupboards in the kitchen. He could offer no comfort, because in some way he could no longer be bothered to comfort himself.

## III

The following day after lunch, when nothing was happening, the Consul said to Tripp: "The new Governor has let them reopen the Calle Fernando Barriga."

The Calle Fernando Barriga—the old "zone"—was right down the social scale when compared with the establishments near the Calle San Martin. Years ago the "zone" had been in the center of the city; then it was banished beyond the railway line. During the last administration it was closed altogether.

"I suggest we go and have a look," the Consul said. "I hear it's lively in the afternoons."

The Consul had his camera hidden under his coat. He and the Press Officer took a tram to one of the big railway stations. After walking a while they came to a wide street. A cordon of police was strung across it, and the men who went through were being examined for lethal weapons. The two Englishmen thought it better to retreat, but at that moment the cordon broke up, and a whole bunch of men went through. The Calle Fernando Barriga was at right angles to this street.

A shuffling line, mostly young and poorly dressed, with one or two old men and a few little boys, moved down one pavement and back up another. The late afternoon sun came into the street, which showed nothing unusual until you were actually in it. The doors and windows facing the pavement were lit by electric light. Each was solid until about three feet from the ground. Then there was a sort of slatted grille, so that the faces of the women behind were crossed with lines, like the horizontal bars of a cage.

Tripp heard a scraping sound behind him. A legless man was

pulling himself along on stumps, gazing up at the windows above. The effect of cages grew stronger as one advanced into the Calle Fernando Barriga. The women's voices were inarticulate and hoarse. Tripp was reminded of the cries of birds of prey—goshawks, vultures, and eagle owls—in their quarters at Regent's Park. In addition, several of the women had their arms held up and their fingers entwined in the slats above their heads; they rocked to and fro, with their faces sullen and silent, while their fat cheeks and arms were shivering, their breasts swinging and shuddering in gaudy half-transparent blouses. There was a mirror on the wall behind each of them.

As the Consul passed, one of the women called out: "I want a man of refinement, a well-educated man." People laughed in the crowd on the pavement. Then a pimp came up from the bedrooms behind and slapped the woman on the buttocks with his cupped hands and shouted an obscene invitation. Beyond there was the chalky whiteness of neon lighting, and more women were sitting on frail gilded chairs.

Tripp was beginning to feel a prurient conflict of emotions. Then he looked at the Consul: he was in his element, neat, bright-eyed with the glow that comes to people who are doing exactly what they want. But the Press Officer could not help understanding the invitations that came through the bars. He could not keep his eyes off the men who detached themselves from the crowd and went, in a moment of horrible isolation, through the doors.

At the cross street, more houses stretched on either side. The sun at this point came through a rose-gold aura made by the snorting steam trains in the railway station. Here several women were threading their way through the crowd. A big Negress, dressed in shiny silk of an asphalt-purplish color and tufted with feathers, turned to smile at the two Englishmen, one hand on her hip.

Then Tripp heard this: a thud, then the splintering shock of something heavy, with glass in it. He looked down and saw the Consul's camera on the sidewalk. The policeman's truncheon was still in his hand; another policeman blew his whistle. The Consul and the Press Officer stood waiting. The Negress had gone.

People began to disappear in the street. A green and white patrol wagon slid up to the curb.

The policeman pushed the Consul into the patrol wagon. He had not yet spoken; his face was shaken more with violence than with fear, and he looked like someone who has had a slight stroke. They asked Tripp if he would get in as well; after a moment's hesitation, the Press Officer climbed in beside the second policeman.

The streets near the station were crowded and the car moved slowly. Torn election posters still hung from the buildings; the walls were still chalked with slogans.

Inside the car no one spoke. The Consul remained silent because he did not wish to betray his nationality; Tripp, whose Spanish was almost perfect, because he could think of nothing to say. Sitting in the rear seat, he looked in front of him at the Consul's head with its scattering of sandy hair, between the round mulatto heads of the policemen. Tripp wondered what the Consul was thinking.

Suddenly, almost physically, he realized that everything in the past months had led up to this moment: the row about Candida, the fuss with Nora and his wife, the letter terminating his appointment. Tripp's hair prickled and his skin crawled. He had only to jettison the Consul now, let him face the Police Court alone, let him show his diplomatic identity card. Thoughts of the power he had been given blazed through Tripp's mind. The last few moments in the car were a triumph for him; his lethargic temperament was aroused, alive as it had not been for years.

And then, as the car drew up in front of the Police Headquarters, he knew that he would not do this. He still had himself to deal with—his own primitive notions of "good form" and "not letting another Englishman down," about whose existence he had never guessed. The Police Headquarters were a castellated fantasy in the style made popular by Sir Walter Scott. There, on the steps between rampant plaster lions, Tripp looked at the Consul again. But the tired papery lids hooded his eyes, and it was impossible to tell what the Consul was thinking.

The building's interior was like a school the day before term begins. There were suitcases, bicycles, even an iron bedstead, in the corridor. An unshaven police officer, with gummy red-rimmed eyes, sat beyond a counter. When he saw him, Tripp knew what he had to do. He leaned over the desk and asked if he could speak to the man in private.

While Tripp and the officer were away, the Consul sat quite still between his guards, and stared at the broken camera on the table in front of him.

After ten minutes the police officer returned with Tripp. He undid the camera and took out the film, then handed the camera back to the Consul.

Everything happened very quickly. The policemen melted away behind the marble columns; the officer went back to his newspaper. All the two Englishmen had to do was to walk across an empty hall and out of the building. Tripp looked down at the Consul. Nevertheless, I've got him, he thought; I've fixed him in a human frame, he'll have to realize that.

They had reached the crowded streets before the Consul spoke. "How much did you have to give him?"

"In the end, two hundred pesos."

The Consul took out his wallet. He searched for a moment, then handed Tripp a hundred-peso note.

"After all, you were in this too," he said.

# *The Matchmakers*

"But, Staszek, only wait until you have seen for yourself. A real beauty, you can tell at once. Just think how delighted your mother will be!"

The speaker was the former Countess Milewska, an elderly woman, heavily made up, wearing a round fur hat, a shabby coat and high-buttoned boots. Her nephew, in a black beret and duffel coat, stood beside her, smoking a stub of cigarette in a glass tube between his discolored teeth.

"My dear Aunt, how on earth shall I broach the subject?"

"It will be easy. I have suggested it already. Besides, she is a charming young woman and everyone tells me your English is quite excellent."

"But these Englishwomen—one cannot speak to them of such subjects, I believe."

"Nonsense!" The old lady chuckled and coughed. "All the English aristocracy are brought up in the country. She will be able to speak frankly about these matters, I assure you."

"Very well, Auntie."

Nevertheless Staszek Kopczinski, a music critic with a precarious position on a large cultural newspaper, was somewhat worried by the old lady's scheme. They were standing together at the top of a slope in one of the parks of the capital city. A quiet luminous afternoon in early spring: you could see right down through the bare branches in the chestnut trees to a little eighteenth-century palace in the hollow. The lake had just been refilled and was crowded with swans. A squad of female gardeners was raking the gravel paths and scraping up the last grayish lumps of snow.

"She takes a walk here almost every afternoon. She promised to come today."

"Is that her?"

Staszek had noticed a young girl approaching down one of the avenues. Her red-blonde hair was loose, her raincoat hanging open and, as she trudged energetically towards them with a curious stride which Staszek at once classified as typical of Englishwomen, she was whistling to herself. She addressed Pani Milewska in schoolroom French, and then turned to him:

"I'm Diana Teffont. You speak English, don't you? I'm so glad; I mean my French is awful and I find these things terribly difficult to discuss in a foreign language."

The girl turned and looked back down the path she had come along. Already Staszek was enchanted by her, by her coloring, as natural as a bird's egg or a leaf, by a naïve gruffness in her voice, and by her clothes. To him, all these things gave her that delightful consistency one finds in people who are completely exotic.

"I wonder where he's got to? It'd be terrible if I'd lost him just at this moment." She frowned, then put two fingers to a childlike mouth and whistled piercingly and with practiced skill. It was all Staszek could do to prevent himself laughing from sheer pleasure.

"Here he comes. He is really rather beautiful, isn't he? Your aunt was simply crazy about him."

A golden cocker spaniel came ambling up the path, snuffling among the last snowdrifts and yelping, though unseriously and with only half his attention, on the trail of a little red squirrel which hoped to be fed by the passers-by.

"Come on, Wooky. You'll never catch one in years."

The girl spoke shyly now, in the way people address dogs when they can think of nothing to say to the human beings around them. The spaniel responded by greeting them all in turn:

first the old lady, whose parchment cheeks were by now quite flushed with excitement, then the girl and the young man.

Staszek bent down and took the dog's wet muzzle in his hand, feeling the soft mouth, delicately frilled like an oyster, and the blunt sleek nose. From under brows that seemed perpetually wrinkled with amorous anxiety, Wooky looked up at him and wriggled all over, lithe and silky, like a dragon made of golden feathers.

"My aunt is quite right. He is very beautiful." He was thinking that the girl and the dog in some way continued and complemented each other, and there was in both, if not the achievement, at least the possibility of being exactly right. This possibility did not exist any more for the women of his own country; anyone who possessed it would seem entirely foreign.

"I think you know my mother has one of the same breed."

"Yes, of course. That's how we got talking the other day." The girl looked down at the dog and went on: "You see, poor old Wooky doesn't have much of a time. He will have to stay here when everyone goes on leave in the summer, because of the quarantine. And he hasn't any friends among other dogs here. The only dogs we ever seem to meet on our walks are boxers and he hates them. Anyway, the books say we ought to get him a wife as soon as possible. He's two years old already and he may get to be no good, besides being frightfully neurotic. His father was a champion, actually."

Staszek felt a twinge of family loyalty. "My mother's bitch is the daughter—can I say that—of two champions. My brother brought the pair of them from Germany in 1945. They are both dead now, of course. My mother is devoted to Liszka—'little fox'—as she calls her. You see, my brother died in prison and Liszka is, may I say, a kind of memorial to him."

"I see." His reference to his own world had embarrassed the girl a little and for moral support she looked back to Wooky, whom the countess was teasing with an aged black kid glove.

"Of course," Staszek went on, "in this country is already danger of inbreeding. This has been the trouble."

The girl nodded. "They really seem made for each other, don't they?"

"If you wish it, Miss Teffont, I shall let you know when Liszka is—er—ready."

"In heat, you mean?"

"Is that the expression? One never learns these things in grammar books."

Diana Teffont laughed. "Why don't you bring her here for walks? I'd love to see her, I simply adore all dogs."

"Unfortunately, my mother does not live here. But I travel down quite regularly and can bring the bitch back on the plane."

"Oh dear, that sounds awfully complicated."

"Only here it may be. You see, I share a room with two friends. But I can keep Liszka there one night, I think."

Now they were walking slowly down one of the avenues towards the road. The old lady, excluded from their conversation, was still chattering to Wooky in French, which she had decided was at least geographically closest to his native tongue. When they reached the place where a small English car was parked, the girl said:

"Look, the thing to do is to be sure and let me know when she goes into heat."

"Of course. You will give me your telephone number, perhaps?"

"I can never remember it. But it's in the book, the British Embassy residence. My uncle's our Ambassador. Actually Wooky's his dog really, only I look after him."

"Liszka will be honored."

Laughing she got into her car and drove off, with Wooky sitting serious and still beside her, his soft breath just blurring the windshield in front of his nose.

"She is so charming, isn't she?"

But Staszek's brow, like the spaniel's, was of the sort that furrows all over with anxiety.

"Why didn't you tell me, Auntie?"

"What about?"

"That she is the Ambassador's niece. Suppose someone sees me taking Liszka to the residence? It'll look bad."

The old lady was troubled but at the same time largely uncomprehending. "Oh dear, your mother would have been so pleased."

"Very well, I'll risk it." He smiled at her. "But what a situation!"

His aunt gave him her cheek to kiss. He helped her up into a tram, which was so full that her small frail bones seemed likely to be crushed by the pressure of the crowd. She went back to her room on the edge of the town, where she lived by giving lessons in French and music.

Staszek was coming out of the newspaper office a week later when the car drew up beside him. The girl looked out of the window and Wooky was dancing up and down on the seat beside her.

"Hello there. Any news of Liszka?"

"Unfortunately not yet. I wrote to my mother and of course she is delighted."

"Can I give you a lift? Wooky wants to say hello again."

"Thank you." He sat beside her with the dog shifting from paw to paw on his knees. A moment later they were both thrown violently forward.

"Get out of the way, idiot!"

A young man in a dirty white raincoat was spread-eagled in front of the car. When he felt that it had stopped, he began affectionately stroking the hood. Wooky watched, grumbling under his breath, through the windshield.

"Go on, beat it!" The drunk lurched away, and the girl grinned at Staszek. "I am sorry, talking to your compatriots like that. But I mean they do behave rather oddly in front of cars, don't they?"

"They see very few, except for taxis and the Zims belonging to Party officials. They get out of the way of those rather quickly."

"They crowd around to look whenever we stop. I used to hope it was me, or even Wooky, but now I know it's just the car. Fascinating though, I must say. In fact I think everything's fascinating here. I do wish I could stay longer."

"You are leaving? But, excuse me, surely the Ambassador has only just arrived?"

"I know, but I'm off to Germany to see my fiancé. We are getting married in two months' time."

Staszek stiffened. "I see. You are marrying a German gentleman?"

"No, of course not. Someone at the Embassy."

There was a momentary awkwardness between them. Then the girl went on, speaking carefully: "What I mean is, it would be better if Liszka got herself ready before I left, because as you can guess Uncle Bill doesn't really have time to concern himself much with Wooky's sex life."

"Well, we must hope for the best. Excuse me, will you stop here?"

When she had driven away, he felt a small angry sense of disappointment. Of course the girl was leaving, she would not want to stay in his ruined country. But how clumsy of him to imagine that she might be marrying a German! He was already in a bad temper as he crossed the sidewalk to his block, and it grew worse when he saw that the concierge had been observing him.

"Miss Teffont?"

"Yes, who is that?"

"Here is Stanislaw Kopczinski."

"I'm afraid I don't know you, do I?" Obviously she had forgotten his name, but her telephone voice, which was that of her class, chilled and depressed him.

"You remember, the man with the friend for Wooky."

"Oh yes."

"Miss Teffont. Liszka is in heat."

"Yes?"

"Do you remember"—he was sweating a little now, as though it was his own case he was pleading—"I said I would bring her up here?"

"Yes, of course."

"But Miss Teffont?" He wiped his brow and wondered why he was getting agitated. "I will bring her around to you? Tomorrow? The next day?"

"If you like."

He heard her replace the receiver. Puzzled as to whether and how he had offended, he lit a cigarette and then telephoned the airline. There was no place on the flight this evening, and so he booked for the next day, and a return for himself and Liszka the day after. At the airport he rang up Miss Teffont again, to tell her when he would be arriving. She was scarcely more affable than before, and this worried him.

On a sunlit early morning Staszek arrived back with Liszka. She was a solid middle-aged spaniel, but when he let her out for a run by the airport she raced around in a circle, yelping with excitement, and soon afterwards two lean mongrels materialized out of the long grass near some sheds. Staszek picked her up quickly and carried her across the asphalt to a taxi.

They had gone about a mile when he saw through the rear window a black car following them. As soon as they reached the outskirts of the city he asked the taxi driver to stop, while he went to a newsstand to buy cigarettes. He looked back. A car had stopped some distance away, but he could not be certain that it was the same one. Liszka whimpered and licked his hand; he wondered if his nervousness was communicating itself to her.

He paid off the taxi outside the Embassy residence. There were several cars parked along the road here and he could see nothing unusual. Diana Teffont was waiting for him; she seemed as cheerful and friendly as ever.

"Jolly good. So this is Liszka."

"She is a little older, of course."

"Well, Wooky can't be choosy, can he? I think it's marvelous of your mother, keeping a dog at all, I mean."

"My mother has always had dogs."

"Well, let's hope she'll have a lot more. We'll leave them together, shall we? Can you come back this afternoon?"

"As you wish."

Staszek went to a coffee shop and then returned to his room to try to work. He found his roommate Andrzej in bed with a cold. Staszek told him about being followed to the residence.

"What do you expect, flirting with Western diplomats?"

Staszek chuckled at this. In fact, he was strangely enlivened by the whole business: it was innocent, a little ridiculous, but he felt both amused and moved by it. In his grown-up life he had not experienced such feelings often. They belonged to the time before his brother's death.

Diana Teffont met him with Liszka. "Everything went absolutely fine." Staszek giggled. "I'll give you both a lift back, if you like. Hop in, Liszka."

Staszek held the bitch on his knee and sank his face on to the round crown of her head. He was pleased and relieved to have her back again. Then he remembered. Trying not to show Miss Teffont, he leaned back as they were turning a corner by the Palace of Culture. A black car, apparently the same one, was following them.

The girl gave a little snort of laughter. "It's all right, he's still there."

"You mean, you know?"

"I've been watching him in the mirror. We get quite used to them. I hope you won't get into trouble, will you? I mean, I tried to shut you up on the telephone, didn't I? They must have thought we were talking in code."

He realized now why she had been so abrupt. "I think I won't have trouble," he said. "We had enough trouble in the past, when my brother was in prison. Nowadays I try to live like a—like a neutral. Do you understand? Of course it is often very difficult."

"I'm sure you're right," the girl said. "It's just that it's so damned sad, isn't it?"

"Yes, it is very sad," he said shortly.

They stopped in front of his building. "I do hope everything goes well. Let me know, won't you?"

"Most certainly I will."

He kissed her hand, and she drove away. But the other car did not follow her. It stayed, and when Staszek took Liszka for a run that evening, it was still there.

He did not see Miss Teffont again, and by the early summer he knew for certain that she had left the country. Walking in the park he caught sight of Wooky, chasing squirrels.

"Wooky!"

The dog cantered up, celebrating him with affectionate bumps of the nose. Staszek crouched down and rubbed the long soft ears, which reminded him of strips of heavy silk tapestry. He stood up when he saw a plain girl with glasses approaching them.

"Excuse me, Wooky and I are old acquaintances. You are perhaps a friend of Miss Teffont?"

The girl flushed. "Oh no. Actually I'm one of the secretaries at the Embassy."

"I see. I am so very glad to see Wooky. He is—how shall I say—the husband of our Liszka. Liszka has three puppies, but all are black, not beautiful like their father."

The girl stood silent and awkward. She is very unattractive, he thought, and obviously in a different social category than Miss Teffont.

"I would like Miss Teffont to know. Perhaps you may tell me her address. She is married, I think. Do you know her married name?"

"I'm sorry." The girl bent down and clipped the lead to the spaniel's collar.

"Please?"

"I'm not going to tell you anything."

"I do not understand. Miss Teffont asked—"

"I said I'm not going to tell you anything. Actually," she went on, with a little superior distaste in her voice, "us girls are not supposed to even talk to you."

Staszek flinched. "I understand now. Please excuse me."

He watched them go away, the girl pulling at the beautiful dog, which kept on looking back at him, up the avenue between the chestnut trees, now heavy with leaves.

Some time later Staszek received an invitation to attend a music festival in Italy. He applied for a passport but was refused. The reason, he heard from a friend of Andrzej's at the Ministry of the Interior, was not only his brother and an unreliable family background; he had also been reported to be in contact with Western diplomats.

# *In the Dark Years*

In the dark years, there was little excitement in the university city. Nobody traveled abroad and there was nothing unexpected happening at home. By 1953, even the decisions of Authority had something foreseen about them. If you belonged to the older generation you might be appalled but you were rarely surprised. Sometimes it seemed that there were no particular instances of conflict any more: everything had become part of a general abstract case. It was as though gods were at large, competing, as in some baroque allegorical painting, in the empty sky above the church towers of the city. On one side the bearded prophet Marx and the mustached dictator; in the center the God the crowds still quietly and humbly worshipped from a hundred churches. Somewhere towards the edge, Venus Anadyomene, she who flourishes on boredom—she ruled even in the inner corridors of the University, stepping in between student and student in the Socialist Youth Organization, between professor and assistant amid the dust of out-of-date libraries, the bundles of invalidated theses.

"Poor Jurek, he seems so worried," Halina Nowalska said to her cousin, the wife of Professor Stankiewicz. "He is still waiting for his appointment to be confirmed."

They were drinking tea in the elder woman's flat, two crowded book-lined rooms near the center of the city.

"These things get delayed in Warsaw, you know. At the Ministry."

"But we have been waiting four months now. That girl in the Russian department heard six weeks ago."

"Darling, you must be patient," the professor's wife said. It was Stankiewicz, one of the older generation that the University still could not dispense with, who had got Nowalski his appointment as lecturer. Now there was nothing more he could do.

But Halina was a large, graceless woman, whose sincerity and innocence might conceivably be dangerous, and this was why the professor's wife even now felt she must look after her.

"He does not tell me, but I think he has enemies."

"Most people do nowadays."

"Political enemies—and my poor Jurek has nothing to do with politics. It's so unfair."

In spite of the older woman's efforts to dissuade her, Halina went away with this idea firmly lodged in her head. In the days that followed she even developed it into a new reason for worshipping her husband. She believed she had created Nowalski (whose parents had been nothing at all, farm workers from the Tatras mountains) to play his part as a martyr for Western culture, classical languages, the world of scholarship.

When they next met she told Mrs. Stankiewicz: "I was right, darling. He is to be summoned before the Disciplinary Committee." She seemed no longer worried and her eyes were blazing with a dotty pride. "We must help him, mustn't we?"

"Zygmunt has done all he can."

"Let me speak to him, darling. I will persuade him."

As his wife had foreseen, Zygmunt Stankiewicz was furious when she told him.

"Politics! How can she go on being taken in by that peasant. She has no brains. I think you'd better disabuse her."

His wife looked frightened at this. "No, Zygmunt. That would kill her. He is all she has." This seemed to be the truth, for the remainder of Halina's family had been taken to Siberia. "Obviously this is just a minor scandal. If it is not, then I agree we must do nothing. We cannot afford the risk."

"Very well." He accepted his wife's judgment on personal relationships without question. "Tell her to get in touch with me."

Professor Stankiewicz was a buoyant and much-respected figure. An outstanding scholar, but a clown, and something of a tease. Everyone was pleased that he existed; almost anyone, except perhaps a woman as blind to other people as Halina Nowalska was, would have felt it unjust to endanger him by too close a contact with other people's problems.

He found the message from Nowalska at his department. She begged him to meet her at the Literary Café, at eleven o'clock.

Nowalska was waiting for him at his usual table. He kissed her hand, and she seized hold of his arm and would not release it.

"Save him, my dear Professor, save him! He means so much to me, so very much."

To the professor, his wife's cousin seemed not only innocent but a little mad: she was like some great schoolgirl who had never learned the rules, who would always talk out of turn. Besides, she was completely unteasable: there was no joke in the world to make her laugh.

"It's the Party, of course."

She spoke in a dramatic tenor that made him wince. He did not look around him immediately, but he straightened his jaw once or twice as though trying to ease a shrunken shirt collar. In this way he could see the people on both sides of him. There was nobody unusual: an old prince who worked in a museum, with his cronies; two social realist painters at present collaborating on a fresco for the Palace of Youth; groups of the grayish men, drab as the city's pigeons, who worked in state trading organizations. Stankiewicz knew them by sight and they knew him. That was the advantage of living in a small city.

"What can I do?"

"I want to know why. Why are they hunting him? I know my man, Professor. He is outside all this, and besides"—here she turned a little pink—"his social background is a good one. I must blame myself perhaps?"

"Surely not."

"My man is outside all politics, I tell you."

"Mightn't that be the trouble?" Stankiewicz asked. In front of that plain face and direct gaze pity and embarrassment overcame him. He agreed with his wife: how could this woman be told the truth? But in the end he promised to have a word with one of the Vice-Rectors "to clarify the situation."

The Vice-Rector, of course, knew everything about what was going on. "He's been having an affair with one of his students. Her father, a Party official from one of the Silesian mining towns—I forget which—made the complaint."

"Is he important?"

"Not particularly. He might make a fuss."

"What would happen?"

"Nothing much. There have been plenty of others before our little Nowalski. The girl has been asked to leave the Students' Hostel."

"What for?"

"The usual thing. They tell me she's very popular."

They both giggled.

"Then, if nothing comes of it, surely there'll be no difficulty about Nowalski's appointment. You see, my wife and Nowalska—"

The Vice-Rector nodded understandingly. There was a moment of sympathy between them, for they both felt that pushing one's own family was a permissible gambit among the strictures of the official world.

A week or two later the Vice-Rector was able to tell Professor Stankiewicz that Magister Nowalski had been confirmed in his position as Latin lecturer.

"And about the girl?"

"There won't be any more trouble there. The Disciplinary Committee has decided to drop the matter. She has got engaged to one of her fellow students."

The professor felt a burden was lifted from his shoulders. Outside he stopped for a moment to pull on his gloves and fur hat. He was standing in the Gothic archway of the main university building, which was built of glazed brick, a surgical dark-red like the plaster model of a liver you might see in a shop window near the Medical Academy. In front of him wet snow was falling among the bare trees, and a small plump figure was approaching up the steps. With a thump of surprise at the coincidence, the professor saw that it was Nowalski.

They had rarely spoken to each other, the academic gulf between them was too vast. On this occasion hats were doffed, bows exchanged, and that was all.

Stankiewicz looked back at the retreating figure with a certain peevishness. As the leading member of an academic and professorial family, he belonged high in perhaps the only hierarchy which, in a People's Democracy, everyone accepts as valid. Had Nowalski's bow been quite low, quite grateful enough? He had a characteristic, which the professor believed he had noticed among peasants, of taking everything you did for him entirely for granted.

Stankiewicz replaced his fur hat more firmly and decided to have nothing more to do with the problems of so insignificant a figure as Lecturer Nowalski.

The "winter break"—a short interval in February which in recent years had taken the place of the abolished Christmas holidays—started a few days later, and Mrs. Stankiewicz sent her husband away while she and their old servant spring-cleaned the flat. He stayed at a university hostel in the mountains, and there he finished a paper for the journal of the Academy of Sciences.

During his absence his wife and the servant worked hard on the two rooms they lived in, dusting the thousands of books, polishing the furniture that remained of his inheritance, rubbing down the marble bust of his grandfather, the bronze one of his uncle, and reviving the green plants that stood in the window between the room and the world outside. Downstairs there was a stinking entrance, with blistered walls adorned with the tattered regulations of the Block Committee. But here the professor and his wife could sit apart, by a stove bursting with heat, among books and photographs of the dead.

That evening while they were drinking tea, Mrs. Stankiewicz said: "Halina has been worrying me again."

"What is it now?"

The professor was resting his head in his hands. He was tired and depressed by his return to the city. In the mountains you could sometimes believe that nothing had happened to the world, but here there was always a sense of oppression, and the possibilities of hurt and disappointment were infinite and eternal. The only person he wanted to protect from them was his wife, who had looked after him so devotedly. He thought of Halina's problems as a drain on his wife's and his own resistance to the viruses of the age.

"She is going around telling people you saved Nowalski from the Party. She says you are a champion of academic freedom."

"Surely no one will believe her?"

The professor was tired, he had spoken without thinking. His question appalled them both so much that it struck them silent.

There was a sense of shock in the room. It was like waking—as they still sometimes did in the early mornings—from a warm dream of childhood into the haggard post-diluvian world. Like most of their generation they both had an image of the past in which nothing whatever had had the power to appall, when terror had been unknown.

"Poor Zygmunt."

The professor still could not speak, and he felt a lurch in his throat as if he were going to be sick. Then he found himself thinking, with grinding hatred, of the plump little figure of Nowalski, sliding into the Gothic university building like a rat into its hole.

Finally, with his voice hardly under control, he said: "You must tell her the truth about that wretch. This cannot go on."

For Mrs. Stankiewicz, Halina was the only connection with the world before the War. Perhaps this was the moment which had never completely arrived, the moment when one said good-bye to the past.

"Yes," she said. "I must tell her."

When Nowalski went to give his first Latin lecture of the new term, he was surprised to find his way to the blackboard blocked by one of his students. Cautiously he assessed the half-known face, the romantic hair, high forehead and mad, frozen eyes: the young man was of the type that seems to have stepped into our time off some barricade of 1848. Nowalski went down while he was still trying to remember the student's name. Falling, he kicked the easel and the whole blackboard collapsed on top of them both, covering them with a cloud of chalk dust.

The lecturer got up at last with a cut lip and an eye that would blossom later. By now the student was in the grip of his fellows, who privately thought him a complete fool for troubling about his girl's reputation. She was sobbing somewhere in the background.

Nowalski arrived home soon after Mrs. Stankiewicz had left. Halina, knowing the truth about him at last, was white and crazy-looking, like the student who had hit him: it was like meeting two members of the same family, one after the other. He received another black eye and went out once more, only to return at nightfall because there was nowhere else for him to go.

Halina was determined to divorce him. She behaved with complete consistency, though at great cost to herself. But they could not leave each other, for the housing crisis made other accommodation impossible to find. Instead they lived in complete silence and ate in public canteens, so that they were often hungry or suffered tortures of indigestion. At night they lay with their lips sealed and only their protesting bodies gurgling plaintively into the silence.

By the time the divorce came through, Halina was already involved with a young physicist who badly needed looking after. This was a great improvement: because he was a physicist it was most unlikely that he would get into trouble with the authorities. He was high on the list for a new flat. While they were waiting for this to be finished, Halina and he slept in the kitchen of his brother's flat. She was happier now than she had ever been. To help him in his career, she persuaded him to join the Party.

Nowalski, left in their old room, could not persuade anyone to join him permanently. Venus had deserted him, and he was not interested in the other deities. Meanwhile Latin became less and less sought after as a subject, and when the academic year was over he returned to school teaching.

Halina never spoke to her cousin now. Was it for not telling her, or for telling her, the truth about Nowalski? Mrs. Stankiewicz felt disproportionately saddened by all these events. Nothing had happened which would not have been possible in a free society. Suspicions, undertones, fear of the Party, all these had existed only in Halina's imagination. Yet to Mrs. Stankiewicz the breakup of the Nowalskis' marriage was still another of those incidents in the dark years that turned the heart to stone.

# A Young Girl

Maria Forrest, the seventeen-year-old daughter of a prominent civil servant, woke out of a crowded dream, with her wrist lying across her mouth.

When she awoke, she felt herself still to be laughing and crying. Hair had fallen over her face; the greasy warm blanket at her mouth smelt of tobacco. Light from the London dawn filtered through a big frosted glass window, and someone was shouting, someone else banging. Beside her, her young man's back was turned to her: his skin was bluish-white with spots of faint discoloration. She touched him with her finger; he did not move. Then she put her arms around him, bare and hot. He grunted "Wozzat?" and went to sleep again with his mouth open. She saw that his lips were parched and blackened with the coarse Algerian wine they had been drinking the night before.

Maria sighed; the loss of her dream still ached inside her. She stepped out onto the floor, shrugging on his overcoat, which up to now had formed part of the bedclothes. The inside buttons were cold on her naked belly. She was angry with the young man for being still asleep, but she did not care to wake him. And so, feeling the dirty floor rough under her feet, she padded to the side of the room. Water sucked and rasped in the tap and then dashed on to her thin hands. She yawned violently and covered her face with cold water, until the day shivered into her mind, over the ache of her lost dream.

On waking, her young man, Witley, discovered that he had a cold. He sat up in bed with his eyes and nose streaming, and swore dully at the empty space in front of him. "I shan't go to school today"—this was the art school where he was a student.

"You must, you must," she said. "I won't be here, I've a lot to do."

"What've you got to do?" he asked, not suspicious, but stupid with sleep and his cold.

She glanced at the drab canvases stacked by the wall. "I'll go and sell some pictures."

She knew this would please him. It was a ritual in their lives. The galleries, though never buying any of the pictures of Witley and his contemporaries, occasionally proffered a vague promise—a mixed show in the summer, even a one-man exhibiton "as soon as we can arrange it." The young men would leave the gallery elated, and buy drinks on the prospect.

Witley was pleased, but he said he would stay in bed for that day. At ten o'clock she left him, and was soon waiting at the tube station with her heavy bundle. Some of Witley's canvases were still wet and were held apart with wooden pins. She and Witley lived so far from "anywhere" that the tube was still a mere slot when it traversed their neighborhood. Maria waited under a blue and gray sky, there was green on the black earth of the cutting, and the wind brought a scent of railwaymen's gardens, a suggestion of lupins and rambler roses. At this time of the morning the platforms were almost empty: a few women, as solitary as she was, had thoughts which made them wander to and fro on the breeze-swept spaces. The girl must just have missed her train, for she had plenty of time to wait and regret her promises to Witley.

When Maria entered the gallery, tired because of the string cutting her hand through the glove, there was nobody to take any notice of her. She was abashed by the silence of the place, with its neutral shades, the thick beige carpet and the natural wooden frames on the drawings that lined the passage immediately before her. She had hitherto only penetrated to these places in a crowd of young men, one or two of whom would have known and despised the owners of the gallery or the limp young men who sold the pictures. Her friends would sneer at the little red spots announcing a sale that appeared singly on the gilded frames, and in twos and threes on the glass of etchings and lithographs.

Today, too, Maria was still intimidated by what she had promised to do. She had heard of this gallery from a different source, from some cousins who had nothing to do with the painters. They knew the owner. He was charming, her cousins had said, a rich and charming young man. She had not told Witley about all this; he would have sneered at what he called "cheating"—the use of personal relationships to further one's ambitions.

Alone then, the young girl walked along the carpet into a high room with top lighting. At a desk a woman was writing with a short, thick fountain pen. There was a silence of some moments, and then the woman said, "Ya-as?" without looking up. Maria knew, however, that the woman had been watching her and had seen the bundle of pictures.

"What is it?" The woman's pen had stopped about a quarter of an inch from the paper. It did not move.

"I've brought some pictures for you to look at."

"Your pictures?"

Maria watched the close-cropped head in front of her, the gruff refugee accent made her want to speak sweetly and reasonably. "No, they're by a friend of mine."

"What is his name?"

"Tom Witley."

"I have never heard of him. Has he exhibited?"

"Yes, he has, once, at the Gonfalon Gallery in Chelsea."

The woman snorted. She pulled the top from her pen and carefully screwed it on. Now she raised her head. When she looked at the girl her face changed a little; it was as if a headlight had flashed across it.

"Well, let me see them."

Maria undid the knotted string, tearing at it nervously, and pulled the pictures off the pins that held them apart. Some of the canvases were still wet, and the paint was very thick. Witley was experimenting a good deal with texture: it swelled out of the canvases in sticky gouts of cobalt and chocolate.

Maria placed the canvases in front of the woman. Her hands trembled, because she believed so much in these pictures that she could not think about them clearly. But the woman did not speak. Maria put out more of the canvases. Once the woman said: "Let me see that one again" and once she said: "Oh, God." She lit a cigarette and inhaled noisily.

After a long silence Maria looked up and their eyes met. Maria received a little shock from the naked look in the woman's eyes. She felt confused and stammered: "Eric Spreyton liked them very much."

"He would." The woman stubbed out her cigarette; she came around the desk and put her hand on Maria's shoulder.

"How old is your friend?"

"He's twenty-nine."

The woman kneaded Maria's shoulder with her hand.

"If he were younger he might have some chance, but as he is so old I do not think so."

"But surely—"

"I am interrupting?" Both women wheeled around guiltily and saw a young man swinging a rolled umbrella. He had approached silently along the thick carpet. He was not tall, but he gave an impression of bulk; he wobbled a little when he moved.

This, then, was her cousin's friend, the owner of the gallery. But before Maria could speak, he had already ignored her, turning a long cold-white face to the other woman.

"I have something important to tell you, Elsa."

They moved away and Maria could watch them. Without lowering his voice, the young man started to give a long and libelous account of a party he had attended on the previous evening. He waved his hand as he spoke or rested it, between his dark suit and camel waistcoat, in the direction of his heart.

While he was speaking, the woman Elsa seemed to shrink and lose importance. He was obviously one of those whom the noise of their own selves deafens to all contact with the outside world. Elsa twisted about, hunching her shoulders, picking up her pen from the desk and dropping it again. Occasionally she laughed sourly at something he had said. The young man was rich, she herself in a subordinate position; she had not been invited to the party he was telling her about, though it was obvious that she knew everyone who had been there. Her face grew sullen and she appeared relieved when he stopped talking.

Now the young man looked around for something to attract his attention.

His pale eyes found Maria and he stared at her for a few moments with a look of dismay. Then he saw Witley's paintings propped against the wall.

"Pictures, fascinating! I love pictures, don't I, Elsa, darling?"

They laughed their way through a private joke. Laughter is a characteristic that imperfectly defines the sexes; their laughs echoed, but the woman's was the deeper in tone. Maria stood still.

He bent down and rummaged among the canvases, then turned to Maria.

"They're so dull, aren't they?"

Elsa had gone back to the desk and was writing.

"Don't you agree with me? Do say." With his umbrella he made a scribbling movement. "I mean this. And this, this passage here, like—like Sutherland or someone. One's so bored with it. I mean, all one's friends have been through that stage, haven't they?"

With his long face looking up at her, Maria could not speak. She had a violent longing to betray, to detach herself from the pictures, to agree with Elsa and this young man, whom she already hated. But she could not speak and her silence affected the young man who, being as nervous as she was, was willing to take it for an unknown superiority.

He glanced at his watch with a stagey gesture. Then he gave the two of them a smile which astonished with its lack of relation to anything that a smile is usually for.

"My dears, I fear I must leave you to your unpleasant task."

His words suggested more than the pictures; they brought the two women into an uncomfortable physical proximity.

He was gone. Elsa trembled with emotion. She had been

humbled in some way which, in her closed world, she imagined the girl must know of.

"No, we can make nothing with these. We only want pictures that are new and original. Please pack them up."

Before his departure the young man had stacked two of the wet canvases face to face. There was a sickening sound as Maria pulled them apart. She did not stop to look at the damage. She tried to adjust the canvases on their pins, and paint smeared her gloves. At last, with the parcel more or less as it had been before, she stood up.

The woman was watching Maria the whole time.

"He is your man, isn't he, this painter?"—she indicated the pictures. "Take my advice, my dear"—the refugee accent became stronger—"and chuck him."

"Really, is that your business?" The girl was aware that her voice sounded ridiculously refined. But the last quarter of an hour had been bad for her and she was almost weeping with anger. Witley would laugh at her, when she told him; she had done it all wrong, of course, used the wrong approach. But she knew that, on this occasion, he would have been even more angry than she was, and equally unsuccessful.

Nevertheless tears were scalding her eyes; when she got out into the street the sun dazzled her. For a moment she stood, alone and hopeless, on the pavement. A line of cars was turning the corner onto Bond Street.

"Taxi! Taxi! Victoria Station, please." In her confusion, it seemed that it was the pictures she hated more than anything, more than the people in the gallery, more than Witley, more than herself.

Now Maria had left the pictures in the luggage office, and held the ticket for them inside the palm of her glove. She walked across into Victoria Street and entered a public house, where she ordered herself a glass of stout and a ham sandwich. As she sipped the stout she said to herself in cockney: "I must feed meself up," and giggled a little. But while she was eating the sandwich she started crying again. The food would not move in her mouth. She pretended to sneeze into a handkerchief.

"Is there anything wrong, miss?" A weak-looking old man was addressing her.

"No, thank you. No, thank you, really."

Perhaps that woman is right, she was thinking, perhaps he isn't any good, which makes it awkward in a way, because I am finally and completely in love with him.

She blew her nose and drank the dark stout.

"Please will you give me some more stout?"

"Right you are, miss. Are you sure there's nothing?"

"No, thank you, thank you so much."

She put another florin down on the bar. The atmosphere of the place pleased her, the smell of beer and meat sandwiches, and the dark mahogany fittings, which were interspersed with little bits of cut and beveled glass. Serious men in mackintoshes stood at the bar, munching carefully as if unsure of their teeth or their ulcers.

It occurred to Maria that her father might come to a pub like this on the days that he did not lunch at his club in St. James's. She had not seen him for two months, and she knew that he was very unhappy. Her brother, who was ten years older than she was, was also in the Civil Service. Her mother had died of cancer six years before.

A few weeks ago a friend of hers, Jeremy Nayland, who was working in an art school, had taken her to a party where she had met Witley. She wanted him at once. He had spent the War in a munitions factory; afterward, he left his wife and children and came south on a government scholarship. He still spoke with a flat West Midlands accent. A lot of women had been his mistresses but they too were older—some of them even remembered the King's Road before the War. They worked as artists' models, on the edge of the films, or in the small theaters around Notting Hill Gate.

These were the women Maria had once envied, but she could only think of Witley as he was now, as he was to her. At the present moment he was probably still in bed. Whenever he was alone his will suffered from paralysis; when she left him, even if he was well, she often returned to find him half-dressed, unshaven, sitting on the edge of the unmade bed. She hated him then; he wanted her to be indifferent, but she could never find indifference in herself.

"I am too young for it," she decided.

Then she thought of Witley's reality to her, his white body, the foul sweater and corduroys he had worn all the time she had known him, and she realized with a new force that she was truly and violently in love with him. She felt she had betrayed him about his pictures; she wondered what made her inclined to trust the judgment of a jealous lesbian in preference to that of her lover. Accusing herself like this, she felt extremely happy.

But Maria told herself that she would not return yet; she need not always keep to him. And, on the top of a bus that was taking her toward Kensington, she thought: "I can go where I like. It does not really matter." In fact, she wanted to go back to the studio all the time.

"Say if you want something to eat, I never have anything."

Maria's sister-in-law, sleepy and pregnant, was curled in a high-backed chair; magazines and knitting lay around her. An Italian servant, who had shown Maria up to the first-floor drawing room, went to fetch another teacup. Maria could hear the faint thud of the children playing on the stairs above.

For a time neither of the two women spoke. However long it was since Pauline had seen you, she never asked you about yourself; she preserved a private disinterest. In the presence of this unnatural lack of curiosity Maria usually felt herself isolated and uncertain, and she guessed that Pauline still considered her a mere child. But today this lack of curiosity was what she wanted.

Today, also, the room itself, with a picture believed to be by Nattier beside the chimney piece, the pile of books, still untouched, that the brother had bought at the Times Book Club—all these affected Maria with a pang like jealousy. Her brother had a future, he had bought his house, he was putting down a pipe of port, his children were to go to good schools. He was making an attempt at confidence, an attempt at the world of their father. If there was any good in Maria's life with Witley, it was only in their own selves and their being together; perhaps, as she believed, it was in Witley's paintings. There was a time when poverty and oysters went together; nowadays, however, nothing good goes with poverty.

As she drank the tea, Maria thought of the stewed brew, treacly with sugar and condensed milk, that they used to drink when Witley was painting her. They had no money for the gas meter, and she would stagger from the model's throne numb after an hour's session. She shrugged on his overcoat, as she did in the mornings, and gulped the tea and felt it like sleep in her body. A moment later Witley would drive her back to the throne again for another hour. He was full of energy then and he seemed to derive it all from her. She knew she had never been happier than at these times.

The China tea that Pauline gave her had the delicate taste of grass in summer.

Pauline's children came in and looked at Maria. "Hello, Caroline. Hello, Anthea."

The younger child put its face, like a small white moon, close to Maria and stared hard at her, liking her calmness, studying her clothes carefully and fingering her belt and necklace. But Anthea, the elder, was paralyzed by self-consciousness. Even in her moments of stillness she became twisted with affectation; she moved as though anything she touched might turn out to be red hot. From the other side of the room her mother watched her uneasily, ready at any moment to call out.

The child approached a small table, where a wine-glass stood, holding a single rose.

"Now, don't go near there," Pauline shouted. "You'll only upset it." She turned with a helpless expression to Maria. "It's always like this on Nanny's afternoon out. Anthea! Stop it, do as I tell you, stop it!"

But the child ran mockingly away from her. In a second the table clattered to the floor. The child looked at the broken glass and rose petals and shrieked with anger. Pauline went to her.

"Look what you've done! I told you that would happen!"

The child's arms flailed out wildly, hitting the mother in the soft parts of her rounded body. Caroline, the second child, watched in silence.

Pauline rang the bell and the Italian reappeared. Without

waiting for instructions (such incidents had obviously happened before) she picked up Anthea, who had by now screamed herself into the ominous silence of hysteria. The younger child followed, still silent and watching, her fingers gripping onto the servant's skirt.

Flushed and unhappy, Pauline sat down again and pushed a strand of hair back from her face. Through the wall they could hear Anthea start to scream again. Maria was not meaning to comment in her thoughts. "When I have children, things'll be better"—as she began in this way to herself, she knew that things for her were likely to be worse. The thought of what must happen, of how much life she must wade through, appalled her. She felt she must get up and leave, get back to Witley before it was too late.

But Pauline suddenly seemed eager for her to stay. "Of course you mustn't go yet. June and Elizabeth are coming here with their young men. They've been at Hurlingham."

Maria said: "I must go, really."

She did not wish to meet her two cousins and she felt out of place in this house. She wondered why she had come and whether she would ever return here again. Perhaps she had really experienced a craving for sympathy from a woman; in this, she was defeated. She suddenly wished that, rather than the chilly ideal counterpart of her brother, Pauline had been a person with real feelings.

As she turned to go, Maria heard voices downstairs, the shrill rather overconfident voices of her cousins.

Two plump girls came rustling up the narrow staircase, bumping against picture frames on the way. Each had a smooth succulent complexion, but the features were heavy, with thick eyebrows and jowls like young mastiffs. Arriving at the stairhead the girls greeted Maria with fond folly. She returned with them to the drawing room, already feeling the mental relaxation which these two girls gave as the greatest of their charms.

"We never see you," they said. "We heard you'd gone Bohemian or something."

"Last time was at Jeremy's twenty-first birthday," Maria replied.

"But that was ages and ages. We've been to hundreds of parties since then."

"I've seen you," Elizabeth said.

"Where?"

"Only in the distance. It was from the top of a bus, in Knightsbridge. You were with two people, one of them had a beard and a duffel coat and the other was rather a beauty, I thought, sort of hungry-looking." She spoke with an expression of childish greed, which among her friends was how one mentioned a young man.

"Do tell us who he is."

"He's a painter," Maria said. "His name's Tom Witley."

"A painter!" Like two kittens with a scrap of paper, they hurried the word away from her and made something quite different of it. Maria watched them patting and playing with it in their minds, making it social and fascinating.

"Is he famous?"

"We must ask James about him," June said, turning around restlessly in her chair. "He knows all about painters. You know, James Fearne, we told you about him, he owns a picture gallery."

Maria remembered, with some discomfort: the damaged sensations of the morning returned to her. Then the two young men came in. The first, John Morton-Hesketh, she recalled as hanging around Elizabeth for some time. He was tall, fair, wore a Brigade tie, and had a pustule on his lip, which his tongue visited every minute or two. He was what Tom Witley imagined all upper-class young men to be like. For Maria he had no interest: if I had stayed, she thought, I would have danced with him in night clubs and listened to dirty stories which he vaguely hoped would shock and excite me.

Then the other young man appeared. Their eyes flashed together and Maria felt her cheeks pinken. She was glad that he was the first to look away. She herself shivered, as if with cold.

At all costs she wanted to avoid him, but he sat down near her. When he spoke she noticed that he had changed since this morning. In Pauline's house (where unknown to Maria he was a welcome visitor) James Fearne was less strident. What had seemed effeminacy in his picture gallery here became an Edwardian stateliness and charm. This adaptation was well judged. The young man placed his conversational stepping-stones adroitly, telling anecdotes which were almost pointless if you did not know the personalities involved, but full of interest if you wanted to know them. He talked to Pauline about Paris, about Venice; he airily mentioned Osbert and Sachie. His aggression was based on assumptions scornfully assumed and difficult to disprove—for how could one convince such people, Maria thought crossly, that one's own ambitions were different? And was one even sure they were? She stuck close to the idea of Witley, of good found only in love and in pictures.

She felt herself lose ground, however, when a few moments later he started cross-examining her. "Who are you? What do you do?"

Direct questions were what Maria nowadays found hardest to deal with. Perhaps she had sought out Pauline this afternoon because Pauline never asked them.

"Who are your friends?"

"Well, I suppose painters and people interested in art."

"Which painters?"

She replied cautiously: "I don't think you'd know any of them."

He shifted around until he was facing her, with one hand over the back of her chair.

"But tell me, really," he said seriously, "if you like painters why do you stay here? Why don't you go to Antibes and see Picasso? Or Andre?" He turned his head away for a moment. "Andre's so nice, and he's quite gone off boys now, you know. He loves young girls. I'm sure you'd like him. I'm doing his next one-man show."

"I think I prefer living in London." She felt awkward and pompous; but at least she was controlling her enthusiasm, her young girl's desire to plead liking from everyone.

Conversation had died elsewhere. Pauline had asked John Morton-Hesketh to mix a cocktail. Maria sat upright, her tilted features shining a little. But she was only half aware that she had become the most important person in the room.

"But how can you tell?" the young man went on. "You must

travel. Go to Provence, or better, Spain. Spain is the only country where the people still behave like servants."

"Spain?" Pauline said, crossing the room with a cocktail. "Have you read Sachie's new book?"

Maria felt her toes bite hard into the soles of her shoes. Anything, surely, was better than this.

James Fearne said something to Pauline: would it have been about Zurbaran? It was difficult for Maria to spell the word out in her mind. She played with the idea that she had misjudged him. Perhaps he really knew about painting. If so, then Witley's pictures—she was back with her old treacherous fears again. But, shortly afterward, Pauline asked the young man about his gallery. He replied: "All one can hope for is gay things for gay people to put on their walls." Maria shuddered and knew he was all wrong and was not a young man of any importance.

Suddenly she stood up. "I must go, really," she said.

James Fearne followed her. "Come with me. I shall have to take a cab back across the park. Where are you going?"

She thought for a moment and decided on Knightsbridge; she would take the tube from there.

"Knightsbridge," she said. "I have to go to Harrods'."

"But surely Harrods' 'll be shut?"

"So it will. How silly. All the same, Knightsbridge."

She left them quickly. She saw June's face, puzzled and querulous, watching the young man and herself. She had the detached feeling of power that one has from doing a wrong action one is not interested in. But she remembered to kiss Pauline good-bye.

Once in the taxi, Maria wondered if it would be any good mentioning this morning to the young man. Perhaps he would start the subject. Now, however, even James Fearne seemed to draw away from her into his corner, and his fingers tapped nervously on the handle of his umbrella. After hearing him monopolize the conversation in Pauline's house, Maria wondered why he had stopped talking.

His silence, however, did not particularly disconcert her. Tom Witley and his friends hardly spoke at all. When they woke in the mornings they were often ill, and by the evening they were usually drunk or angry. Occasionally, late at night, they would have long venomous arguments about painting or burst out in gusts of childish jokes; but for the most part they preserved a boorish silence.

Now, when he spoke again, James Fearne let his pale eyes slide away from her and found difficulty in finishing his sentences. Maria wondered what was wrong.

She herself could not know. The truth was that she was overcharged still with a sense of triumph, a minor feminine triumph over June and Elizabeth, so that her physical presence seemed uncomfortably to fill the back of the taxi—like a huge bunch of roses appearing suddenly in a surrealist film. The young man felt pushed to one side. He was inwardly horrified by women, with a feeling of nervous fright he had to talk loudly against, especially when they were as spectacularly nubile as Maria at that moment.

Maria remembered that she must buy some food before going back this evening. The thought made her full of hurry, so that, while they were still near the park, she told him to stop the taxi. Before he could ask what was the matter, she had opened the door. She turned and said good-bye. "Thank you *so* much," she said in the voice Witley had always complained about, her Kensington voice. This time she was mimicking herself. She set out across the sidewalk with a boozy look of happiness on her face.

In the studio, Tom Witley and a woman were sitting together in front of the stove. The bare bulb of a lamp glared at them, and the rest of the room was shadowed. The two were in deep conversation. At one moment the woman counted on her fingers, and shook her head.

When Maria came in, the woman called out: "Hullo!"

Maria said "Hullo, Betsy." Witley looked at the stove and did not speak. Maria made her way between the bed and the easel to the other end of the room, where she switched on the light above the sink. She put a parcel of kippers on the draining board. The grease had made the newspapers transparent and the gold-burnished skin of the kippers showed through. Maria looked at them for some time, pretending to be busy so that she would not have to turn back to the room. She had an ominous feeling of what was going to happen.

Tom and Betsy were still talking in low murmurs. Betsy was counting again. It was the end of a long story.

A square of mirror glinted above the sink, where Witley used to shave. Maria peered into it, but avoided her own eyes.

"Tom," she called out, "do you want anything to eat?" Her voice sounded strange against silence.

"No."

"How is your cold?"

This time he did not answer. Maria felt a seed of anger sprouting; she moved quickly out into the room to look at him. Tom sucked his pipe and stared at the floor, he was as sullen as ever. The woman looked up and Maria noticed that she was drunk and had been crying. The mascara was blurred around her eyes.

"Maria, darling, such frightful things happen to me, do forgive me for coming and interrupting. I was just telling Tom."

Maria sat down. Before any violent unhappiness she felt awed and respectful. Sitting beside Betsy she wondered if she, too, would be told about the frightful things. But no one spoke for at least five minutes.

Finally Tom said to Maria: "How much money have you got? We need some more drink."

"Twenty-five shillings."

"I've got some too," Betsy said, feeling in her purse. "No, it doesn't matter, I don't see how I'll need it."

Witley took all the money, put on his raincoat and went out.

When he had gone, Maria asked the woman: "Are you ill?"

"I suppose so," Betsy said. "But forgive me again, it's a very long story. I've already told Tom and he'll tell you."

Maria felt that another door had banged against her. Tom would never tell her, and it would be foolish of her to ask him. There were perplexities for which no explanation was ever offered, at least to her. She often wondered why Tom and his lot treated her in this way.

Maria looked speculatively at Betsy. Who was Betsy? Maria did not even know her surname. In any case, beyond Betsy's tinted hair, her affected voice already gruff with drink, the original personality must have disappeared. Betsy was no one: she lived anywhere, and was always on the verge of being turned out of her lodgings. Maria was jealous, not because Tom among many others had slept with this girl and would do so again, but because Betsy was supposed to understand things that she herself did not. Betsy was on the side of "life." It was Tom's theory that, owing to her upper-middle-class upbringing, Maria understood nothing of "life."

Maria felt herself grow taut with dislike of this woman.

Tom returned with a bottle of whisky. Looking at it, Maria decided to drink as much of it as they would let her.

Later, while they were drinking, Betsy became tearful again and started coughing. A thin, starved hollow sound was emitted when Tom patted her back. She slipped from her chair and her face fell softly and nervelessly against his. Tom replaced her in the chair, but he continued holding her hand, down between the chairs out of sight of Maria.

Maria had hardly eaten anything today. She held her glass up to the light and watched the whorls of whisky spiraling in the water. She had the impression that she saw everything very clearly. She knew Tom's words before he spoke them.

"I'll take Betsy home."

Maria looked hard into his eyes. How strange it is, some buried part of her mind was thinking, that people believe so much in the eyes as a way of expressing emotion. Tom's eyes were nothing to her, nothing. She was a little drunk.

He turned to go, shepherding Betsy out of the door, which slammed shut after them.

And now the studio was dead silent. A violent current of air seemed to have departed, leaving a vacuum. Maria picked up the whisky bottle and shook it. There was nothing inside.

"I don't mind, I don't mind," she shouted to the empty room. Luckily for her, she fell asleep before she discovered that she did.

# *The Palace of Culture*

The night club was large, with a circle of columns and a fountain in the middle of the dance floor. At first sight it was deeply depressing; but in the end, through habit, I began to be fond of it. Here, in flight from more respectable engagements, I seemed to spend most of the evenings of a week or two of my life.

The time was midwinter and gusts of snow swept across the parade grounds around the Palace of Culture. In the portico there was a glass door, unlocked by a commissionaire. A militiaman stood next to him, and one or two drunks were warily circling in the offing. I paid the entrance fee and went down the red carpeting to the night club: down under the Palace, whose whole weight now stood overhead, a weight of offices, of conference rooms with headphones and booths for the interpreters of Asian languages, puppet theaters, educational libraries, corridors, and exhibition halls.

I am sure the three young men had never visited any of these. The night club, however, was the most splendid place they knew, and they loved coming here. Zbiszek, the organizer among them, got them a table near the dance floor. You could see from his dark, excited face that he wanted everything to go right, for the evening to function according to plan. And perhaps he did influence his friends, though they often seemed to be pulling against him. He was nineteen and waiting to be conscripted. Jacek, on the other hand, couldn't have influenced anyone. Tiny, wildly aggressive, he was always getting into fights which he lost. He cultivated his resemblance, which was a close one, to the dead film star, James Dean. Jacek ordered the carafes of vodka in their frosty silver buckets, but it was Henio or myself who ended by paying for them. By the time we got the bill, it was usually past three in the morning.

This night club had become their village. They knew everyone in the place, the waiters, the cloakroom attendants, the young man who sang rock 'n' roll, and the members of the orchestra. When they had no money for anything more than the entrance fee, they smuggled in sandwiches, which they shared with the five girls who did the floor show. Their favorite among these was a tall blonde called Piasecka, who sometimes came over to our table. There was nothing tarty about her; she looked most distinguished. She had a gentle, amused attitude toward the three of them, and they slept with her, they boasted to me, on alternate weekends.

But much of their conversation centered on protest. Jacek had just spent a couple of nights in jail for starting a row on a tram; he was like one of those undersized dogs that feels it incumbent on itself to attack everything larger. School inspectors, militiamen, students in the Union of Socialist Youth, attenders of official rallies—none of the three could begin to accept any of them, especially militiamen. Because their protest was instinctive, almost mindless, they did not come to much harm, and as I watched Jacek and Zbiszek, I felt that they would simmer down and conform later on.

What about Henio, though? Surprisingly he was the richest of the three. He worked at a lathe in a factory. Piecework enabled him to earn more than his father, who had owned a factory before the War. Henio was twenty, born in the first years of the German occupation. Every morning before going to the factory he drank down a tumbler of vodka, which he called an "eye-opener," but his face and his body were still almost unpunished, except for two steel teeth in the front of his mouth. He was tall and very strong; his eyes were green and usually good-natured. To me he was a wood demon, a complete Slav: I could not imagine a Swede or a German, for instance, with that amiable but slightly treacherous look.

In the summer they spent the Sundays following their drinking bouts asleep on the banks of the river. Near the sports stadium there was a sort of *plage*, always crowded by the young, and with an oppressive atmosphere of body-building and athletics. The three of them got bored with this, but they always headed for the river.

The river is one of the great ones in Europe. I could never look at it, swirling past the gray cities on its course, without a lift of the heart: a sensation, it must be admitted, hard to come by elsewhere in that country. At the capital, the river was nearly four hundred yards across, but it was so much alive that, if you looked closely at any particular part of it, you imagined at once a diving bird, an otter, or a big fish turning and twisting under the surface. The river was fringed with islets of willow, which were pulled under and sprang up wisped with floating straw, and with long spits of silver and gold sand, where flocks of wading birds congregated (these were observed through binoculars by a man from our Embassy, whose wife was chronically bored).

After one of their drinking bouts, the young men caught a ride on the back of a truck going to the country. It was five o'clock on a June morning, and at such times the river gave off a light of its own, not yet reflected on the sky. Henio had brought out his "eye-opener," offered some to the driver, then drained the bottle and, standing upright as the truck lurched across the long bridge, hurled it away so that it fell into the miles of whirling water. He was fond of childish gestures such as this, and afterward he sat back, hunched up, half smiling, a good demon germinating mischief. Behind them the city shrank away until they could see only the Palace of Culture (where the last drunken trade delegates had been turned out of the night club an hour ago) standing up like part of a telescope.

The truck driver left them near a village, and they took a sandy track that led to the river. Nearer its banks there were pools of floodwater, loud with the celebrations of frogs. Jacek, the child of a divorced movie actress, felt smaller and even more pugnacious in the country, as though diminished by the huge sky and the dull flat fields. He looked around for violence but only succeeded in silencing the frogs' chorus with a hail of stones. Zbiszek shepherded them to the edge of the river, where they stripped on a bar of sand and slept.

Jacek awoke at midday. The river shone in front of him, there was a clover field and some birds were playing tag through a line of willows. There was nothing for him to look at and so he began to tease Henio, who was sprawling with his alcohol-blistered mouth wide open, completely abandoned to sleep. Jacek fluttered a blade of grass across his face. Henio's massive hand swiped at it and fell back. He woke, sat up, and gazed blankly as an animal. Jacek prepared to duck away. Meaning came back into Henio's eyes like a face appearing at a window; he sprang up and pushed Jacek into the river and dived in after him. He swam like a torpedo.

After a minute they were out again, their hair dark and their tanned bodies shining with water.

"God, I could do with a vodka."

Zbiszek, woken by the noise, said: "You know you can't buy alcohol today. It's Sunday."

"Who says I can't buy vodka? I'll buy vodka."

They pulled on shirts and trousers and made their way up to the village. Like most of the villages on that war-ravaged plain, it did not promise much. The cottages looked as though they had been left empty for about three years and the inhabitants had just returned to them. The dusty air smelt of horses and flowering elder trees and, from time to time, like a sudden blow, the fierce summer stench of outhouses. The villagers in their best clothes were coming out of church.

Jacek shuddered. "What a hole. You won't get anything here."

"Who says I won't? I'll get vodka. You wait here."

While the other two sat under a chestnut tree and smoked, Henio set off alone up the unpaved street. For a young man, his way of walking was curiously imposing, bolt upright with his shoulders back and his arms hanging loose. The churchgoers stood aside to let him pass. He was much taller than any of them.

"He's asking that old man."

"No good. I told him it'd be no good."

"He must have given up," Zbiszek said. "He's talking to a militiaman."

"As I love God, they're going off. It can't be." Jacek slapped his knee and guffawed, as at that moment Henio nodded and waved to them.

The militiaman and Henio reappeared a few minutes later. They were accompanied by a thin boy of about fifteen, and Henio was carrying a transparent blue-green bottle which glittered at the sun.

Jacek threw himself around with delight and astonishment. "As I love God, he's incredible. Getting vodka off a militiaman!"

Henio came up and introduced his new friend.

"He knows an old woman who keeps a stock. Special price though. He's going to show us where to swim."

The militiaman, who was thick-hipped, belted tightly into his uniform, and had wet hands, seemed greatly impressed by Henio. "Of course, swimming is forbidden," he giggled. "But there is one place where it's perfectly safe."

They set off back through the fields. Nobody took much notice of the thin boy, his nephew, who scuffled along in the sand behind them.

Later they were lying by the river, at a place where a stream joined it, forming a deep pool under the willows. They had all swum, and the bottle had passed to and fro and was nearly empty, and now their new friend couldn't stop talking, an endless flow of anecdotes about infringements of minor regulations in the village. Zbiszek and Jacek laughed at him through their hands. But Henio, propped up on his elbows, his green eyes flickering, was nodding and agreeing quite convincingly. "He's incredible," Jacek whispered. The militiaman lolled back on the sand, half drunk and completely pleased with himself.

Suddenly he twitched all over and sat forward. "Dobroslaw!" His voice was squeaky with anxiety.

"Who's he?"

"My nephew. The boy who was with us."

"He was in the water just a minute ago," Zbiszek said.

The militiaman jumped up and began running up and down in his pants, with his belly swaying.

"He'll come back," they laughed at him. "Gone off to see his girl."

"No, no. You don't understand. He comes from a mining town. He can't swim."

They dived in and Henio and Jacek swam underwater. At the edge of the pool they found the full current of the river, like a solid gale blowing under the surface of the water. After some minutes they met again on the bank, dark in the face and with their breath sawing in their open mouths. Jacek bent over, retching, and vomited on to the grass.

Zbiszek shook his head.

"But the boy's family—he was staying with me—his father's in the Party. I shouldn't be here. All bathing is forbidden by order. Strictly prohibited. My God, what will happen to me? I'm finished, that's what it is."

They looked blankly at the militiaman now, but with their eyes full of contempt and dislike. Henio, the strongest swimmer, jerked his head towards the river. "Come on, once more."

This time he and the militiaman let themselves down into the water, feeling with their feet, and moving carefully in order not to disturb the mud and weeds. From time to time Henio dived, but when he came up he always shook his head. The two of them moved farther and farther out, past a line of willows bowed by the weight of water.

Jacek and Zbiszek lit cigarettes. They did not speak. They were involved, but in nothing more than violence and action. They waited to see what would happen.

Henio pulled himself out, stood wet as the river on the short grass, and spat.

"Where is he?"

"How do I know where he is?"

He screwed up his eyes; he might have been only blinking the water out. Jacek began to laugh but they hushed him.

Zbiszek, the organizer, took charge.

"We left the uniform there where it was on the sand. We threw the vodka bottle into the river. When you think about it, there wasn't anything else we could do, not without getting into trouble. We made off through a wood and hit the road on the other side of the village. Nobody saw us. In the afternoon we got a truck back to the city."

"What happened to them?"

"The bodies were recovered all right. The boy's was three kilometers downstream. It was all in the newspapers. Everyone thought he had been trying to save his nephew."

"Well, he had."

Henio was very drunk. He put his hand on my arm, as though like a child I had missed the whole point of the story. "Listen, that militiaman couldn't have saved anyone. He was too fat and he swam like a dog. He'd have been pushed out of the Force and the Party'd have given him hell." He brought his big hands slowly together and hard down on the table, and the vodka glasses rattled against the knives. A smile appeared all over his face.

"As I love God, it was the best thing," Jacek said.

Piasecka and the other girls had long ago finished their song-and-dance routine. The band still played but only a few couples were stumbling around the dance floor; the fountain in the middle was switched off. Soon the night club would be closed and above us, in the Palace of Culture, all those offices and corridors and lecture halls waited for the socially positive activities of the day.

Jacek fished the empty carafe from the ice slush in the bucket. "Waiter! Some more of this! Waiter!"

# Inexperience

The girl stood with her back to the bar, slightly in everyone's way. A pretty girl, she was wearing a dress with a flared skirt that she wore at cocktail parties. She swung her foot to and fro, and looked around her at the dull groups of raincoated men, whom she took to be commercial travelers. Her glances always ended with a little gesture of irritation, as if these people and these places were too boring and typical; then she took up her glass, pretending to drink deeply. She usually sipped a very little, sometimes nothing at all. She let the beer touch her mouth and slide back into the glass. She wanted to make it last a long time.

The young man had on a patched tweed coat and service dress trousers; he was about twenty-two and had just come out of the Army. He was looking down at the top of the bar. Neither of them spoke.

Now another young man pushed his way toward the bar, where, after exchanging a few words with the landlord, he peered around about him until he saw the couple. Their expressions and their way of standing were arranged for the general public, not for each other. He could guess that they had not been talking.

"Hullo, hullo!" the newcomer said. He was tall and had a fair handsome face; his expensive overcoat hung open.

"Oh, Colin. You know Colin, don't you?"

"Of course I know Colin." The girl turned her face, bright with anxiety to be liked, full on him.

"Hullo there, Fred." Colin called girls "Fred," but he seemed embarrassed. "Have I kept you waiting?"

"Waiting?" the girl asked, puzzled, for she had not expected to see him at all. She looked at her young man, but he did not help her.

"I'm sorry," Colin said suddenly, rousing himself. "What are you drinking?"

"Oh, thank you," the girl said, "but I'm all right with this one." The young man was frowning at Colin across her head.

"I see." He caught the landlord's eye, and bought drinks for himself and his friend. "What've you been doing?"

"We went to Curzon," the girl said helpfully. "It was really awfully good, wasn't it, Andrew?"

"You said you liked it," her young man answered.

"Well, you liked it too, you know you did."

"Me?" He made an incredulous voice. "I thought it stank."

"Then why did you take me to it, if you thought it was so awful?" she asked crossly.

To interrupt, Colin said: "What was this film, Fred? You haven't said what it was yet."

She told him the name of the film. "Have you seen it?"

"Yes."

"Well, you liked it, surely?"

Colin looked across at Andrew, laughing. "I must say I thought it stank, too."

The girl made a curious trapped movement of her head. "It was jolly good," she said blinking. "I thought it was jolly good." She examined the stitching of one of her gloves and started humming a little tune to herself; then she came back at Andrew savagely: "It's your turn to buy a drink."

He made a hopeless face at her. "Tisha, you know perfectly well I haven't any more money. I told you."

Color flooded into her cheeks. She had forgotten, and she was genuinely sorry, for she did not want to be unkind to him. Earlier, at the beginning of the whole thing, she had firmly decided not to mind about his being poor.

"Give me a cigarette then," she said quite softly. "Look, there's a table free, why don't we sit down?"

But she felt their resistance as she said it, and again she had the feeling that she had said the wrong thing. They remained standing, and soon afterward the two men began a conversation about people she didn't know. Without listening to them she smoked her cigarette in little puffs, with a slight frown.

"Tom and Maria," Colin was saying. "They're in a pretty bad way. I've been up there all afternoon and I did say we'd go back there. I don't think they should be left alone."

The girl looked from one to the other, her eyes half closed, as if trying in a sophisticated way to sum them up.

"What sort of thing was happening?"

"The usual things. They'll probably be turned out of the studio."

"I see."

"The girl watched Andrew carefully whenever he talked. She was anxious about him. It had been Sunday afternoon and she was aware that all had not gone very well. She had dressed up, but he had appeared in his oldest clothes. He had not spoken much; it became increasingly obvious to her that he reserved his humor for state occasions. One always realized things so much more deeply after the cinema: coming out of the Curzon this afternoon into the cold streets of early summer, she knew that he no longer tried to interest her. Without meaning to, she sighed; but neither of them noticed.

Colin said rather loudly: "Yes, I told them I'd go back and bring you."

She looked up at him. She hadn't known they were going to meet Colin this evening, and there was something not right about his being there. Nevertheless, his presence might make the evening easier.

"We must do that, then," Andrew said. He turned to the girl and began explaining carefully and unnaturally. "Tom and Maria —these friends of ours—you've heard me speak of them? Well,

Tom's wife's been writing to him again and they're both very depressed."

"I see."

"Colin's been out there this afternoon—he only came back again to see us. He said we'd go up there tonight."

"Of course, why not?" Since this fitted in with her idea of being among other people this evening, she let herself agree with what he was saying. "Well, let's go there then."

"But, Tisha, it'll be a great bore." His voice was quieter.

"I don't see why, they're friends of yours, aren't they?"

"But, Tisha—"

"When do we start?"

"Not you, Tisha."

The suddenness of the hurt made her gasp and lose all balance for a moment; her expression became ragged and wild-looking. She had known, perhaps long ago, that they were arriving at this point. It was too soon, though, far too soon.

"Well—I—really!"

"But, Tisha," he was going on saying, "you don't know these people."

"I know I don't. But am I so awful that I can't be shown to them? You'd think I was a pariah or something. Look, I want to meet your friends. I know you don't think I want to, but I do." Suddenly it was important for her to fight, though she hated herself for it.

"Try not to get into a flap. Colin has only just told me I have to go and see these people. I don't want to go, it's a long way and it'll probably be very dull."

"Where is it?"

"Hampstead."

"Hampstead's not very far."

"Well, beyond Hampstead then. Anyway, we're not going to have a gay time, a smart time. It wouldn't be at all interesting for you."

"How do you know?" she asked him. "You think just because I don't belong to your lot and I still live at home, that I don't know anything at all."

"It isn't that—"

"If you mean they won't like me, why don't you say so? Is there something I've done wrong?"

"No, really, Tisha, stop this." He gave a groan of tiredness. "Why do you always put everything onto yourself?"

"Because I believe that's what it's all about. I don't think you're going anywhere. I think you're just trying to get rid of me."

"Tisha, you heard Colin tell me, didn't you? You heard him say that Tom and Maria wanted to see me?"

She gave a little hard laugh, but she could not quite turn and call the other young man a liar. "It all sounds very suspicious to me," she said. "Why don't you let him go by himself?" She jerked her head rudely at Colin, who was looking at himself in the mirror behind the shelves of the bar. He turned, but his glance seemed to slide away from her face.

"They asked me to go too," Andrew said. "I can't let them down."

"What about me? You had a previous appointment to take me out." An idea came to her. "I want to go out with you. Look, if it's because you haven't any money, I'll go home and borrow some from my brother."

There was a silence while Andrew finished his drink. She watched him furiously, twisting her gloves in her hands. He put his glass down and said: "I didn't want to tell you this, Tisha. Tom tried to commit suicide last week."

This stunned her—for a moment he thought it was because she took it as a huge lie. Then he saw that she believed him.

"Oh, I see." Her voice came thin and strained. "Well, I don't see what you can do about it. He's not going to do it again, is he? He probably only did it to show off."

"How dare you say a thing like that?"

"No, I'm sorry—I—"

"What right have you to suggest such things—you, just a spoiled little girl who talks too much."

She looked at him and for a moment she was horrified with herself. She was sure now that she would not see him again, but she knew that she would go on loving him for some time yet.

"We ought to go," Colin said, looking at his watch.

"I don't know where I'm going to go," she said pathetically, "all dressed up like this. I've said I'll be out to dinner. Please couldn't you take me with you—I'll wait outside."

Andrew, avoiding going near her, almost shouted: "I tell you, Tisha, it's not possible."

Their eyes met, wounded, angry and meaningless. They stared at each other for some time.

"Oh, very well, then. Good night."

She went towards the door, her head held up, tottering a little on black court shoes with too-high heels. They watched her until she had gone.

Andrew broke into a sniggering mock-dance.

"Oh, God! Damn, damn, damn! More drink, quickly. You know, you saved me, being there. I thought I was going to give in."

"Let's go somewhere and get drunk, shall we?"

"Yes—look out!"

She was standing between them, her face white and shocked.

"I've left one of my gloves behind," she said.

# *At Home with the Colonel*

When a train entered the tunnel, smoke welled up between some beech trees and died out on the lawn in front of the house. From a window a girl watched it fade. Then she moved back into the room, where she put her arms around another girl, who was sewing attentively, and pressed her cheek on the shoulders and rubbed herself like a cat. Anna, the girl who was sewing, gently pushed her away.

The first girl returned to the window. She yawned.

Downstairs an old man, Colonel Starcross, was sitting before an unlit fire of paper and sticks, onto which people had thrown cigarette ashes, paper wrappings, and tufts of wool. He was thinking: "Those girls up there all day. Don't seem to want to do anything. Only an hour from London. Lots of friends." He stirred uneasily from indigestion. "I'd invite the young men myself, but it's difficult, they mightn't like it." The occupant of an isolated house, he could imagine nobody coming up the drive unless he had lured them there.

"All this dreaminess, introspection! Yes, I'll invite the young men myself, kill a chicken, make up the spare beds," he thought, with the irritable domesticity of an old man who, alone now, his life-work over, enters the world of food and comfort assigned to women, finds himself forced into gossip and women's ways.

The Colonel stood up; he fastened the buttons below his waist that he always undid when alone after lunch. He shuffled to the stairs and called.

Bridget Starcross came out onto the landing and leaned over.

"Yes, what is it?"

He had been lonely and he had nothing to say. The hall clock ticked. His house smelled stale in the dead afternoon.

"What's all this about?" His throat was stretched tight with looking up, and his voice became thin and hoarse. "What's going on? What are you doing all this time?" He was making himself angry because he had been left alone.

Her eyes were sleepily egocentric. "Nothing's going on," she remarked. "Anna is making a dress."

"Dresses!" he said wildly, not meaning to criticize the guest in his house.

"No, a dress," Bridget said, unamiably watching her father at the foot of the stairs. "For me."

He turned away in bewildered anger.

She went back to her room. Passing the back of the chair, she stroked one finger along the clipped nape of Anna's neck. Anna caught the crimson-nailed, rather dirty finger and with mock cruelty began to twist it. Both girls giggled.

Bridget lay back on her bedspread. She rubbed her bare arms together, staring at cracks on the ceiling. She wriggled her feet until the shoes fell off. "A-ah!" she said.

She appeared to go to sleep, but she could hear her father rattling the buckets of hen food downstairs.

The big house threw a darker twilight onto its shrubberies, where the Colonel, carrying a bucket, made his way into the wind toward the railway line. He was early today: the four o'clock train, thundering through the tunnel, found him still at the hen run. He hid from the smoke behind the hen house, his eyes shut. But the smoke made him cough and then his chest started hurting again. Drops of water fell on him—they might have been rain or spray from the engine—and he shivered with cold.

While the Colonel was coughing, the smoke died away. But

his eyes still watered; the young man approaching between the vegetable beds was just a vague blur to him.

"You looking for me?" he shouted. Then he wiped his eyes and recognized his visitor, who was wearing a shoddy demobilization overcoat and black army shoes. He was bareheaded, his fair hair still rawly clipped. But the Colonel registered him as a friend, connected in some way with his dead wife and the summers before the War. When they shook hands, the Colonel realized that he had forgotten the young man's name.

"Glad to see you again. Just back, what? We'll go back to the house—Bridget's at home." The Colonel felt very shy. He opened the door of the hen house and groped around for eggs, although he already knew that there were none. He felt obliged to ask the young man something about his military service; he needed time to beat his fuddled memory until the facts would drop out of it.

The young man, similarly afflicted with shyness, cleared his throat and said: "Are your hens laying well, sir?"

The Colonel could look at him again. "Bloody," he said. "I feed 'em up, give 'em this balancer meal stuff, and they loaf around, scratching themselves." He stared at the hens still fussing around the trough. "I'm lucky if I get one egg a day," he said.

"D-do you give them cod-liver oil, sir?"

"Cod-liver oil!" the Colonel shouted, in such a voice that the young man was sorry for the hens, and slammed the door of the house, raising anguished shrieks and a dusty fluttering of wings. "So they give it to hens now, do they? That's all those bastards want, cod-liver oil and pap for every loafer in the street!" The Colonel was suddenly very angry; however, the young man could not feel offended, for the anger was not aimed at himself or even at the Labour Government. Colonel Starcross looked up apprehensively; his gray eyes were watery like the winter sky. He put his hand on the young man's arm. "Tell you what, come up to the house. Get you some tea."

The old man lit the gas under a kettle on the stove, and brought down two tins, one of which contained tea, the other a slab of grocer's cake. His visitor helped him set the tray. "Why four cups?" he asked.

"This friend of Bridget's," the Colonel grunted.

Carrying the tray, he went through and called "Bridget!" at the foot of the stairs. He continued into the drawing room, while the young man waited. The bedroom door swung open, letting twilight into the landing. Bridget and Anna appeared, arm in arm.

The young man smiled up at them both.

"Hullo, Bridget," he said. "Wonderful to see you."

"Oh dear, hullo." The girl peered shortsightedly into the dark well of the hall. "It's John, isn't it?"

"Get a move on, there," the Colonel called. "I've made the tea." Nervously enthusiastic, he rubbed his hands together. "Everything's ready."

He had switched on the electric fire, but its single glowing bar could not melt very far into the cold air of the room; the empty spaces beyond the armchairs were as drafty as the woods outside.

The conversation at tea was left to his daughter and John, for Anna did not speak, though she ate a great deal of cake. The old man sat with his face drawn and exhausted by the efforts he had made. His thoughts, sour with tiredness, kept on saying: "If only I could ask him to take her away, take her away from my house. I'm fed up with her and her sulky bitches of girl friends"—though Anna was the first guest they had had since the War. "If only I could get that bitch out of the room and leave them together." But he could think of no way to do this. During the week she had been in his house, he had scarcely addressed a word to his daughter's friend; she herself rarely spoke in his presence, though he heard the two of them chattering and laughing behind closed doors.

Bridget sat carelessly unattractive on the sofa. She was completely ignorant of what her father thought of her. Too lazy to find a job, she secretly imagined herself saying later to a critical audience—possibly of relatives, though she had few who would be interested: "I have nothing to blame myself for. After all, I was his only companion through those last years, and pretty dull it was too, sometimes, I can tell you. It's only fair that I should get the mon—" But at this point of her harangue, she usually became slightly ashamed of herself: if she was curled up in an armchair or lying on her bed, she would jump up and pace around the room once or twice, or start hurried sentences which had no purpose except to batter down her own unruly fantasy.

"I often wonder what happened to all our friends," the young man said. "The Shaddocks, the Armitages, the Bentleys. Do you remember when you fell off Heather Shaddock's pony?"

Bridget would not let herself help him. "I can only remember how dull this place was. I know I was always bored stiff really." Her eyes moved toward her father.

She may have succeeded in hurting him. His fingers drummed on the chair, and one of his knees vibrated. "Well," he said at last, "I suppose I'd better go and shut those blasted chickens up."

When he had gone, Anna moved into the deeper recesses of the room. The young man decided to try to ignore her. He turned back to Bridget. He told her about his job at the Estate Agents; he questioned her about the other people they had known. But he found the conversation increasingly difficult. Each of his sentences seemed to be suspended for inspection, even for mockery, in the cold air of the drawing room. Finally he knew that all his gambits would fail because he couldn't make himself interesting to her anymore.

"It's been jolly good to come here again," he said. "I hope that you—and your friend of course—will be able to come over to our place one day. Mother's always talking about you."

"Thanks very much. But I'm afraid our plans are rather uncertain." She began to be as conscious as he was of the waiting figure behind them.

"Or—I come this way quite often. I could drop in, if you like, and we could make some plans."

He couldn't see Bridget's face; she had moved beyond the circle of light from the standard lamp. "Well, if you want to."

"But I thought . . ."

"Perhaps I've got other interests," she said sharply. "Have you read this?" She threw a book across at him. It disappeared behind some cushions and he did not trouble to find it. He felt heat bursting in his cheeks.

"I'm sorry," he said. "I suppose I must be intruding."

She did not answer and he began to humiliate himself. "Perhaps I'm a frightful bore. You used—I mean——" He gulped. "I haven't any wish to stay where I'm not welcome."

"Oh God," the girl opposite him said. But in a moment she would have relented and asked him to stay. He heard a new sound, however, from the back of the room: it was Anna, laughing at him.

The young man went out into the hallway; he was dimly conscious of the Colonel somewhere in the house, but he was too angry to say good-bye. He walked down the drive between the rhododendrons. The village stretched out in front of him; the bus went every half hour through the dull empty fields to the county town where, if there wasn't another war, he would live until he died.

After he had gone, the two girls slipped down on to the floor in front of the electric fire. Bridget, who had a guilty conscience, held her friend tightly by the arm.

"But he was so funny, my dear," Anna said. Her short black hair was coarse, her face shiny in the strong light. Then Bridget laughed too.

When the Colonel came in, neither of them looked up at him.

"Where's that young fellow? Nice young chap, isn't he?"

"He's gone."

"Gone where?"

"How should I know? Just gone."

The Colonel bewilderedly contemplated the young man's bad manners. He was lost and hurt.

Bridget turned away and he began to tidy up the tea things. They heard him fumble and curse his way into the dark kitchen with the laden tray.

Bridget put her arms around the friend's shoulders. She could feel the firm padding in the jacket.

"How dull it all is," she murmured sleepily. "But we'll have our cottage one day, won't we?"

# *Showing the Flag*

At dusk, this part of the South American shore is almost empty. A few men in white suits sit smoking under the palm trees; lovers in pairs help each other gingerly along. Beyond them, the lights of the town rush quietly into place. There are rats among the fallen newspapers.

Two late bathers return across the tramlines and the pavement. They dodge through an interval in the long line of American cars. On the other side of the road, they walk blindly through the crowd, past bars brightly lit and little shops still open, past girls in starched dresses who parade up and down with glistening eyes and soft arms linked together. A humiliated dog crawls toward the two bathers; they spurn it. They part on the steps of the English Club.

"See you in the bar, then, Ronny."

"Righty-ho, Ken."

Ron Lester, a young man who works in a coffee firm, hurries to his boardinghouse further up the road. There he takes a shower, puffing and blowing and whistling the latest samba out of tune. Afterwards, he towels himself vigorously in front of the looking-glass. His dull-red hair is rough, like a mongrel dog's; he has not been long in the country and his naked body has still the unhealthy bluish tinge of living in English cities. He puts on a white shirt with tight cuffs. Carefully he takes a suit off a hanger. It was bought at the London shop recommended by his firm before he came out here.

Ken Hodge is changing in the dressing room of the English Club.

Several Englishmen, some in shirtsleeves, are already drinking in the bar when Ron arrives early, smoothing back his hair. Heat is beginning to creep out again all over his body after his shower; he needs a drink. For a moment he hovers on the edge of the circle, doubtful of his position, but he is soon involved in the discussion that is going on.

"By golly!" little Shuttleworth of De Souza Engineering is proclaiming. "In the days of Queen—Queen Victoria—they'd have sent down a dirty big fleet of battleships and blown this place to bits, by golly."

The others feel that they ought to be concerned about what he is saying. But many are affected by their attitude to Shuttleworth himself. Of course, he is a "good type"—all Englishmen out here are; De Souza's have treated him badly about that new contract. Nevertheless, this sort of talk doesn't cut much ice.

Then another man says: "What can you expect with these fucking Socialists at home?" He has a coarse London voice, and at once his swearing tightens the atmosphere.

Others, finding their feet more readily, join in.

"No patriotism anymore," someone's voice, embarrassed, echoes from his tumbler.

"No guts, more likely," Bagley, the swearer, says. He is tall and stout, and the drink is sweating out of him.

"English prestige out here—years to build up—down the drain," others contribute.

"Palavra ingles," Shuttleworth says. "The word of an Englishman—that used to mean something in this country."

Ron, perplexed by the conversation, turns to one of the others and asks in a high voice: "I say, could you give us the gen, old boy?"

But Stanley Abbott, who works in the same firm as himself, stares blankly at him and does not answer. For a moment Ronny forgets what he has so often been told: "All's fair in the Club. No side. A man making thirty contos a month will have a drink with one who's only worth four, just like equals." He feels that his three months in the country are compared unfavorably with their "twenty years in the old days." His opinion will not matter. He gulps and prepares to retreat to one of the tables to wait for Ken. But Shuttleworth, excited, takes his arm. He even buys him a drink, for the first time.

"These people here—they're worse than bloody animals," Bagley goes on. And again the others take up the theme from him:

"Can't trust them as far as that."

"Shoot you as soon as look at you."

"Filthy minds."

"Women and *futebol*."

"I've been out here thirty years and I'm proud to say I've never had a conversation with one of 'em—apart from line of business, mind."

Another round of drinks is ordered: gin and tonic, or Scotch for those who aren't buying their own. "Cheers" all round, in spite of this.

"Ah, that would never of happened in the old days," Abbott says, glancing at Ron.

"An English sailor, His Majesty's Navy," Shuttleworth says.

"What's the H. M. Consul doing about it?"

"The Consul," several say scornfully, who are not personally known to him. "A newcomer. What does he know about the colony?"

"We had a businessman as consul in the old days."

"That's right. And the Padre. Padre Jackson would have raised the roof all right."

"He was a fine type of Britisher, Padre Jackson was. No side. Wouldn't even have known he was a parson, only his collar."

"I don't go to church myself," Stanley Abbott says, looking around him as though this criticism were final. "But he was highly thought of, Padre Jackson was."

"Yes, we need someone like Padre Jackson now."

"What's happening to the poor bugger anyhow?" Bagley asks.

"The—er—interment's tomorrow. Padre Berridge is giving the whole thing, just as if he'd been a member of the colony."

"Mind you, Padre Berridge is a fine type too, but he hasn't got the touch."

"Too much la-de-da."

"Oxford accent and all that. That sort of thing doesn't go down out here. What goes down is plain speaking."

"I was going to say . . ."

The veranda door opens, and outside the bar some stars can be seen on the tropic sky; fireflies begin to flash over the cricket field. Shuttleworth starts the whole story again to the newcomers: Ken Hodge, Garrett of Kumfi shoes, and Sanderson of the cigarette company. Ronny leans over to try to hear it, but at that moment Bagley, who has been drinking all afternoon, begins telling him a dirty story and, although he has heard it before, he feels obliged to listen.

Shuttleworth finds that this time his news falls a little flat. He emerges and, catching the attention of the whole group, says excitedly: "I agree with Jim, what we want is a showdown."

"Come to think of it," someone says, "if they let us down at home, we ought to do something about it here."

Others agree: "Hear, hear." "We ought to show 'em."

Shuttleworth bursts out: "Right you are, chaps, that's the British spirit. I think the whole colony ought to turn out at the cemetery tomorrow."

He gets into the middle of the group. His face is flushed and a lock of greased hair falls onto his forehead. He is a full head shorter than anyone else, and he stands in the middle like a child about to start "Eeny-meeny-miney-mo."

"Now, who's with me? You'll come, won't you, Les?"

"Love to, old man. Can't make it. There's the rugger match tomorrow."

"Going to be a hard match."

"That's right. Our lads need all the support they can get on the touchline."

Last of all, Shuttleworth turns to Bagley, who merely answers, with a feminine pouting of the lips: "I've got something better to do."

Ron comes into the Club to play tennis the following afternoon. Shuttleworth, in white flannels, is on the veranda overlooking the field. It is a hot afternoon; the sun overhead seems dissolved into a blank white sky.

"Heard any more, old man?" Ron asks, falling into a wicker chair beside him.

"What about?"

"This sailor chap."

"No, no. I haven't. Going to be a good match, this."

As he is speaking, the two rugby teams, squat, rotund, and lanky, walk out onto the brownish grass. A jungle-covered hill, which rises directly behind the clubhouse, throws its cool shadow onto one half of the field. But the other is in full sunlight.

The two teams give up after twenty minutes, before any score has been made.

Later, when the short tropical twilight begins, more English people begin to gather at the Club. Even the plainest wives seem to become mysterious and romantic, as, in twos and threes, their light summer dresses are visible along the asphalt path by the field. They settle down on the veranda, to knit or play canasta or merely to wait for their husbands.

In the bar that night it is learned that the funeral took place yesterday, even before the discussion and Shuttleworth's energetic proposal. Corpses rot quickly in this climate, and are hustled underground and out of people's memories. But those in the bar who, yesterday, felt uneasy in front of Shuttleworth, are justified. They are glad that they didn't get mixed up in anything, in these days when so many contracts come from the state government.

Meanwhile, as dusk falls, trams can be heard going through the still suburb past the English Club toward the living part of the town: the port, the streets of dance halls and brothels. It was here, the night before last, that a local policeman shot a drunk English sailor three times in the stomach. Frightened, he watched him die on the sidewalk at his feet.

# *The Student*

When Marek Pulawski had been learning English for about two years, he had his first opportunity of talking to an Englishman. A foreign research student, the first from the West for several years, had installed himself at the University.

Hurrying toward the Students' Hostel on a late winter afternoon, Marek looked very much like other young men of his age, which was twenty-three. He was wearing a dirty raincoat with a belt, blue jeans, and thick-soled shoes. His brown hair was cut back without a part, so that he needed always to be attending to it with a pocket mirror and comb. Perhaps he would have been handsome if he had looked well, but his face was tired and gray and he seemed younger because of this.

In the black square building which stood on the outskirts of the city, Marek soon found the Englishman's room. He knocked at the door and sidled quietly in.

"May I speak with you?"

"Come in, of course."

"Pulawski."

"Binsley."

After they had shaken hands they waited in silence for something to happen.

Marek said: "You are comfortable here? I think it is a rather bad room."

The room was small and bare, with cracked plaster walls. There was a basin with a cold tap and a lopsided wardrobe. Binsley's reply was determinedly enthusiastic. "It's all right for me. After all, it's what everyone has, isn't it?" Binsley, who was doing a thesis on Polish history, felt pride in knuckling down to the living conditions of a student in a people's democracy.

"Yes, but in the other rooms four or five students are sleeping."

The Englishman seemed put out by this. "You must find it very difficult working."

"I do not live here. I live at home."

"You're lucky then."

"Please?" Marek turned back: his eyes had been wandering off to the clothes on hangers across the corner of the room.

"You are lucky," said Binsley clearly. "Living at home."

"Perhaps. I do not know. There are my mother and my sisters. We have just one room, and the kitchen. They always quarrel, my sisters." He moved across to the corner. "You have good clothes."

"Oh, not really."

"Here a suit like this is worth three thousand. As most persons are getting only fifteen hundred each month, that is plenty of money. How much were those shoes?"

The Englishman shifted about uneasily. "I can't remember."

"I will sell them for you. And the suit."

"But I don't want to sell them. I mean I have quite enough money."

"How much do you get?"

Binsley was silent at this, but Marek went on looking at him, unaware that anything had gone wrong.

"I don't want to do anything like that," Binsley said finally. "I'd feel wrong doing it. I mean, it's a sort of sabotage."

"Please?"

"I mean—" He felt the embarrassment of relieving himself of strongly held ideas in front of someone he hardly knew. "You see, things are really getting ahead in this country—and I feel the black market is a sort of sabotage. I find it very exciting, I can tell you, being able to watch all the changes going on here, all the improvements since—"

"Excuse me, please. You mean you like it here?"

"I'm a complete outsider, of course, but I do believe that a new form of society is coming into being—"

"Perhaps you believe that one day I will have a suit like that? One day I will not have to sleep in the kitchen while my sisters fight next door?"

"Sooner or later."

"Here we do not believe this. There is nothing, nothing for us at all."

"I didn't mean—"

"You can never understand. You are a foreigner, an Englishman."

"I am sorry."

Then they both gave each other a quick raking look across the face, scrabbling for some of the sympathy which a political argument always drains away. They realized that neither wanted to lose the other too soon.

"Not at all. Don't mention it. Are those the correct expressions?"

"Well—"

Marek came nearer. "I hope we may be friends. It is of much value to me to have an English friend."

"Thank you."

He turned wistfully to the pair of shoes. "Will you sell the shoes, Mr. Binsley? There is a boy that lives here that will buy them. I can call him?"

"No, really."

"Thank you." They shook hands again, and Marek gave a smile which should have been brilliant, but his teeth were greenish and broken.

When he had gone, Binsley felt curiously disturbed and walked up and down, trying to batter down his thoughts. He looked out of the window, at a street which was lined with heaps of dirty snow, at a group of ragged people waiting for a tram. He felt depressed. Somehow the things which previously looked wrong for excellent reasons now looked merely wrong.

Marek reappeared the same evening.

"Come out with me, please, to have coffee."

"I'm afraid I'm very busy. I've been to see the professor who's looking after me. He gave me a lot of work to do."

"Do it tomorrow, please." Marek's voice was peremptory. He sat on the end of the bed, swinging his legs, and took his first English cigarette. During the late afternoon he had been wandering around the city thinking about Binsley, and now he imagined, as lonely people are apt to do, that he knew the other better than he did, and that they were friends already, although there had been little in their conversation to make them so.

"What is he called, this professor, please?"

Binsley told him. Marek corrected his pronunciation of the name, and said: "He is a bad man."

When the other did not speak, Marek went on rather sheepishly: "Of course, he is a very great scholar."

Binsley was still silent. Marek felt he had overreached himself again. He was a little drunk with the thrill of speaking English: now he would try to curb his enthusiasm as much as he could.

In the end, seeing that Marek would not go away, Binsley decided to accompany him to a coffee house. In the tram, in spite of his protests, Marek paid for both their tickets.

"All right, it is nothing. We students are permitted half price. I will take you to a very nice place for coffee. There are many nice places but this is the newest one. Have you gone yet to our best restaurant? To the Cloth Hall? To the St. Peter's Church? The Folk Art Museum?"

But when they arrived at the coffee house Marek seemed uncertain of the way in, and later had an altercation with the doorman about leaving his raincoat. It was clear that he had never been here before, and perhaps he had never been to the restaurant, the museums, or even the churches he had spoken about.

The coffee house was decorated with *tachiste* pictures, and the two young men sat on cast-iron stools with their knees touching under a glass table, so that their conversation was, physically at any rate, extremely uncomfortable. Now, too, in spite of his obvious excitement, Marek seemed to be not really interested in what Binsley had to say, but only in the way he said it. He had a fixed abstracted look as he listened not for the meaning but for the sentence construction. Even Binsley, who after a suburban and studious upbringing was socially rather innocent, sensed that the young man was exploiting him. He had failed with the Englishman's clothes; now he was making use of his brains.

Marek had a large Russian watch which he consulted from time to time. At ten o'clock he said: "We may go to the Students' Cellar. There is a jazz band and lots of pretty girls."

They crossed the cobbled marketplace and walked down the Gothic cloister of the Cloth Hall. It was a moonlit frosty night, and Binsley could see the intent look on the bony feral face of the boy hurrying beside him.

Marek's mind was racing ahead again. He was unable to consider the Englishman as a person at all. He was a symbol of the outside world, an audience to be won over, and at the same time a dictionary—and a scribbling block, too, where he could inscribe his wildest ideas in ever more perfect English.

They arrived, a little breathless, in front of the old palace. Marek rang a bell but there was nobody to answer it. Then they both beat with their fists on the huge studded doors. Nobody came. Binsley later found out that all the students of the University knew that the Cellar was closed on Fridays; all except Marek Pulawski, who had never been there. As foreigners often do, Binsley had made a friend who, far from leading him on to other friendships and contact with a whole group, was himself already cut off from his own world: a solitary, a dead end.

Some of the other students had a more sanguine attitude to the world. They devoted their free time to vodka, jazz, smuggling girls into their rooms, and planning to buy motor scooters. But though they were polite they were not very communicative and to Binsley it was obvious that he didn't interest them much. Whenever Marek turned up, however, he felt the existence of a genuine relationship, though a difficult, even an embarrassing one. If other people were in the room, Marek would be silent but would stay, waiting for them to go away, or talk to Binsley in English in a way he knew they would not understand.

The others all disliked him. "You ought to be careful of him," they told Binsley.

And Marek had the same opinion of them. "They are all the same. They betrayed me before, people like them. I do not trust them now. The only friends I may have are foreigners."

"How do you mean, they betrayed you?"

"In the period of Stalinism I was in a work camp. At school they told the teacher of Marxism something I had said and he reported me. Then I had to go into the Army. That is why I am older than the other students and have no friends."

"What about girls?"

"It is the same. They want you to be easy, you know, with the authorities. Then you get good job and money and girls like you. I can only have friends with foreigners. I began to learn English to talk with foreigners, you see."

"You'd like to go abroad, then?"

"That is not possible. I tried once for a student exchange, to Sweden. But they say: 'Never. There are no passports for people like you.'"

"What do you plan to do?"

"I would like to kill myself but I am a Catholic and may not. Also I must work to support my family, whom I do not like."

Like most of their conversations, this one trailed away, leaving them both feeling saddened and inadequate. Binsley was glad that he was going to the Cellar that evening with two young men who were only interested in jazz.

In his room, the conversation of these two young men consisted mostly of mispronouncing the names of Negro musicians until he finally recognized them, then nodding eagerly and miming the playing of instruments. But they were quite different in the Cellar, which was a low Gothic vault hung with abstract paintings and bursting with noise. A tremendous gaiety took hold of them, they produced laughing friends, and plump girls with painted eyes for Binsley to dance with, and they all drank fruit wine until they were tipsy. The place was shut in like a submarine, completely remote from the city outside. One of the jazz fiends toppled gently towards the Englishman.

"Better here than talk to Pulawski, yes?"

"You know him?"

"He was colleague in the school. Fourteenth gymnasium. He is rather mad, I think."

"I'm sorry for him. He's had a bad time."

"In working camp, you mean?" The other shrugged. "He said bad things."

"What did he say?" Binsley asked. He was suddenly interested.

Later another student came up. He was bursting with eagerness to express himself, but could speak no English. The first student interpreted.

"He also says Pulawski is not your friend. He is made to spy on you."

Binsley felt his spine prickle. "I don't believe it."

The other two whispered together. The vaults were ringing with a break on the clarinet, and the dancers beat a centuries-old dust up into the air.

Binsley's friend turned to him again: "He says, if you will try to quarrel with Pulawski, he is coming back. *They* tell him, he must be coming back."

"I'll soon see about that," Binsley said.

For the meeting place they had chosen the Red Army monument on the edge of the city. Perhaps they still felt it belonged to them in a sense that the rest of the city did not. Marek recognized the two of them at once, and he walked with them along the line of the ramparts. It was a place of bare trees, bell towers, and time-blistered walls; there were pigeons, old men, and children enjoying the sunlight on the first warm day of the year.

When the two men left him, Marek was trembling. Couldn't they have given him a few more days as Binsley's friend? But his future at the University depended on his attitude now, and this was what made him tremble. To stop being a student would be to lose his last contact with the world. They had told him the alternatives and given him the afternoon to think them over. They would telephone his flat tonight.

He beat his pockets for a cigarette and found none. He had

left at home, meaning to sell them, a packet of Player's that Binsley had given him. If he went to see Binsley now he might be given another packet. Marek inspected this idea cautiously. In the end he decided that, if he dared not see the Englishman now, he might as well give up the idea of seeing him again.

Marek stopped on a street corner, looking across at the Students' Hostel. Wooden carts were rattling along the road into the country, the peasants and their women lolling impassively behind the glossy buttocks of their huge horses. They had been to the free market and most of the carts were empty, but some contained bits of new furniture and in one there was a big yellow coffin nestling in the straw. Perhaps it was the sight of the peasants, the feeling of his distance from them, which started the violent reaction Marek felt now. Alone and a little crazy with his loneliness, he became convinced of what he must do, and the realization of it made his skin crawl and brought hot tears to the corners of his eyes.

He was going to confess everything to Binsley, tell him that he had been set to spy on him. Then Binsley would have to trust him and let himself be protected by him. Marek was still young and romantic enough to see himself instantly in this double role of spy and protector. Binsley would need him now: they were forced together, finally, in a true situation.

But when he got to the room, he found his friend being remote and pompous. Binsley insisted on talking about a new housing project he had visited. Why did he want to talk about housing projects when Marek was trembling with an agonized pleasure almost like love? Binsley commended the fact that cherries were planted along the streets so that the workers could pick them in the early summer. Marek would have had the buildings razed, the ground sown with salt.

"You won't find many countries where the workers' needs are so carefully considered in projects like this."

"Workers! There are no workers where you go, only Party people." Marek spoke impatiently, eager to get on to the purpose of his visit.

"I was informed they were workers. Of course, some may be members of the Party as well."

"You know nothing how things go on here. Who gives a new flat to a worker? They are for Army officers, Secret Police, people like that."

Marek himself knew very little about the subject and cared even less: he was extemporizing the bad, indulging his vision of injustice because he had come to enjoy it.

"You always make things out worse than they are."

"How can I? I told you what happened to me. How can things be worse than they are, please?"

Binsley was stung by always being told he was wrong. He trembled with anger when he spoke. "All right, you told me what happened to you. You were sent to a labor camp. One of your school friends told me what you said."

"What did I say?"

"'At least Hitler did one good thing. He killed off all the Jews.' You said that, didn't you?"

"Well?" Marek looked genuinely puzzled.

Binsley was silent.

"You do not understand. It is a national problem."

"Have you ever known a Jew?"

"No. Around here they are nearly all dead, I think."

Binsley said: "It was a terrible thing to say. You deserved what you got."

Marek turned on him, his eyes red and slightly crossed like a dog that is going to bite. "You do not understand. How can you understand what we have gone through? I know I cannot be a friend of an Englishman. You come here to make fun of us. I wish I never learn English. Good-bye, Mr. Binsley."

Before he knew what he was doing, Marek found himself outside the building. Carried along by his rage, he strode off down the shabby streets into the long evening. In an hour or so, they would be telephoning him. With his new hatred of the Englishman, he felt glad.

Back at home, however, he sat on one of the beds shivering as though he had a fever. His mother brought him a glass of tea.

"What is the matter?"

"Nothing."

He answered with the sudden turn of the head which nowadays always dismissed her. At first this movement had been intended for her not to see the trouble that was draining his life. But now they both felt that he was expressing his hatred of her for letting him be born into such a world. His mother left him in silence. She was going to the cinema with his sisters.

After half an hour, which Marek out of habit spent in reading his English grammar, the telephone rang.

For a few seconds before he picked up the receiver he felt stricken and afraid. But then he knew what he must do. He was absolutely certain now.

"Yes," he said. "I accept. I'll do as you say."

Then he was alone, exhausted, on the bed in the quiet room. Tomorrow he must go back to Binsley, apologize for their misunderstanding, smoke his cigarettes, and insist at all costs on their being friends.

# Luck

There was silence in the cabin; outside, you could hear cicadas, and the sea catching against warm rocks. But the brother-in-law had stopped talking altogether, and a look of bullish obstinacy was settled on his face. When Rodolfo came in, he was alone at the table devouring a mess of fish and rice.

Rodolfo's sister made a sign to him to keep quiet. They both knew that something had come to an end. By this time he had been in the village twenty-four hours.

The day before, he had managed a lift in a truck that was coming down the Sierra. At his feet were orchid plants which were being taken to sell to people in the holiday towns. The driver and his mate were Polacks. All along the road, blond Polack children played in the dirt outside the shacks, which were decorated with air plants and orchids sprouting from cans.

The air grew hotter and hotter and the road narrowed as they came down through the subtropical forest. At the bottom they passed the remains of a truck in the ditch. It had collapsed into a heap of boards and scrap iron that already seemed a part of the surrounding jungle. Two boys were sitting on what had been the driver's cabin.

"What happened?" Rodolfo asked.

"A car pushed us off the road."

"What happened to him?"

"He drove away."

"Did he pay?" the driver of Rodolfo's truck asked.

"Not yet."

"I'll take some of those plants off you," the driver said.

Rodolfo helped to stack the back of the truck. When they started again he was surrounded by orchids and ferns and philodendrons. The truck was carrying a part of the forest on its back, a trembling mass of leaves with a young man's head among them.

He left the truck at the ferry, where a river ran wide through flat country near the sea. The men who worked the ferry were Negroes, and others were standing around in the shade, their fists clutching the front of their trousers. The Polacks and Germans lived on the Sierra: it was a different world down here, except for poverty, which was everywhere the same.

Across the river he had to jump through mud to the shore. The others were barefoot, and Rodolfo felt the hot mud squelch into his pointed shoes. He felt it soft under his foot all the way along the dirt road that led to the town. The climate was like fever. He felt hungry and ill and sad, and only the thought of his sister's happiness, her tears and embraces when she would see him, kept him going. They were both illiterate and so his arrivals were always unexpected and unannounced, sudden visitations from a different and separate world.

Rodolfo's sister stood by the table watching her husband. He shook the pimiento bottle violently and banged it back on the table. His mouth smacked open and shut, a wet loose sound like the sea on the rocks outside.

*"Que barbaridade!"* Rodolfo thought. He had been a waiter and he knew that this was the wrong way to eat.

"What's the matter with him?" he asked his sister loudly.

"He says we can't feed you anymore."

The brother-in-law's little white eyes slid around but he did not speak.

Rodolfo laughed. He laughed a great deal when he was unhappy. "Oh, it's that. Well, I'll get a job. They want waiters at the hotel. You'll see, I'll go to the hotel and get a job."

He pushed the words out at the man sitting at the table. But the brother-in-law did not look up. He was a big mulatto with hair like a cap of black fur: Rodolfo, who was white, seemed half his size.

One weak bulb hung in the middle of the room. Soon the brother-in-law would switch it off and go to bed. He was a fisherman and the sea was waiting for him before sunrise.

The hotel, a large wooden building, stood in the middle of the curved shore. The hotel keeper had been in this country forty years. Before the War he had been German; now he called himself Swiss.

"Now you'll have one with me, Herr Laumann."

It was the North American's fourth gin. She was alone in the bar tonight.

"Drink. I no drink. Bad, bad." Herr Laumann was an ex-drunkard, reformed by a new young wife. He waved his arms for emphasis. He spoke like this in four languages, including his native tongue.

He knew the North American well. She had been here several times before. She was a good-looking, stoutish woman of forty with a lot of dark blonde hair. She used no makeup and her face was florid with drink. The other times she had behaved herself, but then she had not been alone: first there had been the North American man with the dark red face, the one who had vomited in the dining room; then, after that, often, the young boy who played the guitar. When the boy played she would hum and later dance, with the graceful movements that stout people sometimes have. But tonight she was alone and her loneliness had something dangerous about it. She was drinking steadily and fast.

In the dining room they were serving dinner. She could hear the plates being put on the tables.

"Dinner. Dinner. Better you hurry."

"I just don't happen to have any appetite." She was at the "perfect lady" stage. Her voice was like a little finger crooked.

Rodolfo went slowly up the steps of the hotel. One of the waiters, hurrying past him with plates, recognized at once what he was after. "In there." He jerked his elbow towards the bar.

Rodolfo went through and stood by the bar. The German was marking the woman's bill again. "Yes?"

Rodolfo hadn't expected to see a woman there and he was abashed. He looked down at the grain of the wood in front of him and muttered his request. He squirmed and writhed against the bar, and all the time he kept touching his face with his fingers.

"Work!" shouted Herr Laumann. "What can you do?"

The woman looked up, listening. Her eyes were blue and direct.

"I am a waiter."

"Where you work?"

"Here and there."

"Where?"

Rodolfo laughed. "Oh, I worked in a lot of places," he said airily.

"Lots of places." Herr Laumann laughed too, but the laugh was quite different. When Rodolfo heard it he stopped laughing.

There was silence. Then the hotel keeper said: "Yes, I need a waiter."

"It is true?"

"In January." This was September. He giggled. "You come back in January. The season. Lot of people, then. Lot of money." He pinched the lobe of his ear between finger and thumb.

A waiter came in—the one who had pointed the way to Rodolfo. He was a youth with carbuncles over his face and dirty eyes. He took two bottles of beer from the icebox, clicked them open and wiped them with a cloth.

Herr Laumann put his hand on the waiter's shoulder. "Lot of money. You ask him."

The waiter blushed between his carbuncles. He wriggled away like a dog that does not like to be patted, and returned to the dining room.

"Now, nothing." Herr Laumann wagged his finger to and fro. "Nothing."

Rodolfo was dismissed, yet he still lingered in the bar, as though he could not tear himself away. He saw that the woman was still staring at him with her blurred blue stare. Why was she doing that? Rodolfo smiled nervously and rubbed the tips of his fingers against his face. He had a boy's face and a mustache that was soft and thin, and now his cheeks were flushed as though with fever. He hadn't had enough to eat for a long time, and this had given him a childish sleepy look.

Herr Laumann, making a tour of the bar, sensed a change in the atmosphere. He planted himself in front of Rodolfo: the big Teuton confronting the half-starved peasant of an inferior race. Rodolfo's hands almost covered his face now.

"You can cook? I need a cook."

Rodolfo thought he was being made fun of. "No." He had an access of pride, professional and masculine. He said loudly: "No, I can't cook."

"Then come back January. January I give job. Lot of money." He put up his hands as if pushing the young man out.

At once, the North American woman swiveled around on her bar stool to watch him go. Then Herr Laumann knew what would happen.

Rodolfo took a long time to get through the dining room and out of the glass door. He went across the road under the trees. There was a line of street lamps along the bay, and lights were scattered over the hills.

He felt the stone bench in front of him. It was cold and wet. He stood under the tree and listened to the waves not far away.

After a time, someone came out of the hotel, slithering a little on the steps, and crossed the road and stood at the other end of the bench. A cigarette flew out and glowed on the wet sand for a moment.

Rodolfo knew that it was the woman from the bar and that she was still staring at him. Tiredness and hunger had confused his mind. He would not turn around. He shivered in his thin suit, he was cramped by standing the way he was without moving, but he felt determined not to look around.

Suddenly he heard a strange noise, rough and wild as the sea. The woman was humming, humming deeply and gruffly a tune he did not know.

He turned away and began to walk quickly along the shore.

But it was as though he was holding a ball of string that was tied to the place: the string was pulling and unwinding all the time, falling away from inside him as he walked, and soon it would end and drop back. He would be left alone in the dark. His steps grew slower and slower. After about fifty yards he couldn't take any more steps.

The woman had opened her mouth and was singing quite loudly now. Suddenly she stopped. She had seen him turn back. She came out from under the shadow of her tree and her white linen suit shone in the dim electric light.

She was walking to meet him. Up to now, he had hardly realized what was happening. But now he knew, and his heart and his stomach quaked, not with desire, but with the excitement of his incredibly good luck.

# *A Survivor in Salvador*

I

The airport was far away from Salvador, out in the scrub country.

While the engines whirred down into silence, a steward came around, puffing at the roof and windows with a spray against mosquitoes. Then the door was opened and some rusty steps, which looked like apparatus from a public swimming pool, were trundled up. The passengers descended, one by one, into a bath of soft heat, with the new silence drumming in their ears.

The swept area of dust was bounded by a line of jungle. There was nothing else: no sign of the city of Salvador, with all its bell towers and palm trees, which they had passed over a few minutes ago; and only a rumor, somewhere near at hand, of the tropical sea.

Christophe—Prince Krzysztof Wahorski—was the tallest and oddest looking of the passengers, and his colorless hair and gaunt features made him look older, and somehow more important, than he actually was. He was fifty-three; an amateur painter, if he was anything. He could speak nothing of the language. He walked out of the airport into a world of pure sensation that required an effort of his dazed attention, a conscious recall of the danger he was in. The sun waved a sheet of fire at his screwed-up features, and while he was blinded his precious valise was snatched from him. There was nothing he could do: porters and taxi drivers had decided his fate. With five other passengers, and his valise lost among their baggage tied to the car's roof, he was dispatched on the journey to Salvador.

The other passengers were all men. In lustrous suits of chestnut or dove-gray, they were shiny from their oiled hair to their polished shoes. Approaching the fabled city they began to get excited, like schoolchildren on their way to a treat. Christophe guessed that they were boasting of their successes with women. He was sure of this when one of them, a young man with a squeaky voice, ostentatiously pulled off his wedding ring and put it in an inside pocket of his coat.

Christophe sat cramped, a head taller than any of them, his face twitching a little with heat and tiredness. His life was far simpler than theirs, for at the moment he was merely trying to survive. In his way of going about this he was like many exiled Poles. A sort of arrogance let him stoop to almost anything, as if he believed that his contempt for his associates kept him from losing honor. What you noticed about him was this arrogance, and then also the look of kindness, almost of love, which lay in the eyes blinking on the worn territory of his face. To be an aristocrat, even a minor one, and an artist, although a bad one, cannot leave you untouched in one way or another, and Christophe was helped by both these things.

Today he was wearing his last suit. His shirts, a hair net, and some elaborate toilet gear were in the valise on the roof, and there also was the small package that he believed to represent his future.

Christophe had been living for the last eight months—living on promises, on his title, on his bridge game—among the Polish colony of Pôrto Alegre, in southern Brazil. Something was always going to turn up, and speaking Polish or German he was able to get around easily. When he was finally broke and in debt, a friend told him about Blom. Blom, who was imprecisely described as a "businessman," invited him to lunch.

The house was in a suburb of Pôrto Alegre, with small villas, oleander-shaded gardens, and garages for Fords and Chevrolets. Standing at noon in the red-tiled porch, Christophe already bristled with native distrusts and phobias—of Jews, of the middle classes, and of work. It was only the immediate prospect of a good meal that kept him there. After that, he thought, he might be able to force himself to listen to Blom's proposals.

A black servant girl let him in. He saw walls lined with books and there was a strong smell of the chemical used to kill tropical book grubs. While he waited, he read some of the titles near him: *Zen Buddhism,* the American edition of the works of C.G. Jung, the *Kama Sutra.* Hearing footsteps, he swiveled around. He was still so suspicious that when he saw them he thought for a moment they were midgets. He hadn't imagined Blom having children.

They were a boy and a girl of about ten and twelve. "*Vati kommt gleich.*"

"*Vati! Vati!*"

"*Ruhig, Liebchen!*"

Blom shook hands softly, then he ran his fingers over his daughter's shoulders and her long black hair. "This is Gerda," he said, "and my son Dov. My dear Prince, these young rascals do not speak English and so perhaps we shall do so. Little pitchers have big ears. May I offer you some vodka?"

Mrs. Blom, a comfortable-looking woman, joined them, bringing a plate of pickled herring. To Christophe she spoke Polish with a ghetto accent that made him wince.

"I can understand nothing," her husband said, with great satisfaction. "You see, I am lucky enough to stem from that famous old city of Frankfurt-am-Main." Everything he said was bitten down with deprecating irony, a way in which Englishmen are believed to talk, but seldom do. But his accent, which he had modeled on that of Leslie Howard many years before, was far better than Christophe's.

They ate heavily braised meat, thick with gravy, rice, and sweet purple cabbage, and the little servant girl waited on them. Christophe watched her, his hot eyes inventing her body: she was barefoot, and possibly even naked under the plain shift hanging from her shoulders.

As they filled themselves with the warm heavy food, the atmosphere became easy. From time to time the children looked at Christophe, looked away, and broke into wild pubescent giggles, which the little black girl joined in, staggering around the table with the heavy dish of rice. Christophe laughed back, and with the warmth of the room, and first vodka and now tumblers of Chilean wine, he found that he was enjoying himself. Long afterward, he would remember the giggling middle-class Jewish children and the Negro maidservant as innocents living before the Fall, his Fall.

Perhaps he was off his guard, then, when he was alone with his host. Without any warning—Christophe believed himself a little shocked by this—Blom began to talk business.

"Our friend Mister—I am afraid I am very bad at names—has told me you are anxious to try your luck up north. I believe there are many possibilities there. I was wondering if you would do me a small service? It is merely to deliver a little package or parcel."

Christophe nodded. The room became quiet and still while Blom unlocked a safe in the wall. The children's laughter was miles away beyond the bookshelves.

"In return I should be willing to pay the cost of the plane fare. And my correspondent, Mr. Lemberg, will pay five thousand cruzeiros on delivery. Is that satisfactory? They tell me that life is far cheaper up there."

Christophe lifted the package and dropped it, as if measuring its weight. It was about the size of a can of coffee. "Is it valuable?"

"I think it worth about three thousand dollars." He giggled. "Of course, it would be most dangerous for anyone to try and sell it. For you, a newcomer without the necessary contacts, it would be impossible. That is my guarantee. Also, Mr. Lemberg will know you are coming."

They went towards the door. "For a painter, the city of Salvador should be most picturesque," Blom said. "Tell me, do you prefer oils or watercolor?"

For Christophe, who had been educated for idleness, all ways for making money involved a racket, and up to now his life had confirmed him in this belief. He was an exile three times over:

firstly, from Poland and then, an officer in Sikorski's Army, from France in 1940. After the war he and his brother, who was married to an English girl, started a restaurant in Bayswater. There was black market trouble and Christophe, the unmarried one, had done six months in jail. On leaving Wormwood Scrubs he was deported and obliged to sign a paper saying he would never enter England again. Typically, when recounting this experience, he blamed it automatically and almost without malice on the Jews. Anywhere else he would have needed a lot of forgiving; in Brazil, however, people didn't really understand what he meant.

Tonight, in Salvador, Christophe waited in the taxi until all the other passengers had been left at their different hotels. Then he gave the driver Lemberg's address. It turned out to be quite close, in one of the few modern apartment buildings in this section of the city.

There was a single elevator, by which he ascended jerkily to the seventh floor. Standing there, feeling the package sliding up and down inside his valise, Christophe was overcome with an exhausting sensation of relief. He even yawned several times.

He pressed the doorbell. There was a scuffling sound behind the dark wood, and a woman's voice speaking German, frightened and scornful at the same time.

The door opened a little.

"Mr. Lemberg? I am sent by Mr. Blom."

At this, a small excited man shot out at him.

"*Nein! Nein!* You must go away!" A hand pawed at Christophe's middle, pushing him toward the concrete stairs at the side of the elevator. "Please, Mister. Down here, hurry, please. Police coming."

Christophe descended a few steps. The door slammed shut and the woman's voice started up again, more desperate than ever.

He stood in the shadow, two flights lower down. Then he saw the tacky wire ropes begin to tremble in the elevator shaft behind him, and the cage climbed slowly upward, with three Civil Guards inside it.

Christophe ran out of the building, crossed the road, and stood among the crowd on the opposite sidewalk. A black police van was parked near the curb, but no one took any notice of him. After a few moments, Lemberg came out between two of the Civil Guards. Behind him, weeping, was a plump woman who looked rather like Mrs. Blom.

Standing among the crowd in the upper city of Salvador, Christophe knew that he was effectively stopped in his tracks. South America was the end of the line for him. Now they could not deport him anywhere except behind the Iron Curtain. Again he swung the valise to and fro and felt the package sliding about at the bottom of it. It was his greatest danger, and his only wealth: about this, he was going to prove that Blom was wrong.

The city of São Salvador da Bahia de Todos os Santos is one of those raddled beauties whose poverty has kept them intact from change. Night was falling as Christophe stood there outside Lemberg's apartment block in the upper city, and the bells from several churches clanged discordantly. Around him, streets ran downhill into the darkness. They were filled with women walking to and fro. The beauties of mixed blood, who gave the city one of its reputations, were like flames lit at intervals. Tonight Christophe avoided them. Choosing a less crowded street between two churches, he looked for somewhere to sleep and to leave his possessions. Wherever he went the inhabitants watched him, without hostility or interest, the tall foreigner with colorless hair, whose white face was constructed out of a different set of feelings from theirs.

A fanlight had "Hotel Nova Iorque" written on it. Inside an effeminate-looking boy led him up to a room with a single iron bedstead and a row of hooks on the wall. It was what Christophe wanted, and he paid the boy's mother enough for three days: this used up nearly all his money. Now he was gambling on the package, which he took from the valise and put into his pocket. He was not afraid of Blom: the distance, the half continent that separated them, made it almost impossible to believe in Blom.

Downstairs, he asked the way to the port. The boy accompanied him to the top of the street and pointed across the square with all the churches.

"*Elevador,*" he said. He watched Christophe with humorous, almost patronizing curiosity.

By the elevator, Christophe descended through layers of heat to the lower city. At the bottom there was a tree-shaded square, inhabited by shoeshines and peanut sellers. Old black women with charcoal stoves were selling coconut sweets and mealy cakes fried in palm oil. There were bars and cheap restaurants, but nothing of the type he was looking for.

Christophe walked through the streets of the commercial quarter until he came to the docks. Here there were neon signs: "Scandinavia," "Texas," "Good Beer Serve By Women." He looked into two or three bars, but they were empty, except for women knitting. Evidently he was too early, or there were few ships in harbor.

Finally, in the "Scandinavia," he got into a conversation with two young Englishmen, merchant seamen. They were sitting quietly together near the wall, with glasses of beer in front of them.

"Know this place? Just think we do. Must be our fourth time here, isn't it, Ted?"

"That's right."

They were both large, and seemed very white, with small blue emblems tattooed on their forearms. Christophe pulled out the chair opposite them and sat down. He told them that he had arrived today and knew nobody. He was going to put himself into their hands gently, as one tests a deck chair.

"You want to watch out," the first sailor said. In spite of his massive appearance his voice was refined and finicky, like a tenor's in a cathedral choir. You could imagine him sewing on buttons. "We know all about that, don't we, Ted?"

His friend nodded; he was perhaps stunned with drink.

"What is it you know?" Christophe leaned forward, dropping his voice.

"You don't want to get too friendly, see what I mean?" He indicated the cluster of women who were watching them.

Christophe's interest faded. For him, knowledge of the women came first in one's attack on a place. "What about the other bars?"

"No good," the sailor said. "Never been in any of them. Might pick up something nasty."

"But in the upper city, perhaps?"

"Where's that?"

"I mean, up the elevator." It was obvious that they did not know what he was talking about. "You always stay in this bar?"

"As long as we're in port. We only take the beer, mind. With these other things, you never know what you're getting. That's right, isn't it, Ted?"

The other hardly moved.

"Ted's got one of his upsets again. He had one of these *cuba libres*, rum and that. Never know what they put into them."

Christophe was up against that transparent protective shell which Europeans think they touch on meeting an Englishman. He prepared to go.

The sailor patted his mouth delicately. "Not that the beer's any too fancy. It repeats."

Christophe walked out into the street and followed the tramlines along the dock. He spoke to two Norwegians, one of whom, with mad blue eyes, trembled all over, like an airplane about to take off; they had jumped ship and were as lost as he was. He had a long conversation, completely at cross-purposes, with a mulatto from British Guiana. Then, as he walked on, he realized that he was moving away from the area of bars. The warehouses beside him smelled of foul straw, and on the other side the ships lay quiet under the starlight. Only an American liner was fully illuminated. Christophe could see passengers in white dinner jackets walking on the promenade deck, watching the loading which was going on under arc lights. A booming sound came from the machine, like an escalator, which trundled raceme after raceme of green bananas, creaking and stiff with unripeness, into the hold of the white ship. On the dock, groups of uniformed officials were standing around. While Christophe watched them, guessing that among them, though unapproachable, was the corruption he was looking for, there came a sudden downpour of rain. The loading machine stopped. The stevedores under the arc lights ran to put up their umbrellas. A tarpaulin was dragged over the open hold of the ship.

On the dock, umbrellas sprang up everywhere: all the officials had them. Christophe stood in the shelter of a warehouse roof. His feet were in soft leafy rubbish and the rain beat on the pavé in front of him. He shivered, for the fruitless conversations of this evening had affected him more deeply than he thought. One of Christophe's brothers had been murdered, shot in the neck, at the Katyn massacre; his mother had died during the 1944 Warsaw uprising. Would even they have preferred survival in a foreign city, without money or friends or trust?

He put his hand into his pocket and gripped the hard package. He was beginning to be frightened of it now, and to hate it for the demands it was going to make on his endurance and his courage.

When the rain stopped, he retraced his steps toward the lighted bars. By now, there were a lot of people about and among the soldiers and seamen who crowded the sidewalks he saw some more of the Civil Guards—he had learned to recognize their holstered belts and white truncheons. Who were they looking for? His fears gave him the answer. After Lemberg's arrest they had discovered something, a letter perhaps, that led directly to himself. They had only to throw a cordon across the street and he'd be done for.

It was in a moment of panic hurry that he stumbled against the American.

The American, who wore a fringe of ginger hair and was dressed in a suit of dark-blue silk, held on. He was slightly drunk and obviously lonely, and though he looked far too innocent to be of any use to Christophe, his presence while the police were about was almost as good as an American passport.

Back in the Scandinavia bar, the American beamed at Christophe across a pair of gin and tonics.

"Where you from?"

With a bow, Christophe presented his card, which at first created the impression he expected. But in the midst of his tipsiness the American carried, rather proudly, a few grains of suspicion.

"But if you're a prince, what you doing here?"

"I am a portrait painter, but I have yet no commissions here."

"Ah, that's too bad." The decent, unreal face frowned. "You're Polish. I met up with a Polish lady last evening. Well, no, perhaps I shouldn't have said that, you see, she keeps a house. Wonderful character, though, wonderful personality. . . ."

The American stopped drinking. He was rotating his glass in his hand, watching the wheel of lemon circling slowly around. For a moment, the other was frightened that drunkenness was going to claim his new friend.

"Please go on, I am very interested."

"Maybe she could help you, might want her picture painted or something. These madams here must make out pretty well."

"If you will give me the address I will go there."

"Ah, no." A calculating look came into the American's eyes. "You hold on and I'll come with you. Let's have another of these and stick together."

He probably thinks I can get him a woman more cheaply, Christophe thought. But he accepted this role as he had accepted all the others. He did not want to drink any more for fear he might get careless and lose the hard grip on himself which, at this time, was the only thing he could be certain of. The American, however insisted, and he couldn't desert the American without learning the address. A woman like that would know everything he wanted.

The moment of calculation had passed, and now the American was watching him with increasing affection. The warmth of a lover of humanity had come back into the American's eyes; he was eating life, as though here it had a savor that his native nourishment had lacked.

Then, suddenly and everywhere, shantung suits, pink plump skin, rimless spectacles: the bar was crowded with his fellow tourists.

"My friend Prince—" "Hey, listen, Prince—" "Another of those—"

A quarter of an hour later, among them, almost drowned out by voices, Christophe recovered his friend. He leaned down. "Please, the address. You give me the Polish lady's address."

"Ah, wait a minute, can't you? They'll wait for you, won't they?"

"What address, Rud, what address?"

The first American flushed under his ginger hair. "It's nothing at all. Some idea this guy's got. Who is he, anyway?" Now his eyes had changed again, and were scared and cruel. "You know, I don't credit he's a prince at all. You meet all sorts of people."

Christophe clenched his fist in his pocket. His knuckles touched the package, and he controlled himself.

"Some kind of a pimp," a voice said.

Christophe glanced around him, but none of them were looking at him anymore. Then he walked away between the tables towards the door.

A man opened it for him. *"Bonsoir, monsieur."*

Turning to him, Christophe recognized a life-worn European face. The ground was under his feet again, a tussock in the middle of the bog.

*"La maison d'une polonaise,"* he asked, *"vous la connaissez?"*

*"Mais certainement.* Madame Daisy, Rua Gloria 47."

Christophe knew, the moment she entered the little room with the plush sofas, that he had found what he was looking for.

"Senhor, I am afraid all my girls are busy. If you would care to wait . . ."

He spoke to her in Polish and presented his card. He asked only to be allowed to talk with Madame for a few moments.

"You may talk as you wish. None of my girls understands."

Round-shouldered, almost hunched, Madame Daisy sat opposite him, holding his gaze. Though the tropical night was as hot as ever after the rain, she was bundled up in a cocoa-colored knitted shawl. Her face was powdered thickly but the mouth was unpainted and so thin that the lips seemed to hook together, like the catch of a child's purse: if this was what the American considered a wonderful personality, he deserved to be deluded wherever he went.

Yet, in spite of Madame Daisy's baleful appearance, Christophe felt at home with her. She too was from the Old World, she would understand these little problems of survival. He offered her an American cigarette and spoke to her of Poland. He had not much imagination and, when he told her his recent history, he kept as close to the truth as he could: he had disembarked with an immigrant's visa, and he had something valuable to sell.

At this point, Madame Daisy shifted a little in her seat and pulled her shawl together. But she still held his eye. She had been humiliated by his class in the old days, and now she was not displeased to have him begging for favors.

"If you tell me what it is, I think I can help you. But not jewels!" She wagged her finger. "Here you don't have a good market."

Christophe expressed his profound gratitude. He had known at once, he said, that he had found the right person, and an ambiance in which he was at home. If she would help him, he said, he would like to throw a party, with champagne, for all her girls.

"Then you waste your money. They are poor silly girls, these ones, and don't appreciate a party." The sofa creaked and she stood up. "Well, what is it you have?"

Christophe put the back of his wrist up to his nostrils and sniffed.

"Good. I write you an address. This man will help you and you can trust him."

She went to a table and scrawled a few words on a piece of paper, which she folded up and pressed into his hand.

"No thanks, please. I shall hear very soon what this man will give you, and I shall ask for my share. I do not give information for nothing."

Christophe was not angry at this. Instead he felt the rather masochistic pleasure you get when people revert to type and behave exactly as you expect them to. Whatever happened, he would now be able to sell his package, and even a small part of its value would set him up quite adequately: of an artist's talents, he had at least that of living poor. He left the house and walked some distance to the nearest street lamp, before he opened the paper she had given him and tried to read it.

His first impression was of the handwriting they had taught at free schools in Poland: he had not seen it for many years. Then he began to make out the words. There was no name, but the street and the number were of Lemberg's apartment.

He tore the paper into small fragments and threw them in the gutter.

II

Christophe lay on his bed, feeling the day burn hotter and hotter through the room. Sweat streaked off him in runnels into the mattress and his smell brought in flies, which tried to settle on the corners of his mouth. From outside, he heard the noise of wooden sandals and handcarts on the cobbles. He moved, and felt his hunger. When he sat up, he remembered why he was afraid.

In his mind, the previous day became an area of appalling innocence, an Eden in which he had committed almost every sort of blunder. (Lemberg's clients had been expecting him to receive a consignment. . . . Blom, in Pôrto Alegre, had heard of the arrest and knew who had the package. . . . Madame Daisy had published the fact that she had been offered it.) From the window, dressed in his underpants, Christophe looked out on the eighteenth-century city. Even in the bright sunlight, he was scared. The shouts in the unknown language from the stalls below had a note of menace, and he felt no pleasure at all in the satisfying thump of knives going into the rose-scarlet flesh of papaws and watermelons.

He went back to bed. When the morning was half gone, the boy he had spoken to the night before came in and swept the floor, then leaned on his broom and chatted amiably and incomprehensibly. Christophe watched him, his interest momentarily aroused. Compact and self-reliant, the boy had been able to come to terms with himself more quickly in a society in which there was absolutely no question of being respectable. You could trust him with life, Christophe thought, in a way you could never have trusted the English sailors or the American.

While the boy went on talking, Christophe stared up at the bumps and patches on the whitewashed ceiling, forming them into maps of all the countries in the world where he could never go anymore until he died. "No!" he shouted, suddenly. He was talking to himself, exploding out of pressure within, the ingrowing smolder of his life.

The boy looked up, without surprise.

Christophe pointed to his watch. He made the boy understand that he wanted to sell it. The boy nodded at once and beckoned to him to come out. Christophe pulled on his clothes; he took the package from under the pillow and replaced it in his pocket. When he felt it there, heavy against his side, he knew he was back in his situation once more.

The boy led him across the square to a jeweler's. But he refused vehemently when the other asked him to come in.

"No, no." The jeweler would think he had stolen the watch. Christophe accepted his knowledge and went in alone.

A silence settled around him and staring people made way for him up to the counter. The jeweler, a dark, furious little man, snatched the watch away and a few seconds later pushed across some money. Christophe counted it. It was not nearly enough and he began to object, but the man ignored him, talking to someone else. You got money out of the poor by surliness and anger, when they were too far gone to resist. Christophe bowed his head and folded the thin wad of notes into his wallet. Everyone was still watching him. It was like the moment when madness strikes, but he seized hold of himself and went out into the street into the glare of sunlight and trams.

At the hotel, his friend was standing in the doorway talking to a young woman.

"This is Antonieta," the boy said.

They shook hands and Antonieta smiled, showing small bluish-white teeth.

Christophe looked at her again. Her skin was the color of dark caramel, but she had European features. A ribbon was fastened with a brooch around her neck. She was wearing a black skirt and a white blouse and though these clothes were tight-fitting over the breasts and thighs, there was a primness, almost a schoolgirlishness, about her which immediately interested him.

"He told me you were a foreigner," she said. *"Allemand?"*

*"Polonais."*

The girl spoke French well. Christophe was amazed, for it was as though there was a gap in the wall in front of him: he could go through it, and live.

"This is a good girl," the boy said, poking at her and whistling vulgarly. Antonieta pretended to hit him, and there was a scuffle which ended with her arm affectionately around the boy's neck. The ease of their contact surprised Christophe: there was a quality like innocence about them both, though of course you could not call it that. But it made him remember Blom's children, in Pôrto Alegre.

Christophe invited the girl to come and drink with him.

"Willingly."

She led him to a bar nearby. Though she must have learned from the boy that the Pole had no money, she was obviously glad of his company. He suspected, too, that speaking French gave her a certain status among the other women who came to the bar. Unlike them, however, Antonieta sat stiffly upright, her knees and feet together, her skirt pulled down. She looked charming and entirely presentable. There even seemed a sort of wit, a strong, perhaps unconscious, private joke, about the way she dressed and held herself.

She had learned French, she said, from a Belgian who had been the representative of a shipping line. She never told Christophe his name: he remained always *"le belge."*

"My mother was the cook in his house. At the beginning I was only a child, but he was always watching me and joking with me. It started when I was thirteen and I lived with him five years. He was not always good to me—he suffered from amoebas, poor man, and he had very bad humors—but he taught me many things. He was often sick, and I nursed him, changing the sheets, everything. In the end he had to return to Belgium, he was so sick. He left quite a lot of money for me, as a *dot*, but I did not get married and the lover of my mother, Seu Silvio, spent it all gambling."

"Why didn't you get married? You are very pretty."

"There was no one special. It is difficult, like this." She scratched gently on the back of her left hand as if testing whether the darkness would come away under the nail. "Besides, I cannot have children. When I was fourteen the Belgian gave me one but I was very ill and nearly died." She smiled at him. "Now I do not mind anymore. I am twenty-one and still new. I have kept my figure."

Compared with Antonieta, the people Christophe had met in Salvador, the English sailors, the tourist, Madame Daisy herself, became intangible, part of a nightmare that was over. He spent the rest of the afternoon talking to her and told her something of his past. He soon realized, however, that anything that happened outside this city had no reality for her. Yet their conversation was easy, for there was no need for them to pretend to one another. She pleased him more and more, and if he did not yet desire her, it was because the package still obsessed him. With his hand in his pocket he held it to him, his unadmitted vice. He knew that, sooner or later, he would confess its existence to Antonieta. Already he trusted her enough.

About five o'clock the boy came to fetch her. "The Portuguese is waiting for you at the hotel."

Antonieta was quite frank about her departure. "He is rather old, this Portuguese, but he is good to me. He is a grocer and quite rich. You never know, perhaps he would like his portrait painted. I will ask him."

On her way out, she stopped and looked down at Christophe: there was something else she had to declare. "But the moment I find someone I love, I stop at once"—she banged the edge of her hand like a cutting blade on the table—"like that. It is my character, you understand?"

This little blaze up made her eyes glisten, her features grow taut, and yet it was still a comic passion, which seemed to mock at itself.

When he met her the following day, however, she was in deep melancholy, her face clouded by an African sullenness.

*"J'ai des ennuis avec la police.* But not what you think. I will tell you one day, perhaps."

Christophe was annoyed at her troubles, because today he had meant to ask her help. In spite of her youth and humble station, she knew things about the city which, without her, he would take years to learn. Whereas he still saw only the narrow streets where colored people shouted incomprehensible things, the churches like gold-encrusted grottoes and the gardens dark with aged and magnificent mango trees and palms, Antonieta knew the city as a pattern created out of her struggle to live, a series of shelves down the rock with people scrambling on them, fighting for existence.

"Christophe, I have had enough of it, this life. If I had a room, I could work making clothes for people. But at my mother's there is always Seu Silvio; he doesn't do any work. Perhaps I will go back to Albertinho, it was he who taught me to sew when *le belge* went away and Seu Silvio took my money. Did you know Albertinho was a friend of mine?"

"Who is this Albertinho?"

She was astonished. "But he is famous! They know about him even in Rio, and there was an American woman who put him into a book."

The hotel boy, who had joined them, said something which was obviously derogatory. Antonieta turned on him and they quarreled violently, like two children. Then she said to Christophe: "This one, also, walks in the street with paint on his face. He cannot speak against Albertinho."

The boy smiled and was quiet, preening himself.

"Albertinho was good to me when no one else was," Antonieta went on. "He taught me to sew in many ways. Also, I was a *filha do santo* in his *terreiro*. He receives the *orixá* of Yansan. Yansan has been very good to me."

Christophe realized that she was talking *candomblé*, which is voodoo, but the words meant nothing to him.

"You believe this?" he asked.

"Naturally. Everybody here believes in the old ones. Apart from that, Albertinho is my friend. He knows everyone. If you are ever in trouble, if you need help, I just say that you are my friend and Albertinho will help us. He has great influence, here in Salvador. The politicians go to church but also they go to Albertinho for advice."

The boy began talking to Antonieta again. For a time Christophe watched them with the detachment you can feel from those much younger than yourself, but then his own troubles surged up in front of him again. When the boy went away, Christophe did not come out of his silence.

"You are not there!" She was suddenly jealous, fearing she had lost his interest. "You don't like me?" She smirked. "I am wondering, perhaps, you are not a man at all?"

He looked up at her, his face lined with hatred and strain. It had been one of her professional gambits and she quickly repented of it. Across the table she placed her dark hand on his. "Our fingers look like piano keys," he thought.

He pulled his hand away roughly. "Come with me."

"To the hotel?"

He did not answer, but led her out of the bar. They climbed the narrow street and crossed the three squares to the elevator. They were in the middle of the upper city, at the edge of the cliff. Below lay the roofs of the lower city, the fish market, the little port crowded with sailboats, the streets, mean and squalid with sunlight, where Christophe had wandered two nights ago. Far off in the heat haze, arrivals from an exterior civilization, stood the great aluminum drums of an oil refinery.

*"Chérie, je veux que vous m'aidiez."*

"What is it?"

He told her.

He spoke very low, between flattened lips, although there was nothing but air surrounding them, and the nearest people were at the entrance to the elevator, thirty yards away. She listened to him with her whole soul, and at the end she wept a little.

"Why are you crying?"

"Three thousand dollars! It is impossible to think of so much money."

"*Enfin*, you see I am in trouble."

"You are in great trouble. Of course you cannot make love when you are like this."

Although her taunt had forced him to tell her, it was the best thing he could have done. Now, moving closer to her, he felt himself for the first time alive in the body. But it was like the lust you feel when you are very tired, in a strange town, after a long train journey.

"I thought of throwing the package away."

"You must be mad."

"Well, what shall I do?"

"We will go and see Albertinho tomorrow. He will know."

Christophe nodded; for the moment he was prepared to leave the matter in her hands. A true Slav, he believed that you could never dominate a situation or inhabit a country, unless you first had a woman in it taped. A newfound colonizer, he held her arm with a preliminary knowledge of possession.

Later, he told her about his adventures, about Blom, Lemberg and Madame Daisy. When he spoke of Lemberg, Antonieta said: "I have seen his name in a newspaper, a day or two ago."

They got a pile of newspapers from the boy at the hotel.

"Here it is." She translated for him. The Public Prosecutor, in a statement to journalists, demanded Lemberg's deportation.

"It will be the same for me," Christophe said. "In my case, to the Russians."

Her eyes shone at him in admiration for his importance. He smiled—how grateful he was that such things were completely strange territory to her!

Her fingers touched him experimentally. He put his arm around her and they helped each other up the stairs to his room.

Behind them, the boy crowed in triumph.

They rode to the end of the tramline and got down, under a white sky. The tram rounded the circular track, rang a bell and clanked away, as if happy that its expedition to the interior was over.

There were no houses, only a bar thatched with palm leaves, where some men were drinking *aguardente*. Everyone stared at Christophe, who was the only white man in sight, and at Antonieta walking quietly beside him, picking her way on pin-heeled shoes.

"Where are we going?"

"To his house. The *terreiro* is a long way away."

He now saw that there were several entrances into the mass of vegetation that surrounded them. Electric light poles followed paths that bare feet had trodden, winding between clumps of thorn and castor-oil plant. Antonieta led the way, and small houses began to appear, half hidden behind the foliage of banana trees. Walls of bamboo sticks shut in little patches of maize, but in front of each house there was always a bare patch, running with wastewater and coated with the thin foul mud that is made by the feet of chickens.

When they came to Albertinho's house, dogs started barking. On the veranda, a girl working a sewing machine gave a cry. Other women came running out. They all shouted to Antonieta and then, when they saw Christophe, fell silent.

"You stay here. I will go alone. It is a house of women, *filhas do santo*."

She climbed the steps to the veranda. In a little while she was embracing them all, first a mud-colored old woman with a tightly kerchiefed head, then half a dozen of the girls. A man came out and joined them. He stayed in the shadow and Christophe could not see his face. But he felt a curious lowering of spirit, derived from his own belief in mediums and fortune-tellers, and a memory, from his childhood in Poland, of the servants' stories of witches and ghosts.

Antonieta disappeared into the house.

The women on the veranda had stopped giggling and chattering and were watching Christophe. It seemed to him that there was a peculiar meaninglessness and lack of interest about their gaze: they were like a row of chickens when you turn a torch on them at night. Christophe paced up and down the bare patch of earth. The house and the land around it were in the shadow of a hill. The afternoon stood at a distance on either side, and here everything was in twilight. Bamboo clumps, pathways, the roof ridge, where two buzzards were sitting, the white porcelain insulators on the wires seemed to acquire a sort of luminosity: you got very conscious of the edges of things.

The door on to the veranda opened. Antonieta reappeared with Albertinho, who accompanied her down the steps.

He was wearing a shirt of shiny crimson sateen and white trousers, heavy rings, and a bracelet. Albertinho was the "horse of Yansan" and when in trance his body was ridden by the goddess of winds and storms, and he wore her long skirts and purple beads and received her sacrifice of goats. Apart from the tinge of African blood, he had a face, soft and creamy, from the Place Pigalle or Shaftesbury Avenue.

The meeting was not a success. The Pole was depressed by the atmosphere and impatient at having been kept waiting under the hen-like eyes of the women. The mulatto seemed coy and sulky, fearful of contempt or criticism. Antonieta separated them as quickly as possible.

"What happened?" Christophe asked, when they were out of earshot.

"He knows a man. This man came to him for a cure, but his wife will not let him come again. He is *granfino*, you see, this man, from an old white family, very rich. And because his wife despises *candomblé*, Albertinho cannot help him."

Christophe recognized the usual excuses of the unsuccessful witch doctor. "How would a man like that come to believe in this?"

"Probably from his black nurse. Albertinho says he is now ill and without this stuff he is going mad. He will pay anything for it, if you can get it to him without his wife knowing."

They were back at the tram terminus. Antonieta took off her shoes and wiped them carefully on the grass.

"You found out his address?"

"Yes, when we get back to the city I'll show you where it is. You must go there tonight and speak to his manservant. I will meet you afterward at the hotel."

But when Christophe came late that night to the Hotel Nova Iorque, he did not find Antonieta. By then, he was in despair.

It had all seemed too simple: Albertinho had given the address and Antonieta had told him how to reach the house. But by now, the city itself was working against him. The house, which was established with a sort of brutal dominance at the top of the city, was a standing insult to all who were defeated and came begging. The poor of Salvador are not allowed to forget other people's success.

All along the *avenida* Christophe felt the house waiting for him. Porters were on sentry duty at the gates, and police dogs were ready to growl at any passer-by who smelt furtive. Christophe had to hand his card to a Negro in khaki livery, like a member of a private army.

Christophe had asked to see the owner of the house and at the front door the major-domo received the request and acted without hesitation. He was shown into a high room furnished in the North American taste: low tables with playing cards fossilized under glass in them; some enormous gilt madonnas, such as you still might find in the ruined churches of the interior of the state; on the walls, French pictures, Kisling, Van Dongen, Léger.

Christophe was standing between two doors: the rooms led from one to another in the traditional form of the Portuguese town house. And now he could hear someone approaching along the string of rooms. A woman's footsteps. "The Senhora is coming now." Christophe's heart sank. He knew already that it was not going to be any good.

"Madame."

She was a mere child of sixteen or seventeen. She was holding his card in her hand. *"Vous êtes vraiment un prince?"* she asked, in shrill convent French. "How can I help you?"

She was wearing a shirt and tapered pants. Her eyes, which were slightly protruding, kept looking up and down him. But she was charming—she reminded him of a little frog, one of those pretty, throbbing tree frogs that have almost the delicacy of insects.

"Forgive me, Madame. There has been a mistake. It was with monsieur your husband—"

"My husband is ill again. Please speak to me." She sounded almost as though she were pleading for his company and conversation.

"It is a matter of private business."

"Please tell me." She moved toward him, blinking her eyes: she had lived alone and had become uncertain of her effect on other people. As well as guessing her loneliness, Christophe noticed that she was not greatly concerned about her husband. Perhaps, when it had been arranged for her to marry, she had been told "he will be ill" and had accepted it as a permanent factor in her life.

She settled on the arm of a chair, frowning and swinging her foot, and went on: "I know all about it, you see. My husband has had this trouble a long time, and first there was the German who came here, and later my husband went to a *pai do santo*—you know what that is, the voodoo?—but the priest told me that I mustn't let him go there anymore. Then this doctor came from Rio, with the new treatment, and no one may speak to him, not even me. He has nurses, everything."

Christophe said nothing, and suddenly she asked him: "You come from this German?"

It must have been Lemberg. "No, Madame."

"You don't?" She frowned again, nervous that she had made a mistake. He saw that she was trembling violently: she was desperately frightened, not of him, but of everything her life had brought her.

"I have changed my mind about this. I would do anything to make him happy again."

Christophe was a Pole, a refugee from East Europe. He had to survive. He was a makeweight in the balance of the world: that part of the human race which had never suffered enough, the rich and the untouched, was prey for his exploitation. But not, he decided, this girl. If she had been older, he might have sold his package and survived. But they were not the right people for the situation, he, penniless in his last suit, and she only a child, a little girl with a fat bottom, who couldn't have been married more than a few months. The butler was there the whole time, because her husband could not allow her a minute alone with a strange man.

"No, Madame. The situation is different from what I had expected."

"You won't help me?" She was suddenly angry. "I could call the police, you know. That German was arrested—I saw his picture in the paper!"

Christophe bowed, and drew himself to his full height. It was still an imposing front, and below him on the chair she quailed a little. "I wish your husband every success in his cure."

The major-domo accompanied him as far as the gate. The moment Christophe was outside the dogs were released again, and their breath roared out, like a gas burner, a few inches behind his calves.

By now the thick darkness had settled down, buzzing with crickets and gassy with rotting vegetation. There were fireflies in the gardens along the street. From the echoing distances of the city, faint shouts came from those who were still involved with the world.

When Christophe came in sight of the sea, he knew he was approaching the center of the upper city. Then the shouting turned into the sirens of police cars: the sound was muffled, blocked off by houses, and returned again, swooping up the funnels of the narrow streets.

He was cold with shock, the package bouncing against his thigh. The little frog girl had betrayed him, of course. What else could she do alone there but try to hurt? What other mark could she make on anyone's existence? But he took the blow all over him, shivering and coughing. After this, there came a minute or two when he could think quite calmly. He walked up the steps of a church. He would stay here, and later, at the hotel, he would find Antonieta, and she would have somewhere to hide the package until the opportunity to sell it arose again.

When he sat down in the church his mind was quite empty. The emotions aroused by danger soon faded away. He was getting old, and there were pains and sorenesses in various parts of his body. The night before he had not slept enough after making love, and as he sat in the half-darkness of the church he felt his body groaning and settling down like furniture in a house at the end of a hot day.

While he waited, the church gradually manifested itself around him, the gold carving against the shell-white stone. There was a smell of tallow and incense and dirt. Many years had passed since he had sat long in a church, and it all meant very little to him. When he had been cornered, as he was now, he had always looked for a woman and always found one. It was the thing he did, the way he took out of circumstances.

The streets had grown silent outside and Christophe was

bored. A bell struck nine overhead. It must have been the eve of some saint's day, because candles were being lit and whispering and shuffling drew nearer and nearer to him. He tried to shut out the sounds. But when they were close behind him, he turned around. He almost cried out: it was a violent shock, of awe and dread.

The whole church was filled with people, row on row of dark and white faces in the candlelight. It was as though they had pursued him as far as the shrine. But they meant no harm to anyone. It was his recurrent experience in Salvador: he had looked for evil, had needed it, but each time he had met innocence.

He felt his skin contract, his eyes prickle with tears. For the first time he himself was part of the patient despair of the city, and now there seemed to be no point in trying to escape from it, in being the one man in search of a better fate. The hopes that had been wrecked for Poland and himself had never even been born here. Antonieta too would become one of these work-worn crones, scrabbling and muttering after God. And if he failed, wasn't it honorable to fail in such circumstances? For Christophe, twenty years separated from his country and his class, there was certainly no honor in anything else.

He left the church reconciled to his idea of his fate, which was that God will beat us down until we beg for His mercy. Civil Guards, like the angels of punishment, were still standing on street corners, but they were not stopping anyone.

"Where is Antonieta?"

The boy, who had been asleep in his chair behind the hotel door, awoke with scared eyes; he looked very small in the half-darkness.

"She is not here. She is not coming tonight."

Suspicion hung between them, and the boy twisted in his chair. Christophe took his key and went upstairs.

He threw the package on the bed, hating it. Then, with his head in his hands, he knelt and prayed. Afterward he moved aimlessly about the room for a few minutes, breathing deeply, like a swimmer who has taken longer than he believed possible to reach dry land.

On the windowsill Antonieta had left a bottle of cane spirit mixed with sugar and the juice of green lemons. She had prepared this for him with great pride. Now he poured a little into a tumbler and drank it: it was like some mixture that you use to trap insects. He took another gulp and felt better. He finished the bottle.

The next moment, he was awake in the hot sunlight with the flies buzzing over him. The sun was high in the air, small and concentrated, as though a magnifying glass was directing its heat on the house. The boy had forgotten to wake him.

Christophe found him downstairs. "Antonieta?" he asked.

But it still wasn't any good. The boy looked away, sulking. His eyes were puffy, his face a drab color, and he had been plucking his eyebrows. "She will come back," he said.

"When?"

"I don't know."

The boy disappeared into a room behind, where his mother was lying, and closed the door. Christophe heard whispering.

The boy came out, rubbing his fingers together. "Money," he said. "For the room."

"Tonight."

The boy turned away in apparent disgust, and Christophe felt the angry humiliation the middle-aged feel when the young can dismiss them easily.

Out in the street, he began to be racked by jealousy. He was conscious of the loss of Antonieta as though each cell of his body was shrieking for her. He had never felt like this before, and believed it to be a by-product of his advancing age. This morning he knew that he had outlived his prime, and that Antonieta had abandoned him: the boy knew this, but had been told to tell him nothing. Perhaps the boy and Antonieta were in collusion to rob him.

It was another blinding, dusty day. Wherever he went he could not help looking for her face. In the Rua Chile, which is the chief street of Salvador, there are hotels with big windows, where respectable businessmen sit in white shark-skin suits, reading the newspapers and watching the women. Here she must often have passed, raising the plaudits of eyes: Antonieta was *mulata escura*, one of the dark ones who are the most desired.

At times it became impossible to believe that he would not find her around the next corner, or that, among the incomprehensible voices of the roadway, her voice was not calling his name. But after his heart had leaped with hope half a dozen times, he gave up the effort of concentration. He walked on.

He knew by now he was *cornudo, cocu*. His body began hurting again and he could not trust it with his feelings. He deliberately went away from the part of the city where he was most likely to find her, and spent the middle of the day, the hours of skull-cracking heat, sitting in a square full of carob trees, not far from the big house he had visited the previous evening. The idea that the Civil Guards might be on the lookout for him did not trouble him anymore. The bit of his mind that reacted to danger was numb. He had even left the package in his valise at the hotel. It had become unimportant.

There were very few places in Salvador where you could sit down without spending money. Christophe realized that he was treating the city as an old man must do: an old man does not wander aimlessly, but with the knowledge that, before a certain time, he must reach a fountain with a tap of drinking water, a place to urinate, a bench to sit down on out of the sun. But even here, Christophe thought, the old men had a shelter they could return to by nightfall, where they were expected, though grudgingly and on sufferance.

Heat poured down out of the sky. The parakeets stopped screeching in the branches overhead and everything was held in the grip of noon. And then, at last, the shadows began to stretch. Bells rang. A flock of children in regulation orphanage uniforms were shepherded through the square by a couple of nuns. The whole line sparkled with noise, and Christophe saw the children cling to each other, rubbing their chins on each other's shoulders. Did they too foresee a future of loss? But compared with himself, even the most despised here were not alone; their consciousness was a part of the consciousness of the whole city, a part of it like the churches and the trees. Into this consciousness for him there was only one way, through women, through Antonieta, lost.

When the boy of the hotel came hurrying toward him, Christophe was still marching erect, his coat buttoned, his tie a tight knot, his face shaded by his Panama hat. Only the crumpled shirt collar, the thick dust on his shoes, could give anyone an idea that he wasn't still dominating his circumstances. But he was painfully stiff from his afternoon on the bench and his throat was sore with drafts of water from the public fountain. He knew that to quell the pangs of hunger he'd have to buy more cheap cigarettes, even though they fouled his mouth up and made him gape.

The boy sidled up to him and now his voice was soft and coaxing. He said the words twice before Christophe understood. "You may stay in the room until Antonieta comes. My mother agrees."

"And Antonieta?"

But again the boy shook his head. He walked back to the hotel beside Christophe, looking up at him and smiling, and greeting from time to time the women who already paraded the street. None of these tried to attract Christophe's attention. Before, he had imagined that the boy had told them he had no money, but now he wondered if he was considered to be Antonieta's property, and if she was expected back. Christophe tried to question the boy about this, but could not make him understand.

The boy gave Christophe his key and signed to him to go upstairs. A few minutes later he banged on the door, carrying a big sandwich of bread and meat. Christophe thanked him. "You're a good boy," he said.

But, next morning, there was still no news of Antonieta. Christophe closed the shutters against the torrent of sun, and wondered if he could survive another day.

He took the package out of his valise. Usually he returned to it with boredom, as one returns on a long train journey to a newspaper already leafed through four or five times. But today, for the first time, he saw it with an ordinary curiosity. The desolation of sexual jealousy that he had passed through had killed off the rest of his hopes. He had stopped telling himself that the package represented a place to live, the setting up of a studio with himself as the society portrait painter, complete with smock, Rembrandt hat and mahlstick. He did not think of his own survival with any interest at all.

Christophe cut away the brown paper and revealed a screw-topped bottle. The powder was shifting about inside. He had heard that people like Lemberg would divide it into small envelopes, possibly adulterating it with something else, and sell them one by one. Christophe was no longer interested; until he had freed himself of this thing, he was neither alive nor dead but suspended in anxiety.

Carefully, he unscrewed the bottle and took a very small amount, like a pinch of snuff.

He knew it would be some time before he felt anything, but he did not want the experience or illumination, or whatever it was, to happen here, on an iron bedstead behind the shutters of a dissolute hotel. He still possessed at least his sense of ceremony. He pushed the bottle into his pocket and hurried downstairs into the street.

The boy saw him go and watched, wondering.

Christophe clambered on to the first tram he saw and handed the conductor a small brown coin. Through the open sides of the tram he watched the whirling faces of the crowd fall back; he was leaving them on permanent holiday, his search was abandoned and his ambition forgotten.

The tram passed the tree-hidden big house of the rich girl. It stopped at the square where Christophe had endured the previous afternoon, then, rattling downhill, it gathered speed and he saw that it was going right out of the city. They were in the suburb of Rio Vermelho. Small houses alternated with patches of castor-oil plant or bamboo, and once the tram crossed a muddy creek fringed with brilliant green grass, where washerwomen were toiling over bundles of grayish clothing. The conductor came around on the outside of the tram, hand over hand like a tree sloth, and collected another coin, and then, with its bells ringing, the tram lurched out on to the seacoast at the Barra.

Here the road goes along a curved shore, until it reaches a headland crowned with a ruined Portuguese colonial fortress. In the shelter of a rock, Christophe opened the bottle again and sniffed some more of the powder.

Cars approached him along the coast road and he knew for certain that his hand had only to go out, the wide palm smacking lightly on the windshield, and they would stop. But later, there were no more cars. He returned to the shore, to an endless bed of sand, golden and softer than feathers, where, toward dusk, he slept.

The visions of the afternoon had been of extraordinary intensity, but when he woke it was with the usual sort of hangover. His body was back with him again, and he had fallen asleep on top of the bottle, which was pressed uncomfortably into his belly. While he was asleep the moon had risen; it stood, as if on a pillar of its own light, just above the rim of the sea.

Christophe took his life in his hands and looked at it. The long decline of his fortunes was over. His name would survive—his brother in England had a child—but Christophe himself had abdicated. He guessed that he would die quite soon and in misery but, as a concession to remembered beliefs, he wanted to be free to be chosen by death. Still, therefore, he had to get rid of the bottle.

The sea is untrustworthy: sooner or later its tides bring everything back. He crossed the road and looked at the low jungle stretching out ahead of him. Into it, as far as he could, he threw the bottle. He only imagined that he heard the noise of its fall among the roots and swamp water, cocaine, three thousand dollars going into the eternal mud.

Then he slid back on to the shore and slept.

He fell asleep on some dry sand under the rocks, and when he awoke the sun was high in the sky. He had slept through the night and a large part of the day. At some time or other he had kicked off his shoes, and now, when he moved, he realized that his feet and his calves were horribly burnt: they had been in and out of the sun during the day. He had to throw away his socks because, if he wore them, his feet would no longer fit into the shoes. His mouth was seared dry and his head bursting with pain.

Christophe got off the tram and stumbled across the square by the cathedral. Nobody looked at him now. Well brought-up people believe that if you get dirty and drunk everyone will look at you. But in fact this is the time when nobody does.

Near the hotel, he went into a bar to kill his thirst. Even here, where he was already well known, no one seemed to see him: it was as though at some time during the past twenty-four hours at the Barra he had become invisible. He crossed the street to the hotel. In his mind the small bedroom had become a well, a coffin, into which he had to throw and obliterate himself.

At the entrance, he almost fainted. His hand scrabbled wildly for the key on the hook. The boy heard him and came hurrying out of the back room.

"She is back! She is here!"

But when he looked at Christophe's white-stubbled face, his fatally injured eyes, the boy retreated, respectful at the ruin which had overtaken his friend. He gave up any attempt at getting through to him. He pushed the key into Christophe's hand and then he ran out to fetch Antonieta.

Lying on the bed, Christophe became aware of someone moving near him, and then of the small, subverbal noises which must be the earliest things a man hears: the noises, not of disgust or horror but more of formal disapproval, which a woman makes in the presence of a physical disaster she knows she can cope with. He heard the little chimes of water in a tin basin, his forehead was sponged and his feet cooled almost miraculously with a soft cream. He was conscious too, without daring to observe it, of her sympathy all around him. He delivered himself to it and feared it might end if he once opened his eyes.

He was right.

"Christophe, I have looked for you all last night. Listen, please try to listen. I have found a man, a friend of mine—well, no friend—but I told him about this stuff you had and he is very interested. He will take it and sell it abroad and there will be no danger. Christophe, are you listening?"

He let her take his hand.

"Please speak to me."

"It is no good." His voice came dry and he coughed. "I've thrown it away."

He felt the emotion rushing through her body. "Tell me where. We can get it back."

"No, no." Christophe felt cross at the idea. "I threw it into a wild place and even I do not know where it is now. Having it was killing me."

There was a silence. By now, the lights were on in the street outside and they shone pink through his closed eyelids.

He was the first to speak: "Antonieta, where had you gone? Where had you gone?"

While he was waiting for her to answer, there was a knock at the door, and the boy came in with a plate of rice and black beans. He stayed talking to Antonieta. In the reddish twilight of the room Christophe watched them with half-open eyes, very conscious of their youth, the firmness of rounded limbs: the boy had the paler skin but the short cat head of the Negro, and Antonieta's stillness now seemed a minor miracle, the gift of a peculiar grace.

When the boy had gone, Christophe said: "He has been good to me."

"He loves you too."

She watched him eat the rice, stained with the dark gravy of the beans. She did not refer again to the loss of the package; it was one of those upheavals that shake life to its depths, then pass. Hers was the point of view of poverty: one is more likely to stay the same than to change, and one's life is too.

"He says we can keep this room and I will look after you. I still have some money the Portuguese gave me, before I met you. Later, when you are better, I can get work."

He put the plate to one side, half finished. She was helping him devotedly, without hesitation, and he did not want to damage this by asking questions.

Then, without him having to ask, she began to answer him. "Poor boy, he knew where I was but he was too frightened to tell you."

"Will you tell me?"

"Of course. I think you can understand. It is just that sometimes the police take all the girls they can find. It happened that night after we went to Albertinho. You must have heard the sirens and the girls screaming. They always scream, because they want everyone to know what is going on."

Ashamed, Christophe thought of his fear after leaving the big house, his hours of sanctuary in the crowded church—in flight from a terror that was not for him.

"The police have nothing against me. But there is one of them, a sergeant, who knows me. He used to play cards with Seu Silvio, my stepfather. He has been after me a long time, I think that is why I was arrested."

Christophe flinched. The knowledge of suffering can make you close your eyes involuntarily, like too strong a light.

"They got what they wanted, he and his friends, there in the police station."

"I understand."

He had the truth now. He bit hard against it, as one tries to murder an aching tooth. When the truth came, it was always as bad as you could stand, far worse than you had expected, and so you could never really prepare yourself for it. And there was really no one to blame: Seu Silvio's friend had merely waited for his opportunity; the poor girl had learned not to expect anything else from life. The horror, Christophe knew, was mostly in his own imagination.

He was grateful to Antonieta and she seemed fond of him. But in spite of the warm night, he felt cold. Later, he would open his eyes again, raise his hands, and pat her with a comforting gesture. For the moment he could not bring himself to move.

Then he heard a sound and looked up astonished.

Antonieta was weeping as though she would die. He pulled her down and held her to him, his hands and head doing all they could to convince her of love.

# FINGERS IN THE DOOR

# *The Palladian Bridge*

The balustrades of the Palladian Bridge had been chipped by farm carts and decorated with long wisps of hay. The bridge terminated a landscape gardener's vista, which was formed by the lake and the massed trees of the park. In two centuries the trees had grown huge and rounded like cumulus clouds, and clouds of the same shape hung almost motionless above them. These were split by gulfs of intense blue, and somewhere up there, catching the sun from time to time like trout fry in shallow water, stratospheric bombers proceeded to a daylight raid. The horizon echoed: the boys in the park and the school buildings were ringed around by sunlight, by great trees and the insistent sounds of war.

Up at the school, a cinder path led from the kitchen entrance into a wood scented with mock-orange bushes, and past an obelisk commemorating the battle of Dettingen. The path became a cart track, crossed a steep field, and descended to the Palladian Bridge. For Page-Barlow, the boy standing on the bridge this afternoon, all the track was as important as a vein in his own arm.

Of course he had come too early for the appointment. He waited, trying to concentrate on some lines in the anthology of modern verse he carried about with him. "Issues from the hand of God the simple soul." He knew this was meant to be good, even though it was back to front, but his attention kept skidding off the words and he found himself in the middle of the poem without having understood anything.

Page-Barlow took off his glasses and leaned over the sun-warm parapet of the bridge. Between the water lilies he could make out his rough hair against the darkened sky, but he was too near-sighted to see what he was looking like. If he replaced his glasses, they might fall straight off his ears onto the lily leaves, then tilt slowly off and sink into two centuries of black mud.

He jerked back quickly; for a few seconds he had forgotten why he was here. From his position on the bridge he could see the beginning of the mock-orange wood. So far, there was no sign. He wondered how, when the moment came, he would deal with his glasses and his poetry book. Then he felt foolish, because he was not here on his own account. He was doing Walters a favor. "I've got a squash match but it'll be over by three," Walters had said, breathing hurriedly, in the stone corridor near the changing rooms. "Please, Paggers, please."

Charmless, Walters had power. He was one of several boys in the school whose families lived in Spain or Portugal, in connection with the wine trade of the Douro and Jerez de la Frontera. His parents' marriage had broken up, and during the past year they had been quarreling over his school fees. While these remained unpaid, the school was unlikely to be rid of Walters. This knowledge was useful to him. Examining the school photographs of those years, one longs to say to the confused faces that stare out from behind the house matron's white cap, "Don't worry, you'll survive." But Walters is an exception: he does not look adolescent in any valid sense. Even then he was physically quite completed. He had a behind which stuck out like an African's, and large feet and hands. His fingernails were like other people's toenails. There was something rather awful about Walters under the showers.

And Walters's conversation—it led straight out into the unknown, beyond giggles and speculation, into acheish reality. After talking to him, you felt guilty and excited.

But now, on the bridge, Page-Barlow knew that his position was humiliating. The go-between has to learn the pimp's arrogance, and without it he is only a mess. Two or three times he decided to abandon the whole thing, even if it meant forfeiting the rank pleasures of Walters's friendship. Then he knew it was too late. A bicycle wheel flashed at the edge of the wood.

His instructions were clear: if she was with her friend, he was to greet her, nothing more. He saw her bare legs pumping up and down, her bleached head nodding as she fronted the gradient of the hill. She was alone.

How on earth was he going to talk to her? Here the situation was entirely different from in the school dining room, where she waited at their table. Leaning over them with plates of food, she brought the warm farm smell of herself. She was their waking point and, half relieved that they could get no nearer to her, they celebrated her in unison. She could not talk to them when there were masters or prefects present, but after these had left the dining room she chattered happily to the reprobates who stayed behind: to all of them, that is, except Walters, who had stopped speaking to her about a fortnight ago.

The girl, who was called Edna, was free-wheeling now, swooping down the hill with that winged freedom of girls on bicycles in the war years (they were everywhere, spokes flashing, skirts flying, bare legs pistoning, as they swept past whistling ambushes of soldiers, past elderly gossips in Victory gardens, on their way to work in factories, to buy the rations, to give love).

Gravel ticked against the wheel as she drew up beside him. Now he was sitting on the balustrade, with his glasses tucked into his pocket and the *Little Book of Modern Verse* entirely concealed beneath his buttocks.

"Hullo," she said.

He saw her in a hot mist. "Hullo."

Edna's hair, which needed bleaching again, was like hay with dry plants in it. She wore a scarlet coat with boxed shoulders, and shoes so large that you could see into their sides—the Minnie Mouse shoes that country girls wore at that time. To Walters, knowledgeably apprehensive, she had declared her age to be sixteen, though she looked younger.

Page-Barlow coughed and began talking like an old man. "You may be somewhat surprised at seeing me here, perhaps it will be necessary for me to explain."

She watched him kindly, as if he were a child getting through something he had to recite. "No. Why's that?"

"Timothy, you see, asked me to come, actually."

"Who's Timothy?"

"Walters."

"Oh, Walters." Her voice placed Walters as something inevitable and boring they both were bound to know about, like the blackout or rationing. "What's he up to, then?"

"Playing squash, in fact."

"Whatever next."

Edna settled herself on the saddle of her bicycle, which bit into her small behind, and sniffed the wide air and the large shining landscape which stood ordered around them.

"It's nice here, isn't it?"

Up to now she had not asked whether Walters would be coming or not. She was content with Page-Barlow and he wondered for a heart-leaping second if she might not accept him as a substitute. No, it was no good; even now Walters would be parking his squash racket up at the school and threatening to set off down through the woods.

"Can you wait?"

"What for? Oh, Walters. Thinks I've got all the time in the world, doesn't he?"

She spoke extremely quickly, hardly making an effort to pronounce all the syllables. She had been brought up in a farmhouse kitchen full of men, to believe that in any case nobody listens to what girls are saying.

Page-Barlow shifted uncomfortably on the parapet. She saw the book he was trying to hide.

"What's that?"

"Just a book."

"You studying?"

He nodded.

"You've got two names, haven't you? Why's that?"

He knew it had been something to do with money, in the

past, but at the back of his mind his mother loomed up, telling him you did not discuss money with servants.

"I don't know."

Nothing led any further. With girls in the holidays you spoke the first thing that arrived in your head, relaxing onto that cushioning silliness which does so much to mitigate the discomforts of pubescence. But girls of the holidays did not reek of the Act, of the hot breath of Walters whispering the details from bed to bed in the top dormitory.

Dull-brained, he caught sight of a parcel, wrapped in yellow wartime newspaper, in the basket of her bicycle.

"What's that?" His question echoed hers.

"Just some things I'm taking back for Mum."

At this, his face seemed to catch fire again. Of course he sympathized with the act of rebellion against the school. Then his father's voice took over from his mother's: "So you had to get mixed up with a thief and a whore." No, "tart" was the correct word: it had the sticky sourness of old men's desires. "A thief and a tart." And his mother again: "You can never trust maids." The years before the War, in Surrey, the years of Page-Barlow's childhood, were spent in a running fight with The Servant Problem. You had to get them from the North, from the "distressed areas," which you spoke of in embarrassed tones, as though they had something to do with God or Sex.

Even just talking to Edna meant a reordering of the universe in the interests of love and sympathy. And how could Walters, a brute and in any case almost a foreigner, understand that?

He squirmed off the parapet toward Edna.

"Look out, your book's gone."

"It doesn't matter." This was his brief farewell to art.

As Edna leaned over the parapet beside him, one of her shoes fell off and a little gold chain ran out between her breasts and hung below her face.

"You can get it back easy."

"I can't." The book was lying half open among the reeds at the water's edge. He hated it.

"We can get it. You go on down and I'll give you a hand up."

He accepted unwillingly, for this seemed to turn them back

into children again. He took her small roughened paw and skidded slowly down the bank on the sides of his shoes. Then he let go and swiped for the book. One foot went thrusting into rich blackness and sucked out again, leaving an icy vein of water in his sock. He threw the book up the bank, clutched Edna's hand again, and at the top they faced each other, red-cheeked and breathless. He held on to her hand.

"There's your book."

"Actually, it's done for."

"It'll dry out."

"No, it's done for."

"You are a gloomy one."

"Am I?"

"Yes, you are."

He tried to speak, but his lips had dried and his tongue tasted of meat. Beyond the girl, dragonflies whizzed to and fro, the trees held out their branches leaf-heavy and motionless, and over them the clouds loomed, moving sluggishly as though stirred in an enormous vat. There was still the rumble of airplanes from the ends of the sky. One can dismiss such moments easily, imagining them to be a rehearsal of something to be repeated, but they never are.

Edna spoke first. "There's Walters."

Walters came steadily along the path down the hill; he could look surly at a hundred yards' distance. He did not speak until he reached them.

"Christ, do you have to stand in full view of everyone?"

Neither of them answered.

"Hide your bicycle in the ditch." Immediately she turned to obey him. "Scram, Barlow."

"All right, all right, I was going."

He moved off as slowly as he could, not willing to admit that he had been dismissed. He did not look behind him. As he stumbled among the cowpats and tussocks at the edge of the lake, his mind tried to follow Walters and Edna into the woods beyond the Palladian Bridge, but it gave up at just the same point as it always did in his dreams. His experience would not let him past that point. And now it seemed impossibly far away, because he knew he could never learn to be like Walters.

Through the back pages, through Ruthven Todd and Dylan Thomas as far as Louis MacNeice, the lake water had soaked into the *Little Book of Modern Verse*. Even if he dried it out, Page-Barlow knew he would always hate to read this book again. He threw it as far as he could across the reeds and lily pads into the lake. The pages opened as it flew, and the book fell short into the reeds and slithered down until it was a few inches above the water.

"Someone in a boat will find it there. They will find my name and wonder why I was here. This afternoon will be on record when I have forgotten all about it."

But he knew it would not let him go.

# A War of Liberation

Miss Featherstone, renowned in my childhood for the children's parties she gave, was the retired headmistress of a school for girls. A small energetic woman, with a face that seemed sometimes as intimidating as a clenched fist, she was neverthe-less known to be the soul of kindness.

A great many of the parties we attended were given by old ladies, members of a small colony of the professional classes existing on the edges of a mainly working-class village. The old ladies lived in Victorian and Edwardian villas, whose original plantations of conifers and other evergreens had in thirty or forty years grown so tall that they already blotted out the sunlight. These houses were usually half empty: apart from the old lady and her servants, there might be a maiden daughter, who would slam her library book and flee upstairs when visitors arrived, or a bachelor son who, while showing off his collection of coins or butterflies, would tickle you to distraction. In many cases mar-ried sons and daughters were living abroad, usually in India; it was for their children, spending the school holidays with their grandmothers, that parties were given. In spring and summer the large gardens, the shrubberies, the greenhouses, and the disused stables seemed purposely intended for Easter egg hunts, for hide-

and-seek and sardines, or for complicated games with clues in doggerel rhyme.

The surrounding country was parkland, interspersed with shabby, run-down farms. The country mansions were owned by Jews and Greeks. The Jews went in for fox-hunting, while the Greeks preferred otter-hunting—perhaps, descended from islanders (I have been told that many of the Greeks in Surrey and Sussex came from Syros), they had no racial memory of being looked down on by superiors on horseback, and no need to assert themselves in the same way. In any case, we never went to their houses. The Picton-Dotterels, a mine-owning family from Yorkshire, were also established in the neighborhood, and old Miss Dotterel gave parties for the local children to meet her niece. Pauline was four feet tall, wore a "page-boy bob" and red taffeta dresses, and, like the rest of us, she had a nanny, though this woman was referred to as "Moggy" (she was perhaps a Miss Mogridge). The only difference was that while we were six or eight Pauline was twenty-four. We were told that "she had never grown up" and that "the specialists considered it good for her to be with children." Some of the children protested loudly and were never invited again, but I can't remember their parents objecting to their being made use of in this way. Perhaps Miss Dotterel's condescension was considered to be a reward in itself.

From the other end of the social hierarchy some unexplained child, most often a ferret-like little girl "from the cottages," might be conscripted to some of the parties. She would be expected to help and be grateful, and in return she could carry home for her smaller brothers and sisters a box of battered cakes and uneaten sandwiches with the cucumber slipping out of them.

Heather and Olive Willock, the twin sisters whom Miss Featherstone had adopted before coming to live at Furzecroft, did not belong to this last category. Yet there was always something pleading and unprivileged about them. They overflowed to an unusual extent with that extraordinary goodness, clear and pure as spring water, which affects little girls immediately before adolescence. But to us, several years younger, the twins were not little girls at all but big girls. Surely nobody could be more mature than Heather, who pushed you higher and higher on the

swings at the Victoria Pleasure Ground, until the Jubilee plantation of pines and poplar trees hung upside down, and the sky lay under your feet like a lake; or Olive, who was both bossy and gentle as she dealt with a dreadful performance of my own when, at the age of four, I had been lent to the girls for the day without being provided with the formula for asking the way to the lavatory. Both Heather and Olive were natural leaders and in picking up sides they vied with each other in giving preference to unpopular sniveling children. They were full of moralistic sayings: "Talking to yourself, first sign of madness!" "Writing backhand, first sign of madness!" The twins both wrote a rounded hand, using brilliant blue ink. They had been given autograph albums, in which everybody contrived, by hook or by crook, to be first or last, the middle pages remaining almost empty.

In due season, they became Girl Guides and talked mysteriously but with hot affection of "Captain" and "Leffie." Heather was Captain's upholder, but Olive devoted herself to extolling the merits of Leffie. In this she showed her translucent kindness still more clearly, for the role of Lieutenant was held by a forbidding female, the unmarried sister of an Indian Army colonel. Later a kind of coup d'état occurred in the Guide troop, with Captain, always nervous and delicate, retiring to have some sort of a breakdown and Leffie emerging as Captain.

For Olive and Heather these had to be transient passions, their greatest loyalty being dutifully given to dear "Feather." Miss Featherstone provided them with a home at Furzecroft and paid for their education, on special terms, at the school to which her own life had been devoted. With her encouragement, their futures were already planned: on leaving school, a training college for teachers, to be followed by careers as much as possible like her own. Armed with the capacity to give girls a good grounding in general subjects, they would have no difficulty in finding employment. Sharing digs with a sympathetic friend, one could save enough money to enjoy the long holidays which are the privilege of schoolteachers, with trips to the Black Forest, the Engadine, or the Tyrol (farther south, Miss Featherstone indicated, was inadvisable for women traveling on their own). Heather and Olive had already shown that they could take responsibility, and there was

no reason why they should not get headships in the end, as Miss Featherstone herself had done. They would have the respect of their colleagues and get a very good screw. Like many old ladies, Miss Featherstone had an unfortunate way with idiomatic English.

Careers like these could be mapped out with confidence because, for the past century or so, the reasonable expectations of reasonable people had usually come true. The people I knew in my childhood were not, perhaps, happy, but they dosed their unhappiness with little nips of self-esteem. They had been through the War; they had served their country in the Empire; they gave employment to gardeners and indoor servants in this agricultural slum, and got very little gratitude (when they left India, they told you, the native servants had wept).

Even so, beyond the rambler roses and the macrocarpa hedges, leisured lives sometimes threatened to disintegrate. Then the wives came to our house in the afternoons, for my mother radiated a sort of generalized sympathy and benevolence. From time to time, walking past the drawing-room window I would catch sight of a female face that looked as if it had been rained on all night, and hurriedly turn away. My mother was told of the ingratitude of husbands, a number of whom, to make up for real or imagined sufferings in the War, lived comfortably off their wives' private incomes. She might be the first to be informed when "something inside" proved inoperable, or of the trouble people had with children, so often sulking, difficult, or impossible. Sons could manage to get away, but daughters at this date found escape much harder. Pretty girls especially, growing up, felt increasingly trapped. They clumped around in tweeds and brogues, exercising Sealyhams in the empty woodlands of winter, and thinking how much they disliked their mothers.

The Willock twins were never, I am sure, like this. My difficulty is that I cannot remember them at all at this time. I have a vague recollection of their appearance at the Drill Hall in amateur theatricals produced by a throbbing woman in a cloak, Miss de Saumarez. Then they vanish again, and for several years I do not think I would have recognized either of them in the street.

By this time I already realized that, except in the eye of God, none of these people was very interesting. After I had gone to school they merely belonged to a casual comedy, a series of interrupted scenes played out in the holidays, while my own life as well as the life of the world went on elsewhere. Even the outbreak of the Second World War left local people very much as they were. When "the gale of the world" blew, it was to find them comparatively well wrapped up.

Soon, however, the presence of troops in the neighborhood tightened the atmosphere, so that even middle-aged spinsters stopped having dyspepsia and headaches. One night, after her bicycle tires had been punctured, Olive's former friend, the Captain of the Guide troop, was attacked by a French-Canadian private. She knocked him out. In the part of the village known as "the cottages" the forces found a more friendly welcome. During one summer the local doctor, who was my father, was to encounter nine cases of parthenogenesis, all personally vouched for by the mothers of the virgins in question.

By this time several of the old ladies had died, and others went away to live with married daughters or in what were known as "safe hotels." Their houses were taken over. From a turreted villa close by, now a sergeants' mess, radio programs of a rather desperate cheerfulness resounded all day. The conservatories and greenhouses were smashed and then used for firewood, and a treasure hunt in the shrubbery would have produced only a hoard of empty Spam tins and the white, deflated balloons from the private celebrations of grown-up people.

In the second winter of the War, it was learned that Heather Willock had become engaged to a soldier and that she had, in another of Miss Featherstone's unhappy phrases, "thrown up everything." She was merely protesting at Heather giving up the prospect of a teaching career. Now there was only Olive to reward Miss Featherstone for all she had done for the girls. Luckily Olive had always been the more sensible of the twins.

During the Easter holidays Heather brought her fiancé to meet my mother. He was a Canadian Army dentist called Bob, though he himself pronounced it "Barb," which held the suggestion that, like a spearhead or a fishhook, he could not be removed without causing injury. He was quiet and polite, speaking out of a cloud of professionally disinfected breath. His clipped hair was orange-red, and his complexion had the shade that, many years later, was to be known as "shocking pink." These two colors were to show up well in the Kodachcrome snaps which Heather sent from Vancouver every Christmas after the War. Bob's hair and features were echoed in the row of children, their grins all decorated with the golden proofs of his skill, posing first of all in front of the station wagon, and in later years on the deck of the sailing yacht. By that time Heather had traveled, having accompanied her husband to Dental Conventions in nearly all the big cities of the United States. In her letters, though filled with good news, there lingered something of the pleading unprivileged note which had marked her as a child. But by now there was nobody to plead to.

Today when I remember the Willock twins it is only in the bright enclosed aquarium of childhood, where the thick air is like clear water holding everything in its place. I remember lying on the grass of the lawn, looking at the sunlit sky and watching the tear bubbles trickle slowly across my eyes (I thought them to be a special private vision, like angels), while nearby the big girls are climbing higher and higher inside the dark-green cone of the sycamore tree which I'm too young to attempt.

My memory of Miss Featherstone, on the other hand, is of a much later date, a wartime summer when I am sixteen, about a year after Heather and Bob came to visit us.

The house is open to the August afternoon, the high Victorian rooms reflecting light from the garden outside. I am alone in the drawing room and am, I suppose, dangerously detached from everything that is going on. At school we are unconcerned with the War, which still seems to take place at a great distance from our lives. My friends and I have just discovered that a previous generation of writers has made bourgeois life interesting by turning facts into symptoms. "The game is up, for you and for the old gang!" I recite, bicycling past the Picton-Dotterel estate, with its befouled rhododendron thickets and its greensward torn up by Bren carriers. At the end of each term, we sing "Lord, dismiss us with Thy Blessing," and I come home to dismiss everyone else. Yet at the same time I am dumb with a shyness from which there is no escape, for when I try out the words I have to read and use, people at home say "Oh God" under their breath, and if I consciously make things simple, they think me a fool. Shyness and boredom, feeding on each other, turn me back to my proper task: climbing the interminable ladder of books which leads to the next examination I must take. This activity seems to immobilize an entire lobe of my brain as it stores the facts from the pages I race through, with the intention, never to be fulfilled, of returning to them later.

Whoever it is who is ringing the doorbell, then, will find me completely the wrong person to answer it. I cannot really face anyone.

The opening of the door lets in a flood of light, a view of the laurustinus and the gravel drive. Miss Featherstone is standing there (for once the awkwardness of the historic present seems justifiable, because to me she is standing there forever). She wears a black straw hat and a striped summer dress, of the type then worn by schoolteachers, but now only seen on women in the Soviet Union. She has walked some distance, for her house is on the other side of the village.

Of course, in spite of my adolescence, she knows who I am because of where I am. I can remember her rather vaguely; for some years she has been spoken of, rather than seen.

"Is your mother at home?"

"I'm afraid not. She is taking someone to the hospital in her car."

I tell her I don't know when my mother will return. I am cautious about this, because there is a great atmosphere of strain in the house at this time. My father, recently released from the Army because of his senior partner's death, is overworked. My mother is out for a large part of the day, doing voluntary service of various kinds. There are no more of the prewar parlormaids; a daily help comes in for the mornings, bringing her illegitimate child. My instructions are to keep importunate visitors at bay. When I fail to do this, there is usually a scene, and I am too inexperienced to reconcile the acrimony with which my parents refer to such people with the extraordinary generosity with which in fact they treat them (in later years, when people no longer ask for help, neither of my parents will find any further reason for living).

Miss Featherstone peers past me into the long dark hall, to the table with its bowl of calling cards, the grandfather clock, and the carved chest containing motoring rugs.

"There is nobody at home?"

From her point of view, nobody. To Miss Featherstone I must possess all the conceivable disadvantages of my age and sex except that, by some oversight of the universal architect, I don't suffer from acne.

Perhaps some emotion shows on her face, but the spectacles, the wrinkles, and the pursed lips of age make this impossible to identify. She has hardly altered since I first knew her. Even for Heather and Olive, it must always have been difficult to tell what she is feeling.

Miss Featherstone looks once more past me, as though in the hope that the green baize door at the end of the hall will suddenly open and one of the servants of long ago reappear.

I could ask her to wait in the drawing room, but then shyness and boredom would agonize me, and I should risk my mother's displeasure.

"I'll tell them you called."

She sighs, but does not speak again. She turns away from me and stumps off down the drive.

To me at this moment she was part of the casual comedy, like one of those "old maids biking to Holy Communion in the mists of the autumn mornings" in George Orwell's new pamphlet, *The Lion and the Unicorn*, which we had read delightedly at school. When I told my mother that Miss Featherstone had called, she said: "You should have let her wait. An old lady like that, walking a long way on a hot afternoon."

"But you told me not to let people in."

"I wonder what she wanted."

A week or two later, it was learned that Olive Willock was engaged to be married. Like her sister, she had chosen a Canadian officer, called Bill, a friend of Bob's and in peacetime a solicitor in Edmonton, Alberta. Whether this was the news that had brought Miss Featherstone to our house on that August afternoon was no longer to be discovered, because by that time she had been found dead.

Later my mother would sometimes say: "I wish I had been at home that afternoon when Miss Featherstone called. I might have helped her." Equally, if it had been anyone else who had answered the door, a chain of cause-and-effect might have been severed. Possibly I am present in this story only as a small punctuation mark in a sentence that was already hurrying toward the full stop. And, possibly again, if I had been able to speak to her she would not have died. But like everyone else, I too was a symptom, a part of the evidence: we classify in order to deal with one another, and then we die. At that date many others were dying by categories and by classes.

For years afterwards this generalizing habit would prevent me from thinking of my childhood, of Heather and Olive, and of Miss Featherstone herself. In the face of proletarian necessity, such lives were of no interest at all: they were "unreal." Wherever I went in Europe after the War, the English were to be classified in the same way, by people who had grown to be connoisseurs of their own suffering. The end of this process occurred for me in communist Shanghai, where a woman guide indicated, almost unintentionally, that a fountain pen, a wrist watch, and a camera were caste marks for which one was to be dismissed out of hand. I realized that I had become a sort of coolie in reverse: I was free. Before that, however, I had begun to suspect that the idea of God is the only escape from the categories and the classifications.

This is all I can derive from the memory of that unlucky afternoon, almost three decades ago. But what about Heather and Olive, so kind and so grateful to their dear "Feather"? If the War had not taken place, would they ever have snapped the emotional bonds by which she had bound them to her? Trying not to disappoint her, their careers would have progressed from term to term, from scholastic year to scholastic year, while they hoped always that the next holidays would break the pattern. Life would have been over while they waited for it to begin. For the Willock twins, this war had certainly been a war of liberation. Bob and Bill had caused their escape, but this death was to set them free forever.

A year or so after the War, the Nuremberg Trials took place.

The subsequent executions were bungled disastrously. Only Goering escaped, by biting a capsule of potassium cyanide, and people considered him lucky.

"He didn't have much luck," my father told me. "It is a horrible way to die. It is what Miss Featherstone did, and I had to go and see her. It was an appalling sight."

And so I have another image to add to the one of the figure in the doorway on that summer afternoon: the small body in the upstairs room at Furzecroft, clenched and distorted with the final pain.

# A Life Membership

One cold Saturday in March, soon after the Second World War, a young man appeared at a street corner near a bus line and started shouting.

He shouted continuously for about four minutes.

The line was composed of women, squat in Utility winter coats, shuttered off behind glasses and under knotted head-scarves. Because buses came seldom, they had rested their laden string bags and baskets—the rations at the bottom, fish to one side, lettuce hiding the lavatory paper—on the sidewalk. The women looked impersonal as pieces of furniture, but occasionally one of the man's words showed as a little spasm on their blank faces.

He wore a white silk muffler and his shirt was unbuttoned. He seemed less poor than outcast, as if he had been away from ordinary life for a long time. He walked up and down the line like a busker begging for silver, but the women turned their backs on him. Defeated, he scratched his head. He let out one final burst of invective, then he saw the bus approaching and stumbled off.

He stood at the corner of another street, an explorer surveying new territory.

The street was like many others in West London at that

period. The houses had balustrades and porches painted gray and dull yellow. Some already showed traces of reconstruction and conversion, paid for out of grants for war damage. Ex-naval officers were to be found here, decorating their own converted basements with pots of distemper, putting everything shipshape in their spare time. But there were Indians in the street too, and a sprinkling of Poles, and most of the houses had rows of bells at the door, with a visiting card or a label in rain-streaked ink beside them.

At eleven o'clock on this Saturday morning the street was almost empty. A couple of Central Europeans in blue overcoats and tan shoes went past, pleading to each other.

The young man watched them pass. He seemed tired after his orgy with the bus line.

Now the street was entirely deserted in the wintry sunlight. Along the pavement a cat stood licking one of the unwashed bottles, blued with milk.

"Fucking cats," he said.

A door opened on the other side of the street, and another young man came down the steps and began walking with a scuttling motion along the sidewalk. He wore a tweed jacket and corduroys, and had a curly pipe in his mouth.

From his side, the first man saw the newcomer. He stepped off the sidewalk and began to cross the road, so that he would cut off the other's advance. The man with the pipe saw him approaching too late. He knew he would speak.

"Hi, boy."

Momentary perplexity and curiosity crossed the other's face. But he continued walking until he had gone by.

"What are you running away for?" The man caught hold of his arm.

The other removed his pipe and said in a privately educated voice: "I assure you I have no intention of running away. But I happen to be in a hurry."

They stared at each other.

"You don't have to be scared of me. I know your type—Conservative like." This took place near a general election.

"No, I'm not," the young man with the pipe said.

"That's right, you don't have to talk to me."

The pipe smoker looked at him again. He was undoubtedly drunk, but the War had left the other without any of the set reactions about drunkenness which might have made the encounter shorter and more definite. Nevertheless he could think of nothing to say. He walked on. He heard a confused shout behind him, but he did not turn around.

Twenty minutes later the young man with the pipe, whose name was Michael Winch, came out of the telephone booth at the Post Office, and went into a pub. The saloon bar was empty. He took a pint of mild-and-bitter and went to sit by the window. He read *The Economist* and drank slowly.

"Hi, boy."

When he heard the voice again, he knew he was lost. He waited until the greeting was repeated, and then looked up. His acquaintance of half an hour ago was signaling to him from the public bar.

Because his girl had refused to lunch with him and he was bored, Winch surrendered immediately. He grinned at the man, drained his glass and went through into the public bar.

"Thought we'd be meeting up again. What is it?"

"Mild-and-bitter," Winch said.

"Two pints of mixed, Miss."

He pulled a long white envelope from inside his jacket and rummaged in it among tightly packed wads of notes.

"Christ, what's that?"

"Insurance money. They gave it to me yesterday. Five hundred."

Michael Winch gulped some beer. He made his voice sound calm. "What was it for?"

The man held up his right hand and Winch saw that one of the fingers was missing and the rest were mangled and shortened. "Construction job—bleeding Festival of Britain." He stared at Winch with small bright blue eyes and laughed.

Much later, Winch saw a friend enter the other bar. He beckoned to him.

"Hey, what's going on?"

The newcomer was tall, fair and seemed fretfully self-important. He needed quieting down.

"Jim, this is Peter."

Jim swiveled unsteadily around from the bar and appeared to have difficulty in focusing his eyes. "What are you taking, lad?"

Peter Bryce looked at Winch and said: "Well, actually—no, really I—"

"Come on, boy."

"Well, I suppose a bitter. Only a half."

"A bitter, miss. Same again for Mike and me."

The long official envelope was produced again. There was a deep silence while Jim pushed it back into his inside pocket. He and Winch drank to each other's health; their eyes were full of the instant affections of the drunk.

Jim put down his glass and headed away through a door beside the door.

"No, not that way," Winch called after him. "Outside and around the back."

"He's a good chap," he said, when Jim had gone.

"Where on earth did you meet him?" Peter asked.

Winch explained.

"Good God."

"He's got it all on him, in that envelope. Five-pound notes mostly."

"They shouldn't have given it to him," Peter Bryce said pompously. "Those sort of people are not responsible."

"He's got a perfect right to do whatever he likes with it."

Bryce retreated at once. "Yes, but I mean the first tart that comes along will roll him for the lot."

"I know, Peter, I know." Winch scratched inside his pipe for a moment and then said: "He's already offered some to me."

Bryce asked casually: "Did you accept his offer?"

"Not yet. Would you have done?"

"Someone else will, before today is much older. Have you told him that?"

"I hinted as much, but I don't think he really minds. It's probably what he expects, after all."

"What do you propose to do?"

"Stay with him, anyway."

"What's the point of that?"

"I can help him to keep it as long as possible."

Winch realized how unconvincing this sounded. In fact Bryce and he suspected everyone's motives, including their own. Both of them lived the same sort of life, which they had found in London since demobilization. It was a London in which one drifted, spending the mornings in pubs, the afternoons in the circuit cinemas of Fulham and Kensington. They ate a great many luncheon-meat sandwiches. Both of them had parents, retired and living angrily in the country. Bryce and Winch disappeared home at intervals, returning a few days later with a dozen eggs and the rations they could not afford to buy, to find dust on the crumpled sheets of the bed, a fur of mold in the frying pan, beer stinking in a forgotten glass. For the moment they adopted in behavior a Bohemianism they really despised. They believed they were waiting for something, for their generation to ripen and their expensive education to pay off.

"I want you to take over part of the time. I have to meet Barbara this afternoon."

"I can't, Michael."

"Of course you can, why not?"

"I've got to go home. There's an uncle there who may give me some money. I simply must be at Waterloo at four-thirty."

"Hell. I suppose I'll have to get Barbara to meet us somewhere. Difficult, though, you know what she's like."

Lack of money gave a continual tension to Winch's relations with this girl. Usually he met her in the West End, went to foreign films with her there and ate in the cheap restaurants of Soho. Today she was lunching with school friends.

Before the pub closed for the afternoon, Bryce bought him a drink. Jim still had not reappeared.

"That's the last of him," Bryce said. "Now I can go to Wiltshire and you can go to Barbara. Honor is saved."

"All that money going out of our lives. The *pissoir* is only around the corner."

Bryce pulled long cavalry-twilled legs from under the table. "No, you've seen the last of him all right."

"You needn't sound so bloody relieved about it."

Out in the street Winch was suddenly dazzled by the March sunlight, and he realized he was drunk. He had not eaten anything since the previous day.

"Hi, boy." Through a blur of light and noise, the voice caught hold of him.

Jim was sitting in a doorway. With his head against the wall, his face drawn and unshaven, he looked younger, more defensless than before.

"Leave him. He'll be all right," Bryce said.

"Why the hell should I leave him? He's my friend." Winch pulled Jim to his feet. "This pub's shut. We're going on in a cab."

"It's much better to leave him," Bryce said.

"No need to be an utter shit, Peter."

A taxi approached and Bryce signaled with his rolled umbrella for it to stop.

Jim sat between them on the back seat. He was quiet, his eyes were half closed, his head fell limp on his shoulders. The taxi went fast through the empty streets and out into the park. When it turned a sharp corner he slid down on to the rough matting on the floor. Winch tried to lift him, but he seemed to slip through his clothes.

The taxi stopped in Chelsea, and Bryce was standing pompous and fretful on the pavement.

"You'll have to give me some money, you know."

Jim handed him another big, white, five-pound note. "I've still got the cash," he said. "They always look after you if you've got the cash."

Bryce said: "Well, actually I know a kind of club near here."

Winch crowed with laughter.

The door was between two shops. A gondola, some bulrushes, and the words "Gondola Club Members only" were painted above the staircase. There was a red stair carpet and the radio was playing below. Bryce scribbled three names into a dog-eared visitors' book.

Downstairs, illumination came from buff-colored vases in niches in the walls. Underfoot the carpet was thick and gritty. An orange-haired woman was knitting behind the bar.

"Peter!" A man slid off one of the bar stools, buttoning his double-breasted jacket, and padded towards them on crêpe soles. "Years since you've been in. And who are these boys? You've signed them in the book, have you, Peter?"

"This is Michael Winch, whom you know. This is Jim."

"Do I know them, Peter? I'm not really sure that I do." He looked them up and down. "Well, Peter, what can Lily give you and your—friends?"

"We're drinking whisky."

They sat on stools by the bar. Behind a Chinese screen the woman poured out whisky from an anonymous bottle. "Hullo, Lily," Peter said. She did not answer, but put the glasses in front of them and went back to her knitting.

The man put a hand on Bryce's arm and began talking to him quietly. "Peter, you manual laborer chum! You old thing, you."

Winch looked around the airless cellar, the little dance floor surrounded by tables. Then he watched the man next to him, trying to remember. "Good God," he said suddenly. "You're Webb-Brabazon, aren't you?"

The man turned around. "Yes, that happens to be my name."

"You and Peter were in the same house at school."

"Who is this, Peter?"

"Michael Winch."

"I don't remember him."

Their gaze tested each other for hostility. Webb-Brabazon turned away first, drumming his fingers distractedly on the bar.

"David," Bryce said, "would it be a bore if you chalked these up to my account?"

"No, boy, I'm the one as does this today."

"Is it all right if he pays?"

"It's my cash, isn't it?"

"Yes, but you have to be a member."

Webb-Brabazon saw the wads of notes in the envelope and looked away quickly. "No, that'll be all right. You boys just order anything you want."

They had two more rounds. Webb-Brabazon turned to Winch and said in a formal, pompous voice: "Of course, I'm really only filling in time here. My people insist I have some lucrative employment, hence The Gondola. I'm by no means unwilling. One meets a lot of interesting people. Last night Robert Newton was in with a party."

Bryce, who had been preparing to look at his watch for some time, now did so.

"Christ," he said. "It's four o'clock. I'll have to hurry if I'm going to get to Waterloo." Suddenly good-natured and enthusiastic, he said good-bye.

"Where's he gone?" Jim asked, emerging from dumbness a few minutes later. "I like him. He's a good lad."

Winch explained.

Jim indicated Webb-Brabazon with his foot. "He's a funny one, that one. You don't want to trust him. I'm lucky to of found you and Pete. There's a lot of jokers around who'll do you down if they know you've got cash."

Winch said: "If there's two of us, they can't get it."

"That's right."

Winch was moved by the simplicity of his relationship with Jim. They were encompassed around by people who would try to get the money out of them. Drink brought out moral streaks in him. Apotheosized in his own estimation, Winch looked warmly toward Jim and his eyes filled with drunken tears.

Suddenly from the pit of his stomach, he remembered the girl he had to telephone. He left Jim and lurched towards the booth at the foot of the stairs.

"Hullo."

"Could I speak to Barbara Fedden?"

"Who is it?" A girl's voice, hard and bell-like.

"Michael Winch."

The voice remarked entirely audibly: "Barbara, darling, there's a person here called Wench." There followed a series of small noises that create anxiety: shoes clicking over polished floors, telephone directories and lampshades being shifted.

"Michael, where have you been?" Barbara was using the other girl's voice. He knew what sort of day she had been spending.

"I said I'd telephone you."

"You're late. Look, this is very important, are you listening?"

"Yes, Barbara."

"Well, this man I had lunch with, he's a friend of Miranda's, and he's starting a new business. It's an economic survey or something for businessmen, but connected with the government."

"Christ."

"Oh, please don't say that. I've arranged for you to meet him here at six."

"I can't come."

"Michael, you sound drunk. Are you?"

"Fairly."

"Oh, Michael, this is terribly important. I've been pumping for you like mad all through luncheon."

"I can't come. There's a chap here and I said I'd stay with him."

"Who is this chap?"

"You don't know him. I met him today. He's very rich though."

"Will he give you a job?"

"No, I don't think he will."

"Well, this one might. Look, Michael, you must do this. Please."

"I can't, Barbara."

She began to lose her temper and her smart voice started cracking. "Why is it you never try to help yourself? You stonewall everything—"

"Barbara."

"If you don't come I'll never speak to you again. I've promised for you, you'll make me seem a fool."

"You had no right to do that."

"Well, I did. I'll be here at Miranda's till six. If you don't come, I'll know what's happened."

There was a clanking sound and he found himself listening to silence.

Winch trod slowly across the thick carpet. "Jim, I have to go. I've got to see my girl."

"Bring her here, boy."

"No, I have to go." He turned to Lily. "Will you look after my friend?"

"That's all right, dear."

"Webb-Brabazon, will you look after my friend?"

"Only too delighted. One'll have to make him a member, though."

Winch watched them while they brought the membership forms and a fountain pen, which Jim refused to touch. Watching Lily persuade him, Winch was reminded of an A.T.S. officer he had once seen coaxing a private soldier to do an intelligence test: it wasn't his sort of thing at all.

Michael Winch left them.

(He was too drunk to be presentable when he arrived. Later he quarreled with the girl, but arranged to meet her the next day and the day after.)

At the foot of the stairs he turned. Webb-Brabazon and Lily were standing over Jim, who looked around and waved to him. Webb-Brabazon put his hand on Jim's shoulder, and Lily got the pen into his hand at last.

"Write it here, dear. Yes, just your own name. Let me see, it was the twenty-guinea life membership you wanted, wasn't it?"

# The License

Aunt Cynthia rarely made personal use of the chairs in her London drawing room. She was kneeling now on the hearth rug, and poking at the grate from time to time with a pair of tongs. When she turned around, her face would be full of endeavor at sympathy and understanding. It is a great effort to talk to boys of Peter's age.

Awkwardly waiting for her to speak again, he looked as if he might break the chair he was sitting in.

"Does your father write to you?"

"Yes, of course."

"Often?"

"Yes." Adolescence still made Peter's voice thrum like a slack guitar string. "At school we're meant to write home every week, so, as I usually do, he pretty well has to; I mean he writes something, not much though."

His aunt struck a heated coal and it split satisfactorily, emitting branches of flame. "What does he write about?"

Peter laughed oafishly. "About my future mostly."

"Surely that can wait. What about himself? Has he told you any plans?"

"We're going to Austria this summer. He wants me to learn to drive."

"You're too young."

"I won't be then." He laughed again, to help things on.

She was agitated and fussed. The boy had a train to catch in half an hour's time. Though partly impelled by curiosity, her sympathy was genuine; but he deflected it at every opportunity.

"Please don't always try to shut me out, Peter."

He looked at her with hatred and desperation.

"I suppose it isn't any use. You're just a child."

Her husband, a barrister, came in with the evening papers.

"Hullo, Pete, old boy."

"Hullo, Uncle Raymond."

Raymond Pelham issued a big grin: everybody felt they had to start off cheerfully with Peter.

"Darling, Carla's been pressing your dinner jacket. Do go and see if it's all right."

"What did she want to do that for?"

"Because we're dining at the Messiters. Darling, please."

"I expect it's all right. Is Pete old enough to have a glass of sherry?"

"Darling, please," Aunt Cynthia went on signaling until her husband left the room, first winking at Peter on the way.

She put a hand on Peter's knee.

"This housekeeper, Mrs. What's-her-name."

"Mrs. Macdonnell."

"Yes. What does your father write about her?"

"Nothing much. Why?"

His aunt turned back to the fire, armed this time with the poker.

"He got her from an agency," Peter said, trying to help.

"Oh, God. How difficult it is!" Aunt Cynthia hit a smoking coal with some violence, but it failed to crumble. "He's my favorite brother. I was fond of your mother too. She could be a very very sweet person."

At this, Peter was locked in silence.

"You'd better go to your train. I'll ring for a taxi."

"I can go by tube."

"With your squash racket and record player and everything?"

"Oh, all right."

In the hall, they listened for the taxi. When they heard it stop outside, Aunt Cynthia kissed him. He still reeked of boarding school, as men do of prison; in her arms he held himself quite still, like an animal tense and ready to leap away at the first relaxation. She let him go, with a hurt little laugh.

Afterward she said to her husband: "I sometimes think he hates me."

"He probably still feels like hell, poor Pete."

"That's no answer. It's five months now—I was counting this morning."

She moved into his arms. Raymond knew that for her the problem was, not Peter, but her own childlessness.

Because his father had evening surgery, Peter could not be met at Shereham station. He took another taxi to the house, which lay a mile away, among bird-haunted shrubberies. The drive spat and crackled with new gravel.

"There he is at last! I expect you know who I am, don't you?"

The woman in the doorway spoke in a soft Edinburgh voice. She was about forty, and wore a knitted suit and her dark hair done up in a bun. On her bright, bird-like face, the lips were thin and scarlet.

Peter dropped his squash racket to shake hands.

"I'm Mrs. Macdonnell. When you've got over your first shyness, I expect you'll want to call me Helen. Come along up, then."

Peter picked up his bags again and made off up the stairs, with Mrs. Macdonnell following him.

"There's a big strong laddy."

The room was small, on the sunless side of the house, a museum of Peter's past. He put his record player and a case of records on the bed.

"Those'll be all the latest smash hits."

"No," Peter said.

"What are they then? Dixieland?" She was showing him she knew all the modern words.

"Bach mostly."

"Gloomy stuff, eh? Well, I never."

She seemed put out, and left him, shaking her head as though she knew he'd be growing out of this phase. "You'll be coming down when you're ready."

Peter's trunk would arrive later. He unpacked his suitcase quickly and put the clothes in the drawer; if he left it, she might do it for him. He hid under his handkerchiefs the photograph of his mother, and the letter she had written to him before she died.

Dr. Hesketh was standing in front of the drawing room fire with a whisky and soda. He had reddish hair, which was growing colorless, and a bristly mustache. He always looked ruffled and embarrassed; everyone over the past few months had conspired to expect too much of him.

Peter and his father shook hands. It was, nowadays, their only way of touching, and they hardly glanced at each other.

Mrs. Macdonnell said: "You know I think he's got quite a look of you, Jack. Quite a look."

At the sound of his father's Christian name, Peter flinched visibly. His father stared at the logs in the grate.

"He's taller, though. The wee bairn's taller than his daddy." She drained her sherry. "Well, then, I'll be going through to get you your supper. I expect you two have lots to talk about."

Relieved of her presence, they could talk to each other quite easily.

"Aunt Cynthia's got seats for Covent Garden next week. She wants me to go up."

"You go then. It's no fun for you now, moping around down here."

"Have you thought any more about my driving lessons?"

"Yes, I don't see why you shouldn't begin as soon as you can."

"Mr. Beaman—he's the history master—let me practice stopping and starting in his mini. On the school grounds, so I didn't need a license."

"Well then, you know the rudiments."

"Yes."

Both Peter and his father knew they would over-discuss this

subject: they exploited to the utmost the few topics for conversation that now remained to them.

Mrs. Macdonnell called them.

"Not much for supper, I'm afraid. Today's the day I have my hair done."

His father ate in silence, pouring tomato ketchup onto the thawed-out fishcakes. When they had finished, he whispered to Peter: "Give her a hand with the dishes, there's a good lad."

He went through to the kitchen.

"That's nice of you, Peter. I see they look after your manners at that school, not like some of these places."

Peter seized a cloth and began drying plates strenuously.

"How do you think Dad is looking?"

He did not answer.

"Lost your tongue, have you? Never mind. As I say, you'll soon get over your shyness with Helen."

"Actually, I call him Pa."

She laughed, "Do you now? Old-fashioned, aren't we?"

"He's all right, I suppose."

Mrs. Macdonnell put down the dish mop. "Your father's a fine good man, Peter. He wears himself out for those patients of his, but they're not grateful, not a bit of it."

She poured bleach into the basin.

"They don't know they're lucky. I was an ill woman when I came here, Peter. You're not old enough to know about these things. Your father's been a trump to me, a real trump."

She unbuttoned her apron. Her sentimentality was full of menace.

"There's not many like him, these days. People down here don't know they're well off. And all these foreigners that work at the big houses!—they're not healthy, you know. I wouldn't have one of them in my house. And they don't do the work, either."

Peter ducked away as soon as he could. Upstairs he lay flat on his bed, and put a Haydn quartet on the record player. A few minutes later she was at his door.

"D'ye like the sound o' the pipes, Peter? D'ye no like the sound of the good Scots pipes?"

"I don't know much about them," he said politely.

"There's nothing to beat them."

She gave no signs of going away. Soon she tried whistling and humming a bit, to help Haydn along; it was the allegretto, however, and he was too quick for her.

"What do you have, Peter?"

"What?"

"What! Did ye never learn to say 'pardon'? What'll you be having for your nightcap? Will it be Horlick's or Ovaltine or cocoa or hot milk?"

"Nothing, thank you."

"Ah, come now. Not even a nice cup of tea? Won't you join Helen in a nice cup of tea? She always has one, this time o' nights."

"No, thank you."

Huffed, she finally went away. Peter raised the arm of the pickup and put it back to where it had been when she first came in.

Later Peter stayed awake, listening. But the silence in the house was absolute. There was only a faint ringing sound out of the spring darkness, which might have been the blood encircling the walls of his own brain.

And then across the corridor, a small regular noise: Mrs. Macdonnell snoring. A guileless innocent murmur, it seemed to fill the whole house until Peter went to sleep.

Coming out of his bedroom, where he had been rearranging his long-playing records, Peter bumped into a small gray figure armed with a feather mop.

"They never tell me you was back! How are you then, dear?"

"I'm fine, Mrs. Parkes. How are things?"

"Oh, it's not the same." The old woman's eyes sparkled with grief and mischief. "It's not the same by a long chalk."

Mrs. Macdonnell called upstairs: "Mrs. Parkes, I've left the vacuum cleaner out, so's you can give downstairs a proper doing today."

Mrs. Parkes made a face at Peter. "See what I mean? Only I'm loyal, see? I won't let Doctor down. I said that to your poor mother, I won't let Doctor down."

Relishing this, she was going to repeat it, but Mrs. Macdonnell had come halfway up the stairs, her head raised, scenting trouble.

"Your father's just off, Peter, once I've made his list out. You're going with him, aren't you?"

"Oh, all right."

Dr. Hesketh was downstairs drinking a cup of tea. Mrs. Macdonnell stood dutifully beside him with his list. She gave Peter a little smile, which indicated the regularity and reliability of this event.

Peter's father pointed to one name. "Who's that?"

"I can't spell the foreign names, Jack. It's that cook at Shereham Hall."

"Right-ho. Nothing going to hold us up for long there." He pocketed his stethoscope.

"Now, boys, don't you go being late for lunch. One o'clock sharp, mind."

Peter followed his father out to the garage.

"It's probably only corned beef, anyway," his father said, starting the car. Peter giggled.

The houses around Shereham were bright with new paint and daffodils and pink cherry trees were in flower in the easily run gardens. On the few remaining bits of pasture, horses and ponies which belonged to the daughters of London businessmen were frisking in the sunshine. Dr. Hesketh visited two or three council houses and a thatched cottage, in which a family waited for a grandmother to die; they had already an offer from London people. Sometimes he stopped for a moment behind the car, out of sight of the windows. He came out of the last cottage whistling, and drove to Shereham Hall.

"Got something to read, old man? I may be a bit of time here."

"Is the cook very ill?"

"No, not really. Be a bit of time, though."

Shereham Hall was a square Palladian mansion built of pale sandstone. In the portico there were croquet mallets and some hooded basket chairs. The garden was very large and would soon be opened to the public, in aid of the District Nurses.

After half an hour, there were voices, especially his father's, which sounded louder than before. Mr. and Mrs. Tyrell Bailey, both with pale hair and long whey-colored faces, came out with him.

Mrs. Tyrell Bailey leaned towards the car. "So this is the boy."

"Oh yes, the boy," Mr. Tyrell Bailey said.

Peter was trapped, like a fish under observation in an aquarium, but before he could get out of the car, they had lost interest in him. With the slow saunter of garden viewers, they had crossed the drive and were approaching a large magnolia tree, which stood in full blossom near the lake. Mrs. Tyrell Bailey was telling his father about the tree, and his father was nodding a great many times.

After a few minutes Peter's father returned across the lawn, smiling to himself and mopping his hands with a handkerchief. He got into the car in silence. As a child Peter had once said to his mother: "Pa smells like the cocktail cabinet." This joke had not been funny a second time.

"Well, off we go."

Gravel roared under the tires, Shereham Hall, the basket chairs, and the magnolia tree spun around, and, the car raced toward a wall of rhododendrons. Beside the lake, the faces of the Tyrell Baileys flashed by, identically aghast. The car reached the bottom of the drive, swooped into the main road, and came to a halt.

"Get out, get out, you little fool," Dr. Hesketh shouted. "See what it is."

Peter scrambled out and ran to the front of the car.

A schoolboy, several years younger than himself, was kneeling on his hands and knees in the road. The wheels of his bicycle were still spinning furiously.

"Are you all right?"

The boy got up. He wore shorts and a county school cap, and his overfed face was white with fear. His smooth knees were grazed and the palms of his hands pitted with the marks of stones.

"I think so . . ." Tame, neuter-looking, he was ready to apologize. "P'raps I should've rung my bell."

"Are you sure you're all right? My father's a doctor, he could probably help."

"No, I'm all right." Nearly crying, the boy wanted to be left to himself.

Peter rummaged in his pocket and produced five shillings. "Here, take this."

Startled, the boy said, "Thank you, sir," and they both blushed. He picked up his bicycle, spun the pedals once or twice, then mounted and wobbled slowly away up the hill. Peter watched him until he had disappeared around a corner.

In the car Peter's father was leaning forward with his forehead resting on the top of the steering wheel.

Peter sat beside him in silence.

"Sorry, Pete. Sometimes, I can't see things—I can't—"

"Let's stay here a bit."

His father leaned back, showing that his cheeks were wet. "No, better get back. Helen'll be waiting lunch." He took out a cigarette with violently trembling hands. Peter pulled out the dashboard lighter to help him.

"Now, you see, Pete, why you'd better learn to drive."

"I want to, anyway."

"Peter, you'd better know about this. I've been under a lot of strain lately. Very private strain."

The expression sounded peculiar. After a moment he inquired cautiously: "Is it about Ma?"

"No, it isn't."

"Oh," Peter said.

Late that night Peter heard somebody moving about the house. Without thinking, he put on his dressing gown and crept to the end of the corridor. Mrs. Macdonnell was standing at the top of the stairs. Wearing no makeup, with her hair hanging in two long braids down her frilly white nightdress, she looked both archaic and sexy, like somebody out of the Brontës.

"Who is it?"

"Hesketh. I mean, Peter."

"Must I be always after you two laddies? Somebody left the light on in the hallway."

He shivered, clutching his shrunken fawn dressing-gown—someone at school had pinched the cord years ago. His large grayish feet were cold on the floorboards. She came closer to him.

"Off to bed with you now."

Her eyes were an entire shock: they were hard with hatred, like little darts of steel. He turned and without dignity made his way back to his room. She was watching him the whole time, and his hair prickled and his skin crawled.

"So you're off today, are you, dear?" Mrs. Parkes said. Peter was wearing his London suit. "Well, I can't say I blame you. That auntie of yours, Mrs. Pelham, she's a kind soul. She spoke quite nicely to me after the funeral. I told her I'd stick with Doctor, and I done it up to now. But this isn't a happy house. You're well out of it."

Peter's provisional driving license had arrived by the morning's post. He showed it to his father at breakfast.

"Good man. I'll fix up those driving lessons before you come back. You may as well have something to do in the last week of the holidays."

"Do you think I'll be able to drive in Austria?"

"I don't see why not." His father was silent, buttering a piece of toast. "It probably won't be Austria, in fact. Helen thinks she'd prefer Switzerland."

Their eyes failed to meet across the tablecloth.

"Oh, I see."

When they had both finished, Peter stacked the breakfast things and carried them through to the kitchen. Mrs. Macdonnell was standing at the sink, doing the flowers.

"Well, you're off now, are you, Peter? No doubt that aunt of yours will be spoiling you again. Funny, I thought you were a nice polite boy, first of all. Well, we live and learn and that's our misfortune."

She cut through the stalks of a bunch of jonquils; they fell stickily, one by one.

"No, don't go yet. Listen to me a moment, Peter." Her voice dropped. "Now, young feller me lad, don't you be talking out of turn. No telling tales out of school, got it? Because if you do, laddie, you'll live to regret it. You'll live to regret it very much. Helen can be real nasty, when she's the mind to it. And one thing she doesn't take to is dirty little sneaking eavesdroppers. There's your daddy calling. Now remember what I said."

Peter got into the car beside his father.

"I'll ring up about the lessons today. And you can start driving me around for practice."

Peter did not answer. His father accepted this and looked straight ahead, his face twitching with guilt.

Cynthia Pelham had been taking Peter out to lunch.

She had made an immense effort to stop making remarks like "I suppose it's no use suggesting you do something about your hair?" She had refrained from straightening him up altogether, apart from insisting he get his shoes cleaned by the man on the corner of Piccadilly Circus. He bought the clothes he wanted, including two frightful ties. In the restaurant she had let him order what he liked, and allowed him, with certain afterthoughts, to drink a glass of wine. Now she pushed money under the table at him, whispering: "The man pays."

"It's obvious you're paying," Peter said. "The waiters all know."

They returned home exhausted.

Tea was waiting and with it, by prearrangement, was Juliet, Cynthia's oldest friend.

"Washing his hands."

"How are things?" Juliet asked.

"Worse, if anything. Of course, I scrupulously refrain from mentioning, and all that. But really, it's been half a year now. And it isn't as if everything between Jack and Elizabeth had been so absolutely marvelous, because I happen to know——"

"What on earth difference should that make to Peter?"

"No, none, I suppose." Cynthia sighed. "I'm sorry, darling, I'm tired. He'll be down in a minute. Try a spot of charm, will you?"

"I'm sure he's a perfectly normal boy," Juliet said. "It's just that——"

"It's just that he's going through a phase. I know. Jolly long phase. I wonder if a psychiatrist——"

"I'd leave him alone if I were you."

Kneeling on the rug, Cynthia bit into a piece of bread and butter. "Nobody helps."

"Honestly, I'd skip it. What good bread you always have—though of course I shouldn't be eating it."

"He's impossible."

"I can remember when everyone said 'Cynthia's impossible.'"

Peter's aunt blushed a little. "You know perfectly well that was about something quite different."

The stairs shook overhead and the pictures began rattling.

"Peter, darling, come and have some tea." His aunt had not called him "darling" before, and this embarrassed both herself and him.

He shook hands with Juliet and sat down. Fair and gleaming and beautifully dressed, the two women filled the immediate view. They tried to talk about Covent Garden, but since Peter was the only one of them with any knowledge of opera, conversation did not progress. Juliet had been to Glyndebourne three or four times, but couldn't remember any of the names.

"When do you go back?" she asked him. "I'm sorry, I don't mean school—I know everybody always asks that. I meant to Shereham."

"The day after tomorrow."

"So soon!"

"Peter's having driving lessons," Aunt Cynthia said.

"Yes?"

"My father wants me to drive when we go on holiday. We're going to Austria." He stopped, then continued: "At least, I mean, Switzerland. Also he wants me to drive him when he visits patients."

To Juliet, Cynthia made a tiny elbow-lifting gesture, which Peter observed.

"I think that's marvelous," Juliet said. "Your father will be pleased. How's he getting on with his new housekeeper?"

Peter stared at the floor between his feet. "She does her job."

Cynthia, collecting the teacups, muttered: "Yes, but what job, that's what we'd all like to know."

Peter got up and walked out of the room.

"Darling!" Juliet said.

"Have I said something awful?"

"Yes, you have."

Cynthia went scarlet. "Well, everything one says is awful. It's absolute hell, you don't know what I've been through."

This evening Peter's father was waiting for him at Shereham station.

"Hullo, old boy. Got your luggage?"

"Yes."

"How's Aunt Cynthia?"

"She's all right," Peter said. "She sent you her love."

He handed in his ticket and followed his father into the parking lot.

"Not too tired after all your junketings?"

"No, of course not. Why?"

"I thought of going over for a bite at the Ram at Chillington. They do quite a decent meal there. It's outside my parish, so there's no risk of meeting patients. We used to go there a lot in the old days."

"That'd be lovely."

"Mrs. Parkes has been leaving me something in the oven, but I told her not to bother tonight, as you were coming down."

His father spoke excitedly and rather fast, and Peter had to wait until they got into the car before asking: "Where's Mrs. Macdonnell?"

His father was silent a moment. "I—I gave her the sack. We had a bit of a bust-up, so I said she could leave at once. Come, now, her cooking wasn't so fancy, was it?"

Peter giggled. "It certainly wasn't."

His father drove very slowly through Shereham and swerved out onto the dark Chillington road.

"Pa, can I have wine at dinner?"

"Well, that's not really the object of the exercise, but I should think so. In moderation."

A minute or two later his father drew up at the roadside.

"Got your license on you?"

"Yes, I have."

"Like to drive?"

"Yes, I would."

"Good man. Hop out then, and I'll move over."

Peter let in the clutch perfectly and the car slid off toward Chillington.

# A Reprieve

Luckily Sister Marsh herself was on duty. She was able to have a word with Miss Peacock on the way into the Surgical Ward.

"I'm afraid you'll find your brother a bit depressed this afternoon."

"Oh dear, how disappointing." For a moment it almost seemed that Miss Peacock was turning to leave. "I do wish he would make an effort. I have to come all this way—I change buses twice, you know. And my friend's not at all well. I've had to leave her quite alone at the cottage."

Sister Marsh tapped her pencil on a pad of National Insurance Claim forms. "Miss Peacock, we expect visitors to help us keep our patients cheerful. Not the other way about."

An ungraceful lip movement revealed that Miss Peacock possessed a crowd of nicotine-stained teeth. This might have been a smile: Sister was joking.

"It is a most difficult situation for me."

"I hope you resolve it soon. You see, we want you to have him at home with you for a bit."

"I am afraid that is out of the question. My friend is so very delicate."

Sister Marsh hissed a little, like an offended swan, but said nothing further, merely drawing in her bosom to allow Miss Peacock to pass through to the Men's Ward. Once in there, Miss Peacock appeared odd but perhaps not entirely exotic, for she was "Eton-cropped," and her sports jacket and corduroys might have been bought at any school outfitters'. With her plump body and curiously wrinkled face, Miss Peacock sometimes reminded you of a midget, an extremely large one, male.

Sister Marsh knew she was up against a conspiracy between the sick man and his sister to defeat the hospital's plans for him. The previous day she had accompanied Mr. Rossiter, the surgeon, on his rounds. Cheerful Mr. Rossiter, with flat feet and Khrushchev-like trousers showing beneath his white hospital coat, spoke to all his National Health patients as though they were deaf or mentally retarded. He slapped Captain Peacock on the knee and said: "Well, old chap, now we've all had a good look at you, don't see much point in keeping you here anymore. He can go home when he likes, can't he, Sister?"

A mountainous silence greeted this suggestion. Captain Peacock's features were like his sister's, only much larger, sadder, and slightly dewlapped, and nearly six feet of him lay stretched out under the bedclothes.

Sister Marsh handed Mr. Rossiter the folder which contained the history of the case. The patient was fifty-eight, retired after thirty years' service with the police of an island colony. When the vomiting attacks began, he was warden of a London Boys' Club, and since then he had undergone two series of tests. The interval between them had been spent at his sister's.

"Let me see, where is home? Oh yes, lovely part of the world. Bit of country air should cheer you up no end." Mr. Rossiter slammed the folder shut. "Right, when is it to be?"

"I can't go there."

"But you give it as your home address, old chap."

"I know that."

Captain Peacock turned his head away and stared at the night table. There were two tumblers, one for water and the other for his teeth at night. All down the ward other tables were laden with fruit and flowers, but his sister, being hard up, did not bring him anything.

"I can't live at my sister's."

"Come on, flesh and blood, you know. I'm sure she's looking forward to having you back."

Captain Peacock said precisely: "I do not wish to be an imposition on my sister." Then he embarrassed everyone by bursting into tears.

While they were waiting for this phenomenon to cease, Sister Marsh said: "He wants to go abroad again."

"So that's it, is it? You're certainly not fit enough to travel anywhere like that, old chap. Might get all manner of bugs in the old tummy."

"I must go back."

"Besides, things can't be so comfortable out there since we hauled down the flag. Let's see, it's four years since you left—"

"That makes no difference. My friends have written to me, and they want me to go back. They'll look after me there. They'll know what to do. My sister does not want me. I decline to go where I am not welcome."

"You're imagining things, old chap. The trouble is, we have to keep an eye on the old tummy. You can't just go running off to foreign parts."

"Then I want to die."

After this Mr. Rossiter, Sister Marsh and the house surgeon moved on. Because Captain Peacock had used a shocking word in public, he was left alone by the ambulatory patients in dressing-gowns who passed gossiping from bed to bed. Throughout the afternoon and evening he stared ahead of him, paying no heed to the television set, which spluttered with noise and light only a few feet away. From time to time he murmured "Stavros," but nobody knew what he meant.

On Miss Peacock's arrival the following day, he managed to smile.

"You heard they want to turn me out of here?"

"Yes, Freddy."

His sister was ill at ease. She had never sat up with children or attended sickbeds, except that of her friend, Laura, formerly a viola player with a well-known orchestra, who had always been delicate and was likely to be so for many years to come. Miss Peacock came here from a quiet world where people often had headaches and you could hear the petals dropping from the bowls of flowers that Laura arranged so beautifully. She was intimidated by the loud cheerful families whom the other patients were able to summon up for visiting day. In the nearby beds, heroes in striped hospital pajamas grinned proudly as they held court over their scars, and conversation was unceasing. Miss Peacock could not think of anything to say.

"I told them I can't leave until I'm ready to travel," her brother said.

"Of course not."

"They say they need the bed. It's all the government now, you know. And those medical students keep coming around and asking impertinent questions."

Miss Peacock did not have anything to add to this.

After about five minutes, her brother asked: "How are things with you, Phoebe?"

"Laura's not a bit well."

"I'm sorry about that, Phoebe."

Miss Peacock knew how much he disliked her friend, and she herself was irritated by the name "Phoebe," which now only her brother used. To Laura, Miss Peacock was always "Jock." "Oh, Jock," she had wailed, when Captain Peacock was staying at the cottage, "I've tried and tried but I can't stand it any longer." The cottage was tiny; the presence of the sick man made it reverberate with noises it had never known before. "Jock, darling, I can't stand it. Please tell him to use the one out in the shed." And so Miss Peacock told the Captain, and was too child-like to realize how enormously, how finally she had wounded his feelings. But they both understood that he would never go back to the cottage again.

Captain Peacock said: "I had another letter from Stavros."

"Oh, you did."

"Yes."

He did not really need any response from her. While he groped under his slippers on the night table for the letter, he was already half smiling to himself. He was no longer imprisoned in the Surgical Ward on a darkening November afternoon, but driving out on early morning patrol through the olive groves, and later he would stop at a village for a glass of wine with the mayor and the priest. Beside him, compact and smartly turned out, Stavros his driver seemed every day as freshly created as the new crop of tangerines or a mullet brought in from the sea. "A most astonishing fellow, that driver of mine," the Captain used to say, with a tremor in his voice; even he soon noticed that, in the club at any rate, this remark never led to any further conversation. Once, rather drunk at a party, he had cornered Mrs. O'Malley, the newly arrived wife of his superior officer, and explained about life in the mountain villages, the olive harvest, and the panegyrics when they roasted a sheep and everybody danced. "How fascinating, Captain Peacock, I insist on your taking me to see one." By their next meeting, however, her interest had vanished. A day or two later she was heard talking of "these beastly Wogs," and Captain Peacock blurted his feelings no longer. During the War, with elephantine kindness, he used to ask the plainest of the W.A.A.F. officers to dance, because they had fewer opportunities and it made no difference to him.

His worst shock came when Stavros lightly announced his forthcoming marriage. "You understand, Captain, I must have somebody to look after me in my old age." Captain Peacock's heart was frozen; he had not believed that Stavros could be callous, or that he would ever grow old. In the event, the marriage changed their lives hardly at all. Vassilia was plain and quick-tempered. Stavros would come creeping out of the house, a finger to his lips. He and the Captain still spent hours together under the plane tree, playing backgammon or talking. The Captain was *koumbaros* to their son, Kostaki.

Miss Peacock looked at her watch, while her brother smoothed out the thin sheet of writing paper. Vassilia and Stavros were extremely pleased with the idea of the Captain's return, and Kostaki was longing to kiss his godfather again. Now the political troubles were over, he would find things unchanged, except that prices were rising. Could the Captain bring some nice English cloth, three meters would be enough, for a suit for Stavros?

He translated the whole letter, omitting the last sentence.

When he had finished, he wiped his eyes carefully and said: "Once out of here, you won't see me for dust, I don't care what the medics say."

After this, Captain Peacock suddenly looked very tired and ill. They were again sitting in silence when Sister Marsh came swinging down the ward, with her hands tucked together under the starched bosom of her apron.

"Well, then, I hope we have made up our minds."

Two versions of what must have been the Peacock family face, one large and one small, both finely wrinkled, watched her with apprehension. To Sister Marsh they were just a couple of egoistic elderly children, "taking advantage" as such children will. The Peacocks, however, made few claims for themselves and were quite prepared to get out of Sister's way. Because of Miss Peacock, Laura had been saved from half a lifetime in an institution for nervous complaints. With dowries from the Captain, Kostaki's two little sisters would not have to face perpetual spinsterhood in their mountain village. One must do what one can, even if it be secret and not respectable. Because they had done exactly this, Captain and Miss Peacock felt they had a right to dig in their heels.

"I shall not be going to my sister's."

Sister Marsh had expected this. "Very well then, the house surgeon says we can allow another week for you to think it over. You'll be here next weekend, Miss Peacock?"

"Well, I really shouldn't, with my friend not well."

"I want you to come. Next Sunday we'll be able to discuss things properly."

By next Sunday Sister Marsh expected the results of the bronchoscopy to be ready; already it was known that Captain Peacock was incurable, but not how soon he was likely to die. Sister Marsh whirled around and was gone down the river of linoleum between the beds. When she reached the door she rang the bell for the visitors' departure.

While the bell was ringing, Captain and Miss Peacock exchanged a brief smile. Perhaps they had won; in any case, they were reprieved for a further week from sharing each other's lives.

# *The Trap*

"That is Mr. Haworth?"

"Speaking."

"Here is Marysia Rodzinska."

"Oh yes."

"Here Marysia Rodzinska." The voice grew shrill with anxiety and fear of disappointment. "You are remembering me? From your lectures."

"Of course. Nice to hear your voice."

"Mr. Haworth"—she was pleading now—"I have brought with me a present for you. When may I give it, please?"

Haworth had left her country six months before. At the last moment, among tearful farewells, he had distributed his London address to anyone who asked for it, knowing that nothing he could do for them would be enough in the effort to redress the appalling imbalance of the world. In London, however, this Iron Curtain euphoria did not last. It was not only that new interests claimed his attention, but he discovered that, of the half-dozen of his friends he really wanted to see, two would never get passports for political reasons; others could not leave the relatives they supported, or simply dared not face all the formalities which foreign travel involved: the visa form from the British Embassy, the application to the police in a building which still held the aura of terror, the rare passage on the only boats for which you could pay in national currency. Often by the time you received your passport, the British visa form had expired; by the time you renewed your visa form, the boat had gone: you handed your passport back to the police, until such time that you might summon sufficient energy to start the whole process again.

Marysia Rodzinska said she was staying with refugee cousins in West Finchley. No, she had no idea where it was, she had no map, she had been staying indoors the past three days, too nervous to go out. She knew nobody else in London. With some sense of foreboding Haworth arranged to meet her for a drink three days ahead. And since she had no landmarks to guide her, he suggested that they meet at the exit to the underground at Piccadilly Circus. She had only to get on to a train and get off it. She assented dubiously to these proposals, said that she would get there somehow, and rang off, leaving him with the impression that he had failed her expectations. But what could she have expected? He barely remembered what she looked like.

He was on time at Piccadilly and waited for a quarter of an hour in that bright underground limbo inhabited by police constables, Somali students, and elderly German tourists with pleading eyes. He wondered whether he would recognize Marysia Rodzinska. He could not remember if she was married or not, since in her country the title by which you addressed women did not indicate their status.

"Mr. Haworth! Mr. Haworth!"

There she was at the barrier, carrying a large parcel and waving to him with her free hand. While doing this she mislaid her ticket, and now turned to shout with every evidence of contempt at the West Indian girl who asked for it. A middle-aged couple standing behind her stepped forward and resolved this situation. These, when she got through the barrier, she introduced as her cousins, who had been in England since the War. They smiled delightedly and while shaking hands both uttered their names, which Haworth did not catch. But he was heartened by their presence, which would mitigate the greedy enthusiasm of Miss—obviously Miss—Rodzinska. There would be time for polite conversation, conducted slowly because their English was less good than hers.

Haworth was to be disappointed. After some consultation in their own language, the couple shook hands once more.

"You're sure you won't join us?"

Small, square, they beamed at him. "Marysia is so pleased," they said and went back through the barrier. They had return tickets.

"They were bringing me here because I was so frightened. They are very kind."

During his lectures Miss Rodzinska had always chosen to sit in the middle of the front row. She was an indefatigable note-taker: when one of the women behind her asked a question, she would lean back to listen, without turning around but with an occasional frown or shrug, while her pencil quivered with impatience to continue. Sometimes she interrupted him and he checked her with "One moment, please"; she then assumed the ironic expression of a clever child who is scolded, but this was only her idea of a joke. As teachers do when they are carefully enough flattered, he had concluded by considering her intelligent.

Now, as he tried to move off, she stood still. He looked inquiringly at her, and she thrust the parcel into his hands.

"It's very kind of you to bring it. Who is it from?" From the shape, it was probably a bottle of vodka, or even *spirytus*, which is twice as strong.

"Open it, please."

Trying to stand out of the way of the crowd at the ticket machines, he tore apart the rough brown paper and revealed a cardboard box. She watched him; people bumped into her, but she took no notice. Where he was, she was, humbly. He lifted the lid from the box and found two dolls, elaborately dressed in folk costume, dancing together on a wooden box. To him the folk dances of European countries were indistinguishable and their costumes unaesthetic, but he knew the cost of the gift. These objects were specially fabricated for presentation to friends or relatives abroad who had sent food or luxuries for sale, or dollars which ought to have been spent on necessities.

"Who's it from?"

Smiling and writhing, she directed his attention to the lid. "To my very dear teacher from his humble pupil and admirer, Marysia Rodzinska."

He closed the box quickly. "They're very nice, but you should not have done that. I mean it seriously. These things are extremely expensive. I cannot possibly accept it." He was annoyed with her at once. She had wasted money on a gesture that seemed almost self-destructive, like a gambler's final throw.

Her eyes blurred. "Please, please, Mr. Haworth."

He put the parcel under his arm, to be decided about later on.

In the bar of a nearby hotel they sat face to face. Watching her, he repented his harshness. Her dark-blonde hair was thin and she had a face that hard work and a poor diet had driven quickly from prettiness into pathos. Though she would pass in any English crowd, to him her appearance was unmistakable to the point of nostalgia. She was wearing a salmon-pink coat with a single button, a gray suit, with sandals of a different gray; her handbag was gray plastic. She belonged in fact to the Plastic Age of communism, when people no longer look proletarian but lower middle class. She had either bought the outfit at a State store or had patronized one of the dressmakers who work privately, sometimes using cloth from abroad, but most often altering, transforming, and hermaphroditizing clothing within the circuit of a given family. Whichever it was, no taste was involved because there was no real choice, and all the effort and considerable expense had only led Miss Rodzinska to look like a gym mistress on her afternoon off. Had the consciousness of this made her stay at home up to now?

Since telephoning him, however, she had made a first sortie into the alien territory that surrounded her. Accompanied by her cousin, she had visited the Victoria and Albert Museum.

"I was shocked."

"Why on earth?"

"There are many beautiful things there but no people. With us, a place like this is filled all the time by excursions."

Haworth had forgotten about the whole generation of prigs,

created by the competing puritanisms of Church and State. Miss Rodzinska was old for a university student; there was some pretense at gentility in the family, and for several years she had been refused entry to the University, working in a factory. He remembered her telling him this last year, her loud droning voice full of all the egotism of someone who feels socially diminished. She had few friends, which was why she thrust herself so ruthlessly into the front row at his classes.

At first she would drink nothing, then accepted orangeade, which she tasted and put down with a shudder.

"It is not good." Then she smiled to show she was being naughty; if he was English, he must defend English orangeade.

Haworth tried to keep the conversation going, but she had only disapproval for those of her compatriots he inquired about, and soon he was wary even of mentioning their names. And she had no evident interest in England. Already he had had to ask her to dinner, and he perceived he would have the utmost difficulty in getting rid or her, either tonight or later. She had what was called "Dean's Leave" from her university; she would be in England for six months.

She had come here for no other purpose than to see him.

"Please, I will have exactly what you do."

He ordered two steaks *pizzaiola* and a cautious half-carafe of wine. Miss Rodzinska kept trying to catch his eye, and he went on talking, aware that she was not listening to him so much as inhaling his physical presence. He thought of the tiny distance that divides the great peace of mutual attraction from the warfare of that which is not mutual. Now his knees were almost painfully spread apart under the little table in order not to come into contact with hers.

"What are those, please?" she asked in her loud, childish voice.

"Chianti bottles."

"Why do they hang them up there? It does not look nice."

She tried to challenge him on everything from the restaurateur's taste in interior decoration to commercial television, which her hosts kept permanently switched on. "People like it," he answered each time, but she could not feel any force in this argument. And for her, defending one thing involved defending everything: hers was a Hegelian universe in which all things hung together.

After a time he noticed that she was not eating. "Is something wrong?"

"I do not like meat."

Her countrywomen rose at five in the morning for the butcher's line or else a peasant would arrive in the middle of the afternoon with a furtive parcel in newspaper, his motorcycle hidden in the reed beds outside the city. I am not demanding gratitude, Haworth told himself, only that the gifts should go to the right people.

Miss Rodzinska was still in the first stage of refugeedom: she thought herself powerful and important through having come from where she did, for having lived the way she had, through those long, hungry winters in which it always seems to be six o'clock on a freezing morning. She believed the unfortunate could make bullying demands on the fortunate, whoever they were, and was ready to try this out on him.

There are claims, however, which are quite illicit; sometimes in her country you came across Dostoevskyan beggars, refugees into insanity, whose argument appeared to be: "You owe me a dollar because Roosevelt was a dirty Jew who bribed Churchill to hand us over to the Russians." But no historical debts, whether forged or genuine, can be charged to the account of private individuals. Nor can you be forgiven at the same time both as a refugee and a private person. If Miss Rodzinska wanted to be loved, she must try at least to be as nice as other people. And poor, poor girl, she was not.

He was still arguing to himself like this as he prepared to take her to the nearest tube station.

"Oh, not yet, not yet, let me stay with you, please."

"Then you'll have to take the train, by yourself. I live in Chiswick."

She did not answer, but entwined her arm into his. Her bones were just under the coat; it was the stick-like arm of someone thin with desperation. How could things have got so far? They passed a cinema with a French film showing. "Let's go and see this," he said hurriedly. "I've heard it's very good."

She sighed, "If you wish it."

She leaned against him throughout the film, breathing heavily through the long crescendo where the heroine and the motorcyclist wandered through the château gardens. After the climax (tilted nipple and dark areola in profile against tangled sheets, hero zipping up jeans) he was aware that she was staring at him and had been doing so for the past ten minutes.

When they came out into the street, everything was much worse than it had been before.

"Why did you make me go to that, when all I wanted was to talk to you?"

"Didn't you like it?"

"It was *horrible*." She was nearly crying. "I am pleased that such films are forbidden in my country."

He spoke very clearly. "Now I'll put you on your train."

"No, no. Let me come with you."

In one of the white-tiled corridors of the underground, Haworth pulled Miss Rodzinska away from the stream of passengers hurrying to the last trains. Neither of them had any natural presence; they were the sort who are always being bumped into by old women who mutter, by men in raincoats who stare, by smaller men carrying unwieldy musical instruments, by a group of Hindus in ocherous tweeds.

He tried to haul her out of the current, but in her avid concern with him she kept stepping back into it and getting jolted. This only added to the feeling that everything was being shaken apart in their hands.

"You were so kind before. You have changed."

"I endeavored to be nice to everybody in the course," he said crisply.

"I came to England especially for you."

"That's quite absurd. You know that's absurd."

She turned away. "I hate England. What is going to happen to me? I cannot go back home now."

"Really, you must try to pull yourself together." Sensing that this expression might be too idiomatic for her understanding he amended it to: "Cheer up, please." The wrongness of everything he said had stopped mattering. The poor thing was looking with an abstracted gaze into a future in which she was determined to see only defeat. Why couldn't she find someone in her own country? He knew the reasons: a generation of men slightly older than herself either dead or in exile; worse, a new crop of girls, lively and far less priggish, who had grown up in the last few years. This was her last throw.

"Where is your parcel?" she shouted.

He glanced down him, at the sudden lightness of nothing under his arm.

"You left it in the cinema. You want to lose it."

"I'll go back for it when I have seen you off."

"No, no. I want you to come with me. I am so frightened."

"That's impossible. I told you I live on the other side of London."

"But I'm frightened."

The train took long to arrive, and while they waited he felt invaded by her panic, which was the only one of her feelings he could share. Hysteria was beating around them when at length he pushed her toward the door, and said: "You'll get a taxi at the other end."

"Please, I am frightened."

The doors slid shut. There was a minute before the train started and he watched her standing there. She did not look at him anymore, but was making small half-blind movements, like an animal searching incredulously around the walls of its trap.

# *Fingers in the Door*

For Caroline's sixteenth birthday her brother sent her a paperback copy of *Silverclaw.* She considered a paperback a trifle mean, but obviously old Christopher, enduring his first term at Marlborough, hadn't enough pocket money for the hard cover edition to go with the other works by the same author on the shelf above Caroline's bed. Still, she was glad to have the book. She was equally glad that, from now on, Christopher would not be at home for her birthdays. Months ago, at Caroline's insistence, her parents had bought three stalls for the musical they were to see today. This show she expected to be too adult in every way for a thirteen-year-old brother. While she dressed, she felt excited. Not too excited, for she was trying to convince herself, as she tried to convince her friends Jennifer and Sara and Claire, that a trip to London, hot lobster at Wheeler's with a matinée afterward, was a normal and to be expected thing. It was something Daddy had to give her, like all the other things she simply had to have. When she looked at the works of her favorite author—*A Bomb From Russia, Dying is Forever*, and the rest—she thought that Daddy was jolly lucky she liked things which were so cheap; Claire's father had flown Claire to Paris for her birthday.

This morning neither parent commented when Caroline

breakfasted off black coffee and half an apple. She gave her mother a look of admiration; she approved of Mummy's hair that new way, bouffant, lacquered, almost exactly like a wig. Mummy might be a bit out of place on Basingmere station platform this morning, but by the time they reached London she would seem perfectly all right. Daddy, by a stroke of great good fortune, always looked distinguished.

Beryl Ringsett gave Caroline a smile and a little wink. After the hammer and tongs of early adolescence, complicity was growing between them.

"What was it Christopher sent, darling?"

"*Silverclaw*. It's marvelous. I'm dying to read it." All Caroline's pleasures were prejudged in this way, by the trio of fat, well-off girls with whom she shared private coaching.

From behind his newspaper, Andrew Ringsett grunted something.

"*What* did you say?"

"I think you ought to be reading something better."

"Well, I think you're *beastly*. I did hope that today, of all days—"

By taking Caroline's side, Beryl managed to smooth them down. Andrew was so difficult: you would have thought he liked his daughter best when rage lent a flame of animation to her somewhat static features. All was calm by the time they got into the Jaguar to go to the station. Caroline had brought *Silverclaw* to read on the train, and if it hadn't been for horrid old Daddy she would have had nothing in the world to complain of. It was a translucent March morning, the crocuses were up, and the house, one gable of which dated from the seventeenth century, appeared at its best. On a morning like this, Andrew thought, you could have slammed two thousand onto the price and got it.

Andrew Ringsett was an Estate Agent on the way to becoming a Property Dealer. If anything held him back it was a nostalgia, of which he was ashamed, for the War, for friends in his regiment unlike those he had made in this part of Surrey, and for girls rather like Beryl, who, once you had finished exploring their merits, were somehow no longer there. Beryl, after seventeen years, was still there. True, she had come a very long way from the typing pool and, though Andrew had reason to feel proud of her, it was he who was tired after the journey. Her ambitions had somehow made his own worthless, and nowadays his energies needed more conservation than hers. It was she who drove them to the station, nearly four miles among woods and gardens and fresh-painted houses. A Power & Ringsett notice stood outside Brazewood, one of the best small Georgian houses in the neighborhood. "Of course it will all need rewiring," Andrew's partner had told the owner. "A shame about the bathrooms. All our clients expect colored bathrooms."

Caroline did not look out of the window but sat flicking through the pages of her book. She still had every confidence that it would be a marvelous day. Mummy would see to that. More and more she realized that she and Mummy were after the same things. They both had to be careful of Daddy, though; recently, by unspoken agreement, they had dropped that old joke about Daddy being in the doghouse. "*The Korean's crocodile-sheathed toe jerked forward*," Caroline read, with her eyes swooping up and down from the motion of the car, "*and pain flashed upward through Rand's body from his groin.*"

Basingmere is less melancholy than most of the stations on the former Southern Railway. Its porters and guards are given to whistling; every spring they are praised for their flower beds. Regular travelers to the capital are recognized and greeted by the ticket collector, and for them there are posters for the London theaters, including the musical show the Ringsetts were to see. ("A gale of hoots"—*Daily Mirror.* "Ought to complete its lustrum"—*Sunday Times.*) Caroline spotted this at once. "Look!" she cried. "Isn't it marvelous?" Andrew, affected by the euphoria of Basingmere station this fine morning, felt a heave of love as he watched her. It had been worth living to have produced somebody so charming and so silly.

While he was off buying newspapers, the London train drew in. Caroline selected their carriage and settled herself at once into the best seat. "*His rear wheel caught the recumbent Mexican dead center. 'Lover boy won't be much use to the girls anymore,' thought John Rand grimly.*" As she read on, Caroline kept glancing upward in the way small birds do when they drink, with an air of approbation for the surrounding world. The prettiness of this gesture brought an encouraging smile from Beryl and a beady stare for the only other occupant of the carriage.

This was an elderly woman, in a mink coat of unfashionable shade and a grimly determined hat, who had joined the train farther down the line, where the Home Counties become the Shires. Caroline took no notice of this fellow passenger, but Beryl's pursed lips, the nervous positioning of her handbag, and the conscious straightening of her posture in the corner seat showed the resentful tenor of her conclusions, which were something like this: "Even if there is a war and civilization comes to dust, this woman will never invite me to be a voluntary helper in her canteen."

A whistle blew. Caroline bit at her gloved finger. It would be typical of Daddy to miss the train now. Patiently she was about to inquire who, please, had the theater tickets, when he appeared in front of her, carrying papers and magazines. One of Basingmere's blithe railwaymen moved down the platform banging doors. As the train started to move, the door of the Ringsetts' carriage slammed dully. There was a scandalous yelp, umbrella and newspapers flew sideways, and Andrew pitched forward onto the floor between the nyloned legs.

For an instant the fingers of his right hand had been trapped, down to the second knuckle, in the iron door. One moment he was in the bright commonplace landscape of the Home Counties. The next he occupied some limbo of red clouds, of brokenness and screaming. His pain made no concession to the modesty of the circumstances: it raged there as it does before indifferent eyes in police cells and hospital wards. This time it had chosen to make its howling declaration in a first-class carriage of British Railways.

Andrew got up and sat heavily on the seat beside Beryl. Through a scalding mist, he attempted to discover what had happened to his hand. Beads of blood stood out around the nails and more blood was beginning to surface under the skin, which had broken only on the knuckles; in a short time the whole business would turn black. He experienced the first wash of self-pity; everyone hurt feels himself retrospectively to have been beautiful, feels as though the damage were a blasphemy to his natural godhead. Then the pain jarred his entire body again.

He blew on his fingers and chewed his lips, remembering the women present. If only they would leave him, or give him permission to yell out like a child. But they were talking. Their voices throbbed in and out with the blows of his pain.

"Poor man, what a terrible thing to happen! That porter should certainly be prosecuted. Of course you will report him."

"Oh no, I don't agree at all."

"I beg your pardon?"

"I feel it is we who should apologize really. I mean, I'm sure it was my husband's fault. Daddy's always doing things like this, isn't he, Caroline? Remember that fuss we had over the power mower?"

Some women were like great artists, Andrew thought, they continually astounded and yet still were the same. He could accept that she would attack him in the presence of others, rather as domestic fowl attack one of their number which has been injured. But how could she be as unwise as she was now? She was asking for confidences about what great clumsy creatures men are; if it were not for us wives, where would they be? The old woman merely glared at her.

Beryl recognized this glare only too well, for Andrew's aunts had been free with it in the early days of her marriage. In the past it had made her cry, later it had hardened her to what she was; now it caught her off guard.

"You see, we have this power mower——"

"I am not interested in that."

"I mean—"

"Your husband is in pain. Aren't you going to do anything about it?" The old woman had risen to her feet and bent now to speak to Andrew. "I feel I am in the way, and so I'll move to another carriage. You have all my sympathy. I do hope you get medical attention as soon as you can. It must be exceedingly painful."

When their fellow passenger had gone, Beryl put her hands over her face.

"Oh God," she said quietly.

Andrew watched her with some detachment. Less than five minutes had passed since the door closed on his fingers, his whole body was still echoing with the blow, but it had become a part of his life. He could almost set it to one side while he entertained the problem of Beryl. He thought that if she had refrained from comforting him, from putting her arms around him, even from touching him, it was less through coldness of heart than false gentility. Poor Beryl, she could be all right sometimes on the rare occasions when nobody she considered more important than herself was watching her. Snobbery, which she believed to be other people's but was her own, had laid her life waste and reduced whole prospects to ash and cinders. People who watched her, smart and competent, could not imagine how the obsession burned deeply at the core of everything she did.

Now, of course, she would realize that she had behaved in the wrong way from the old woman's point of view, just as unfailingly as she had acknowledged the old woman's superior status in the first place. Of course, Beryl was thinking now, a woman like that would know what to do, from the hunting field, from polo accidents. But it was too late. Couldn't she perceive, Andrew wondered, that the old woman didn't give a damn, but merely relished the opportunity of snubbing her? Alas, no. Beryl always took it straight between the eyes. She was a slave to unimportant tyrants merely because she insisted on recognizing their existence. It was all nonsense, but her lacquered head was bowed, her trembling hands still concealed her face. Her pain was worse than his.

Andrew put his good arm around her, and held out his injured hand.

"Look, love, there's an interesting yellow tint coming up."

"Don't be disgusting." Beryl blew her nose. "Really I was quite ashamed of you. In front of a stranger—" She could not go on. She picked up one of the magazines he had bought her and fiercely pretended to read it.

Andrew turned to his daughter.

She was gazing out of the window, her paperback forgotten on the seat beside her. Poor kid, she looked quite white. "Caroline!" It was like calling to somebody from an immense distance. "Caroline!"

She did not answer.

"Caroline," Beryl said.

"I knew it would happen." Without moving her head the girl spoke in a small cold voice to the windowpane. "I knew it. Just when I hoped everything would go right for once. He's ruined my day. No, I don't want to talk about it, it's ruined. I'd like to go back on the next train, really, but I suppose you want me to stay. It's absolutely no use expecting me to enjoy myself."

"Caroline!" Beryl said.

"I don't know what I'll say to Jennifer and Sara and Claire." She took a deep breath. "God, oh God, why can't we be like other people?"

Her mother put her arms wide to comfort her, but she twisted away. She had no use for comfort. She continued to stare out of the window. The three of them sat separately, not touching each other at all, while the train moved slowly through a wooded landscape toward London.

# *A Floral Tribute*

For the first time in his life he had taken a sleeping pill, which had stunned him for some hours and then dragged him clear away. When he awoke into the dazzling morning, he found that Priscilla had gone from the bed beside him. Across the landing was his mother's room. He heard the two women talking and the telephone being picked up.

"No, I'll do it, Ma."

"I'm quite all right, Cilla. Please let me. Bardfield 32. You must let me do things for myself, Cilla."

"Of course, Ma."

It was curious how much their voices had altered since his father's departure for the nursing home three days earlier. Before this Priscilla and his mother had never been easy together; their conversation had been limited to subjects such as babies and clothes and central heating, and even with these they skirted, for Graham's sake, large areas of disagreement. Now in their complicity they held nothing back; they caressed each other with sentences.

"Wintle's Florists? Mr. Wintle, please. It's Mrs. Corbett."

While Graham cleaned his teeth he could not hear what his mother was saying. He spat and rinsed his mouth out.

"Oh, the *Telegraph*. We don't take it but my son must have put the announcement there as well." Now her voice changed its tone and rang with emotion. "Yes, he was a wonderful man, Mr. Wintle. Yes. That was what I was telephoning about. Oh no, not a wreath. He would have hated anything so—"

Graham brushed his hair and put on a dressing-gown. When he went across the landing, his mother was still talking.

"We asked for no flowers, only donations to the— Yes, I knew you'd understand. Something really simple, *a spray*, to go on top of the— Well, what is there? Delphiniums, larkspurs, and— That sounds nice. Something simple. Thank you, Mr. Wintle. And thank Mrs. Wintle too, will you?"

Priscilla was holding his mother's free hand.

"We've been having such a talk about things," his mother said.

How strange they both looked, shiny-eyed and important. Neither of them, to Graham's knowledge, had wept after the telephone call from the nursing home yesterday evening. In fact, once it had become clear that his father was to die, he had watched them assume their roles; Ma was going to be wonderful, and Priscilla was going to be perfectly sweet to her. Evidently there was some glandular secretion which adjusted his women for the encounter with death; in grief they flowered a little, as though they were pregnant. Because of this he was pleased with them and loved them, even though their virtues might not be their own fault.

So far Graham had felt himself to be excluded, for his job was to face facts and he had none. His mind was in an improper mess; it nagged him to know whether his mother had yet wept; he had guilt about his stunned sleep all last night, dodging his own responsibilities to feeling; and now he was watching Priscilla in her nightdress and wondering how soon after the funeral he could make love to her.

"Ma has decided she prefers not to go to the nursing home this morning."

"I want to remember him just as he was."

These phrases sounded like quotations from somewhere else, perhaps from some traditional drama that had begun to take over their actions. Graham knew he had a role in it, but it seemed he had never learned the words.

"I'll go," he suggested. "I want to go."

This was right and was accepted. But what would they be up to in his absence? In the traditional drama there would be ritual actions to be followed by the womenfolk, the washing and laying out of the body, the drawing of blinds and burning of wild herbs, the ceremonial wailings and the choice of mourning clothes. But in the southern part of Great Britain today, these were all obsolete or only to be performed by professionals. Graham had to discover what remained of the ritual, now that people died alone under hygienic conditions.

"I'll hand in his card at the National Insurance Office. There's twenty pounds to collect."

Not being traditional, this had the power to shock. Priscilla frowned at him and Mrs. Corbett said: "Oh dear, it seems so—"

"He contributed, didn't he?"

His mother looked miserable. Priscilla, taking charge, made signs for him to leave them.

While he dressed, Graham knew that he had spoken too roughly, but he had to make his own facts: born too late for the War, he had reached the age of thirty-four knowing nothing of death.

Before he left, Priscilla came downstairs and kissed him.

"What've you been talking about all this time?"

"Absolutely everything, she's never been like this with me before. She told me all about how she married your father. Apparently she held out until he left Birmingham and got a partnership near London."

"She always pretended to have a strong influence on him, but I don't think she ever did." Then, seeing Priscilla might be disappointed if these new confidences appeared insignificant, he went on: "He was terribly detached, wasn't he? Sometimes he hardly seemed to be here."

"He was perfectly sweet. You know the children and I adored him."

Perhaps somebody is going to weep now, Graham thought, and examined her closely.

Priscilla said: "Gosh, there's his hat still hanging there. I must hide it before she comes down."

Pushing open the garage doors, Graham still felt ignorant and unprepared for what lay ahead of him. He was reduced to ransacking his memory for a real corpse and could only find a motorcyclist decapitated in an accident on the Italian Riviera. One would have been sorry for the poor man, Priscilla and Graham decided, driving past, if only one had known what his head looked like. They were on their honeymoon, a terrific success, and confidence was overwhelming. Ten minutes later, they were giggling.

Today he had no confidence at all, and he knew his father would not have blamed him for running out on this particular responsibility. Mr. Corbett had possessed no beliefs, and what he had joked about as "the disposal problem" was to be resolved as undenominationally as possible. As a solicitor he knew that death gave a lot of trouble and the instructions in his will had been designed for nothing more than the avoidance of difficulties. Graham's mother was equally undenominational. When questioned, she would mumble something about living on in beautiful memories and gardens. Her gospels were seed catalogues, with their promises for a blossoming future, and the songs of birds. Plenty of birds were around the garage this morning, but their utterances were functional and unmusical and could not have given his mother much comfort. In any case she was again talking to Priscilla upstairs.

While he drove through the gleaming countryside, Graham went on bruising his thoughts together. Perhaps death was a mystery, but he peevishly did not want to cope with anything, even a mystery, that interrupted his life with Priscilla and the children.

In the hallway of the nursing home he got through his little talk with Matron. He was conscious only of a white floating cap and an oddly monolithic bosom while her voice, refined and musical like the dinner gong on a cruise ship, went chiming on: "Rudge's are our usual firm. I expect you'd like to see them this afternoon, and so I'll be phoning them straightaway. You'll go up for a moment then?"

Graham nodded, silent.

"He's looking so nice, Nurse and I both agreed."

The windows of the nursing home were shadowed by a mass of leaves. In this place Graham's tonsils had been removed one December when he was nine years old, and he could remember the winter branches cutting the sky into shapes which were the heads of wolves and storks. In the afternoons his father would arrive from his office in the town to spend half an hour or so in the creaking armchair, while the boy lay in bed hot with embarrassment. It was sad now that, twenty-five years ago, there had never been anything to say. Memories swarmed in his brain; it was their season for swarming and they made him buzz all over with the consciousness of self.

Now he stood in the room which was green from the tree-light outside. Under a sheet the deliberate shape of the body was an accusation to him: you were too trivial to know it, but this is what it is like to be dead. He went over to the bed and drew back the sheet. His mind was razed clean.

There was no gesture he had been given to make, and no approach. He could not kneel. He said to the waxen caricature "Good-bye" and to himself "I don't understand." But already he felt there was nothing to understand. He replaced the sheet.

Outside in the car, Graham lit a cigarette. His buzzing memories had all cleared off. Instead there was an infinite feeling of weight: his fingers were heavy, the steering wheel was rock, a torn carton under the dashboard was carved marble. He tried out the sentence to tell Priscilla, "The dead are—" but found he could only end it with the word "dead." There was no other qualification. He had been in the presence not of a mystery but of an unarguable fact. The sheer weight of the fact was so appalling that for the moment he was thankful that neither his mother nor Priscilla was here to learn it.

Shoes creaked on the gravel and in the corner of his eye white wings were floating. He had forgotten all about Matron. Now he turned his head unwillingly toward her. He didn't want her there at all, for it seemed to him she must be expecting congratulations on the nursing home's completed product, the monstrous effigy which lay upstairs.

"I just caught you," she smiled. "Mr. Rudge will be with you at half past three."

She never asked me whether it would be convenient, he thought as he drove off, but at times like these there appears after all to be nothing important to do.

At the National Insurance Office Graham received from a clerk with leather-patched sleeves a check for £20, which could be cashed at any post office.

He got home to find chops grilling. The women's voices seemed shriller, but their light movements still belonged to a predetermined rhythm of exaltation.

Priscilla came out and kissed him. "She's being simply marvelous. I do admire her, really."

"I need a drink."

"I think there's some beer."

"I'm going to have a very dark brown whisky."

Priscilla was watching him intently and he longed for her to question him about this morning. Instead she spoke of the children.

"I telephoned home and Gabriela said they were being *molto gentili*. Natalie even insisted on going to school just as usual. Wonders will never cease."

Graham sat down in an armchair with his whisky, feeling haggard. Priscilla picked up an ornament she had seen a hundred times before, stared at it, and put it down again.

"Give us a sip, will you? Darling, it's rather awful, I didn't want to tell you this but—"

"Yes?"

"It's about Gabriela. I suppose she meant to be helpful, but—she asked me where the children's *mourning clothes* were."

"Oh." He stretched out his legs, relaxed. "Probably they all have them where she comes from."

"Well, this isn't Italy. She ought to respect our customs. After all, she's here to learn about English life."

"What did you tell her?"

"A whole lot. But I don't know how much got through—her English is pretty putrid on the telephone. I said, would she please discuss the subject as little as possible with the children. I said I knew Natalie'd be sensible, but Adrian's quite imaginative enough as it is."

"They'll want to know, surely."

"Of course. I said, Gabriela, we'll explain all about it to them when we get back. That was right, wasn't it? Actually, I thought we'd tell them that Grandpa Corbett has gone away somewhere where he's going to be very happy and they won't see him again."

"But he hasn't gone anywhere," Graham objected. "He's dead."

"Darling!" She glanced from the glass of whisky to his face.

"Very dead indeed and looking awful. You musn't tell them lies."

"Darling, please don't let me down."

"Why don't you tell them he's gone to Madame Tussaud's? That's what he reminded me of. The children will understand because Gabriela took them to Madame Tussaud's, didn't she?"

"You're getting morbid." When he emptied his glass, she took it from him firmly. "I'll go and see to the chops."

"He certainly isn't happy. He isn't anything but dead."

"What was that, Graham?"

"Nothing, Ma."

To him in fact it was everything. But once his mother had appeared downstairs, the chance to explain was gone. Up till now he had tried to protect his women; he began to suspect that they were naturally successful at protecting themselves.

He grew surer of this in the afternoon when young Mr. Rudge, with black coat, striped trousers, and socially oppressed manner, came and dangled his professional suggestions in the air like bait. Mrs. Corbett, with Priscilla beside her on the arm of her chair, had to be enticed into confronting them.

"Lined or unlined? Oak is usually preferred."

"We hadn't really thought—"

"And the handles?"

"Whatever is usual. Something really simple."

While Mr. Rudge made notes, the women squeezed hands

and gave each other little encouraging smiles, which worked, for they both looked encouraged.

"And about the wreaths and floral tributes, where are they being sent?"

"We asked for no wreaths," Priscilla said quickly. "Just a spray."

"A spray on the—" Mrs. Corbett began and gave up.

Mr. Rudge retrieved the word that insisted on escaping. "On the coffin," he said. "That's always nice."

Ruffled by the brutality of this encounter, Mrs. Corbett and Priscilla settled down again, while Graham was thinking: we ought to have six horses and plumes, hired carriages and mourners, paid masses for the dead, and Ma and Priscilla helped along, half fainting, drenched in a cloudburst of black veiling. We ought to be declaring that my father actually existed, instead of hustling him out of mind with an unpretentiousness that is conveniently inexpensive. But thinking this he had nothing to say. The women had taken over and everything was as it should be.

"And the ashes? To be returned in one of our special caskets?"

"Oh no." This was far too much for his mother.

"Interred is nice. With an inscribed plaque, set into the grounds of the crematorium."

"We hadn't thought of anything so—"

"Scattered then?"

"Scattered?"

"In the Garden of Rest. It's such a lovely spot, all birch trees and daffodils."

"I like the thought of the daffodils," Mrs. Corbett said.

"The daffodils are over, anyway." It was the first time Graham had spoken and they all turned to him, as though he could lead them to decision.

"Which shall it be?" Mr. Rudge's pencil was almost showing impatience.

"Which is usual?"

"Some families like it one way and some the other."

"It's so difficult to decide," Mrs. Corbett moaned.

"Scattered," Priscilla said.

We could have tossed for it, Graham thought.

Mr. Rudge recorded the decision and snapped his notebook shut. "Scattered is nice," he said. "Many families favor that these days."

When he had left, Mrs. Corbett gasped: "What a nice man!"

Priscilla was making tea, and Graham walked out through the kitchen without looking at her. In heavy sunlight the garden was full of bees and hovering insects. He made his way toward the sheds. "The broken sheds looked sad and strange" was one of his favorite lines of verse, and among the apparatus the smells of gardening, carborundum and tarred string, yellowed newspapers and boxes of withered corms, he could mourn his father without tears, without words, without grief even, by facing all the facts, by remembering the arrogant wax mask in the nursing home, the nostrils plugged with cotton wool, the feet jutting at an unreal angle. We have lived too long with our genteel procrastinations. His father must always have known this: like a parent who is accompanying schoolchildren to the cinema, he had watched a second-rate performance which he had no intention or expectation of enjoying.

Graham smashed a flowerpot and said aloud, "Father." (Though in life, according to the custom of their class, he had been Daddy.) "I know what it is like." But he was too late. His father communicated more this morning, by the fact of lying there dead, than he had done in all the later years of his life.

That night Graham swallowed another of Priscilla's sleeping pills, but this time he dreamed. He dreamed of endless conversations that led nowhere and hurried explanations it was far too late to give, like instructions shouted to someone who is driving off in his car. Occasionally he groaned and woke Priscilla, but then slept on with his mouth open. When the doorbell rang in the early morning he was still heavily asleep.

"Graham!"

He made an odd noise. Before he could speak he had to reclaim those parched areas in his mouth which had dried out during the night.

"Come down, please."

"Why?"

"Come quickly."

In a dressing-gown he joined her. "It must be a mistake," she was muttering. "I'm certain it's a mistake," as though like him she was still half doped.

The deliveryman stood concealed by one of the largest wreaths Graham had ever seen. Into a vast wheel of cypress, interwoven with gold and silver tinsel and maidenhair, were wired a dozen cabbage roses, rubbery and half deflated like balloons on the morning after a party. The wheel was backed with palm fronds and across its diameter was strung a banner with "In Loving Memory" in gilt Gothic script.

"There's an envelope attached, madam."

"Very well."

Priscilla, signing the receipt, appeared to be furiously insulted about something. Since there was no perceptible evidence of grief in this household, the deliveryman went off whistling.

For a second only Graham experienced the odd feeling that he himself during his garrulous dreams had ordered, perhaps by telephone, this most extravagant of floral tributes to fill a gap in the ceremonies attendant on his father's death. He opened the envelope: Priscilla and he read the card together.

"Oh no," she breathed. "How dreadful!"

Graham's eyes were jabbed by unshed tears.

She gave him a fierce look. "Whatever happens, we mustn't let Ma know."

"What do you propose to do with it?" Propped on the ground against his hand, the wreath looked the least disposable of objects. Stiff and creaking on its wire framework, it glittered in the early light.

"Get rid of it. Out in the shed. I'll take some of the best roses and put them in a bowl."

In the shed he looked at the card again. "Poor little things! I wonder how they afforded it? It must have cost the earth."

"Pocket money. They'd been saving for an aquarium."

Priscilla's nails disentangled the roses from their wiring and pulled the cypress foliage away from the frame. "We must hurry. Ma is bound to have heard the doorbell." He watched her kneeling there working away furiously; in a short time she was surrounded by wreckage. She hugged the frame to her until it was no longer a circle but a half-moon. At length she stopped, exhausted, and her head sank down.

"Darling!"

He put his arms around her. She was trembling. Her breath sobbed like a saw racing through the final half-inch of wood.

"I'll kill Gabriela! How dare she? How dare she?"

He held her more tightly, resting his chin on the top of her head. From the door of the shed he could see almost the entire garden. The herbaceous borders were coming into bloom; this would mean a lot to his mother. In his arms Priscilla buried her face against him and went on crying and crying.

# A Special Relationship

Roland's first decision on leaving St. Audrey's was entirely conventional: the nurses, who had been wonderful, should share the largest and most beribboned box of chocolates he could procure. Sister Grainger, however, was different; with her he had enjoyed something of a special relationship. He decided to invite her to the theater.

The nineteen other patients in Chest Surgery (Male) had seldom wanted information about their condition. They had handed over their health, like the education of their children, to the authorities. Staff Nurse Andrews was quite put out when Roland first questioned her. Later Sister herself had lent him some medical magazines with articles on the operation he had successfully undergone. At the same time she had whispered instructions to him not to show them to the other patients, who might get upset. From this, he felt, began his special relationship with Sister Grainger.

What would have happened to it after an interval of two weeks?

At first, deprived of the floating cap and the starched barriers at cuff and bosom, Sister seemed hardly recognizable. Taking her raincoat, Roland saw that she was wearing a low-cut black dress, carried a white paisley stole, and that tonight she surprisingly marched on the highest of stiletto heels. Her appearance embarrassed him; he hadn't expected her quite so, well, so orchidaceous.

Pulling in her shoulders and rubbing her hands, she waited for the warmth of the electric fire on her bare arms.

"What lovely blooms!" she exclaimed.

In the middle of asking whether she would have a sherry, a dry martini, or what, Roland interrupted himself to begin a little disquisition on the cyclamens she was admiring. His mother had a greenhouse full of them down at Windleshaw, he told her, and then he sensed a need to scale this assertion down:

"Of course, she does them all herself."

"Green fingers! I'm hopeless, I'm afraid."

She sipped at her sherry. Inactivity seemed to chill her and she again began warming her hands, the only visible part of her that she had brought unaltered from St. Audrey's. Strong hands, scoured until they felt like rubber gloves, a month ago they had tweaked the stitches from Roland's recently shaven abdomen.

"I thought we'd leave here fairly soon, actually."

Sister did not reply. The white cyclamens still had something to give her.

"I thought we'd eat first. The curtain doesn't go up till eight."

"I thought we'd—" this was his personal variation of the imperative mood. What was hers? "Perhaps you'd like to—" "Perhaps you'd like to roll over." "Perhaps you'd like to give us a specimen." "Perhaps you'd like to wash yourself." It was the form of edict under which her territory was administered, and Sergeant Withers in his prime couldn't have been more effective. Later, Roland would inquire after Sergeant Withers, who had occupied the bed next to him. For the moment news of those who remained in Chest Surgery (Male) would have to wait.

"Does that sound like a good idea?"

"Whatever you say." She sounded coy. "I'm getting lovely and warm here."

Passing behind her chair he saw that her shiningly set head had fallen forward a little. Without its cap, the nape of the neck looked dangerously exposed above the woolen stole. He returned with a plate of cocktail biscuits.

"Blotting paper!"

"Pardon? Oh, thanks. Delicious!"

Sister's eyes circled the room. The Venetian mirror, the majolica plates, the new picture (French, seventeenth century) obviously daunted her. She returned to the cyclamens, which continued to occupy her until their folded ears were twitching under her gaze.

"I don't know when I've seen such gorgeous blooms."

The ball was in Roland's court, but he had to fall over backward to return it. "How about those truly magnificent flowers that used to come to our ward?" Every two or three days his fellow patients used to whistle with admiration as Nurse Hammond, who had taken a course in arrangement, bore in yet another towering pagoda of carnations or chrysanthemums.

"Oh, those."

"Yes?"

"You know all about those, surely?" Sister Grainger appeared unwilling to go on.

"No?"

"They send them on from the Crem, as we call it. The Crematorium, you know. The relatives often ask for them to be forwarded to us when they—they are no longer required." Sister gave a polite laugh. "Just think, when I first arrived at St. Audrey's, the hearse would come straight up the drive with them, on its way back, sort of thing. Of course, I soon put a stop to that. Patients might have seen."

"I suppose so."

The disillusion was sharp. Roland was immediately convinced that the other patients had known the origin of the flowers, even young Arthur. Only he himself had remained in ignorance, because of a bourgeois capacity for recognizing benevolence where none in fact exists. His fellow patients were far more wary.

In the same way Roland had entered Chest Surgery (Male) assuming that everyone was intended to recover. Later Mr. Frace, a tough-minded garage proprietor, had murmured that he himself and half the others were there to die of cancer. After that, one's own recovery seemed an unfair privilege, like having been to a Public School, or enjoying a special relationship with Sister Grainger.

"I thought we'd take a taxi. It's difficult to park near the theater."

Too early, they settled down in their circle seats. The evening was moving ahead extremely slowly, like the last hour before a boat docks. Sister Grainger remained on her party behavior. In the restaurant she covertly inspected the décor and the people at other tables, turning away each time with a little laugh. She'd have something to tell the nurses. For the most part it was like entertaining a large and appreciative schoolgirl, and he supposed that for her all reality lay at St. Audrey's, where the word "theater" itself had a far more important connotation.

Between the restaurant and the theater, however, she sat in the corner of the taxi, withdrawn from him and with the white wings of her stole folded. Lights from passing cars and shop windows flashed into her fine eyes: he knew she was observing him. Then she was like an enormous bird, perched in meaningful silence in the shadow of its cage, imprisoned and passionate, waiting.

Once she began to say something.

"I'm sorry?"

"Nothing. It's just suddenly you reminded me of someone."

His diaphragm gave a small howl of boredom.

Since leaving St. Audrey's, he had retained a curious hyperesthesia. Returning to work at Bullett's during the past week, he had noticed that some quite minor pictures had acquired a beckoning quality, as though they had been painted in a state similar to his own. People, on the other hand, were diminished; he found Adrian and Peter infuriating, and wondered whether he wouldn't one day murder Mrs. Rheingarten, whose field was the Late Renaissance.

He had bought chocolates and a couple of programs. "The Sundays gave it very good reviews."

"It looks lovely," Sister Grainger said, leafing through the program.

"You must tell me some news about the other people in the Ward."

Her eyebrows were raised a little. "I don't think I quite remember who was in with you."

"Mr. Frace, for instance."

"Old Frace is still there." She laughed lightly, as though Mr. Frace were a "character."

"And Arthur?"

"Arthur too. He's going out quite soon, just as soon as he's got a little stronger."

"How about Sergeant Withers?"

"Sergeant Withers has gone."

Without looking at Sister, he guessed what she meant. Every Sunday Sergeant Withers had been visited by three tall sons, two of whom had been parachute commandos, and three flashing daughters-in-law. On visiting days during the week, Mrs. Withers was always first through the glass doors. It took her two hours on the bus from Edmonton. "She's an awful-looking old bag really," the Sergeant used to say, "but I'd like to have a good few more bashes at her before I go."

Sister Grainger handed back the box of chocolates. Roland was staring in front of him; his face was stiff and his throat hurt.

"Of course, you were our very special patient. Andrews and I always used to say you must have got a lot of amusement out of the different types in the Ward."

Blast you, Sister Grainger, he thought. May you rot in hell.

The curtain rose.

*A Rat with Horns* had already been running for three months; given a single set and only four players, production costs were low. Dame Kitty, cast against type as the Mother, was coping gamely with an improbable accent, a shabby quilted dressing gown and a brass-blonde wig with bluish roots. The play contains a triangle situation involving herself, her eighteen-year-old son, and her son's boyfriend, whom she succeeds in seducing by the end of the first act. There is also a "running gag" concerning the fourth character, a crippled old uncle who suffers from enuresis. The entrance of the two young men, traditionally attired in jeans and leather, occurs eight minutes after the rise of the curtain. The son's opening line is addressed to his lover: "Don't take any heed of my mum, she's going through the change."

Sister Grainger gasped aloud, but immediately controlled herself. For the remainder of the act she stayed completely still, while discarded chocolate papers rustled from her and fell to the floor.

Roland glanced at her from time to time but she was always watching the stage.

In a sweat of despair, he accused himself of trying to show gratitude without giving it his full attention.

He ticked off the list of his errors. A box of chocolates, ordered and dispatched unseen from Fortnum's. A patronizing invitation for Sister Grainger, first to his flat, where the evidences of his good taste had struck her silent. (And he'd had his operation on the National Health Service solely in order to be able to afford the new La Tour.) Then to a restaurant, where she had left half the escalope on her plate (though that perhaps was party manners). And now this excruciating play, chosen because he was acquainted with the actress and might meet her at one of Bullett's auctions fairly soon. He had always suspected himself to be an awful little man; surely the case was proved.

In the bar at the intermission, he forced himself to ask: "What do you think of it?"

"It's very modern, isn't it?"

"Why don't we get out of here?"

"I'd simply love to." She gave him a curious look. "Funny, I somehow thought you'd be enjoying it."

"Of course not."

As though escaping from some tentacular monster which might haul them back again, they hurried down past the doormen and the blown-up eulogies from the Sunday papers and out into the street.

What will I do with her? What will I do with her? "I thought we'd go back and have a drink at the flat."

He hailed a taxi.

"Well, well," Sister Grainger exclaimed. "I certainly shouldn't wish any of my nurses to see that."

On her second arrival at his flat, Sister walked around, peering intently at his statuettes and nonsenses and turning from time to time with a quizzical look, as though with the aid of a word or two from him she might be granted a clue to his real identity. The change in her, although this often happened to women in his rooms, surprised him.

"I am most awfully sorry about tonight," he said. "I can't imagine why Kitty, of all people, should take such a part."

"Don't you worry. In any case, Sister Bryce—she's the one in Physiotherapy—saw it and enjoyed it very much. But, then, she's got a filthy mind."

He looked at Sister Grainger with renewed surprise. It was a moment or two before he got around to offering her a drink. "Er—would whisky be all right?"

"Lovely."

After this he retreated, to moan gently at himself in the bathroom mirror. He wondered if he would have enjoyed the play if he had gone with Adrian. The laughter coming from the nearby seats had been harsh and embarrassed, reminding him of Adrian's and Mrs. Rheingarten's laughter, a mechanical reaction like a death rattle. You had to be in a particular mood, and he felt that the mood had gone forever.

When he returned, Sister was bright-eyed and sociable. By some curious process of reasoning which he didn't quite care to follow, the play had liberated her.

"I never thought you'd live in a place like this, somehow."

"Yes?" In the past two weeks he had become tired of the flat.

"We got you all wrong. I well remember Staff Nurse Andrews saying: 'I bet he's thought of reading for the Church.'"

"Did she?"

"I suppose nurses don't know much about people. Who would have thought of you liking that Sergeant Withers?"

"I did, very much. And after all I spent two months in his company."

"The nurses all thought he was a dirty old man."

"Yes, he was."

"The younger ones didn't like washing him. His hands!"

"What was wrong with his hands?" Roland asked.

"They were all over the place."

"He didn't want to die a bit. He got the most tremendous kick out of life."

Sister laughed. "I don't mind what people get their kicks out of, as long as it isn't my nurses."

Her voice had taken on a rougher, more countrified, tone and her weathered face was beginning to shine a little. He had been right about her at St. Audrey's in the first place. But in ordinary circumstances it was impossible even to think of such encounters except satirically; irony had a very diminishing effect on his life.

"Sergeant Withers wasn't sorry for himself, like some of them," Roland said. "You remember when that old man burst into tears because he didn't want to be sent home and cause trouble for his family?"

"He was a real old moaner, wasn't he?"

"Wasn't it true?"

"We needed the bed, we had no choice."

He rose to fill her glass. On the way back he looked at the new La Tour and said: "I spend my life making choices."

He had often thought during the past fortnight that it would have been better to have forgone the La Tour and chosen private treatment. From the London Clinic, Adrian had emerged unscathed, still Adrian. But Roland felt unutterably changed.

"You're one of the lucky ones," Sister Grainger said.

He hated to be called "lucky." "Suppose I don't want to go on as I am? Suppose I hate what I do?"

"What do you do exactly? The nurses could never quite make out."

Roland said carefully: "I work at a place called Bullett's. They sell things, works of art mostly. We also do valuation for probate." This given, he watched Sister Grainger with some apprehension: he never expected anyone to approve of what he was.

"Things like these? I suppose you'd call them curios, wouldn't you?"

"Not exactly. Things like these, though. I travel around quite a bit."

A twinkling Sister Grainger now: "No ties. Lucky you!"

That word again, rubbing salt into his misfortunes. "I'm fed up really."

"I expect you need a change."

"Yes, that's it. I'd really like to start doing something for other people."

Her amusement was obvious. "I meant a holiday," she said. "At this time of year?"

"You could go abroad, couldn't you? No ties. I envy you." She evidently found him a great joke.

"Where would you suggest?" he asked testily.

"I don't know." Sister Grainger was silent for a moment. "Believe it or not, I've only been abroad once. I went to Interlaken on my honeymoon."

He almost dropped his glass. "I didn't know—I mean—"

"Oh yes. I was Nurse Byrne before I married."

Before he could quite recover from this, he realized that she had started telling him about it.

"I was doing private nursing at the time. Some nurses prefer it, you get more interested in the cases. I never thought much of this one, though he made a splendid recovery. Then, just as I was leaving, I had my things packed upstairs, he asked me to marry him. Of course all the other nurses were up in arms. 'Byrnie, don't think of it,' they said. I was off for my holiday next day, and it rained every day, so I had plenty of time to think of it. And I did."

"Is he—Does he—"

"He should never have married me," Sister Grainger said.

Sitting unobserved in the shadow, Roland blushed.

"After that I couldn't face the Nurses' Home. So I went back to hospital work." She put down her glass. "No, no more thanks. People don't change much, do they? It's no use pretending they do."

The Buhl clock struck eleven. It served to make their two lives echo a little, as though struck like bells, and was followed by silence.

Roland was remembering Adrian's single visit to St. Audrey's. He brought fruit, which looked embarrassingly expensive, and was clamorous with gossip, to which Sergeant Withers and young Arthur listened in from adjacent beds. After a short time Roland had felt exhausted; he had even raised a slight fever. He was exposed and condemned, as though he could never re-enlist in the comity of the ward. That night, however, old Mr. Pierce took a long time to go. Sister Grainger and the night nurses moved swiftly to and fro, while for hours the death rattle sounded beyond the screens. When the lights were switched on next morning to show the empty bed, the whole ward was united in the curious well-being that followed such public deaths. Ambulatory patients in dressing-gowns came to Roland's bedside to discuss the news. By that death, life was somehow enhanced. After it, Roland thought, one could never be quite the same.

Like Sister Grainger, however, he had obviously made a mistake.

Humming a little, Sister stood up to leave. "That was that, anyway. I was a juggins, wasn't I? Nurses never know anything." She smiled. "Tomorrow's a theater day. Mr. Pratt."

The words had only a meretricious attraction for Roland now. "I'll drive you home," he said.

He brought Sister her mackintosh, but she refused his help with it. The bare shoulders and the black dress were hidden away. She stood before the looking-glass, buckling the belt and tucking in her chin as she fastened the top button.

"There," she said. "You couldn't mistake me for anything but a nurse, could you?"

Leaving her to go ahead, Roland turned and saw in the glass a dark suit, a silk shirt, and a pert, blanched face; and beyond him, inside the sitting-room, the La Tour. He hadn't looked at its reflection before; pretty good, really. Mrs. Rheingarten was right, it would be worth double in three years' time.

Outside in the square Sister Grainger was drawing deep healthful breaths.

He said: "There was one thing I meant to ask you."

"Oh?" He could see that in mind she was already back at St. Audrey's.

"If it's true about Mr. Pratt operating on himself."

Sister laughed. "Those old men in the ward love to have something to yarn about. Old Frace told you that, didn't he?"

"I expect so." He didn't feel like mentioning Sergeant Withers.

"Mr. Pratt's a very brave man."

Roland waited for something more, but she was silent.

He unlocked the car door. Although they would spend the next half hour together driving back to St. Audrey's, the special relationship was at an end. She was already standing a little apart, a nursing sister under the stars and the bare branches, inside the order of things.

# Thunderbolt

The Stone Lions is really the only place to eat in Kilminster. According to the guidebook, "Colonel and Mrs. Stopham aim at providing 'traditional fare with variations of our own, as the whim takes us.' Booking advisable."

Near at hand, a bridge crosses the local chalk stream, trailing long swathes of water crowfoots. You expect to see trout darting above the pebbles, but discover only a sardine tin and the wheel of a pram. In the distance the ramparts of Kilminster Castle withstand the fierce assault of purple aubrietia and yellow alyssum. It is high summer, and the sky is bright with huge clouds.

The visitor walks between the eponymous lions into a house also of stone, probably dating from the early sixteenth century. Among the brass and the timer a red-faced gentleman with an untidy mustache looms up, blocking the way.

"Did you book?"

"No. Have you got a table?"

"How many?"

"One."

Colonel Stopham's expression is surly. He does not answer, but after looking you up and down, he stands aside to let you pass.

The dining room is completely empty. The chairs are wheel-backed and the place mats are decorated with hunting scenes. Near a mullioned window, half hidden from the rest of the room, a table is set for one.

The solitude does not last for long. From outside there comes a rising clamor. It is of women, who are apparently meeting each other after a long separation. The noise continues for some time before they enter the line of sight, two large and well-fed ladies in tweed suits. Clearly their loudness is neither the baying of extreme social confidence indigenous to these shires, nor is it the precarious cheeriness of those who feel ill at ease (Colonel Stopham need not be afraid of getting an order for a pot of tea). The ladies are the wives, at a guess, of solicitors or private school-masters. They are making a lot of noise because this meeting is not just an ordinary occasion. They blink rather fast, look into one another's eyes and look away, and each is surprised at her own happiness. With their clear skins and bright springy hair, they manage to illuminate the varnished rusticity of the surroundings.

As they settle themselves down, the ladies go on discussing which of them it was who kept the other waiting. They conclude that they must have arrived at exactly the same moment. They remember, when they were at school together, how one would often guess the other's thoughts, and how they had often begun to say precisely the same thing at the same moment. They think of this as an example, not of limited mental resources, but of mutual affection and sympathy.

They suggest a glass of sherry to each other, and then one of them remembers that she has to drive.

"I'll get squiffy, but you have one."

But the other, whose son will be driving, says that she won't bother this time. To their amusement they discover that they both need spectacles to study Colonel Stopham's "Bill of Fare."

When the women speak again, the past is not mentioned.

"What have you done with what's-her-name?"

"*Dans le cabinet*. What about Justin? Oh, Pam, don't say he's let us down?"

"He's picking up some tobacco plants for me. Lime-green ones! We're making giant strides in the garden this year." She looks down, fidgeting with the cutlery for a moment. "Rosemary, dear, don't expect too much of old Justin. He's being coached for A levels, you know, such a business. Dreadfully shy, too."

"Not to worry," Rosemary says. "Every little bit helps. I felt I simply had to give the child a treat. I can always charge it, 'said she naughtily.'"

"What *is* her name? I'm sure you told me in your letters."

"Chantal. Her family are *crème de la crème,* my dear, and rolling in money." Rosemary's voice drops, more out of respect for such wealth than because of the presence of a stranger. ". . . guineas a week. *And* she's on a diet. Hardly eats a thing. Ronald and I think they sent her to get over some affair."

"How's her English?"

"Not much. Obviously thinks Ronald and I not worth talking to. You try, Pam. You were always tops in French."

"What a memory! I suppose I was, actually."

During this conversation a girl had been wandering through the dining room in the general direction of their table. At first one can only see long swathes of hair, like the trailing water weeds in the chalk stream outside. Falling apart, they frame a small face which contrives to hold in permanence the look of being recently awakened on some sunlit post-coital morning. A turquoise-green dress reaches a quarter of the way down her thighs. Perhaps she is seventeen, perhaps younger.

So far, neither of the two women has seen her. "Poor you," Pam is saying. "She sounds quite dreadful."

With their eyes, they caress each other again. They would love to be left alone to gossip, but responsibilities weigh them down.

Meanwhile the girl lingers, waiting without interest to learn of other people's intentions for her.

At last Rosemary looks up. "Chantal," she calls out. "*Ça va? Ça va?*"

Since they have separated only a few minutes ago, the question appears pointless. Perhaps Rosemary, energetic and jolly, feels it her duty to be didactic at all costs: she is drawing attention to the superiority of the plumbing at The Stone Lions to that in French restaurants she had known.

The elderly waitress has reappeared. Her tapping pencil tries to intimidate the ladies into making their choice without waiting for the fourth member of their party. This they finally decide to do, but first of all the menu must be rigorously translated word for word.

While this is going on, Chantal offers only two comments: *"C'est vrai, on mange ça en Angleterre?"* and *"Tiens."*

Pamela—who has by now been introduced as Mrs. Proctor—turns to the girl. *"Mon fils vient,"* she tells her. *"Il est très jeune pour son âge. Et très timide. Extrèmement timide."*

After this lukewarm recommendation, Chantal says *"Tiens"* again and chews some bread.

Pamela tells Rosemary: "We're getting pretty fed up, I can tell you. He simply doesn't seem to have any sense of gratitude."

"They say they're all like that these days."

From the sudden awkwardness between them, it is evident that Rosemary is without children of her own.

The waitress brings them brown soup and a jug of water. Chantal does not touch her soup, but the other two have hearty appetites and their plates are empty by the time the latecomer arrives.

Mrs. Proctor greets him without affection.

"I do think you might show a little more consideration, darling."

"I had to park the car up at the Town Hall."

"But you can park here. I told you."

"I couldn't find the parking lot."

"Really!" She is on the edge of losing her temper when she remembers the others. "Rosemary, you remember Justin. Of course, he was only a baby—" She shrugs, as though there had always been some disadvantage attached to him. "And this is Chantal. I'm afraid I didn't quite catch—"

Chantal's surname is produced in a mispronounced form. Neither of the ladies regards it as anything manageable or important.

"Well, sit down, darling. You'll have to hurry up, we've started."

Justin takes the chair opposite his mother. He bears her rage with good humor. It is quite evident that she has underestimated him or has failed, in her busy existence, to follow the alterations of his adolescence. A year or two ago Justin must have been pretty, but now his snub features have coarsened with a sullen, rather contemptuous look. He has the air of a stableboy, which is probably all right since he isn't one. His contemporaries will find him considerable rather than likable: he will not always be welcome, but he will not easily be left out.

Justin has large, long hands with square-tipped fingers. His unkempt hair is straw-colored; exactly the same color, in fact, as Chantal's.

At first he and Chantal stare at each other without speech. It is too early for them to try out any language they may have in common. The girl has stopped pretending to listen to what the two women are saying. She has drawn herself a little away from them. Except by watching, she cannot tell what is going on.

The waitress brings a plate of soup, which Justin consumes in three mouthfuls. His eyes return to Chantal's. Both of them start to smile as if they have just realized a private joke, but where he is concerned the smile stops as a sort of twitch in the corner of the mouth. After this neither of them smiles, but they go on looking.

Mrs. Stopham's "traditional fare" is roast chicken, which in appearance and taste resembles splinters of rotting wood; the gravy is thickened, the roast potatoes are soft and dead-cold at the center. Like many others in this part of the world, the Stophams have used their pretension to gentility to perform the usual confidence trick. In this they are at one with the hard women with cigarettes dribbling out of the corners of their mouths who breed toy poodles or run antique shops in Kilminster and other country towns. Or with Rosemary herself, for that matter, charging in guineas for rudimentary hospitality and the English way of life.

Now, in the dining room of The Stone Lions, none of this has any importance at all. Pamela and Rosemary go on talking, but anything they have to say has became as irrelevant as a television set switched on in a room where two people are making love. Attempts to draw either Justin or Chantal into the conversation have been rejected out of hand.

The world of the boy and the girl is completely silent. They try to eat, but forget they are doing it in the middle of each mouthful. They are deaf as though after a huge explosion. In every way except physically, they are already in bed together. In short, a classic case of the *coup de foudre.*

A whole summer lies ahead: the car borrowed without his parents' permission, headlong drives through the darkness along roads lined with cow parsley, each assignation with its prologue and epilogue of family quarrels, the A levels neglected, the university place in forfeit. Perhaps in the end, too, Chantal dispatched home early (her board has been paid in advance, however, for the full period and is not refundable). Envisaging tennis and outings, Pam and Rosemary have assumed the traditional role of bawd and go-between. They have drawn aside the curtains; the bed is ready, waiting.

At this moment, the dining room of The Stone Lions, which up to now seemed a place anybody would escape from as quickly as possible, is no longer quite that. The four people at the other table have achieved a curious equilibrium. The women's conversation still ranges back over the past. The questions they ask each other are not probing, for their lives have obviously been less interesting than either of them expected or would like to admit, and the true joys came earlier, when they were both at boarding school. Meanwhile, Justin and Chantal, alike with their blond hair and carefully picturesque Christian names, are held in the present, staring over cold plates and the debris of chicken. They have no demands to make of anyone else. They have nothing to remember. They know exactly what is going to happen next.

# *Discontinued Lines*

On this autumn morning, Commander Allardyce did not need to wear the duffel coat which had done him much signal service since his retirement. Prematurely "bowler-hatted," he had in fact never bought a hat. In addition to his pension, a little money of his own had prevented him from being pushed out into the cold of commercial life. He remained navy-blazered in summer, duffel-coated in winter. His clothes, like his rank, were a constant reminder of the past.

Every morning, for the sake of the exercise, he walked the mile or so from his lodgings to The Fisherman's Creel, the very successful restaurant which was run by his sister, Mrs. Kingham. Mrs. Kingham, with her hard face, brick-red hair, and sharp, tilted eyeglass frames, was known as an excellent businesswoman. The Commander merely lent his sister a hand. Nobody knew if repayment was ever made for this loan. Some people, among them the Commander's great friend Mrs. Gilray, considered him to be exploited, while at the same time admitting that it was probably better for him to be made use of than to be useless. The increasing celebrity of The Fisherman's Creel had long priced it out of the reach of the local retired people. Every season Mrs. Kingham was obliged to take on extra help. She still had the

Austrian cook on whom her reputation had been founded. At the beginning, the waiting had been done by local girls. These had been replaced by Cypriots, but nowadays she more usually employed Spaniards or Portuguese.

About a quarter of a mile from his lodgings at Hillcrest, the Commander was due to pass Cedar Lodge. From the top of the hill he was able to see whether Mrs. Gilray was at work in her garden. He always exchanged a word or two with her, but he was a shy man, and years of service life had rendered his vocabulary meager. Whenever he saw the small figure, dressed always in mauve or gray, among the rosebeds, he felt his face warm through slowly as though he was in front of a stove. He was afraid his first words would blurt out at the wrong volume; it was like switching on a radio disused for some time.

This morning, Mrs. Gilray was filled with controlled rage, a favorite emotion among gardeners. She had just discovered that creeping buttercup, with its hairy purple stems and serrated leaves, had pushed its way right in among her dianthus plants. The stems of the dianthus snapped easily in her small hands, which were made large and clumsy by the leather gardening gloves. She realized that the whole lot would have to be sacrificed. She might save a few cuttings, but it would be a long time before they spread into ice-green cushions like those that had fringed the bed of hybrid tearoses.

These battles with various parasites had persisted through ten years, since they had bought Cedar Lodge, a small Regency house on the edge of the village of Limberhurst. They had found the garden neglected since the War. Ground elder had been the first problem, and they had managed to defeat it before her husband died. But the creeping buttercup seemed to return whenever one's attention had been distracted. It was like a moral weakness, one of those bad habits one had been taught in Mrs. Gilray's generation to be on guard against. Evil to her was untidiness and neglect, and in dreams she discovered ground elder and buttercup all over the garden and right into the house, up the stairs, and around the pedestal in the bathroom.

Mrs. Gilray rose from her knees with a tangle of plants and

weeds surrounding her. She pushed back a lock of white hair with the still unmuddied back of a glove, and sniffed, because it was much too complicated to take off the gloves and extract a handkerchief. At this moment Commander Allardyce appeared beyond the gate.

"Oh, hullo," Mrs. Gilray said—they never addressed each other by name. "Look at this. Did you ever see anything like it?"

The Commander was stuck for a reply. He was no gardener, and they seemed to him to be perfectly ordinary weeds.

"I see you have visitors," he remarked coyly.

Farther down the road a large car of European make was half visible. Like an Alsatian sniffing at a terrier bitch, it had pursued Mrs. Gilray's small Morris right to the back wall of the garage.

The Commander's tone of voice, heavy with intention, indicated that it was well known who was visiting Mrs. Gilray.

She took no notice of this. "It's my son. He only arrived last night. He had to spend the whole week in London."

"So we all knew. We saw him on television. That debate on—on . . ." He sieved and riddled his memory for a glint of ore, but was unsuccessful.

"On the Greek Colonels."

"Exactly." He blushed. "Very outspoken, we thought it." His heel ground into the asphalt road. "Trenchant." The word came out like a squeal of static.

Alasdair Gilray's field was the eastern Mediterranean, and the opinions he expressed on television were calculated to anger people like Commander Allardyce. Commander Allardyce had, after all, been out there during the War and he knew a thing or two, if anyone had asked him. But words were not his medium. He could have discussed it with Mrs. Gilray, but she might have taken it as a personal attack on her son. He remained silent.

To help him, Mrs. Gilray said: "Of course, Alasdair's had a lot of practice."

"That must be it. Once you have the practice—" It is one of the tenets of retired people that most activities are a matter of getting the knack; one could have done it oneself, too, had the occasion arisen.

"Staying long?"

"I think it's only a day or two, this time. Perhaps we'll be coming down."

"Coming down?" The Commander looked startled.

"I've told my son a lot about The Fisherman's Creel."

His face grew darker. "Oh yes, I see. Well, must be off now."

He swiveled awkwardly on his heel, and marched away, as though on stage.

Mrs. Gilray watched him for about fifty yards. "Poor old fellow," she thought, although he was some eight years younger than herself. Her married daughters teased her by referring to the Commander as Mummy's boyfriend. She found this irritating, although she pretended to be amused.

Soon after he had gone, her Siamese cat, who was perhaps even shyer than Commander Allardyce, descended head first from the mock-orange tree. She landed heavily, with a shocked, squeaky noise like a toy teddy bear being dropped from a height, and the same sound continued as she trotted through the wet grass.

The cat walked in figure eights between Mrs. Gilray's legs, trampling the toes of her gum boots. Hale voices and the heavy footsteps that had entered the house last night made her uneasy, and she rubbed against Mrs. Gilray to find confidence. When the old woman gathered up the heap of vegetation into a prickly armful and carried it down to the rubbish heap, the Siamese hurried after her, accompanying each footstep with a small interior cry of affection and concern.

The garden at Cedar Lodge was sufficiently small for it to resound with any disturbance going on in the house. The clatter that came from downstairs indicated that it was Mrs. Hobbs's day for doing the drawing room. Now that Mr. Alasdair was at home, she had been forbidden the use of the vacuum cleaner. Nevertheless, by pulling the armchairs around on their squealing casters, she contrived to make a good deal of noise, a token show of violence to break down the barrier that surrounds men and their activities. In spite of this, the sound of the typewriter upstairs continued unceasingly, as level and monotonous as a sewing machine.

Mrs. Hobbs had finished the drawing room by the time Mrs. Gilray came in from the garden.

"Any tea going, Mrs. Hobbs?"

"I've got the kettle on."

The two women sat with their cigarettes at the kitchen table, while they waited for the Indian tea to draw.

Mrs. Gilray fidgeted with her teacup. "I'll never get any more of this pattern," she said. "I asked in London, and they told me it was a discontinued line."

"Such a shame," said Mrs. Hobbs, who had often heard this complaint before. "I don't know what they're thinking of."

"The same with those nice pillowcases. They said it was the end of the range. I've been getting them for years."

Mrs. Gilray poured the tea.

"I haven't bothered with the stairs today," Mrs. Hobbs said. "I like to take the vacuum to them."

"We must come to some arrangement. We can't just leave them."

"Mr. Alasdair wouldn't let me get into his room."

"These are the hours he works, Mrs. Hobbs. We must respect that."

"Nor the other one, either. He was asleep, you could hear him."

Mrs. Gilray stared out of the window. "We'll have to see how it all works out later."

"Am I to wash those undies what you left out?"

"Yes, please do that."

Skillfully Mrs. Hobbs had again found a way to fill out her three hours.

"Those other rooms'll want a proper doing out sooner or later. How long are they staying, then?"

Mrs. Gilray did not answer because she had not been told. She wanted to keep the whole thing on the edge of her mind. Her thoughts had other places to go—to her married son in Washington, to her daughters and their families in London. Now she wandered off, carrying her cup of tea, and Mrs. Hobbs watched her go, thinking: "Well, one thing, however vague she's getting, she never forgets my money and the extra for the stamp."

But perhaps Mrs. Gilray's vagueness was not quite genuine. It had been taught to her class and generation by half a dozen distinguished actresses, matinée favorites of the thirties and forties. They remained a platonic idea in her mind, those wise and gracious ladies, forever drifting in through the open French windows, bearing baskets full of cut delphiniums.

Panayotis was standing immediately outside the kitchen door. He was scratching himself, and yawning from the sunlight. He was barefoot and wore striped pajamas made of some prickly felt-like stuff.

Mrs. Gilray recovered enough to remember the Greek words for "good morning."

Panayotis grinned. His mustache lifted to show white, powerful teeth.

"Would you care for a cup of tea?"

He made the national gesture which involves shaking the head quickly three or four times while leaving the eyes staring wide open. It expresses incomprehension, though often without much desire to understand.

"*Tsai,*" Mrs. Gilray offered.

She glanced hopefully in the direction of the staircase, but the sound of the typewriter continued without interruption. They were unlikely to see Alasdair before noon.

She led the young man into the kitchen. While tap water drummed into a plastic basin in the sink, Mrs. Hobbs presented a back rigid with disapprobation.

Mrs. Gilray fetched another cup. Panayotis lowered himself into one of the kitchen chairs, which creaked in protest under his weight. His feet were huge on the tiled floor; gaps appearing between the buttons of his pajamas showed the blackness of hair underneath. Averting her eyes, Mrs. Gilray perched herself on the edge of another chair and filled the teacups.

Panayotis poured his tea into the saucer and drank it with appreciative noises. He smiled. Another smile hovered and left Mrs. Gilray's face.

Panayotis picked up the Georgian teaspoon and examined it,

first one side and then the other, blowing between his teeth and puzzling over the hallmark.

"Silver," Mrs. Gilray told him. Then immediately she wondered whether it had been quite wise to proffer this information.

"Very nice."

Bleak-faced, Mrs. Hobbs approached in order to hang Mrs. Gilray's underwear on the dryer above the stove. "That's my three hours, then."

Mrs. Gilray looked vague again. "Thank you so much, Mrs. Hobbs."

Mrs. Hobbs buttoned herself briskly and tightly into her raincoat. Whatever the world is coming to, one must protect oneself as best one can. She jabbed a glance, quick as a knife, in the direction of the young man, and then departed.

Panayotis finished his tea and returned upstairs. In the garden Mrs. Gilray renewed her attack on the weeds. She worked with violence until the last of the dianthus was uprooted. The natural rage and aggression of the gardener were now in part directed at Alasdair. Why did he have to leave her alone with his friend, when he knew perfectly well how awkward and embarrassed she must feel?

By the time she heard the grandfather clock strike twelve, she had made herself quite exhausted. In the hall she kicked off her gumboots and left her gardening gloves. She went into the drawing room.

Panayotis was still the only occupant. Now he was wearing his best clothes, a dark suit and white shirt. His short socks were a violent orange color and his shoes were sharp-pointed, polished, but cracked and flattened. It was a question perhaps not only of the wrong shoes but of the wrong feet. As a child in Macedonia he had gone barefoot, and as a Palace Guard in Athens he had worn army boots.

He smiled at her, but he did not stand up. Suddenly she saw that he had got hold of the Siamese cat. Trapped securely in his large hands, she was spitting and growling with fear.

"Prunella!"

Panayotis laughed.

"Let her go at once!"

Since he didn't seem to understand, Mrs. Gilray went and pulled the cat away from him. Prunella stayed in the old woman's arms a moment, cross-eyed in panic, not knowing where she was. She struggled free, leaving long scratches on Mrs. Gilray's wrist, and raced for the door.

Mrs. Gilray followed into the garden, but the cat had vanished, to reappear a moment or two later as a shaking bunch of foliage at the top of the cypress tree.

When she returned to the house, Panayotis was still laughing; as much at herself, it seemed, as at the cat.

Heavy footsteps sounded on the floor above.

Mrs. Gilray went to meet her son as he came downstairs.

"Alasdair, please tell him not to bully Prunella. I can't stand it."

Mrs. Gilray held on to her son somewhere around the middle, and he bent to kiss her good morning.

At his Public School, Alasdair Gilray had been nicknamed "the Walking Bust." Since then he had grown but downwards, as it were, from his great slab cheeks and Roman nose. He was now six feet tall and, with the help of a toga, his whole figure could have adjusted easily into Portland stone. At Cedar Lodge, wearing a pale blue suit, made for him by a Beirut tailor, and black-and-white shoes, he was as exotic a presence as Panayotis.

"I assure you, Mother, that he intended the animal no harm. I have instructed him as to your susceptibilities."

"She's not at all used to strangers. And remember in Athens the dreadful things they do to those poor kittens."

Without answering this, Alasdair handed her a glass of sherry.

"Panayotis requests your forgiveness. And as a recompense we are taking you out to luncheon."

"But Mrs. Hobbs left everything quite ready."

"It can be consumed on another occasion."

Somewhat appeased, Mrs. Gilray glanced timidly from one

man to the other. "In that case, I'll really have to go and change."

"There is no cause for haste. I suggest we patronize the local restaurant."

"The Fisherman's Creel? But it's frightfully expensive, dear."

"No matter."

"That will be lovely." By now her eyes had brightened and her face had become warm with the sherry. "Perhaps it would be better if I telephoned for a table."

The Commander himself answered the telephone. "There will be three of us. Do try and give us one of the tables near the window."

"Three, did you say?" He sounded confused.

"Yes, of course. My son and I and—and my son's chauffeur-companion."

"I see." A pause. "Three, then."

"Yes, that's it. For one o'clock."

She replaced the receiver and came back to the fireplace. "That was Mrs. Kingham's brother, Commander Allardyce."

"Your boyfriend, Mother?"

Mrs. Gilray looked annoyed. "That's only the girls' joke, dear. What was I saying? Anyway, he gets rather muddled sometimes, poor old thing. But it's all right about our table. Now I must go and change and put on a hat."

The Mercedes, which had a left-hand drive, still smelt grandly of its newness. For the first time, in Mrs. Gilray's eyes, everyone was in a suitable relationship. She herself sat in the back seat next to her celebrated and prosperous son, and Panayotis was at the wheel. She could begin to forget that he had walked around the house in his pajamas like a peasant, had omitted to flush the toilet, horrified Mrs. Hobbs and scared a life or two out of poor Prunella. He drove beautifully.

Almost silent, the car swung through the dry gleaming autumn landscape. The road went downhill from Limberhurst into the valley, where The Fisherman's Creel stood among its gardens on the riverbank.

Alasdair made a stately progress across the gravel, while his mother trotted beside him.

"Mrs. Kingham's Korean chrysanthemums always last longer than mine. It must be because it's so sheltered down here."

In the "Jock Scott" bar several elderly couples were sitting, the women lacquered and jeweled, their husbands in ready-made tweed suits. These were not local people; they had driven here for lunch from the big hotels on the coast. As constant watchers of television, Alasdair Gilray's face was familiar to most of them. There were stares and a discreet murmur of voices. These quickly grew quiet when Panayotis ambled through to join the Gilrays.

"Isn't this nice?"

Though he was fond of her, Alasdair did not respond to his mother's enthusiasm. In public he usually wore an air of mild impatience, as though he was already overdue somewhere else.

Mrs. Gilray and her son ordered sherry, and Panayotis asked for Coke.

"Will you please inform Commander Allardyce that we have arrived?"

"Not here today."

Mrs. Gilray repeated carefully: "Commander Allardyce."

Without answering, the Spanish waiter went away, and Mrs. Gilray said to her son: "I know he would like to meet you. He was in Greece and Egypt during the War."

Alasdair's interest remained unaroused. "I don't think your message got through, Mother."

"Oh dear. These boys come here to learn English, I believe, but Mrs. Kingham tells me in some cases it's quite hopeless."

After she had said this, the old woman suddenly became shy and avoided looking at Panayotis. He sat with a half smile on his face. Only his left leg was vibrating rapidly, so that it looked as if it was being shaken by a small machine.

The waiter returned with plates of potato chips and peanuts.

"Where is Commander Allardyce?" Mrs. Gilray asked in a loud, clear voice.

"No. Not here."

"But he must be here. I have only just spoken to him on the telephone."

"No." The Spaniard appealed to Panayotis as a possible ally, but they had no words in common. The Greek shrugged his shoulders and laughed.

By now Mrs. Gilray was fretting with irritation and impatience, like a child who is unwilling to settle down. Her mind raced through the various possibilities of what might have happened. Was the Commander drunk? Had he perhaps suffered a slight stroke? He had appeared perfectly well outside the gate this morning.

Finally she announced: "I'm going to have another try."

"Mother, don't upset yourself. It is of no importance."

"It is important to me. I must find out what is going on. I am not accustomed to being treated this way."

Mrs. Gilray went up to the bar and rapped sharply on the wood. This move was noticed by the other customers. Now they turned their attention from Alasdair and Panayotis to the old lady, whose head in its straw toque hardly came above the level of the bar. They began to expect an embarrassing scene.

A different young Spaniard appeared.

"I wish to speak to Commander Allardyce."

"Sorry, madam, he is not available."

"Is Mrs. Kingham here, then?"

"Mrs. Kingham is in London today."

"There must be somebody—"

"Just one moment, please—"

The young man went away and Mrs. Gilray, believing she was on the way to success, turned, and nodded to her son.

This gesture was recorded by all the commonplace bespectacled faces in the "Jock Scott" bar, and produced the hope that someone who demanded special attention would be frustrated, even humiliated.

This seemed likely to happen when, to Mrs. Gilray's clear disappointment, the Austrian cook came through the kitchen door. He was wearing the tall white hat which Mrs. Kingham had instructed him to put on in public.

"Good morning, Mrs. Gilray. Can I help you in any way?"

The mention of her name was a final confirmation of Alasdair's identity.

"It is about Commander Allardyce. We were expecting to meet him."

"He is not feeling so good, I am afraid so."

"But I spoke to him, not half an hour ago. Did he leave a message?"

"No, no message. Perhaps he went home."

"That is not possible. We would have passed him on the road."

"What are you wanting for lunch, Mrs. Gilray? I have very nice chicken today, also *Wiener Schnitzel*."

Mrs. Gilray had almost forgotten that they had come to The Fisherman's Creel for lunch. Looking into the stone-pale eyes of the Austrian, she realized now that the mystery was not going to be resolved. She blinked quickly several times. Moments like this came frequently in old age; instead of being listened to, you were humored. Where you had expected friendliness, there was a glint of impatience or a stare of hostility.

"I must ask my son and his friend. Thank you, Mr. Schneider."

In defeat, she returned to their table, where Panayotis had finished the potato chips. She sat quietly, as though the spirit had suddenly deserted her. "I can't understand it," she murmured to herself. "So rude. So extremely rude."

"I have ordered you a sherry, Mother."

"No, really, dear. I musn't have another."

"It is already done."

When the waiter came with the drinks, he nodded and smiled again to Panayotis. There was complicity between them, both being dedicated to the proposition that the English hardly exist as people; they are paper-thin, but their third dimension is money.

Mrs. Gilray was frowning, and, as sometimes happens with old people when they are thinking, she appeared to be chewing something.

At length she said: "Of course, Commander Allardyce is dreadfully shy, poor old fellow. I expect he was afraid of finding his opinions out of date. We live so far away from everything down here."

But Alasdair did not seem to be listening. His eyes were unfocused, glazed over with self-regard. Panayotis's left leg was still vibrating quickly up and down.

From the other side of the room, two women stared at them blankly, like large animals looking over a gate. Mrs. Gilray gave the two of them a little smile, perhaps as a tribute to her famous son. The women quickly turned their heads away.

She soon realized that this was going to happen whenever she looked at anyone. She had only to glance up to see all the heads moving, the faces shifting with feigned attention elsewhere. It was as automatic as flicking through the pages of a book.

Mrs. Gilray felt sad. Then she finished her glass of sherry, and this made her feel better.

"Well, I suppose we'd better eat, hadn't we?"

She herself had no appetite. An indigestible lump of experience lay inside her, somewhere near the heart. But she knew she could get rid of it. One always did, sooner or later, and this was perhaps one of the few blessings of age.

She stood up and, marching bravely ahead, she led her menfolk into the dining room.

# Ructions, or A Historical Footnote to the Cold War

In spite of her many aliases—for she was to adopt during her career the surnames of Gorsley, Pratt, Hemridge, Charleston and Bunsenburger, besides several others that history has left unrecorded—it has been established that she was born Sybil Pettifer, the only daughter of a warrant officer serving in Hong Kong. Commentators have sought to connect her formidable destiny with the example afforded by the Chinese amahs, that remarkable group of women who put up their hair, wear special clothes, and abjure marriage and male contacts in favor of a life of service. This hypothesis may be discounted. In the China Station, the Pettifers would hardly have had much contact with the amah-employing classes. And in any case, after the warrant officer's demise, Mrs. Pettifer and her daughter returned to England. Sybil (a name by which she can but rarely have been known) was then seventeen.

Her ambition was "to look after children." Entering a training college, she acquired such complicated lore as testing the bathwater with your elbow, and emerged as a uniformed member of her curious cadre, ready for her first "post." They were always "posts" from the very beginning, as though she were on sentry-go at some invisible frontier between the social classes.

The available evidence shows that she found employment with a young family called Gorsley, who lived in Bayswater. The Gorsleys belonged to "the New Poor," they were chronically "hard up," according to the expressions then current. They even had a secondhand perambulator. On her first expedition to Kensington Gardens, Nanny Gorsley was at once made aware of this defect. "You must *force* them to get you a new pram," hissed another nanny, the same age as herself, yet already glinting and fierce as a young basilisk. "Otherwise, hand in your notice immediately." Peter and Wendy Gorsley were ignored throughout the morning by the resident team and their charges. Almost weeping, Nanny took them home. As yet, she was too lacking in confidence to give notice. Instead she avoided returning to the Gardens, and henceforward the Gorsley contingent took exercise furtively in the squalid back streets of North Kensington. One afternoon, a strange gentleman asked Nanny to step in and have a cup of tea. She would have liked to accept, but Wendy was sniffling and they had to get home, otherwise there would have been ructions. However, she expected she would be passing that way again, and noted down the odd gentleman's address: 10 Rillington Place. But somehow she never had occasion to return. Even at that time it was clear that history had a different destiny in store for her.

Whether Peter and Wendy Gorsley were permanently affected by their lack of social contacts remains obscure. Nanny left them soon afterward, and no one knows what became of the Gorsleys. They pass beyond the gaze of research; it is as though they had been atomized. There are plenty of Peters around still, but whatever happened to all those Wendys?

Mrs. Gorsley must have given her a good reference, because she went straight on to the Pratts in Chester Terrace, who were, from every point of view, satisfactory.

Violet Pratt was a fluffy-haired, bird-like little thing. Giles Pratt was a fine figure of a man with a flat stomach and excellent teeth, who wore his clothes well. He was a first-class shot, and played an excellent game of bridge. People watching the Pratts always thought what an affectionate couple they were. And indeed they might have been, if they had not stepped, brand-new, out of one of the best-equipped fiction factories of the day. Their disappearance in the late thirties in the pine woods near Cap Ferrat created no sort of disturbance; it was to be assumed that they had stepped back into the factory, to be repulped and used again. Their role as the parents of Gervase, and the employers of Nanny, became a mere puff of smoke in the incinerator chimney.

Gervase, their only child, belonged to quite a different order of reality. Indeed, Nanny herself was often to wonder if some mistake had been made at the fashionable nursing home in which Violet Pratt had become sufficiently three-dimensional to produce him. He was a small, scornful child with rough hair and flaky skin. Each of his front teeth, when it appeared, was independent of its neighbor, and this added to his look of an arrogant chipmunk. He was a heller at children's parties, a bully to his contemporaries in the park. There, however, Nanny was now an esteemed and respected figure, on friendly terms with the Royal Nannies of the era, to the extent of supplying them with witticisms and anecdotes which, when their memoirs were later published, they attributed to their own lackluster charges.

It was the golden age of nannies. Half the jokes in *Punch* were about them. In allegorical representations of English life, painted by Royal Academicians, they appeared in the forefront, wheeling prams, while beside them were scarlet guardsmen and aristocratic ladies in silver-fox capes, and in the middle distance a genteel scrubbed band of unemployed ex-servicemen played street music. In those years, before the armies marched once more, there can have been few more terrifying sights than a squad of huge nannies (all nannies seemed huge to those over whom they had power and dominion) reinforced perhaps by one or two bossy, long-tressed big sisters (whose sharp pinches were at once a pain and a privilege), all advancing and retreating like a herd of bison before summoning out, after a whispered consultation to make sure they had got his name right, some wretched child who longed to be left out of the whole business, to bestow on him the dubious title of "Nuts in May."

Nanny already knew that, whatever the future brought, Gervase would remain a favorite among her children, and the only shadow on those years was that they were fated to be so short. Gervase was down for Summerfields and Eton, and it was clear that he would have no successors in the nursery at Chester Terrace. Violet Pratt, however, had several cousins who had recently married and it was improbable that Nanny would be without employment.

Nanny spent several years with Violet Pratt's cousins, years in exile, they were later to seem, while she waited for her summons from history. She grew stouter, and her hair, still shingled, began to turn gray. Belted into her raincoat, velour-hatted, she was now one of the most respected and experienced nannies in the park. When Stella and Vanessa, her newest charges, invited her to run races, she was ready with the classical excuse, that "she could not run, for she had a bone in her leg." The War came, and, under heavy protest from Nanny, she and the children were evacuated to the country, where they were to live with Stella's and Vanessa's grandmother.

The house was in a remote shire—so remote that Lady Hemridge had refused to accept that a war was in progress. She knew perfectly well that the soldiers, even the American ones, had only been called in to combat the Workers' Revolution. No wonder there were pillboxes along the railway lines and sandbags outside the Post Office—there might be an outbreak at any moment.

One night everyone was kept awake while the local cathedral town was being bombed.

"There must have been serious trouble," Lady Hemridge announced at breakfast, "in the slum areas. I hope the working classes have learned their lesson by now."

"Boots the chemist got a direct hit," Stella said. "The postman said so."

"Jolly good," Lady Hemridge said. "It was always a hotbed of revolt."

"But *Boots,* Lady Hemridge," Nanny ventured. "I mean, surely not—"

"Of course it was, Nanny. At one time they only sold red sponge bags."

Since Lady Hemridge was not to be contradicted, her theories remained irrefutable. Nanny's position was curiously isolated;

Jonathan was too young for rational discussion, and Stella and Vanessa were emotionally identified with horses.

When the War ended, young Mrs. Hemridge was found to have disappeared with an American colonel. While the divorce was going on, the children were to remain in the country. As though conscious at last that her destiny lay elsewhere, Nanny gave notice.

Lionel Grist-Miller was elected to the House of Commons in 1945, and became a Parliamentary Secretary two years later. The Grist-Millers lived in Kensington Palace Gardens, and Nanny, escorting Fabian and Artemis, returned to the scene of her former humiliation by the Round Pond, now triumphantly wheeling a magnificent new pram.

She had not been long at the Grist-Millers before she met Gervase Pratt again. She had lost touch with him during the War, and it gave her quite a start to see him coming into her nursery. He had been at Eton with Lionel Grist-Miller.

Once he invited Nanny to lunch on her day off.

She met him by arrangement outside Swan & Edgar's, and he took her to a quiet restaurant in Soho. When she looked at Gervase closely, Nanny had to admit to a sense of disappointment. For one thing, his nails were in mourning, and you could have grown potatoes behind his ears. Whoever was looking after him didn't know the first thing about washing collars.

Some authorities have read significance into her desertion of the violently reactionary world of Lady Hemridge and her entry into the circle of the progressive, politically active Grist-Millers. But this seems to underestimate the influence that Gervase Pratt had always held over her. In support of the latter contention, the crux would seem to be this lunch in Soho, though of course the subject of their conversation will never be known.

In the light of later events, it is at least tenable that they discussed the literature which had delighted them over twenty years before. In this case, Gervase would soon have indicated the development of his ideas. Under the orthodox Marxist interpretation of the Milne canon, of course, Rabbit's friends-and-relations represent the oppressed proletariat. The intellectuals, Owl and

Eeyore, have abdicated their responsibilities, Eeyore choosing complete cynicism, whereas Owl is enmeshed in Alexandrian subtleties: in his hands a simple birthday message becomes, with its Joycean overtones, a classic example of language in disintegration. C. Robin, who seems to represent the feudal alliance of King and People (a "Prince Hal" figure, his Falstaff is Pooh, and his Ancient Pistol, the fantasizing Piglet), retreats into an alliance with the hereditary aristocracy ("Arise, Sir Pooh de Bear"). Even his study of Factors, which might be assumed to indicate a nodding acquaintance with post-Newtonian scientific thought, is fraught with ambiguity: "Factors" may mean "one of the numbers which multiplied together produce a given number" but it also means "one who buys and sells for another." Education, in short, is education for the entrepreneurial system; betrayal could hardly go farther.

If Nanny was unsatisfied with this analysis, Gervase may have indicated the revolutionary element in the work of Potter. In *Jemima Puddleduck* the two foxhounds who assist in the rescue of Jemima, a proletarian production worker, end by eating her eggs. It is a textbook example of how the bourgeois liberal supports the Revolution to further his own aims. Here the Grist-Millers were exemplary, though it is improbable that, at this juncture, Gervase cared to test Nanny's loyalty by mentioning them. All the historian may postulate is that by the time Nanny returned to Kensington Palace Gardens she had, however unwillingly, withdrawn her support from Pooh and Piglet and taken a stand in support of Rabbit's friends-and-relations.

Only once did Nanny forget herself and reassert their old relationship. "Gervase, you haven't finished what's on your plate. It's no use trying to hide it under your knife. Millions starving in Russia." It was something that she had always said, without thinking.

"Pure counter-revolutionary propaganda," Gervase snapped. "We have work to do." He had drunk nearly a whole bottle of wine, since Nanny never touched anything. But she now agreed to take a sip and even to drink a toast. What was the toast? We shall probably never find out. To the Revolution? To the Workers of the World? Or to Rabbit's friends-and-relations?

Lionel Grist-Miller carried a briefcase stuffed with papers and left it all over the place. Once, quite by chance, Nanny found it in the lavatory and was able to return it to him the following afternoon. The Grist-Millers were busy people, but insisted, masochistically, on breakfasting with the children. Nanny was there to interpret and also to intervene.

"What are you going to do this morning?"

"Speak to Daddy, Artemis."

"No."

"We're going upstairs first thing, aren't we?" Nanny proposed the order of priorities.

"I don't want to."

"Then we're going out to the park, aren't we?"

"I don't want to."

"Now then," Nanny menaced.

"Are we going to see your nephew again?" Fabian asked.

"Fabian, I don't *think* somehow Mummy and Daddy would be interested—"

"He wears awful shoes," Artemis said. "They're like dog's do."

"That will be enough."

"He's got a Bulgarian accent," Fabian said.

"Where do they learn such words?" Mrs. Grist-Miller murmured through her headache.

"Fabian, dear," Nanny interposed, "finish up your milk."

Fabian went on: "It's jolly boring, we have to go right over to the Physical Energy to meet him."

Lionel Grist-Miller put down the file he was reading. "What's all this about, Nanny?"

"My sister's boy, Mr. Grist-Miller. She married a foreign gentleman, ever so many years ago now."

"A Bulgarian?"

"I think that was what was mentioned at the time."

"How remarkable! Most interesting." He gleamed at his children in his instructional manner. He embarrassed them horribly, and they tried to duck out whenever they saw him begin looking enthusiastic. Artemis curled her toes up and Fabian crossed his legs hard. "Listen to that, children. At a time when we are striving to advance our knowledge of these wonderful achievements in Eastern Europe, which they quite correctly wish to keep from purely destructive criticism, here is somebody who has gone forward to clasp the hand of friendship. Nanny's sister." (Giggles.) "Someone from a simple, unassuming background has taught us a lesson which we will ignore at our peril. When will we learn, I wonder?" (Opposition counter-giggles.) "I am doing everything, children, and I want you to remember this, to ensure that the bonds of friendship grow ever more meaningful. But the future is in your hands—" At this point Lionel Grist-Miller felt his neck hairs prickling and hot tears, occasioned by his own sincerity, scalded his eyes. Overcome with emotion, he left the table and staggered out of the room. They heard him blowing his nose outside.

Fabian and Artemis let out flatulent sighs of relief. For once Nanny omitted to correct them; sharp-eyed, she had noticed that Mr. Grist-Miller had left one of his files behind.

And so on that morning, as on so many others, Nanny would take the children as far as the Round Pond. There, after the nice policeman, the nice park-keeper, and the other nannies had been greeted, to establish as it were her alibi, she would put on a surprising turn of speed. Up and down went her sturdy legs in their lisle stockings, while her large feet, shod in shoes so sensible that they verged on bluntness, beat the green turf until it shuddered; her face grew flushed under the bowl-like velour hat, and Artemis, who was three, began to shake up and down as though the stroller had become the ejector seat of a jet fighter; behind them, Fabian hurried and stumbled, half sobbing in his efforts to keep up. As the warm air spun past them, the statue of Physical Energy, their goal, became the very shrine of the god whose spirit they incarnated.

Nanny was always punctual, and she expected punctuality in others. At the prearranged moment, the young Slav, horribly conspicuous in his capitalist disguise of a white mackintosh, pointed shoes, and a porkpie hat with a salmon fly on it, stepped out from behind the appointed elm tree. The passwords, arranged by Gervase, were exchanged.

"I—ers—oh—i—ay—or," remarked the Bulgarian, to which

Nanny replied, with meticulous articulation: "Tiggers *don't* like haycorns." And, after a moment's rummaging in her handbag, another mission was accomplished.

Two general elections came, the government fell, Lionel Grist-Miller was out of a job. And so, Gervase promptly informed her, was Nanny. It was something of a blow, for she had quite taken to Artemis, and a new baby was on the way. The decision, however, was no longer her own, and her new post turned out to be in the British Embassy in Kurdistan.

During nursery tea at the Residence, an impending Royal Visit was the subject under discussion.

"I can't think why everyone makes such a fuss about photographers," Lady Charleston remarked. "I always think with a Box Brownie you can take perfectly good pictures."

"I want a Nikon F for my birthday," her son, Paul, said.

His mother put down her teacup and looked at him for a moment as though she had never seen him before.

"Those that ask, don't get," Nanny contributed.

"Yes, I know, and those that don't ask, don't want," Paul said. "I merely offered it as a proposition, although I admit, to use Russell's terminology, a proposition in the optative mood. In any case, Nanny," he continued, "how did you come by your own camera? Which of the alternatives led to the acquisition, if in fact they are mutually exclusive, which empirical evidence leads me to doubt. We all know you got it. Didn't you ask for it or didn't you want it? If you didn't want it, in that case why don't you sell it? You could get plenty of Maria Theresa dollars for it in the bazaars, you know. Please explain."

Paul put his hands on the edge of the table and twiddled his thumbs, while over his head Nanny and Lady Charleston exchanged the wildest of glances.

"Finish up your milk, Paul," Nanny said.

But his temper was high and he now had an addition to his audience. Sir Beale Charleston had come upstairs to see what all the noise was about.

"I should like it to be known," Paul shouted, "that Nanny

possesses a Nikon F Photomic T and a bellows focusing attachment set."

"Now, Paul," Nanny said. "There's no need to go into details."

"I am merely wondering how she got it. We know she didn't ask for it. Are we to presume, therefore, that she didn't want it? If she didn't want it, why does she possess it? I was merely posing the simplest of conundrums."

Across the nursery table Nanny and Paul glared at each other. Outside the temperature was over a hundred; in here, the air-conditioning hummed and you could hear flies, stunned by a lethal spray, fizzing to death under the French windows.

Lady Charleston suddenly yelled: "Stop it, all of you. I can't stand it another moment." She began sobbing feebly, but nobody took any notice of her.

"What *is* all this noise about?" Sir Beale inquired testily, after there had been a silence of about a minute and a half.

"Nanny's got a Nikon F Photomic T with bellows focusing attachment set." By now the words had taken on a demonish chanting sound.

"Is that so, Nanny? How very interesting."

Nanny thought highly of Sir Beale. As he spoke to her, the ground was firm under her feet again.

"My brother-in-law's a permanent invalid, Sir Beale. He'd never forgive me if I didn't take snaps of all the countries I visit."

"Where do you get them developed out here?"

"I take them to a man in the Old City. One of the other nannies told me about him."

"How very interesting," Sir Beale said again and lost interest at once.

"Paul, finish up your milk. We can't wait all day for you."

Paul was looking oddly at her, his eyes glittering with triumph. Too late she realized that she had once told him that she was an only child. She saw that concessions had to be made, to ensure his silence, and she made them.

But there were rather few privileges one could offer Paul, who usually got what he wanted in any case. She let him urinate in his bath several times, and twice on the Embassy lawn, as an experiment, to see what it did to the grass. The whole business was terrible. By nature she was an absolutist; once her laws had been broken with impunity, the power seemed to drain out of her. Sometimes Paul watched her so strangely that she wondered if he had been set to spy on her. And if so, who by.

On her next leave in London, Nanny insisted on changing her job. Perhaps to express official disapproval in high places, she had to spend several years with the family of a Conservative politician. Though the children were dull, the post itself was not without interest. The politician's private papers surprised Nanny considerably, especially some of the photographs; they went into details.

It was during these years that Gervase Pratt disappeared and turned up in Moscow some time afterward. By now Nanny had nothing to connect her with the Pratt family, beyond her own photograph album, which she kept under lock and key. For a few weeks she was worried lest some of the senior nannies would remember the old days in the park with Gervase. But apparently nobody did.

Reassuring messages were transmitted to her, and for two or three years she waited, biding her time, until she should be summoned again. Then, quite out of the blue, a most interesting post was offered her in the United States. She was not quite sure that she wanted to go there, but the family in question seemed to be very well connected.

Alas, it was not to be. The new baby, which was to have been Nanny's charge, died soon after it was born, and not long afterward the gentleman himself was killed in a motor-car in Texas. The historian, looking on, falls silent as History, having teetered toward a pothole, lurches off again in a different direction.

Nanny went to Washington all the same, to an American diplomatic family. Bradford and Caroline Bunsenburger had three chidren: Joy, who was a boy; Kelly, who was a girl; Ritchie, who was the youngest, and who didn't like to take baths. Later, Nanny accompanied the Bunsenburgers to several capitals in the Middle East. It was all very interesting, and she was able to take a great many interesting snaps.

In her ghosted, garrulous memoirs, syndicated in forty-eight countries in twenty-two languages, Caroline Bunsenburger attempts to show that she guessed there was something strange about Nanny all along. This claim, however, will not bear the most cursory examination. Any differences between the two women were of other origins. Like Cortez and Montezuma, like Perry and the Shogun, Caroline and Nanny balefully regarded each other from the standpoints of opposing cultures.

At this point the advantage was surely on Nanny's side. Experience, age, the baroque splendor of her references (together with the slight phosphorescent glow still surrounding her after that missed opportunity in Washington), all these had merely added to her charismatic quality. Like some aged Master of the Tea Ceremony, she rejoiced in a tetchy sensitivity to the smallest hindrances, the almost imperceptible variations in her accustomed ways. Trays sent up to the nursery were as significant to her as the Victorian language of flowers: with one glance at the food or the cutlery she could detect hidden meanings, unwarranted assumptions, blatant insults. Safragis and dragomans, fawned on by the Bunsenburgers, went in awe of her—it was as though she alone still wielded the Imperial scepter. She was assumed, however, to be on the verge of retirement, and already she had acquired a sort of sunset glow.

Perhaps, though, toward the end she grew careless. The chronicler can never know exactly what led to that final, ghastly afternoon—it was in Teheran, at the beginning of the hot months. On such days Nanny was in the habit of taking a somewhat prolonged siesta. At first the children had listened awestruck to her snores, which would peal out, inexorable and yet somehow plaintive, as though anarchic powers imprisoned beyond the world were crying out for release. Nowadays Joy and Kelly and Ritchie merely went on with what they were doing. They did not even notice when the thrumming reverberations had ceased and quiet re-established itself in the night nursery. Nanny lay awake for a while and she listened. Today the American mutterings were joined by the shrill notes of some English children from up the road and the juicy chuckle of the Ghanaian ambassador's son. She recognized all the voices, but it was a minute or two before the words began to make any sense. Then realization dawned on her. Horror-struck, she rose, outrage lending her movements an unwonted speed. They had got hold of her album of snaps.

They were reading out Gervase's name when she got to the doorway.

"That's the spy," one of the English children said.

"Why didn't she tell us she'd looked after a spy?"

"Because she's a spy, too, that's why."

Then they saw her and they all turned to her and shouted: "Spy! Spy! Spy!"

"Sticks and stones may break my bones," Nanny declared, "but words can never harm me."

They were fierce, an infant mob, in no mood to accept proverbial wisdom. "Who said anything about sticks? Fellers, we got a spy on our hands."

But, once aroused, her ferocity was the equal of theirs. She had the lion tamer's eye, and soon she had divided the children among themselves, found her quislings and reimposed her mandate. The effort exhausted her, and it was then that she realized that the end of her career was at hand. That night she sent messages to the Old City. Luckily Brad and Caroline were away in the mountains. When they returned, they found the three children in a doped sleep, and Nanny had departed, had simply vanished into the circumambient air, taking her album of snaps with her.

"Establishment Figure Secedes!"

Where had she gone? Speculations swarmed and flourished like ground elder in a neglected garden. Questions were asked in Congress. Brad Bunsenburger lost his job and, because of his reduced income, Caroline was obliged to divorce him. In the House of Commons, Lionel Grist-Miller made a great ass of himself. The repercussions spread farther and wider: ideas, concepts, the whole structure of past experience seemed to be called into question. Nanny, viewed in retrospect by reactionary and revolutionary alike, represented tradition, deference, hierarchy. Members of the upper-middle classes started looking doubtfully at their children, wondering whether they had been suborned in the nursery or on brisk walks. To Gervase's contemporaries of the Left, all nannies had been due to disappear when the Revolution came. Yet here, years afterward, someone who was almost the Platonic Idea of the profession was suddenly exposed as a surf rider on "the wave of the future." There were no certainties anymore.

Yet all this time there was no "hard news." Even her escape route remains uncertain. Did she take some unknown mountain road into the Caucasus, or was she smuggled by sturgeon-fishing boats across the Caspian Sea? Or perhaps she merely took one of the desert cars to Baghdad: since velour hats and belted macs would be conspicuous in the world of Islam, it is to be assumed that she traveled in disguise. Once this idea of disguise had been bruited abroad, there was to be no limit to her legendary reappearances—she was recognized as a veiled but bulky concubine in the Trucial States, as a market woman in Damascus, and a German tourist in the ruins of Ephesus. In Greece an elderly British novelist, observed loitering near the naval base on Poros, was stripped and searched at Police Headquarters and found to be an elderly British novelist. Later Nanny was reported to have been seen bathing off the island of Brioni. And the following year, when the spring winds were blowing tall curtains of red dust over the gray roofs of Peking, she was seen on May Day, standing in line on the great reviewing stand in the Tien An Men Square in front of the Forbidden City. But the only evidence we have is a blurred photograph, taken with a telescopic lens by a Swiss journalist, and a careful examination, including comparison of the earlobes, shows the identification to have been mistaken. The Chairman was making one of his rare unscheduled appearances.

She herself has never reappeared. From time to time, Gervase and other defectors have given press conferences in Moscow, under the auspices of the KGB. Of Nanny, however, nothing has ever been learned. Years have passed now. Occasionally there have been rumors that, somewhere beyond the Berlin Wall, she has been seen, heading west. But already she is entering into mythology. Perhaps her ultimate reappearance will evolve into an article of faith, like that of King Arthur or Don Sebastian, and throughout the tattered end of this century there will be mad-eyed fanatics prophesying her second coming: a fine summer morning when she will manifest herself in all her splendor in Kensington Gardens, put to flight the rabble of unsuitable *au pair* girls, and re-establish her kingdom under the chestnut trees. But even this, too, will become a vague dream, a consolation for those hours of twilight when it becomes possible to believe that "time will run back and fetch the age of gold," or that far away, in some corner of the Siberian forest, Nanny and Gervase will always be playing.

# Live Bait

# A Summer Pilgrim

Carrying pruning shears, Imogen Roper moved in from the garden. She picked up the receiver of the telephone to hear the insistent tone from a telephone booth. Then coins clunked down and there were strange grumbling and hissing sounds, both human and mechanical.

A nervous voice asked: "Mistah Ropah?"

She might have guessed. It is the unwelcome caller who always chooses the inconvenient moment. Summer is a-coming in, she murmured, and then longen folk to goon on pilgrimages. Oh dear, she was afraid she was rather naughty sometimes: she teased, she played little tricks.

"Mrs. Roper," she said.

The owner of the voice seemed stunned. "Mistah Ropah?" it pleaded.

"Mrs. Roper," she replied.

There was another hissing sound; improbable but without doubt human. The question was repeated and received the same answer. Finally the caller managed to produce at least part of a sentence, "Wishing to speak with Mistah Ropah," but at that moment his money ran out, and Imogen Roper visualized, not without private pleasure, the frantic search for further coins, and the effort to identify them, with myopic eyes, in the stuffy confines of a telephone booth.

In the meantime she straightened her face to find her best half-profile in the looking glass above the oak chest where the telephone rested. She pulled in the top of her skirt to prove to herself how slim she remained: the wife of one of our best minor poets—apart from Graves and Blunden, perhaps the only one to have appealed to three or four successive generations of readers. She was staunchly loyal to the reputation that had been founded on the early verse, with its pellucid pastoral images, its evocations of owl calls, and the smell of crushed water mint. A long time had passed, though, since Dunstan Roper, "the last of the Georgians," had written anything but school texts or children's books; he didn't even follow the county cricket anymore.

What would he do without her? She had met the poet when he returned to England after the death of his first wife. The *Collected Poems* (1960) had earned him a literary prize or two. Imogen was working at Rheinau and Masterton, his publishers. How the sparkish, waistcoated young men had groaned whenever his name was mentioned. Whenever Dunstan Roper telephoned, they mimicked his voice to their debbish secretaries, who laughed, shortly and sharply. But Imogen, who had read English at Cambridge, passionately admired Dunstan Roper's poetry. Her colleagues, to whom she was just good old Imogen, who took over and coped, were astounded when she decided to marry him. She even succeeded in charming his middle-aged son and daughter, both unmarried schoolteachers. "Imogen," they told her, "we can never be sufficiently grateful for your goodness to Dad."

Whenever she remembered how good she had been to Dunstan, she was filled with fondness for him. Now she decided to call him to the telephone. These pilgrimages gave him pleasure, and she respected this. She was the guardian of the secret springs of his inspiration.

The poet came through from his study. He was small, upright; his hair was silky and white, and he was wearing a blue sweater that perfectly matched his eyes. When the telephone rang again and he picked it up, she watched him with affection and pride. She removed a thread of white cotton from his shoulder.

"*Moshi-moshi*," he said. She was amused to see him at his old habit of smiling and bowing even when on the telephone. His ability with the Japanese language always ran out after a few phrases.

"*Ah so*," he said, and then "Yes!" and "Yes" again.

Imogen made funny faces at him. What was he letting her in for? He put down the telephone and dabbed at his eyes. Perhaps it was a wateriness of old age, perhaps a tribute to a time of personal happiness now past.

He had lived for eight years in Kyoto, and had gone on living there after his first wife's death. Those years had given him all the store of small impressions, longings, and pleasures connected with minor occasions like moon-viewing, river excursions, watching the scarlet maples in autumn, which had gone into *The Blue Magpie* (1957). The Japanese had appreciated the presence of the poet among them: he had left the country with the Order of the Rising Sun (fourth class).

"That was old Ukai-sensei," he said. "My colleague at the University."

"Oh, he's an old man. I'm sorry, he sounded just like one of those ghastly students."

"He's bringing one of our former students with him. Norko Hitomi. I remember her. She was a lovely kiddie."

"Bringing, darling? When?"

"Lunch on Wednesday."

"Couldn't you have made it tea?"

"It seems so little to offer, dear." His rich voice took a darker shadow. "These people were wonderful to me at Ellen's passing."

Imogen relented. Like most people who have lived abroad, he had acquired the habit of repeating himself, and his phrases still betrayed the South London respectability of his early years. Like his Georgian predecessors, he was a townsman: he had known the country on bicycle trips, or in borrowed cottages on weekends, until she herself had brought him down here to live.

Professor Ukai was an old man, though not quite as old as Dunstan Roper. No one had tried to make him beautiful: he wore a dark suit, round spectacles, and a whole balcony of front teeth.

When he returned to the hotel foyer, he was twitching a little after his ordeal. It would have been simpler to permit Miss Hitomi, an assistant lecturer, to telephone, since she spoke English far more fluently. But he had expected Mr. Roper to answer, and it would have been disrespectful for him to be addressed by a woman. Miss Hitomi would have her chance when their group returned from Stratford-upon-Avon. Then he and she would travel down to Sussex together; she would buy the tickets and ask directions.

Now, while they took the ritual "English tea" in their Bayswater hotel, Professor Ukai repeated some of his reminiscences of the poet. The strong stewed tea and the damp bread and butter seemed already to bring them closer to Dunstan Roper, although he himself had rarely spoken of such mundane things.

What had he spoken of? Dunstan Roper's colleagues in Kyoto had possessed little skill in the give-and-take of conversation. Instead, surrounding him while he held forth in the teacher's common room, they had sought to improve their English by a process of inhalation. And thus it was that they had listened to his criticism of English poets whose reputations (boosted, according to him, by a homosexual clique) by now surpassed his own. His hearers, who had sometimes spent years researching into these very poets, went away abashed, unable to look each other in the eye. With students, with Noriko Hitomi and her contemporaries, Mr. Roper had been matey and jocular. Like most foreigners, he prided himself on being "different": his students would just have to accept him, warts and all. They had indeed accepted him, Miss Hitomi remembered, but as a typical English gentleman. Belonging to a nation of unwitting Platonists, they generalized from this single example to the ideal. When he tried not to be a bore, he bored them beautifully; followers of the Noh theater and the Tea Ceremony, they were connoisseurs of tedium. Dunstan Roper was sufficiently old (it is nearly impossible to guess the age of a Westerner), he was a poet, he was boring. They delighted in him. For some, it is true, there was more than delight: there was a sort of faintness at the cheesy presence of the foreigner; the oddity of his protrusive face, the clumsiness of his hairy body.

Then his first wife, a dim, brownish lady, had died. Later the poet returned to England, and then the news came that he had married again.

Professor Ukai and his colleagues in the English literature department thought often of the poet's pleasure in his new wife. They imagined him living quietly, failing a little but free from care, while a subservient young woman attended to his needs. Mr. Roper mentioned cricket as one of his reasons for returning to England, and Professor Ukai and the others visualized the poet perhaps listening to the song of crickets in his garden, while his wife crouched in deference on the ground beside him, offering tidbits, solace, and cups of wine.

Dunstan Roper's new address appeared on his New Year card, and the following spring the pilgrims began to make their way to the cottage. On their return to Kyoto, they reported that Mr. Roper had many daffodils, in honor, it was to be assumed, of the poet Wordsworth. They were not used to commenting on personalities and so the second Mrs. Roper went unmentioned.

Professor Ukai was a fatalist, and he was not surprised by the difficulties of his telephone conversation this afternoon. But he possessed all the timidity of the scholar and the experience left him severely rattled. One can hardly lose face in front of women. Where Western women are concerned, however, there are exceptions even to this rule. Western women scared him dreadfully. Professor Ukai had once had a nightmare in which Mrs. McGillvray, the wife of the British Council representative, was brandishing a long dark-crimson phallus, like a young samurai in a pornographic "spring picture."

Accompanied by Miss Hitomi, Professor Ukai traveled to Stratford-upon-Avon with the rest of their group. In the evening they attended a performance of *Measure for Measure* at the Memorial Theatre. He listened for a few moments in blank incomprehension, and then removed his spectacles and slept undisturbed. The following morning, in front of the Birthplace and Ann Hathaway's cottage, he handed his camera to Miss Hitomi. She watched through the viewfinder until he assumed a strutting pose, drawing himself to his full five and a quarter feet, his spectacles and teeth flashing in the summer sunlight.

Tribute had been paid to the dead poet. But Miss Hitomi was conscious that something had gone wrong with the pilgrimage to the living poet. Next morning Professor Ukai telephoned to her hotel room to say that he was unwell; he would not be accompanying her on the visit to Sussex. Miss Hitomi would have the honor of making a full report on her expedition to their assembled colleagues back in Japan.

Miss Hitomi bowed her head to the telephone and accepted the responsibility. She set off alone and Professor Ukai spent the afternoon in astonished fascination in one of the strip clubs in Frith Street, Soho.

Miss Hitomi wore a white shirt, a classic coat and skirt, and one of those beret-shaped hats that suit the Japanese face. Her outward aspect was modest, as though of one of the Brontë sisters applying for the post of governess, and, as with them, it concealed a strong and passionate will.

She brought two presents for the poet, Professor Ukai's and her own, and several books for him to sign. She wrapped these together in a *furoshiki*, the square cloth that is used for parcel-carrying. She caught a bus to Victoria, and at Bambridge station she took a taxi. The journey gave her immense pleasure. She had discovered that things went far less fussily, and conversations were much more interesting, when she was free of her male compatriots. In addition she found, like Dunstan Roper in Japan, that nobody guessed one's correct age. She was nearly thirty, but could have passed for a young student had she wished.

Exactly at half past twelve, as had been appointed, she marched steadily up the brick path to the front door of the cottage.

Her small neat figure was observed simultaneously from two windows. Before she could touch the brass knocker the door had opened.

Mrs. Roper, who was wearing an orange kaftan, was so tall that her head was half hidden by the lintel of the door. But of course Miss Hitomi's eyes went first to the poet. The five years since she had last seen him had enormously improved his appearance. "His golden locks Time hath to silver turned," she quoted to herself, although Dunstan Roper's hair previously had been mouse-colored.

The poet and his wife both began speaking at once. Miss Hitomi stood before them in some confusion.

"Darling, let the girl get a word in edgeways. What's become of old Ukai?"

Miss Hitomi issued the official communiqué. "He is not so well, thank you. He will stay in his hotel."

Her host's blue eyes twinkled. He knew better than to make any comment, but his wife protested: "I do really think he might have telephoned."

The poet chuckled: "And get his ear bitten off?" He winked at their visitor. "Welcome to our happy home. Keep your shoes on and come on in."

In the hall Miss Hitomi unwrapped her carrying cloth and apologetically handed over the two parcels. He laid them aside with a murmur of conventional thanks. His wife, however, at once picked them up and began to undo the ribbon.

"Darling, I've told you so often. You don't open them now."

Miss Hitomi giggled with deprecation.

"Why not? I want to see my present." Imogen Roper held up a lacquer bowl and a pottery jar. "How nice. I suppose they're quite old."

Appalled by this suggestion, Miss Hitomi laughed wildly.

"You must excuse my wife. She is ignorant of Japanese customs."

"I am sorry that they are such poor things."

Mrs. Roper turned the jar in her hand. "I can just see it full of primroses. What would you use it for, in your country?"

"I think it may perhaps be a teacup," Miss Hitomi said. She meant that this was what it was. "A man's teacup," she added more firmly, in the hope of restoring the gift to its proper recipient.

"No, primroses. Lovely, lovely primroses. I must get lunch. Do you want to wash or anything? Darling, you'd better offer her some sherry."

"No, no thank you."

"Come into the sitting room." Miss Hitomi stood aside but

the old poet propelled her forward with his hard fingers on her shoulder.

Without listening to her refusal, he poured her a glass of sherry. She sat on the very edge of an armchair, with her knees pressed tightly together, a posture as near to kneeling as is possible with Western furniture. When he came toward her, the color of his eyes astonished her as it had done the first time she saw him. Very small children, even, stared hardest at foreigners with blue eyes, feeling an almost hypnotic mixture of repulsion and attraction.

"It is very regrettable that Professor Ukai is unable to be here."

Mr. Roper appeared to have no regrets. "Poor old Ukai. I wonder if he ever finished his work on Andrew Marvell. He'd got quite a lot of interesting stuff together, as far as I remember."

"I think perhaps he wishes to complete his research while he is here."

"If he's not too ill?"

Miss Hitomi giggled again.

"Never mind. We've got you with us, and that's the best part of it. By Jove, your English has come on."

"I think you don't remember me. Perhaps I was the smallest and shyest of your students."

"Of course I remember you. Let me see"—he ran a forefinger through his silver-white hair. "You attended my course on Thomas Hardy. Right first time?"

"You have excellent memory."

"You sat in the front row, on the left near the door. I'm right second time."

Miss Hitomi laughed with pleasure. She covered her mouth with her hand, and her cheeks turned a delicate pink, caused neither by embarrassment nor the single sip of sherry she had tasted.

There was a sudden silence, which seemed to drag them both into it. It shook them, like an inaudible explosion. The old man blinked and laughed. The girl was trembling. She despised the cultural training which made her look down at the carpet instead of directly into his blue eyes.

Then the light from the doorway was blocked by the tall wife in her kaftan, carrying a kitchen spoon.

"Well, lunch is ready whenever you are."

Miss Hitomi felt another hand on her shoulder. This time it was a comradely push from Mrs. Roper which propelled her into the dining room. She sat down where she was told. She watched Dunstan Roper unfurl his table napkin, and she copied his actions as best she could. She still felt stunned and rather deaf; it was like a change in the atmospheric pressure, high up a mountain.

"I wonder if you had opportunity to climb Mount Fuji?" she asked.

"We tried, but my wife—my first wife, of course—was wearing the wrong shoes. Perfectly hopeless. We had to come back from the eighth station. How about you?"

"I have climbed. Last summer. It was very interesting."

She fell silent. It had been a modest attempt at conversation, but he seemed pleased with it.

Mrs. Roper stood carving at the sideboard behind them.

"I hope you like lamb."

"Thank you."

Miss Hitomi pushed her chin down to control a shudder. She had eaten lamb once before. With some colleagues she had visited one of the Genghis Khan restaurants in Tokyo, where cooking is carried out on iron grids in the Mongolian style. The evening had been unexpected and enjoyable, but the lamb with its gluey texture and musty smell had made her feel rather ill. Now she was challenged by the pale gray crescents of meat lying on the plate in front of her. Reflecting that all happiness is transitory, and must be fought for, she went to work, listening while she ate to the poet's inquiries after his friends and former students.

Miss Hitomi was deeply conscious that her replies would disappoint him. She was not used to discussing people in the Western way, and she found, as so often, that the English she had been taught had provided her with nothing much worth saying. Some years ago, Karl, an American novice at the Zen monastery in Kyoto, had tried to help her to enlarge her vocabulary. Now, while Mrs. Roper shoveled further slices of meat onto her plate, the only part of Karl's instructions she could remember was the verbal idiom "to throw up."

"How do you like the lamb?"

"Thank you, it is very delicious." Eating it had been an endurance test, and she had been trained to survive such things.

She had just laid her knife and fork to rest, when she was aware of a touch on her knee. At first it seemed accidental. Then it happened again.

A moment later the intruding hand had established its intention by sliding gently up the nylon-smooth inside of her thigh. It remained there without moving, while Mrs. Roper returned from the kitchen with a bowl of gooseberry fool. She went back for cream and sugar.

After proceeding immoderately far, so that Miss Hitomi gasped, the hand withdrew as stealthily as it had come. For a moment she was quite shocked by its absence. Having reached its goal once, the hand made no effort to return.

She stared down into her plate of gooseberry fool.

Afterwards Miss Hitomi excused herself and went to fetch Professor Ukai's camera, with which she had been commanded to record the poet in his setting. She also brought some copies of *The Blue Magpie* and *Collected Poems* for his signature. When she returned, she found Mrs. Roper alone in the sitting room.

"He's gone to lie down. I always make him lie down after lunch. His health is pretty good on the whole."

Mrs. Roper looked irritated when Miss Hitomi showed her the books. "Afterwards. We'll do all that afterwards. Come on, I'll show you the garden."

In Miss Hitomi's eyes an English garden had the wild beauty of neglected places. But she had not been called out merely to admire it. An arm was locked in hers, although a disparity in heights made this arrangement difficult. Miss Hitomi had not encountered before the type of woman who likes to link arms and saunter, talking about life.

"As you can see, we live terribly quietly down here. It's really only the Japanese who find their way anymore. Dunstan still writes a lot of letters, but most of his contemporaries are too old to get about much."

They stepped off the lawn on to a brick path led between rosebushes. The poet's wife went on talking in her rich, deep voice. "I must say, I never thought I'd end up like this. I have to laugh sometimes, when I think what my parents would say if they saw me now. Daddy was in the Army, of course—he was killed after the War, in an air crash in Palestine. He never wanted me to go to Cambridge, especially when they'd started to let in all sorts of people. When my headmistress insisted I try for Newnham, all Daddy said was 'I don't see why my Moggy wants to meet a lot of counterjumpers.'"

This last sentence attracted Miss Hitomi by its very obscurity and she made a mental note to look up the words "moggy" and "counterjumper" in her dictionary. But for the most part she understood very little. Issuing from about a foot above her left shoulder, the rich voice wavered and got lost among the rose leaves. She was still disorientated from the sexual stimulus at lunchtime, and now the after-effects of the food began to be felt, and she realized that she must hold on to herself with conscious control. The effort of doing this made it impossible to concentrate on what Mrs. Roper was saying.

Their path led to a stream, where there was a garden seat. When they had sat down, Miss Hitomi tried to believe that she was feeling better. Mrs. Roper spent a good deal of time arranging her kaftan.

"Of course, after Daddy was killed, one was glad of any qualification. . . . I joined Rheinau's because I was keen on writing. That was how I met Dunstan, years later. I'd always loved his poems. I don't suppose you know, I used to write too. Under my maiden name, of course. Several people thought I had great talent. Not Dunstan, though. At least, not after we married. Aren't men extraordinary? He never for one moment, one single solitary moment, took the slightest interest in my work."

She was hardly addressing the visitor anymore, but staring across the stream. Miss Hitomi watched her handsome clear-cut face, her brilliant clothes, outlined against the dark green of branches.

Miss Hitomi guessed herself to be present at one of those compulsive bouts of self-exposure that Westerners go in for: she remembered reading of how the wives of British and Australian officers had walked about naked in the presence of Japanese prisoners-of-war. It was difficult to learn about Westerners. Some people hated them because, with their big noses and bad manners, they set the nerves on edge, "spoiling the atmosphere." Yet Miss Hitomi had always loved Professor Roper and now, because of Mrs. Roper's eccentric single-mindedness, she began to love her too.

But before Miss Hitomi could speculate further, her physical resources at last let her down. She felt salty water gush into her mouth: the signs were unmistakable. She tried to say something, but it turned into a sort of moan. She stood up and ran swiftly across the lawn.

On the way out to the garden, Miss Hitomi had heard a cistern gurgling. Now at once she opened the right door and, neatly and desperately, she was sick. With a number of paper handkerchiefs, the damage was soon repaired, but she was deeply humiliated and terrified some odor might cling to her. Horrified, she saw herself in the mirror—her face was damson-colored, her eyes full of tears. She leaned her forehead against the cold glass. It was no use telling herself that the food had been intolerable to her system. There can be no sense of proportion to such things. A story was told of a Japanese bride who, after breaking wind at her wedding ceremony, killed herself.

Mrs. Roper was waiting for her outside the lavatory door. "My poor child, are you all right?"

"Thank you."

The woman put her arm around Miss Hitomi's shoulder and led her into the sitting room. The poet himself was already there, seated in an armchair, still looking blank from his afternoon sleep.

"I'll get you both some tea."

The old man watched Miss Hitomi with caution, but in the end he came over and sat beside her on the sofa.

"You mustn't mind, my dear. I know how much Japanese

people blame themselves when things go wrong. Please don't worry about anything." While he spoke he took hold of her hand and began gently stroking it.

Miss Hitomi was furious. Their sympathy was quite unacceptable to her. What she herself felt did not matter at all. People were not needed to be kind; it is our responsibility to see that things go right. She had to get the books dedicated, the photographs taken, and to return to London, having carried out her responsibility to Professor Ukai, to the department of letters, and to the race of which she was but a tiny splinter. Everything else was unimportant.

Mrs. Roper returned with glasses of tea and lemon. "I've put the poetry books in the study, ready to be signed."

"Excuse me, I must take Professor Roper's photograph."

"Afterward. There's still enough light."

The two of them were watching her while she drank the tea. She felt that they had been making decisions about her. Mrs. Roper was examining her closely, humming a little impatiently, as though annoyed perhaps at having betrayed herself to someone who could hardly have been paying much attention. But Dunstan Roper watched Miss Hitomi with affection, and she was ashamed that her physical weakness should have been a trouble to him, in his untroubled old age.

She put her glass down on the tea tray and followed him through into his study.

There, the window opened on to a border of iceberg roses, all in full blossom. They threw light back into the room between the dark shelves of books. A hanging scroll and some dolls in glass cases testified to his years in Kyoto.

Mrs. Roper quietly closed the door, leaving them together.

Some framed photographs stood on the work table.

"That's Walter de la Mare. Great friend of mine. A lovely poet. I don't suppose many people read him nowadays."

For a moment the old man sat very still, staring ahead of him. Then in a hoarse voice he said: "Well then, tell me what to write."

When Miss Hitomi approached his chair, he quickly put his arm out and secured her around the hips; in spite of her sickness, he had no time to waste. Trembling, she let him explore where, in the dining room, he had explored already. His hand was pulling at her tights and his fingers were cold and rough. She stood beside him quite still, with her eyes closed. Then she opened her eyes and watched his silver head with its long straight part, leaning against her stomach. His mouth was open and she could smell his breath as it rose to her. When at last he looked up, his eyes were blurred with tears. She tried to smile and she stroked his head a little. The hair was fine, like none other she had ever touched. He was very strange to her, not like a human being but a friendly animal, or something rude you encounter in a pleasant dream.

Miss Hitomi held Professor Ukai's camera up to her face and squinted through the viewfinder. Her taxi would be arriving in ten minutes. The poetry books had all been wrapped up again in the *furoshiki.* (That evening in the hotel she would be faint with embarrassment to find in all of them dedications to herself.)

Mrs. Roper, who had led them out into the garden, now told them what they should do. She implied that many such photographs had been taken, that portraits of the poet abounded in the albums of pilgrims from all over the world. Her movements had become remarkably stagy and self-conscious and her voice ranged up and down the scale, even becoming a little shrill. She pushed the old man into place in front of a pergola, and smoothed down his hair with her hand. She indicated to Miss Hitomi where she should stand.

Miss Hitomi knew that Professor Ukai had set the camera exactly as he had wished, and so now when she looked through the viewfinder she saw only a pink and green mist with a splash of blue in it. Then she adjusted it, and instantly Dunstan Roper was in front of her, blinking a little but calm, like a rare animal that has grown used to its cage. In that framed world, the sun was darkly bright, the sky was as blue as his pullover. Miss Hitomi wanted to laugh because he looked so exotic, so interesting, so completely himself. Professor Ukai would be pleased. But the moment before she clicked the shutter there was a broad flash of orange, and Mrs. Roper stood beside him, with her arm around his shoulder.

# *Nocturne with Neon Lights*

In the "Well-Wishers' Lounge" at Tokyo International Airport, several parties were performing the rites of farewell. Everyone was ready with smiles, with whole sentences on the tip of the tongue, with new, folded handkerchiefs specially for waving good-bye. Middle-aged ladies in black kimonos bowed precariously low, whispered a chain of compliments and came up smiling. Office colleagues in dark suits fidgeted with the lenses of their cameras. Whenever one of these was brought into action, feet shuffled obediently into line, glasses and teeth flashed with rivets of gold and silver. A pause, while the viewfinder found exactly the anticipated view. Click! And the smiles were there forever.

The English couple who stood nearby were to remain unrecorded. Exotic enough already, with their great height and their wispy sand-colored hair, their gloomy cast of countenance marked them off still further. Seeing them like this, a Japanese friend would have felt offended and embarrassed. But the Prescotts had few Japanese friends and none of these had come to wish them well.

Gillian Prescott looked in fact as though she could not stand it all another moment. She had spent six months in this country and impatience had got ingrained into her. She and her husband had done everything possible to keep her amused. Together, they had come to view her problem as though she were a third person inflicted on them. Jointly they had decided on courses in flower arrangement, in doll making, in brush drawing. She had even tried teaching "English conversation" but, after her students had been shouted at once or twice, they did not return. In a very short time Gillian had exhausted all the activities considered suitable for foreign ladies resident in Japan.

Prescott had often come home from the office to find her in tears. "God knows, I've tried," she howled, "but it's impossible." The American doctor she consulted laughed at her: "That's nothing, my own wife wept for a whole year." This enraged Gillian. If she could not be cured, she at least wished to be a special case. She did not return to the American doctor.

Rescue seemed at hand when she believed she was going to have a child. Gillian's new physician, Dr. Takahashi, reappeared from behind the screen buzzing with felicitations: "No, all is okay, Mrs. Prescott, you are not pregnant."

If they had been at home in Surrey, it would have been tolerable for Gillian to find out that she loved a man whom no one else much liked. As for Prescott, he knew he could be perfectly happy in Japan. Gillian's presence only made him feel guilty. Guilt, he thought, was bad for his health and his job; the business world was quite tough enough without further complications.

The Prescotts reached the decision that Gillian must leave for home. Once her departure was fixed, she snapped the few threads that bound her—American women she had gone shopping with, an old school friend who worked at the Embassy. Far too early, she arranged her possessions for packing. From now on, too, Prescott made all the arrangements even in the house, because she hated speaking to the maidservant.

"I can't make out whether she's malicious or just stupid. What do you think? Oh, of course, you're a man. They know how to suck up to men."

All along, Prescott had been wonderful; Gillian hated having to leave him, really.

"I wonder what Reiko will do, now you're giving up the house?"

"I expect she'll find another job quite easily."

"Some people will put up with anything. Americans might take her, they're not used to having servants. All the same, I worry about you living in that hotel."

"The time will flash by," Prescott said cheerily.

From the pastel-colored walls a crackling voice announced the departure of the BOAC flight. The Prescotts kissed.

"One thing I wanted to ask you, darling."

"What's that?" He immediately looked wary.

"Easy on the drink."

"Oh, that. No cause to worry."

Gillian turned away to join the British businessmen with their raincoats and porkpie hats, and the Japanese commercial delegation, armed with bunches of flowers.

She was soon out of sight. It was all over.

You did it, old boy, you did it!

Ecstatic with self-congratulation, Prescott ascended a little escalator which delivered him at the airport bar. He felt he deserved a drink, my God, he did.

"Double, sir?"

"Double."

The customers sitting at the bar faced a long window; beyond the shelf of bottles, they could survey the whole concrete apron in front of the airport buildings. After a few moments Prescott saw Gillian in her fur coat, head down, pecking her way on quick feet to the vanguard of her group. She peered upward, trying to catch sight of him, but she had lost her sense of direction on all those ramps leading downward. All contact was broken—he did not even raise his hand.

Touching his mouth to the cold gin and tonic, Prescott felt only a second's compunction. Considering everything, the whole business had gone off extraordinarily well. He had watched events clicking into place, not daring to trust his luck, hardly daring to breathe. At the last moment something might have gone wrong, she might have decided to stay after all. Even now, he hardly dared look over his shoulder in case she might have doubled back out of the docile group he had seen set out across the asphalt.

No, she must be on the airplane by now, first and into the best seat. A stewardess brought *Country Life* in a blue Leatherette folder. Gillian did not smoke but watched like a well-brought-up child while the sweets were brought around. When the engines started throbbing, she fastened the seatbelt over her small round tummy, which she had for long hoped to be distended with their child.

Prescott rotated the moon of lemon in his glass. Old Gillian knew how to look after herself. She didn't travel well, that was all. Whereas, for himself, he preferred the *vin du pays*.

The window glass opposite him started thrumming loudly. The noise increased and from the end of the runway the airliner ascended like a heraldic dragon into the Japanese sky.

*I hope it crashes. I hope she gets killed.*

He didn't mean that at all. He was forgetting that this was a temporary arrangement, that he fully expected their marriage to be reincarnated in their Blackheath bedroom six months from now.

In the meantime, he had himself to consider. That was the whole object of the exercise. He really owed himself a good time—though he could not readily have explained how this curious debt had been incurred.

The barman moved up and down beyond the counter, touching the luridly colored bottles as though making sure they were still there. Sometimes he whistled and cracked his knuckles, as though he needed proof of his own existence as well.

On one of his comings and goings, his glance coincided with Prescott's. His young, soft face formed a polite smile, then shyness made him frown and he began vigorously polishing a mark on the counter. Unable to keep this up for long, he reappeared in front of Prescott, beaming like a sunflower.

"Where you from?"

"England."

"*Engurandu*. Are you a gentleman?"

Prescott was no longer to be put out by this question. This time he derived a distinctive pleasure in answering: "No, I'm not."

The barman looked disappointed and snatched away his glass. "Double?"

"Yes."

Not a gentleman. When he finished this drink, he was going to take a taxi back to Tokyo. There Reiko, the Prescotts' intransigent maidservant, was waiting for him. On his instructions she had found a place to live—a room with *tatami*-matting, a sunken bath, cupboards full of mattresses, perhaps a little kitchen for making coffee. On the floor would be one of those electric lamps with a large bulb and a small one: the large one for ordinary illumination, the small one for the act of love. Whenever he returned there, Reiko would be kneeling at the edge of the *tatami*, ready to help him take off his shoes.

Suddenly in a hurry, Prescott paid the bill for the drinks. Everything was going to be all right; this was not just a squalid intrigue with a housemaid. After all, Reiko was a university student who had come to them to improve her English conversation. He was not just another foreign businessman treating Japan as a sort of Disneyland of sex. He was joining in, not opting out.

He left the bar and was halfway down the escalator before he realized that he had chosen the side that was coming up.

The taxi driver opened the rear door by pushing a button on the dashboard. When Prescott climbed in, the door automatically closed behind him. He pulled from his wallet the sheet of paper on which Reiko had printed the new address. Since Tokyo streets have no names, this was a vitally important document. The delicately inscribed characters, piled box-like on top of one another, meant nothing to him.

The taxi driver too, appeared to be in some difficulty. He stared at the writing, first with his glasses in place and once again with them pushed up on to his short rugose forehead. He exhaled sharply through the gaps between his teeth. A moment of ruminative silence. Then he threw down the paper. The gears clashed like medieval armor as he jerked the car into action and hurled it into the stream of traffic on the airport freeway.

Prescott was thrown backward with his legs in the air, then suddenly forward so that he gripped the front seat, almost touching the driver's neck.

They were off. Everything was going according to plan. Someone once said that, in Japan, all the difficult things were easy. How right they were!

The first time Prescott had arranged to meet Reiko on her afternoon off, he had felt horribly squalid and furtive. But the girl herself at once took control. Together they went to the address he had been given. The street of "Avec" hotels had gardens of twisted pine trees and washed stones. There was no squalor here. An old lady unfolded from the floor to take their shoes. She led them along a corridor dark except for an illuminated floor, under which a stream was flowing, full of bright pebbles and goldfish. In the room, a Western bed of wrought iron and scarlet drapes filled a whole alcove. The sunken bath was surrounded by rocks and ferns. There was an air-conditioner, a refrigerator, and a television set.

Here they made love for the first time. Exploring the childishness of her nacreous warm body, comforting the cries and tears following her climax—it was all as innocent as a game. They were playing house in a roomful of consumer goods.

Afterwards he peeped into the refrigerator to see what restoratives might by custom be provided. It contained a can of chopped pork and a can of tunafish, and some bottles of beer and cola.

A fierce gust of sulphur invaded the taxi. Prescott quickly wound up the window.

From some factory chimneys on the left of the freeway, huge plumes of smoke the color of ice cream were welling up into the twilight. To the right dredgers and bulldozers were filling in the bay. The sun was setting behind the hills; toward the Pacific it illuminated a flat stretch of mud where a flock of sandpipers ran quick as mice, the last wild things on this industrial rim of the world.

Over there in the darkness Mrs. Prescott was winging her way toward Alaska and the polar regions. Soon she would cross the date line; she would re-enter yesterday, where she properly belonged.

*My wife's a neurotic, she's in need of treatment.*

He must have spoken aloud. The taximan swung the car over to the curb.

"No, no. Okay. Okay. Let's go."

Prescott could not see the driver's expression; some Eastern faces are so shaped that they are invisible unless you are directly in front of them. He sensed, however, a slight lowering in the atmosphere. There is a barometric pressure in all relationships in Japan; below a certain point, the indications are thundery.

The driver increased his speed. Prescott was thrown from side to side. They had several close calls before they finally left the freeway and descended into the center of the city, where night had already begun.

The women in the greengrocer's shop were dressed in long-sleeved white aprons and some had sleeping children strapped to their backs. From beyond stacks of white radish and Chinese cabbage, they watched Prescott furtively. When he looked at them, they turned away.

The taxi driver's question had created consternation. One woman pointed one way, one another. Reiko's bit of paper was handed around. They all shook their heads.

The driver returned to the car.

Till now, his detachment had appeared to be complete. When the car had lurched down winding streets and raced up to blank walls, he had merely grunted and reversed out again at equal speed. The driver was like a glove puppet, his face immobile, the whole small body furious in action.

Two or three times he stopped the car to stare at the paper: like the koans of Zen Buddhism, it might reveal its meaning only after lengthy meditation had led to enlightenment. Twice he had gone into shops. He preferred to inquire from women, for in front of men the admission of ignorance is more painful. But his walk, as he returned to the car, became always more dejected.

The morale seemed to be leaking out of him like sawdust.

It was clear now that among the unnamed streets and unnumbered houses of the giant city they were completely lost.

For Prescott the urgency of the journey was almost intolerable. He shifted to and fro, sick with anxiety and physical desire. Reiko, I'm wild about it, Reiko, Reiko.

At a traffic light, he suddenly could stand it no longer. "Stop, stop," he shouted. The driver made a calming gesture. Futilely he rattled the rear doors of the car, but because they could only be opened from the dashboard he was the driver's prisoner, walled in by the shabby houses, the bicycles, trucks, and scribbles of neon. Yet at every corner he expected to see Reiko, as though by a miracle.

Perhaps it would have to be a miracle. Perhaps from the very beginning of the affair his caution had wrecked his chances. Too carefully he had kept open the channels of retreat. Did Reiko even know the name of the company he worked for? Even if she knew, she would never search for him, for she had been brought up to accept rejection and defeat—at what cost to herself, it would always be impossible to discover. In her life, there would be no time for fears and headaches in back rooms. Tonight, when he did not arrive, she would simply disappear forever. Even if tomorrow he managed to discover the house, she would no longer be there. It was a national characteristic to accept defeat and cut your losses.

The excitement had died out of Prescott with the waning glow of the drinks he had had. He was sure that, if he did not find Reiko tonight, he would never see her again. When the full force of this struck him for the first time, he shuddered all over, like a dog that recognizes the vet and smells its oncoming death.

Once more the driver came back to the taxi; once more he crashed into gear, but less loudly this time. He turned around to face his passenger.

"Police," he said.

The three policemen laughed ruefully. Inside their harnesses of belts, holsters, and truncheons, they were slight figures, with eyes remote and dreamy behind heavy-rimmed glasses. Their laughter was caused by shame at the intractability of things.

One of them spoke English. He pointed to the piece of paper, by now frayed and impalpable from many fingers.

"This Chinese character. Perhaps we can read it in many ways."

"Yes, but which way?"

"Perhaps we read it '*shutsu*,' perhaps '*ten*.'"

Another policeman intervened importantly.

"My colleague is saying: 'Perhaps also *"de."*'"

"Which is it?"

The English-speaking policeman bit his lip. "This is difficult problem in Japanese language."

"But you must know the place if it is near here."

"Just a moment please." They retreated into the police box again. Once or twice one of them peered out to look at Prescott, large and awkward on the pavement. His insistence, though they did not know what it was about, was somehow rather indelicate.

The first policeman came back. He pointed with a thin finger at one of the Chinese characters drawn by Reiko: it was like a little stick insect, lying on its back and waving its legs in the air.

"This character, for instance, we may read in three ways."

"Yes, you told me that."

The policeman looked at him intently. "You want to go to this place?"

Prescott managed to nod.

"It is not near here."

"Then where the hell is it?" Prescott shouted.

It was as though he had waved a blowtorch in their faces. Their attention shriveled away from him. All three of them turned their backs.

Prescott could only shout, and so nobody could hear what he said. He waved his arms, and so nobody could see him. By losing his temper, he had entered the solipsist's nightmare in which everything exists except yourself.

He returned to the taxi. He was cold sober now. His throat was bruised with rage, his diaphragm ached with frustration. He had nowhere to spend the night, and no idea where he was.

The taxi driver turned to face him. "Okay," he said. "We go."

The driver stopped in front of a small house in a side street. Prescott took out a handful of money and pushed it at him. The rear door of the car whirred slowly open, and Prescott stepped out into his freedom.

He tapped at the door and waited. The throb of traffic came from a distance and over the rooftops the huge city glowed and flared.

There was a shuffling of feet, soft as seal's flippers on the polished boards of pine. The door slid open and he stepped into the pebble-floored entrance. In front of him, an old lady clucked and bowed.

"Reiko-san?" he asked.

She unfolded herself and slipped away. He waited. Ahead of him, in the middle of the house, there was a small garden where a trickle of water continually fell on to stones.

The old woman's place was taken by a tall girl with a hard, calculating look.

"You wanna Reiko-san?"

"Yes."

She disappeared. Whisperings and more footsteps followed, and then a girl in kimono collapsed in front of him, quivering with low sobbing giggles. He could see only the glossy interwoven tower of her hair.

"This one Reiko-san," the tall girl said. "You pay American dollars okay."

The girl in kimono looked up at him. Her face was broad and dull, white-powdered like a marshmallow. Yet the strange coy look in the eyes gave him a weird sensation of having encountered them before, in an entirely different face. He tore himself from her gaze.

"No," he said. "Not Reiko-san."

"You no got dollars?"

"Not Reiko-san. It's all a mistake."

More women had gathered in the doorway. "Reiko-san," they said, mimicking his accent. "Reiko-san. Yes."

"No," he shouted.

Their laughter rose up and fell, like a sound of scared birds. "Reiko-san. Yes, please."

Back in the street, Prescott realized that the taxi driver had brought him here in order to get rid of him. When he had walked a little further, he realized that the decision must have come not from the driver, but the three policemen: they assumed that the foreigner was out for what all foreigners wanted.

Not knowing his direction, Prescott aimed for the lighted streets ahead. Mightn't the address have been wrong all the time, mightn't Reiko be rejecting him by giving him a false address? The taxi driver had driven off with the paper, and so it was too late to find out.

Rain began to fall. The feeling that he had been dismissed and got rid of expanded inside him. His throat hurt and his eyes burned.

Perhaps after all it was Gillian. Her sole idea had been to leave him, all along. Now, while she crossed the Arctic Circle, her husband was stumbling through a narrow street in the northern section of Tokyo. It was raining quite hard now. He had no idea where he was. Rage and disappointment filled him, so that there was absolutely no chance of his asking the way with any likelihood of success.

# *The Broken Bridge*

"Hi, there." A young American hailed me outside the building of the Faculty of Literature.

Although we were in the middle of Tokyo, he was wearing clothes that seemed more suitable for mountain climbing. He looked, in fact, as though Nature had created him for austere and difficult tasks. She had been conspicuously unkind to him, giving him one shoulder higher than the other, a raw beak of nose to hang his glasses on, and a scalp already losing most of its reddish hair.

He held out his hand and said: "Larry Breitmeyer."

I had seen him around before, and had thought him to be a student following the short course on Japanese Civilization which the University provided. But now he said: "Professor Nakamura told me your name. I teach at this place too."

I was prepared to be friendly. To have been hailed in this way, even for a specific purpose, had something exceptional about it. In Japan I had found that the members of that strange tribe known as Caucasians ignored each other warily. (In this, we are quite different from Negroes, who, even if complete strangers, nearly always exchange greetings in the alien streets of European cities.) Perhaps the other Caucasians were up to no good at all, and expected you to be in the same situation. More probably they believed themselves to be in possession of some incommunicable truth about a mystery of Japanese life. This might involve Aikido or Zen Buddhism or merely flower arrangement. Whatever it was, they knew all about it already, and your ignorance would only cause them pain.

"Your students just asked me to help with this British play you chose them."

"I didn't choose it. And, as a matter of fact, none of them are my students."

Later, it was to become clear that Breitmeyer was one of those foreigners who are obsessed by the Japanese theater. But the play he spoke of was to be performed in English as the local contribution to this year's interuniversity drama competition. It was a dim little farce, of the school of A. A. Milne and Ian Hay. The choice had been imposed on the students by Professor Nakamura himself, whom they much respected. The professor had seen the play performed during his visit to London in the 1920s, and it had left an indelible impression on him.

While I was telling him this, Breitmeyer appeared distracted. He stared intently at the crowd of young men who jostled past us into the building. He could hardly have been looking for a previous acquaintance; in a university with thirty thousand students, it was exceptional to meet by chance anybody one knew already.

When I had stopped talking, he said: "It's a lousy play."

"They insisted on doing it."

"I told them it was a lousy play. I've been giving them a few of the basic technical things. Their movement is awful. I'm not too thrilled with the casting, either. Those two girls ought to change parts." He aimed a look at me, as if to show that this was my responsibility. But this was not the case.

By now the students had been rehearsing the play for about two months. A few days after my arrival at the University I had received the committee involved in the production.

There were seven or eight of them, and they came into my office in a closely packed phalanx. The way they stood, quiet and tense, seemed to indicate both shyness and aggression. They muttered in consultation for a bit, and then their spokesman stepped forward from the group.

He was equipped with the kind of Tom Sawyer vocabulary that the Protestant missionaries still teach, though presumably they do not use it themselves. "Gee, sir, I guess we're in some kind a fix. You see, our instructor chose this British play and, gosh, we're stumped to know just how to speak it, on account of we mostly learn American English in high school."

By the time he had spoken, the young man's primrose skin was flushed with mauve. He bowed and was absorbed again into the group, from whom there came a sort of susurration—whether of disquiet or acclaim, I could not tell.

I made a little speech. When two or three Japanese are gathered together, discussion is difficult: you have an audience. I confessed that I knew next to nothing about the theater and that any help I gave them might jeopardize their chances of success. I begged them to seek advice elsewhere and offered to ask around among the numberless English-speaking foreigners who devoted their spare time to amateur theatricals.

All this, however, was taken to be conventional modesty. In the end the students got their own way. I was to make tape recordings of the whole play, reading all the parts.

Later on, as I had promised, I attended some of their rehearsals. From the very beginning the whole cast was word-perfect. They spoke in faint parodies of my own voice. Even now, two months later, they were running through the entire play two or three times a day. They undertook the whole project with the extraordinary concentration and discipline which they brought to every task in which honor was involved.

It was obvious, too, that they had recently followed my suggestion and sought advice wherever they could get it. I was surprised to find the Earl and Countess, the Young Heir and the Burglar all speaking with refined Sydney-side acccents.

Soon after Larry Breitmeyer had been conscripted to help, I attended another run-through. As I approached, a thunderous noise was issuing through the closed doors of the lecture hall. The room itself was foggy with clouds of dust that had risen from the floor. In the midst of this the team of actors was jumping into the air with outstretched arms, then crouching down and rolling over and over. Among them stood Larry Breitmeyer, in a sweatshirt, Levi's, and sneakers, with one hand on his hip and biting the nails of the other.

From time to time he bawled out instructions. Once he organized a mock battle, boys against girls. This was an awesome sight. From the quick gasps, the tight-drawn facial muscles of the participants, you could see that he had called into being that intense fury of the will which hides behind all the decorum and docility.

There was a good deal of this insistent will in Larry himself. His appearance and his manner were enough to risk distrust or even ridicule. Yet he was closer to these young people than I would ever be. He thrust himself at them, and they had no resources to repel him. Perhaps they did not want to. There have been few foreigners in Japan, however fraudulent their pretensions or scandalous their behavior, who have not gained at least a handful of admirers to speak fondly of them in years afterward.

Watching Larry Breitmeyer one was impressed with the idea that the Japanese and the Americans often find exactly what they want in each other. Theirs is a marriage, born under clouds of disaster, that has proved to be of great convenience.

At the Kabuki Theatre the great Utaemon had just performed a solo dance which involved a parasol, much fan-fluttering in imitation of butterflies, and finally a fall of snow on the stage. In the intermission I made my way out to the foyer, between rows of elderly ladies in kimonos who were picking away with chopsticks at the wooden lunch boxes they had brought with them. For this audience feminine perfection could only be transmitted through the medium of an *onnagata,* a female impersonator. Utaemon himself enjoyed at this time a reputation equal to that of all our great theatrical ladies put together.

It was the first time I had been to the Kabuki Theatre. I had been given a ticket as a reward for the minor task of correcting a translation.

Larry Breitmeyer was standing in a corner of the foyer. He wore his usual jeans and sneakers, a pea jacket over his shirt. He was accompanied by a young man elegantly dressed in a dark suit and a wide silk tie.

"This is Yoshi," Larry said.

Now that I had gone up to him, I found myself disinclined to hear Larry's opinions. I imagined, quite wrongly as it turned out, that they would be conventional and insensitive.

Instead, I questioned his friend, who was unhelpful. "I think that Kabuki Theatre is not so interesting for us, these days."

"Isn't that just typical," Larry broke in. "What have they got, if they haven't got this?" He hunched his shoulders, twisted, and stared away from us.

"I am enjoying it so far," I said to Yoshi.

"I think it is more interesting to the foreigners."

I felt the usual irritation at being lumped together with an undifferentiated group of outsiders. "Everybody sitting near me is Japanese."

"I think they are only the old persons."

Larry was ignoring Yoshi. Perhaps they were having some form of domestic row. But suddenly he turned to me: "You liked that?"

"Yes, I did."

"It was superb, but really that's only run-of-the-mill stuff. Just wait for *Kanjincho*. Utaemon plays Yoshitune, the young prince. It's always an *onnagata* role, because of the high voice. Crazy, of course, because he doesn't speak at all. But just watch his hand on the staff he holds. He doesn't move, his face is hidden by his hat. Only his hand is there, acting. It's fantastic."

Larry Breitmeyer had fallen for the intricacies of Japanese culture, for "the fascination of what's difficult" (Yeats's line keeps coming back to one in Japan). I could imagine him going on to learn more and more about it, whereas to myself in my ignorance the Japanese tradition seemed like an elaborate and gorgeous impasse. Nothing you learned here, it seemed to me, could be genuinely related to anything similar outside, and perhaps this was why Yoshi and his generation rejected it.

I never heard Yoshi's opinion of the play for the interuniversity competition, in which he took the minor part of a footman. Until now I had thought it would be impossible to bring the antiquated little farce back to life. Yet on the night of the performance it was suddenly revealed as something charming and even amusing. I wondered how this had come about. Perhaps, after all those countless rehearsals, some kind of Zen illumination had descended on the cast. Perhaps Larry Breitmeyer was a director of genuine talent.

The play didn't win the competition, but the actors won the best acting awards. They were greatly elated. As the Japanese do at moments of triumph, they wept.

Larry Breitmeyer himself was modest about all this. A part of his attention was elsewhere, because he had invited two American ladies.

Meeting them, I could not help being reminded of the severe shock a Westerner's appearance must have given to a Japanese seeing one for the first time. There was, in fact, an inordinacy in the aspect of these women that seared the gaze. It was not merely their height—neither was much under six feet—but the bouffant wigs, orange in one case and blue in the other, the eagle noses, and the costume jewelry. The owner of the blonde wig was Harriet Brine, who did the gossip column for the *Japan Mail,* an English-language newspaper. Blue-topped Mrs. Kirshenbaum was the wife of the managing director of the Tokyo branch of ABM.

About the play, Mrs. Kirshenbaum was conventionally ecstatic, whereas Miss Brine was bored; she rarely mentioned the Japanese in her column. Larry fussed between them, in a cockled misshapen brown suit that had come from a PX store some years previously; he barely reached up to their shoulders.

The University was so large that the paths of the foreign teachers rarely intersected. It was some time before I saw Larry Breitmeyer again. A new academic year began, and our classes were on different days and in different buildings. By now he was producing another play, *A View from the Bridge.*

This well-known populist tragedy had got into trouble with the British censorship a few years before. There is a scene in which one man kisses another on the lips. It is a test of virility which in the event both characters pass with honor.

The present director however rejected this interpretation. "All right, that's what you're meant to think, on the surface. But there's this strong ambiguity running all the way through the play."

Larry was sitting in the staff room with a small group of our colleagues. Old Professor Nakamura was present but unspeaking, like some sacred object of the Shinto cosmography, a rock or an ancient tree. On the other hand young Mr. Kawai, the assistant lecturer and specialist in George Gissing, appeared to be in a continual state of subterranean disturbance, like his native land: private earthquakes and typhoons kept twitching him and ruffling his hair, hot springs steamed up his glasses. Pretty, tiny Miss Ikeda sat folded together between them; she never spoke in Professor Nakamura's presence. The unwavering attention of the three of them formed a sort of enclosure, an arena in which Larry was at present holding forth.

"There's this character Eddie. He is jealous of his niece, right? Well, that statement has two interpretations. First"—Larry numbered it on his finger, as though we might lose count—"Eddie is in love with his niece and Rickie, this illegal immigrant, has got her. Right? Second"—here he employed another finger—"Eddie is in love with Rickie and Catherine has got him. His niece is his rival, right? Eddie destroys Rickie for the same reason that Iago destroys Othello, because he is in love with him. There is this wonderful masculine flame burning through the play. That's what I want to identify and bring out."

There were wordless exclamations from his Japanese witnesses. Neither Professor Nakamura nor Miss Ikeda moved, but Mr. Kawai trembled and thrummed like a kettle on the boil. I tried to feel like an outsider in this purely American-Japanese situation. Nevertheless I was embarrassed for Larry and for the whole race of Caucasians. Some minutes later I left him there, caught in the triangle of their polite concern.

After the next class Larry Breitmeyer was still in the staff room, alone now, hunched in his chair. He seemed pleased to see me. However rewarding one's friendships with Japanese people may be, there are times when both sides want to cry halt.

"Old Nakamura looked rather shaken by your account of the play."

"Shaking is what he needs. He can't pretend to be that innocent, can he?"

"Perhaps it's difficult on the stage. There are only a few themes in the Japanese theater."

"Look, if I can get pleasure and fulfillment out of Kabuki, out of the Noh plays, even out of Bunraku, though to my mind those puppets are a dead bore, why can't they understand the conventions of the modern American theater? After all, it leads the world."

He glanced to see how I took this, then continued, allegretto: "I've got this great cast together, none of that draggy lot from last time. You should just see my Eddie—he's a living doll."

Perhaps Larry was right to go ahead. Since the American play was alien ground, they would accept whatever he told them about it. And in the casual comedy of American-Japanese relations, I reflected, mutual incomprehension has a cushioning effect and nothing is ever as disastrous as it seems at first sight.

Taizo Hitomi's composition was written in pencil, with frequent rubbings out. It filled up one side of a page.

> I don't know how to write an essay like this because we are not taught in Japanese school. I wish to write, dear teacher, about some things great problems for me. Almost of the time I am thinking these problems.
>
> By the way, this semester I am taking part in our university's play for the competition. I am chosen to play Eddie, which is a man in a great play by Mr. Arthur Miller.
>
> It is difficult to me to understand this great play called *A View from the Bridge*. For example, there is one time where a man is kissing the other man. I think this is not known in Japan. This man is Eddie, which is my part. It is very difficult for me to make this scene.

We read how Mr. Miller used to marry Miss Marilyn Monroe who killed herself. Also this is great problem for Japanese people.

If I keep very calm and have a relaxed mind I may be successful. I think so.

With a red pencil I underlined the last use of "think." There is no verb in the Japanese language for "hope."

Rather gingerly I replaced Taizo Hitomi's paper in the folder with the others and went downstairs to the lecture room.

The new third-year students were waiting for me, all forty of them. This was only the second time I had seen them. I went into the room and they stopped talking and stared at me. I noticed once again the extraordinary variation the Japanese face achieves within its limited range of components. Which of these alert, benign faces belonged to Taizo Hitomi?

At least half of the compositions had been confessional. The difficulties of the English language had induced shy young people to be more candid than they had meant to be. A note of gloomy resolution was present in several of them. If Mr. Hitomi seemed more desperate than the others, it may only be because I had an accidental insight into his situation.

I began to call out their names and, as these were acknowledged, I handed back the compositions. In this way I hoped names would attach to faces and individuals begin to emerge from the anonymous group.

I walked down the aisle between the students, letting my eyes wander over the sleek shining heads of the girls, the boot-brush or hippy-thatched skulls of the young men, and watching for each limpid face as it was raised in response to the spoken name. It was an odd feeling, like creating a new world from an indifferent chaos. Everyone began to get more and more cheerful. Given personal attention, they tended to flourish.

Then I called out Taizo Hitomi's name. There was a sound of breath drawn in between closed teeth, followed by a small hard silence. Two or three others failed to answer. I replaced the papers in the folder and the ordinary work of the class began.

The following week two hot-faced girls claimed their essays.

Previously they had been too shy to announce their identity in public, but in the intervening week they had plucked up courage. They scuttled back to their seats, chattering and laughing.

Hitomi's was the only composition that remained. When the hour ended, I read out the register of names. After calling out his name, I paused a little. A rough loud voice from the end of the room shouted out "Absent!"

After a time one gets oversensitive to possible oddities of behavior. I was suddenly convinced that it was Hitomi himself who had spoken. Embarrassed by what he had written, he was sheltering among the still anonymous ranks at the back of the lecture room.

I spoke in the direction of the voice. "Could you tell him I've still got his essay? It's useless to correct it if he doesn't see his mistakes."

At this point a terrifying silence settled over the room. It was as though the barometric pressure had plunged several degrees. Nobody looked at me. I read the remaining names as quickly as possible, slammed my books together, and left the room. I blamed myself for what had happened. I had spoken in entirely the wrong way. I had held Mr. Hitomi up to ridicule in front of his fellows. If he had felt unsure of himself before, his situation now was much worse.

Mr. Kawai, the assistant lecturer, had his office next door to mine.

When he saw me, he blushed fearfully, but this was his habit. Otherwise he was quite obdurate.

"We do not worry about what a student does. If you like, you may fail him in the exam. It is up to you. If he is absent, it is his fault."

"I thought there might be something wrong. I wondered if I could do something to help."

Mr. Kawai's features stiffened. I had made another mistake. For the foreigner in Japan, there is no blame: there are only mistakes. In the strange, impersonal language they inhabit the air between people. There is nothing to be done.

Of course I should have sought out Larry Breitmeyer himself. But I did not know his address, and neither did the university authorities. He called for his letters twice a week at the department that dealt with foreigners. I left a note for him there, but it remained unanswered.

One's life in a foreign city consists in following several threads, narrative lines which one may either pursue or neglect. People appear whom one imagines will become friends, and then disappear forever. Others retain a sort of marginal existence, present but never close. Larry Breitmeyer stayed on the edge of my thoughts, like a bad tooth which one is determined to have seen to sooner or later. Meeting him so rarely, I might have forgotten about him, if I had not read his name one morning in the *Japan Mail*. It was in "Tokyo's Brite Nites," the column written by Harriet Brine:

> ABM's Tex Kirshenbaum and gorgeous Gaye (she of the thousand bangles!!) hosted a stand-up send-off last eve for Larry Breitmeyer. Larry, swinging theater buff, Noh-man and Kabuki expert, hies him westward this day on a wing-ding tour of Europe's capitals. Bon voyage, Larry, and *Sayonara*!

This was very puzzling. Had the performance of *A View from the Bridge* already taken place? Little Miss Ikeda, who was reputed to be interested in the drama (she was writing a thesis on The Theater Audience in Restoration England), knew that Larry had left the country. But about the play itself she was unhelpful. Perhaps some other American director had taken it over.

Meanwhile a national holiday had interrupted classes for two weeks. When the third-year students reassembled, it seemed easy for me to read out Taizo Hitomi's name from the register. It remained unanswered, and I read through the rest of the names.

When I closed the book, nobody moved. They were all watching me.

"Professor."

The same thundery atmosphere returned, and for a second I felt conscious unmixed dread. I suppose this is the origin of racism: I am alone and all these faces are without good will. We cannot tell if our reactions to the same events will be similar. We are lost.

But it was not like this at all. Three young men stood up at the back of the room. They walked down the aisle between the desks. One of them had assumed the samurai swagger, which indicates unsureness. They were a posse, but not a frightening one.

"Professor, please do not read Mr. Hitomi's name again. He is not here anymore."

"Has he left the class?"

"He killed himself."

Where so much went unspoken, a statement had been made. Suppositions withered out, possibilities were deleted. We were silent in the presence of this fact.

I told them how very sorry I was and at the same time (for at such moments of distress one's mind is unremittingly meddlesome) I determined to destroy Taizo Hitomi's essay. Had it been an appeal for help?

From now on everything would be easier. A mistake had been made and we shared the knowledge of it. Perhaps, even, we felt about it in the same way. The girls in the front row were giggling, a wild unhappy noise. I blinked. A grief was burning my eyes, for someone whom I may have seen but could not, in any case, have recognized.

# *Windows*

Tonight they were there again. Like fish in an aquarium, they flashed in and out of sight. Long limbs, tits splendidly aureoled, bouncing globes of hair: two black girls in a white room with a Japanese paper lantern hanging from the ceiling.

He had discovered them the evening before. Returning to his hotel he had gone to the window for the first, ritual view of the city at night. From his room on the fourteenth floor he gazed across at other blocks, huge and dimly sparkling at intervals between here and the East River. Then, a little giddy from all that emptiness, he had looked down at the deserted street, then across toward the dark opposing building, up a network of fire escapes, to a square of light directly opposite his own. And there they were. Were they expecting to be watched? Probably the idea lay warmly on the edge of their minds. Were they lesbians? They appeared not to touch each other, but slipped past like fish. No, they were celebrating a self-love which was entirely justified; they were girls to whom mirrors could only afford delight.

Tim Harman, editor for a London art publisher, was on his annual visit to New York. He could still enjoy himself here, especially midtown on sunny afternoons after a protracted lunch. Then the disproportions did not matter, the weight of the tower blocks overhead was forgotten, for down below there was a diffused brightness over everything. The inhabitants, with their weird clothes and the avid look on their blunt faces, seemed to glitter. It was curiously exciting, he thought, to be alive during this later stage of man, when we shall have lost the discriminations that inhibit our survival. At night, however, mere appreciation became risky. Then he heeded the warnings of his friends and returned to his hotel after dinner. He went to the icebox to fix himself a nightcap. Then he flicked automatically through the TV channels, shooting down one by one the giggling participants of the talk shows. It was after this that he leaned on the closed window with the air-conditioner humming beneath it (those girls, fortunately, had none, otherwise their window would not have been open to the night). At this hour when the streets were banned, you could imagine a new sort of society evolving—communication would be by signals across the gaps between buildings, and sex would take the form of exposure at windows. Perhaps this culture was already beginning: visions like that of the two black girls would be extremely rare elsewhere. Yet even while he stared at the brownstone opposite, he was remembering another lighted window and a similar scene. The memory was like turning to the early pages in a family album, where the photographs are sepia and people seem to live in twilight. That vision had taken place in a seedy area of London, not long after the War, over a quarter of a century ago.

Tim Harman had just left the Army; most of the time he had been drunk. London then had seemed awash with drink, with soapy pints of mild-and-bitter, with tooth-glasses of mouth-puckering Algerian red, and, when anyone got hold of some money, with bottles of whisky and gin. Though he had a government grant to attend an art school, he remembered those days being marked by the curious rhythm of the licensing hours; how you emerged from the pubs into the stinging afternoon sunlight and stumbled down a flight of ratty stairs to an afternoon drinking club; how at night you joined in the migration across Oxford Street, from Fitzroy Street to Soho—or was it the other way about?—to fit in an extra half hour's drinking time. Then, after eleven, if one of you had paid his membership, you ended up at the Gargoyle, an antiquely grand night club. Of course there were girls in all this and they earned merit according to just how much of the racket they could stand. At the art school there were bossy virgins from Kensington, immaculate in their New Look dresses, or lachrymose problem children from the provinces, who worked as artists' models, went from bed to bed and were known as "Chelsea mice." Another ex-soldier, small and brisk, sat next to Tim in life class. His name was Stephen Rossiter. He was involved with one of the mice, a sad wild girl called Sheila, and he talked about her most of the time.

One night when they'd stayed late at the Gargoyle and had no money left for a taxi, Tim walked home with Stephen, who lived with his father in a vicarage in the East End of London. Stephen led him up a long bare staircase, smelling of floor polish. He made up a bed for his guest on a leather-covered settee in the Gothic drawing room.

When he got up the next morning, Tim opened several wrong doors until he found an old housekeeper cooking breakfast. She showed him the dining room, where a tall thin man was standing near the fireplace, reading *The Times*.

From Stephen's account, his father had been a steeplechase jockey and sportswriter before taking Holy Orders. God, it seemed, had given him a rough ride, leaving a thin battered face above the dog collar, a constant twitch of the eyebrow as though of incomplete control.

The vicar folded *The Times* and inquired how the guest had slept.

"Perfectly, thank you."

Tim's voice emerged too loud for the shadowed room. He was relieved when Stephen joined them. But Stephen said nothing at all; he had a habit of leaving things unexplained. They approached the breakfast table. Tim started to sit down, but the vicar began saying Grace, and so he stood with his chair half out from the table. Then they all sat down and embarked on plates of cornflakes. Five minutes passed to an intent sound of mastication and the clink of spoons. The amorous chortling of a pigeon came from outside the mullioned window.

Tim was certain he was going to giggle. He forestalled the first splutter with speech.

"Christ, that pigeon. It kept me awake half the night."

"I understood you to say that you had slept perfectly."

"A manner of speaking."

A few moments later, while they were eating kippers, the vicar suddenly put down his knife and fork. He stood up, glaring ahead of him, and then turned smartly around and left the room.

Tim looked cautiously at Stephen, who seemed to have noticed nothing unusual. He did not begin speaking until afterward, when they were leaving for the art school together.

"I've got to see Sheila tonight," he said. "She's in a jam. Her landlady's given her notice. And that bloke she knew in Birmingham has been bothering her again."

Tim remembered going, a few weeks later, into a pub in Chelsea, the Pier Hotel. There he found some of the well-known drunks of the day, a surprising number of whom went on to survive into the more prosperous decade ahead. Tim saw his friend John Shelmerdene, sitting by himself at his usual table. In front of John there were a pint of beer and a carefully eclectic stack of books. He read extremely fast, and these were to keep him going when he was not addressing his numerous acquaintances.

"Tim," John said. Then he was silent. At length he said: "I was hearing about you the other day."

John Shelmerdene's small features were set in a large blank face on a large body. Some preliminary adjustments suggested he was about to mimic somebody. Tim leaned forward to hear better.

John's eyebrow twitched.

"'Know that boy Tim Harman?' 'Yes I do,' I said, 'and so will a lot of other people, sooner or later.' 'He has an immoral influence.' 'How interesting.' 'He has taught my son to paint pubic hair on women.' 'My dear Ned,' I exclaimed, 'what the hell are you talking about?'"

John Shelmerdene chuckled deeply. He dabbed his eyes, which were producing tears of delight. Tim waited.

"Apparently his son—Raymond, is it? Stephen, then—brought home some life drawings Ned disapproved of, and also some of yours, and there was the evidence. I said to him: 'My dear Ned, my wife has pubic hair, and I presume yours does too. Why all this fuss?' But I don't think I really convinced him."

He wiped his eyes and finished his beer. Tim bought him another.

Tim laughed as well, but with a certain constraint. This was not because of the pubic hair, but because John was unaware that Mrs. Rossiter was in a private home. Though this did not preclude the supposition, it did effectively undermine the joke. John Shelmerdene had once quoted a dictum of Chekhov's, to the effect that, whereas Tragedy is life seen close at hand, Comedy is life seen at a distance. Probably there were a lot more jokes if you kept your distance, as John seemed to.

These were things that troubled Tim in those days: girls crying, people who went mad, and also the fact that mentioning any of this would make one seem gauche and immature. And so he said nothing.

As Tim got up to leave, John Shelmerdene said: "Aldous is in London. Do you know him? If not, would you like to meet him?"

Couldn't John see that, for him, before he had done anything himself, such a meeting would be abject and undignified?

In retrospect, Tim knew that he had turned down this invitation clumsily. In those days you continually adjusted yourself to the world of experience and maturity; you felt judged by it. Yet when you looked back, that world had never arrived. As Yeats said, life seemed "a preparation for something that never happens." You were still the same, and you still trod carefully, with folly on all sides.

By now the black girls had switched their light off, and in his imagination Tim followed into their musky slumbers. Those girls in the other vision would be middle-aged housewives by now. When he had been an art student, the 1970s belonged to science fiction. In those days people claimed to expect nothing ahead, beyond a possible Russian invasion or an atomic waste. Yet here he was, pushing on toward the end of the century and fixing himself another drink for the journey.

Looking out of his window at the foreign city, he thought how the mere act of memory is like awakening the dead. The vicar, Stephen Rossiter's father, had died a year or two after Tim's single encounter with him. John Shelmerdene, assiduous but never sycophantic in his pursuit of the talented and famous, had earned his posthumous mention in the literary memoirs of the forties. For Tim he had been a mentor, someone who had believed in him and whom therefore he had disappointed: you grew up by surviving people's hopes for you. Poor Stephen, after a stormy marriage to Sheila, had died six years ago.

Such a listing of casualties was given an added resonance because of the intervening distance of the Atlantic, because of the apprehensions of the New York night, and because of the vision of the naked girls in the opposite building. The individual dies, but the girls are prancing by lighted windows. Not the same girls, of course; like the cuckoo returning in spring, *the* cuckoo, but not the same bird.

The night he had seen the other girls, he had been to a party in Fulham with Stephen. Sheila had promised to be there. Stephen waited until after midnight before he telephoned her new lodging; her brother had turned up from Leicester unexpectedly.

"I didn't know she had a brother," Tim said.

"Neither did I. I think it's another of her lies. Would you mind coming back with me tonight? I don't really want to be alone. It'll save you a taxi."

"If it'll help. Won't your father mind? I don't think he liked me much."

"Why should you think that?"

It was not possible to explain John Shelmerdene's story about the pubic hair. "He walked out in the middle of breakfast."

"That was his new teeth. They don't fit very well, and things get stuck under his plate."

"Oh, I see."

"Anyway, he's away tonight. There are clean sheets on his bed. You can sleep there."

At the vicarage Tim listened to Stephen discussing Sheila. "She's her own worst enemy. I feel sure I could help her, if she'd only let me."

Tim felt himself drift into unconsciousness. He belched to resuscitate himself and said: "Frightfully sorry. Rather tight."

Stephen apologized and showed him where he was to sleep. The vicar's bedroom was austere. There was a washstand with a jug and basin. The iron bedstead had a dark-brown blanket.

When Tim was alone, he pulled open the curtains. A few seconds later, a square of light sprang out on the wall opposite.

He couldn't believe it at first. He thought he must be suffering from some sort of alcoholic hallucination. Now that the blackout had ended, a window bursting with light communicated a sense of luxury, an assertion of freedom. Yellowish light poured onto the two girls who sat framed in the window, chatting to each other over the benign stare of breasts. Then one of them, short and plump, stood up and amazed him: she was plumaged to the limits of credibility. It was one of the surprises of the physical world that make you want to laugh, in the same way that dogs laugh when they are hunting—it was evidence of a wild baying glee at the center of things.

Tim pressed his forehead to the cold glass of the vicarage window. He tried to pull up the sash, but it was jammed with rust and pigeon shit. He knew the girls had heard him, because they were now both standing. He saw their peroxided perms, dark at the roots like a shaving brush, their sharp faces, and those big breasts and the feral aprons. They laughed and waved to him. Then suddenly the lights went off. The show was ended.

A strong peculiar sense of delight was with him when he awoke the following morning. Then he found Stephen, worried and unhappy, at the breakfast table. The cosmic, physical joke died.

The girls, Tim realized later, had been hostile. They had thought the vicar was watching them and had used their nakedness to deride his enforced solitude. They were two sirens tempting a celibate Ulysses, two Susannahs turning the tables on a lonely elder. Perhaps the vicar had come into conflict with them in his parish. As tarts always do, they had expected to be forgiven and they had not been; they were getting their own back.

Nevertheless, the physical vision had not been lost. In his memory it connected with the bushes on the life drawings, with

Stephen and Sheila, and with the benevolent gossip of John Shelmerdene. And now the first vision, the cosmic glee, was re-created by two black girls in New York (though in them, of course, the special physical characteristics were invisible, if not absent). Whatever your experiences are, it is you who choose them to make the pattern. The girls at the windows belonged to him because he was alive. The two separate visions he had been given reminded him that he was unique, and that, because we are unique, we are alone.

# *Evening in Connecticut*

By now he had learned the names of all the guests at the party. Only their Christian names, of course, or rather their "given" names—meaning the name you gave out to strangers. The other guests kept returning his own name to him with individual variation. "Michael" grew three syllables, or shrank to "Mike." In England he was usually "Mick" or "Micky," but he supposed that might have ethnic implications here.

It was easy for them. They were all connected with Barford College and knew each other already. They were many, and he, unaccompanied by Tessa on this exploratory visit, was only one. He had a whole hand of given names to shuffle and pair off. Bernice went with Gene—they were the couple who had picked him up at his motel. Their host was Russell Barford, whose grandfather had founded the college, a small, white-haired old man in a velvet smoking jacket. But who went with Russell? Since the very rich are able to prolong the appearance of sexual activity for as long as they wish, he might still have attachments. Did Mary-Beth, the sleek blonde girl who had just arrived, belong to him? Could she be his daughter? And who was Lois, the handsome woman in a tapestry dress who was cooking dinner? Was Mary-Beth perhaps Lois's daughter? Or what? The given names they shouted in mock surprise were no help at all here. Nor were the embraces, the squeezes they bestowed on each other, for after all one didn't know how much value they attached to physical contacts.

One thing seemed clear: none of the women belonged to Brian, a stately man with a Charles I hairstyle and a Chairman Mao tunic. Brian took him out on the terrace to see the view. The Barford house, about two hundred years old and of white clapboard, overlooked an inlet of Long Island Sound, and around it the sparse woodlands were bursting into leaf. Here in New England the sudden transition of the seasons was violent, steamy; you were immersed in "depraved May, dogwood and flowering Judas." Brian thought the other trees were hickory. He wondered why British people always asked about the trees.

"I suppose because a lot of us are brought up in the country," Michael said.

But that wasn't the whole truth. They couldn't appreciate, could they, how much he had got to grab hold to feel he was here at all. This afternoon on the campus, when shown the house he and Tessa might occupy, he had been deaf to instructions concerning carports, interior heating, and trash disposal. In this battered Eden he wanted names to be given, not only to people but to things. In New York he was always looking for solidity beyond what Henry James had called "the expensive concert of the provisional," and he ended up staring at outcrops of blackened nineteenth-century brickwork in search of a lost world. Just because things were nameless and provisional, America was curiously productive of nostalgia; you felt that when all our mistakes have been rectified the past might really return. Finding names, learning facts, you were protesting perhaps against the abstract quality of life here. All this made you feel important, the way visiting Europeans feel, sniffing out the exact moment when the world's best hope had been betrayed.

The naming of trees being disposed of, Brian proceeded to a subject that obviously interested him more closely: his boy, to whom, oddly, no name was given. Brian couldn't speak too highly of this boy of his.

This was all right. This was fine, it showed that here they were situated at the liberated heart of liberal America.

"It's too bad you couldn't meet him this time around. I've let him go off to Mexico. He'll have himself a whale of a time there. He's popular wherever he goes. He's a good athlete, got this great physique. Everyone goes for him."

Michael said cautiously: "I look forward to meeting him in the autumn—fall, I mean."

Brian shook his head. "Not possible."

"I'm sorry about that." The abruptness surprised him. But then intonations were misinterpreted more often than words.

Brian's eyes were moist with affection. "We're off to the Orient in September. Japan, Fiji, the Philippines. It seems the least I can do for him. He's such a great kid."

"I see." It is not the wealth, but the freedom from necessity, that makes them different from us, he noted.

Lois called them in to the table. Michael followed in Brian's ample wake. Once on the move, he felt the effect of four heart-stopping martinis, genuine Dylan-killers. The stone steps approached him like a line of waves proceeding shoreward; he stepped on to the first of them as though he would go through up to his knees.

At the round table he was settled between Bernice and Mary-Beth, confronting Brian, who winked at him affectionately. Michael dodged this with a split-second reaction, as a cyclist going downhill dodges a stone. More cautious now, he began to observe the others at the table out of the corners of his eyes.

He got the odd impression that everyone was gleaming, and that this was not merely the high shine of well-kept hair and skin, but some form of Pentecostal transfiguration.

He supposed they had a right to gleam. They had raised themselves up, hadn't they, from grim towns in the Middle West, full of huge-assed men and women with their hair in rollers. They had risen to the Barford residence, the habitations of the blessed, where everything looked expensive, the Bauhaus chairs they sat in, the pre-Columbian sculpture crouched on shelves behind them; beneath their feet the polished floorboards were partly obscured by the kippered hides of large African ruminants. In unison, these people created an atmosphere of sexy bonhomie, which had nothing to do with what they were saying but was perhaps the randiness of money, that pungent whiff you get occasionally at auctions or at the races.

A wave of alcohol rose gently and exploded behind his face. His mind was skidding, he was in peril of letting his hands and feet go crazy under the table. He stared down at his avocado pear. If it had not been stuffed with shrimp, he would have been able to get in there and hide. Instead, he ate some hot garlic bread and, feeling better, turned stiffly to his left and prepared to launch a conversation with Mary-Beth. At the same moment she turned to him, and her prettiness was like a brush of warm air over his face. When she turned away, his attention was held by the loop of her hair and the small nacreous ear beneath it. He seemed to wander around inside this for a time, while his voice asked her what she did at the college. His wanderings continued while, in a tired edgy voice, she told him that she was doing her Master's and that it was devoted to two contemporary novelists, Cohn and Schine.

The weariness in her voice lent it a curious erotic quality. He felt a pizzicato "ping" of lust, the prostatic swoop and its attendant discomfort. Dismissing it, he asked why Cohn and Schine, and why not—he offered her some other much-circulated names. This was merely something to say. She could ignore it if she liked. But she didn't.

Mary-Beth's adviser had suggested the subject and right then she couldn't think of anything she wanted to do. Cohn, she told him, had betrayed the heritage of his immigrant forebears, whereas Schine had introduced Talmudic symbolism into the mainstream of American literature.

This, he reflected, might well be true, though as a proposition it made him again want to inter himself in his avocado. Was Mary-Beth typical of the students he'd be meeting in the next academic year? Perhaps she wasn't too bright. Perhaps an infinite emptiness lay between this small pink ear and its fellow, which was in the purview of their host, Russell Barford.

Perhaps it didn't matter. This was not really a conversation: she was filling him in, so that he wouldn't make a mistake another time. Like all of them, she was under the impression that information was what he most needed. And he managed to make the correct comments from time to time. But when one is adapting one's remarks to someone who is beautiful and stupid, one would rather not be overheard. And he saw, to his chagrin, that Lois and Gene and Brian were all listening, drinking in his carefully filtered words.

Luckily there was an interruption. The plates and the empty husks of the pears were collected, and Lois brought around the beef Wellington. Holding forward the dish, she leaned on him, a warm, herbally scented presence at his left ear.

"Just love your accent," she murmured.

Barford came around with the wine. "You all right?" he inquired, inserting a stiletto point of unease.

Turning to his right, Michael found that Bernice was concluding a long story for Brian, and so he had time to meditate. As he started on the beef, he wondered how Tessa would take to all this. It would be her first time in America; she drank very little, and was too good-natured to let conversations slide past. Bernice and Gene seemed likely to become their closest friends at Barford. The journey here tonight had been given up to Gene's account of their English trip, which had passed through the conventional trajectory of praise for the theaters, the restaurants, the unexpected reception by a titled personage, to the inevitable disappointments, the climate, the hotel, and then the rueful admission of the final row, about dollars of course, in which a misapprehension was represented as an injustice. Michael hadn't listened with much attention, for he liked Americans to get over this bit and talk of other things. Tessa, he knew, would have stopped Gene in mid-career, cross-questioned and argued with him. Gene would have loved it; boyish, spry, he gave every impression of a man eager for interesting conversation. Bernice, on the other hand, had sat silent between them, huddled in a fun fur; he had taken her silence to be ominous, expressing disapproval on a fairly fundamental level.

Now she seemed friendly, as she said to him: "I was telling Brian the latest on my family."

"Oh, yes."

"You see, I work for the State Government and they're trying to fire me. If I lose my job, that's the end of my family."

"How awful."

"They say I spend too much time with them."

"Who do?"

Her voice assumed a sort of helpful patience; like Mary-Beth, she was filling him in.

"The State. My family. I tell them they're being racist and sexist. Well, shouldn't I?"

He found the question unanswerable. He watched her consume a last forkload of beef Wellington.

"They're Puerto Ricans, see? They moved here from New York because Social Security is easier, there's no residential qualification."

"But you were here already?"

"Naturally. I graduated from Barford. Gene was my instructor."

"Oh, I see."

He was still in confusion when Russell announced their removal to another room, for *gâteau,* coffee, liqueurs. Lois and Gene appeared beside hm, Lois the creator of the feast, a strong Demeter in her tapestry gown, and Gene avid to talk seriously, urgent as a man trying to pick up a whore in the street.

Gene said: "Tell us, Mike, who in your estimation is the finest contemporary novelist, American, I mean?"

Why does one's mind curl up and turn silly? He answered: *"Hélas! C'est Nabokov!"*

He was at once contrite. For one thing, they mightn't know any French. For another, they might pronounce the writer's name quite differently (after all, they always made Durrell rhyme with Pure Hell). Furthermore, he wasn't quite certain that he had pronounced it correctly himself. Russell Barford was observing him with a renewal of interest which might indicate contempt.

He said: "I'm sorry but I think it's Nabokov."

Gene gripped his arm in a manner that seemed to congratulate him. "We must discuss this sometime."

Michael found the end of the large sofa and, sitting down,

was engulfed in the steatopygous upholstery. He was surrounded by leather, tanned and soft like non-Caucasian skin.

Bernice descended beside him. With a pneumatic sigh she sank in, and rose again with her knees up. This slapstick entrance did not, however, discompose her in any way.

"It's wonderful," he said. "Like sitting on flayed slaves."

She ignored this. "I was telling you about my family," she said. "Well, there are these six children. It's the eldest boy I'm truly concerned about. He's fourteen and has this heroin problem. He's got these scars all over, needle scars in addition to stab wounds. He's been into heroin since the sixth grade. I only got to him two years back. I'm trying to earn his trust, right?"

While she continued to instruct him, he retreated into British diffidence. Of course, she wasn't talking about her own family. Nobody talked of a real family like that. She was a social worker or something. This was her job, she was talking shop. What the hell did he care?

"What happened to the father?"

"Fathers. None of them around."

At this point his wife would be asking the right interested questions, probing and agreeing. Whereas he was made slothful by the mere idea of other people's people.

He was just thinking what a bore she was, when evidently a similar idea occurred to her. He turned to find she had slid away, neatly as a seal off a rock. He was relieved yet somewhat chagrined, until Lois, the one who had done the cooking, an altogether more comfortable presence, descended to join him.

This time he was determined not to be on the receiving end: if Lois liked his accent, she would get the full benefit of it. He complimented her on the dinner and then, suddenly finding his form and expanding his parentheses, he told her how cooking is an image of art, its categories being discussable, though, with a freedom with which only dukes or millionaires can discuss art, who can consume or dispose of it at will, whereas nowadays our values only truly operate at this lower level where we have the power of choice; to be a cook, moreover, was to hold in view what always eluded the artist, the possibility of getting something completely right—which is possibly why cooking is not a true art but only an image of art.

Lois survived all this pretty well. With her, he managed to forget the wry, slightly emetic essence of his Britishness, like an overdose of angostura in a glass of gin. But how right they were to regard him with distrust, an unwilling client who accepted their support at the same time as he disparaged it; he was reminded of himself as a child, needing thumbscrews to force him to say thank you to an important relative. Now, in benign company, he passed in full sail through dessert and coffee and liqueurs—bless her, Lois even found him a brandy in that trolley load of miscellaneous stickinesses—until they were aware of increasing calms and silences in the other parts of the room: people were leaving.

No, not everyone. He had uncurled from the fetal posture exacted by the furniture and, after hauling himself back into the upper air, started saying good-bye to the wrong people.

Bernice assumed control: "You wait right here. Gene's dropping off Mary-Beth at Campus Heights. He'll be back for you. Lois already said she'd drive Brian."

"We'll let them get out of the driveway," Brian announced, and he accepted another B & B—"since I'm not driving. Lois lives catty-corner from my place," he went on. "Rhona's got my car in New York. She's seeing the boy off to Mexico."

"Who's Rhona?"

"My wife Rhona. She's seeing the boy off to Mexico."

"Oh, he's your son."

"Yes, my son." Brian looked suspicious. "Look, I was telling you about him. Is this some joke?"

"No, of course not."

"I was telling you about him, goddam it."

"Sorry, my mistake. I thought—"

"What mistake? What did you think? No, let's get this cleared up."

But before he could make sure of the implications, Lois had come between them to take them off. She insisted that Michael bring Tessa over for dinner, at the start of the fall semester.

"We'll have soul food," she said. "That's a promise."

Their host had gone to the bathroom.

While he waited, Michael summoned the feelings of mild distaste and wan embarrassment with which it is proper to confront the hereditarily rich.

A storm of water, a new silence, and then the clip-clip of the old man's feet on the polished floors.

"Glad to have this opportunity for a talk. Highball?"

"Thank you."

Russell Barford moved very slowly around organizing the highball. He approached and stood over his guest, who found himself jumping around with unhelpful preparatory movements.

"Sit, boy."

Close at hand, Russell Barford was a neat, well-finished object: white floss hair, skin like wax paper, purple smoking jacket, and the feet of an adolescent in dancing pumps. At the same time you could appreciate that this was an awe-exacting old man, one slowed down less by senility than a consciousness of importance: extraordinary efforts must be made not to interrupt or stampede him.

"You seem to have gotten in some confusion over friend Brian. How's that highball?"

"Fine."

"He's no fag, in spite of appearances." The word cleared the air: it excluded the effulgent sentimentality that surrounds so many silvered transatlantic heads. Once out of that bland Pelagian word, you could say what you meant.

"Cultural differences. One doesn't always interpret the signals correctly."

The old man chuckled at this. "That's true. I myself am fortunate enough to have traveled widely."

This seemed to be leading up to something, but when Barford spoke again he was off on a different tack.

"I was interested in your admiration for Nabokov."

"Oh, yes."

"Of his books, I know only *Lolita*. I vividly recall the fuss when it first appeared."

"Such nonsense. The last thing it is is pornographic."

His host looked disappointed.

"Oh, but you're so wrong, aren't you?"

"Most people wouldn't—"

The old man raised a hand for silence. "I intended to say, if you would allow me, how strange it is that people should be disturbed by something entirely natural, something that, in other cultures, takes place all the time."

His voice gained a new resonance—an obsession was talking. Michael recognized it at once and slid back into the sofa, drawing his drunkenness around him, and let the clear New England voice flow past.

"People say we have the permissive society. Not true. Preferences accepted in many parts of the world cause difficulty here. American parents, though erratic in their attention to their offspring, are apt to be inquisitive. Furthermore, there is this modern habit of sharing everything with Mommy. I do not like Mommy."

Michael had his eyes half closed. If I open them, he thought, I'll see the little feet beating with excitement on the floor.

"I have the good fortune to be able to travel in pursuit of this interest of mine." The careful sentences began to build up into another aria in praise of London . . . "personal friend of mine, who gives me hospitality in one of your suburbs, south of the Thames—doctor in your National Health Service—shares my tastes exactly—obviously well situated to satisfy them—some of these underprivileged families, no objections raised—often the fathers or brothers already—naturally you give only candy, in case the parents find out—last occasion, two dear little things, frilly dresses, not these awful jeans—I always say, ''Course they don't mind, wouldn't come back for more candy if they did.'" At the end he laughed contentedly. "How's that drink?"

The other handed his glass. After all, this was in another country, it was late at night, he was drunk. Did he have to react at all? Probably, yes. Tessa would get it right at once. Indeed, he would scarcely dare tell her about this; she would refuse to come to Barford College, or she would descend like an avenging angel on the south London suburb, ferret out that doctor's name, set the machinery in motion. And you couldn't blame her. Confronted by the violation of children, even eminent rationalists had been known to lose their cool in the public prints, and to bear witness that Evil, after all, does exist.

Yet, arguing with himself like this, he was jabbering down a quite different response. His host's discourse had been directed not only against him but beyond him. It seemed to mean something like this: you are the member of a beaten tribe; back at the kraal, your youngest and weakest are available to be enjoyed by us, the conquerors. This is to let you know.

Afterward, Michael believed that he had been rising to his feet to attack, when Gene's return interrupted them. In fact, though, there was a minute or two while Barford sat smiling at his guest. I can tell you anything because I despise you, he seemed to say. Like all the British over here, you're scared of losing out. And at that moment he *was* scared, being in the presence of a world of palpable monsters he had previously ignored.

In the fussiness of Gene's presence, they shook hands. Russell Barford said: "So you know why I always look forward to my visits to your country." And Gene smiled, reassured, believing the encounter to have been a success.

On the way back to the motel, Gene extolled the Barford dynasty.

"I think he's mad."

Gene nodded quickly, as though anxious not to let an irony escape him. Michael knew that he was being built up into a character, and at the very moment when he felt most hollow and wretched. Without being sure what had happened, he was quite defeated. He looked out of the car window at the night, the clumps of hickory and Judas trees, the filling stations and the mailboxes at the ends of driveways. The headlights turned them all into cardboard, as trashy and impermanent as himself.

At the motel Gene got out of the car to say good-bye. Michael felt a rush of sympathy for him. They'd had to take a rain check on those interesting conversations. Perhaps because of his obvious difficulties with Bernice, perhaps because of some dogged quality of his own, he seemed marked out from his colleagues. Earlier this evening, had he really been gleaming with the others?

The motel was situated in wasteland, remote from the town and the college. There were odd lights up and down the sky, a whistling flight of birds going over, and a freight train's cry, like the last mammoth sinking into a Siberian swamp.

"Have a good flight. If there's anything further you require to know, please write me."

"Yes, of course."

In the motel room, he turned on all switches. When he came out of the bathroom, the television was flickering. He adjusted it, and saw a crowd of peasants with flaming torches rushing toward a castle.

He slumped down in an armchair opposite the set. Lights were flashing in the mullioned windows. Down in the dungeons the monster at last lay strapped, thonged, and fettered, while the scientist who had given him life prepared to destroy him. Gulp-gulp, went the liquid in the retorts; bubbles hiccoughed down glass tubes; sparks crackled like fiery worms. Outside, a dampish-looking blonde rattled the door handle. Meanwhile the shouting peasants drew nearer to the castle, and overhead the dam held in a mountain of water.

Falling asleep, he was surprised to see that this film was to have no sequel. The switches stayed unthrown. Sunlight returned, and the happy Transylvanian peasants began folk dancing. Down in the dungeons the monster lay dead. The scientist and the blonde went trout-fishing above the dam.

# *The Potlatch of Esmeralda*

At last the three travelers, the White Hunter with silver-streaked hair, the American heiress in the bush shirt and her jealous red-faced lover, were able to rest at the edge of the kraal.

"White Bwana welcome!"

On the chief's orders the tribal dancers began to perform. Wielding knobkerries and spears, dangling monkey tails and leopard skins, they shuffled to and fro. They jerked their buttocks, spasmodically shrieking and rolling their white eyeballs.

The whole audience was intent and some were laughing. The exception was Esmeralda, who had turned aside and hidden her face with a neat gloved hand. Vicente, sitting next to her, took a few minutes to notice this.

"What on earth's the matter, girl?"

"It's nothing. I am so ashamed. I can't bear to look."

He shifted his shoulders and made himself comfortable; this was one of her problems, which did not concern him at all. However, since Esmeralda had paid for the seats, he thought it better to whisper: "Do you want to leave?" The cinema, a cheap one in an unfashionable quarter of Paris, was warm and outside there waited a slate-gray winter evening.

"No, no, it's all right."

Already the scene on the screen had changed. Against a violent sunset, the heiress leaned on a tree with her breasts silhouetted. In the nearby darkness a cigarette glowed: it was the White Hunter. Vicente, a self-absorbed young man, grunted with satisfaction. And now Esmeralda's face reappeared from behind her hand. It was black, plain and amiable.

"You must forgive me for making a show," Esmeralda said afterward, "but when I see such films I become ashamed of my race."

They were drinking coffee in a large neon-lit café and watching the rain fall on the street and the little cars roaring past. They had been brought together by loneliness. Both came from Latin countries in which Paris was still regarded as the center of the universe, and they were still appalled at the French faces clenched like fists, the unfriendly prosperity, and the outbreaks of violence in the streets. Vicente, whose features were dead-white as candlewax, lolled in the iron chair in a tight suit of gray tweed—"Principe de Galles" from Madrid—with the trousers cut for virility, and lethal pointed shoes. Like many handsome young men without education, the defeat that was waiting for him seemed to have touched him already and was clearly visible to anyone but himself.

"Why don't you have one of those big sandwiches?"

"No."

"Please, Vicente."

"From you, no. I cannot take any more money from you. I am not that sort. The idea!"

Esmeralda twisted her gloves in her big pale-palmed hands. "But I worry about you!"

"Do what you like!"

"But you are hungry. You cannot go to bed hungry."

This roused him to the ordinary reaction, the jeer from the street corner as impersonal as a whistle. "With you, I must always go to bed hungry."

"Don't be silly." Esmeralda giggled politely. "Have a sandwich."

And in the end he accepted. He exploited her carefully and with as much show of affection as his Spanish pride would allow him. He had even, during the summer, invited her to Madrid, where his mother and his family of sisters had surrounded her with all the affectionate curiosity he denied her. The sisters kept on touching Esmeralda's black skin, they bounded into her bedroom in the morning, laughed all the time she was there, and went on laughing when she had gone.

In spite of this, there was "nothing" between Vicente and Esmeralda. Their relationship was between an indulgent spinster and a boy who had caught her fancy. Esmeralda's compatriots, the clerks and stewards of Southern Cross Airways where she worked, kept on teasing her about it.

"What are you keeping it for, girl? Be modern. After all, this is Paris."

"Just imagine!" Esmeralda's voice became quite shrill, though her face was beaming from the attention she was getting. "Suppose I went back to Rio disgraced like that! My family are strict, I tell you. They'd throw me out at once. I've seen it happen, and what is there left for a girl after that?"

All the same she could not help telling them, with shocked giggles, about the Frenchmen and even Frenchwomen who had tried to make friends with her in the Métro. But for over a year now she had centered her life on Vicente, found him a room to live in, comforted him when he lost his job at Orly Airport, and waited with him through the long hours of doing nothing much, with which Spaniards fill in their lives. When she received her wages she bought him ties and gentlemen's toiletries, and she thought him the most beautiful thing in the world.

They often quarreled. Esmeralda knew that he went with women and indeed she expected him to, but she could never resist attacking him about it. Tonight before they separated, she started questioning him about tomorrow evening.

"I am going to the cinema."

Vicente went to the cinema about five times a week, but she knew his tones of voice and she pounced at once.

"I know. With somebody else. Who is it?"

No answer. Vicente was without a winter overcoat and he turned up his jacket collar against the cold.

The black girl's voice went crowing on: "I know I have no

claim on you, simply because I'm not without shame like those other ones. I merely want to know. I worry about you."

Vicente's teeth were chattering.

"It's that Madame Habib, isn't it?"

"What's it to you?"

"Nothing at all. These Frenchwomen are all the same. At home when a woman behaves as she has done, it is the streets for her and nothing else. Where's her husband, that he lets her do such things?"

"Divorced."

"Divorced! At home we don't even have divorce. They shouldn't be allowed to get away with it. Still, if that's what you want, good luck to you."

Esmeralda, the wise virgin neatly done up in plastic, walked off into rain, jerking her shoulders with moral indignation.

The next time they met she brought him a knitted silk tie he had coveted during one of their walks along the Faubourg St. Honoré. Though he thanked her, he looked depressed. She guessed something was wrong and so she sat waiting, tapping her heels and fidgeting with her umbrella. By the time Vicente began talking to her, anger and suspicion seemed to have made Esmeralda slightly deaf.

"What is it? I can hear nothing, with that piggery coming from the jukebox."

Vicente leaned forward to her and she watched his white face with an obsessed attention. "One must think of the future," he was saying. She noticed a little colony of hairs, like a fine-legged insect, inside the whorls of his left ear. "And I have come to the conclusion, indeed we have often discussed just this point together, that to get on in Paris you cannot be alone. In short, a man must have a woman behind him. It is the women who dominate everything here, isn't it true?"

Esmeralda quivered with excitement. "Of course, Vicente. I have done all I can for you as it is, but if you think we——"

"A Frenchwoman of course. Yvette wants to marry me."

Her voice broke: "Who's Yvette?"

"Madame Habib. I think I mentioned her to you."

"But she's married!" said Esmeralda wildly.

"Divorced. I told you. Her husband was a Tunisian in politics, who couldn't be married to a Frenchwoman."

"Divorced—it's all the same. What will your mother, poor Doña Mercedes, say?"

"Mother cannot understand. Living in Madrid things are different. Here one has to keep up with the times."

The tie still lay in its smart, long envelope on the table between them. After a moment Vicente said in a voice hollow with self-pity: "You won't want to give me this now."

Esmeralda emerged from her stunned silence. "Take it! Take it! I'll give you exactly what it pleases me to give you. You imagine I give you presents because I want something out of you? No, Senhor. Your Madame Habib may demand payment on the nail, not I!"

"Of course I consider that Vicente is undervaluing himself. But if you're going to get on at all in Paris, a man must have a Frenchwoman beside him. It's they who hold the keys, you see this everywhere. Vicente and I have often discussed it quite frankly. I sincerely hope he will be happy. I wish him nothing but well."

The stewards of Southern Cross Airways laughed behind their hands at this. But Esmeralda's private life seemed to have a greater intensity than their own, and they watched her with wary admiration, as though they expected her shortly to go up in flames.

What Esmeralda in fact did was only to astound them further. First, in the corridor, she approached one of the stewards who was on the London flight. After fussily swearing him to secrecy, she said: "Pierre, next time you are in London, I want you to buy something for me. No, it is all right. I have the money."

Later there were errands for those going to Rome and to South America. Unknown even to Vicente, Esmeralda had savings from her three years in France, and now she drew out the last of these, and even tried to borrow ahead on her salary. Rumors spread fast among the stewards, and Esmeralda was a person of such probity that they were greatly impressed.

To Pierre, who kept trying to discourage her, she said: "I

know what I am doing. Now nobody will be able to say I wanted anything from him."

To the others: "You don't believe in Pure Friendship? Well, all I can say is you have been unfortunate."

Her explanations were vague and impressive and they did not nearly approach the truth about her real feelings. Perhaps it is most accurate to say that, as though prompted by some remote Amerindian forebear, Esmeralda was performing potlatch. This, according to anthropologists, is the ceremonial destruction of wealth in order to impress and dominate the neighbors. Esmeralda knew now that Vicente was quite worthless, she knew it as though she had known it all along, but it appeased her pride to throw all this wealth onto one bonfire, in one final extraordinary blaze.

Before much time had passed, Esmeralda found another young man to take to the cinema. Some of the same films were still running. But now tribal dances and documentaries of Congo riots, even the antics of Louis Armstrong, which cause shame to many of her race, no longer troubled her at all. She knew herself as good as anyone in the world.

After the ceremony at the *Mairie* a glass of champagne was offered at the bride's residence. Vicente invited Esmeralda; he was dazzled by all the presents she had been showering on him.

It was a gloomy flat near the Porte de Champerret, full of the hard gilded furniture favored by the French middle class. Most of the guests were women in black, middle-aged and unattached: the only sort in this city who might have made contact with a foreign young man like Vicente. Esmeralda was preceded in the foyer by two shrill-voiced gentlemen, aged *Sociétaires de la Comédie Française*. One said to the other: "I tell you he is extremely beautiful. Yvette has made me furiously jealous."

The bride's mother gave her a glass of champagne. Nobody else took any notice of her at all. A few moments later the happy couple appeared.

The minute she saw him, Esmeralda experienced all the hard triumph she had expected. The suit of tropical mohair from London had been perfectly cut, the shoes and shirt were from Italy, and the cufflinks sparkled with Brazilian aquamarines. Vicente's blanched face, with its neo-classical handsomeness, shone beside his new wife, a scrawny dyed-blonde of thirty-five, half a head taller than he.

"You have known my husband for some time, I believe?"

The black girl looked at Vicente, who smiled sheepishly.

"Known him, Madame, but of course. I feel I've practically created him. Look at the suit he's wearing—it was I who got him that. The cufflinks, the shirt, the tie—all mine. It was just like dressing up a lovely big doll."

The woman flinched and tried to move away but Vicente, too slow to grasp what was happening, hung on to her arm.

"His hair is nice, isn't it, Madame? But I assure you, like most Spaniards, he's got nothing going on underneath it. As to the rest of him, well, you know more about that than I."

Vicente made one move toward her, but Esmeralda did not stop to find out whether it was from weakness or violence. Putting down her champagne glass, she walked unsteadily from the flat, her eyes blurred with pride and virtue, her rituals over and all her gods appeased.

# The Candidate

It is difficult to retain an air of confidence when one's eyeglass frame is mended with adhesive tape. A slight exertion will cause the frail girder of plastic to fold up gently at the point of repair. Once this process has begun, the lenses slip off to one side, often appearing to a spectator to carry an eye or two away with them. In an effort to stop the bridge from slithering down to its jumping off point, the nose wrinkles desperately. Hand comes up, too late. The frame is now in two parts: where once a piece of sticky tape has come unstuck, it will not willingly try again.

All this was happening to Dr. Ewa Rudnicka while she was talking to the English lecturer. They were in the Dean's Office, a high Gothic room in the main university building, where the academic staff were lining up for their monthly salaries, a long and impatient business. George Brady, the English lecturer, was surprised when Dr. Rudnicka, whom he knew only slightly, surrendered her place considerably ahead of him in the line in order to come and speak to him.

*"Elle est vraiment très intelligente, très douée, même."*

Since it was impossible not to be distracted by what was happening to her glasses, his efforts to listen seemed to be giving her greater sympathy than he intended. He was relieved that people nearby were paying no more attention than the speaking of a foreign language usually arouses. Professors, docents, assistants, they had their usual preoccupied air. Amid the doctrinal struggles of the last years, they had chosen scholarship, or perhaps pedantry, and survived.

Gradually they approached the table where a clerk was counting out the money. Dr. Rudnicka continued talking, whereas Brady began to exhibit the symptoms of anxiety that a child shows when a box of chocolates is coming in its direction. He tried not to look at the shabby wads of currency, and so it happened that he was watching Dr. Rudnicka at the very moment when her glasses finally came apart. She caught the lenses and pushed them into a bag she was carrying. All the time she was signing the pay sheets and receiving her salary, one of the plastic sidepieces was swinging to and fro, secured only by a ringlet of hair above her left ear. As the sidepiece touched her cheek, she made a swipe at that too, but it eluded her and fell to the floor, where it snapped into three pieces under the boot of a reader in Old Church Slavonic.

Revealed, Dr. Rudnicka's eyes showed a kindly warmth. Her hair was streaked with gray, and she was still wearing the suit of mustard-colored tweed she wore in the winter. Women here had no choices; you recognized people easily by their clothes, and this somehow gave them a stronger individuality—they were all of a piece.

By now Brady was stuffing the banknotes, sour-smelling and thickened by use, into his wallet. Dr. Rudnicka still stood beside him.

"I am sure you will like her very much. She is shy, I know, but she has studied hard, and she comes of a very good and worthy family."

"I am sorry, but who is this?"

Dr. Rudnicka blinked as she tried to focus on his face. Her smile was very charming.

"But, Monsieur, I am just telling you. My little niece, Krysia Nowalek. She is a candidate in your examination."

The examination season was in late spring—a time of uncertain weather, of chestnut trees in full blossom against a thundery sky, flower women in the market hurrying to protect their buckets of tulips and lilac branches from the hail showers. A feverish atmosphere surrounded the young, who spent whole nights sipping glasses of tea and learning answers by heart, or took despairing refuge in the belief that the examination results were arbitrary and unfair: Does the science teacher like me, will the teacher of Russian remember that I was rude to her?

For the University Entrance, which took place a little later, everyone looked for a friend at court, a personal contact, someone who had the ear of an important figure, some way out of the anonymity of a classless society. A place at the University, which was ancient and grand, might represent a passport from a village slum to the desired uplands of the intelligentsia. It might mean a halt in the steady decline of a former middle-class family. In the Faculty of Literature, there was already a small pile of letters asking, in an obscure and ornate style, for "protection."

Leaving Dr. Rudnicka, the English lecturer came down into the stone-flagged entrance hall. There at the foot of the stairs he saw Jusek Nowrot, assistant in the Department of English Philology, in conversation with Dean Karpinski. Karpinski, a large man with a perpetually good-humored appearance, was the highest Party official in the University. As Brady approached them they checked, and all three bowed—Nowrot in fact was bowing to Karpinski already. Brady walked on into the open air, with the strong impression that they had been talking about something that concerned himself.

Later he sat behind his desk, slitting open some handouts which the Cultural Section of the American Embassy had sent out and throwing them into the wastepaper basket. He waited for Jusek Nowrot to come in. He was afraid that the conversation with Karpinski would have been about something small, unimportant, faintly but distinctly disappointing to everyone. In this gray world of education, things went diminuendo.

Jusek came in.

Chekhov once wrote to his brother concerning the necessity

of "squeezing the serf out of himself, drop by drop, until he wakes one morning and finds he is a real man." Jusek Nowrot had taken a somewhat indirect approach to this problem. Looking at him, you remembered the long periods when the Slav was still the slave. Something of that still affected his whole bearing, the way he held his shoulders and put his feet on the floor and brought his hands together, in gestures that belonged to half-forgotten species of archaic men, ostlers, scriveners, tapsters at wayside inns.

"I am sorry I have news for you. There are to be fifteen new students next year."

"I knew that already."

"Yes, but one of them already is chosen."

"What do you mean?"

"She will take the exam but whatever happens she is assured a place."

"Who says so?"

"The Party. Karpinski says the name is already accepted."

"I thought we were to choose the students we thought best."

"I am very sorry." Jusek chuckled with satisfaction.

"I don't believe it." The Englishman banged the desk drawer shut. He had acquired a reputation for a bad temper he did not feel. In dealing with Jusek one was tempted to be loud-mouthed, chafingly aggressive. But he still thought that Karpinski would not have stated such a decision categorically. As for Jusek, he was always ready to accept the worst in order to prove his point.

"I know the Party has its representative on the examination commission. But it's only people who come up to our standards who go through to them. Nobody else."

Jusek agreed with all this, but he merely said: "I'm sorry, George. I tell you what Dean Karpinski says."

And Jusek would have agreed with Karpinski, too, out of deference to a superior but also from his desire to prove that every man had his price and everything was mediocre. Jusek felt he had a right to his price and his mediocrity, which the presence of a foreigner was in some way denying him.

"What is the candidate called?" Brady asked. "No, better not tell me because I'm sure to be prejudiced."

Jusek laughed, and Brady realized that this was because he too had shown that he was incapable of detachment.

Half an hour later, Halina Barcik, the other assistant in the department, strode into the office.

"I know I'm late." Unlike Jusek, she never made excuses. "Karpinski would keep me talking about one of the candidates. A girl called Krystyna Nowalek."

Her eyes were sparkling at some private joke, and she made a funny face, turning down the corners of her mouth.

She sat down on her desk, as she often did, swinging her legs. She dug around in her bag for cigarettes and lit up, shaking the match long after it was dead. To George Brady, Halina always seemed to go through this process as though it were a sort of pioneering gesture on behalf of women. In the same way, during the cold weather, she would never let you help her on with her coat. She had several of these quirks and gestures which, together with the expressions of her clear-cut face—never pretty but sometimes beautiful—and the way she moved her large-boned body, were enjoyable because, without being specifically funny, they made you want to laugh.

This was in her good moods, for she had some of the manic-depressive taint of her compatriots. Aged thirty at this time, Halina was a survivor of a class and of a generation that had nearly disappeared in the War. It was hard not to think of her surrounded by the ghosts of young men who might have loved her.

Halina blew out a cloud of cigarette smoke. Through it, she gave him her steady, amused look.

"So we shall be having her next year in the department?"

She had a way of watching for Brady's reactions in a way which worried him. Something had happened which he had hoped to avoid: he had become the person who was most capable of being a disappointment to her.

She went on smiling. Jusek was watching. They both liked to continue with a situation until it had been wrung dry of all its possibilities.

"Do you think we shall?" Brady asked.

"If that is what Dean Karpinski says, yes."

"You don't really believe that, do you?"

Suddenly Halina looked gloomy, and crushed out her cigarette as though punishing it for its fire.

In the late afternoon, Brady walked towards the tram stop through the public gardens that formed a ring around the Old City. Sunlight was coming through the new leaves of the lime trees and the paths were crowded. Among the crowds there were coal miners in their gray-blue uniforms, shop girls, pairs of soldiers holding hands, nuns, and schoolchildren.

Was it only the return of spring which produced this curiously intent look on people's faces? Years later he would remember this as the place where you saw undisguised the true face of man. Few disguises were possible here, where everyone knew what everyone else was up to and could remember how, in the testing times not long ago, the others had been tested. In an odd way you were aware of people's identity with a clarity that in other cultures would only come after the act of physical love.

The tram took half an hour to reach the new workers' suburb where he lived. Through the winter, in the half-dark of early mornings, he had ridden squeezed between passengers enlarged by padded overcoats, with the snow bursting softly against the windows. Now that the year had returned, there was an odd translucency over everything: you could see beyond the shabby unpainted brick of the apartment blocks to the black ploughed fields in the countryside. At home in the evenings, he listened to Russian long-playing records and looked out of the window at the sheds where the concierge tended his flock of homing pigeons. A bunch of students came in to talk and drink precious cups of instant coffee. When he went out for a stroll, he would often meet the nice blonde woman who lived opposite him and who worked at the Orbis Hotel in the city. It was she, he believed, who had been deputed to keep watch on whoever visited him.

At the tram stop in the morning, he met Dr. Karcz, another of the deans. Karcz was a small, grim-looking man, but the severity hid a discreet irony. You recognized, not the terror and nostalgia of an Old Believer, but the humorous skepticism of full knowledge.

On the matter of the entrance examinations which occupied

everyone's minds, Karcz had additional discouragement to offer. The inhabitants of the neighboring industrial city, a vast creation of the Stalin period, had made a petition to open their own university. Therefore, Dean Karcz told Brady, we must choose the candidates who came from that city; then they would have no cause to ask for a university of their own.

"Can we just choose the ones who are best?" The question sounded futile in the still morning air.

But Dr. Karcz surveyed the proposal as though it had a rare elegance. He put his forefinger against his right nostril and he smiled.

"Best? There, I think, we have many difficulties. There is the problem for instance of social background, yes? If he is the son of miner and has the same mark as the son of doctor, then he gets the place."

"But nobody ever is exactly the same."

"Perhaps you are right. Though I am afraid all our pupils are rather weak."

Dr. Karcz permitted no confidence in anything; he delighted in being disabused. He got on the tram and paid Brady's fare and his own. The broad-faced conductress, wearing a sheepskin cape, pushed some small coins back to him, but he left them for her to pick up.

"Their wages are still disgraceful," he said. "That is one thing that did not change."

Dr. Karcz seemed to ride the tramcar as though it were private transport of his own. His aspect brightened considerably as they swayed down through the drab suburban streets. Ahead stood a section of the medieval walls, and baroque church towers began to appear above the flowering lime trees. Dr. Karcz's skepticism had its defined limits; it could never extend to his native city, nor to most of the people who lived there.

There was this problem in talking to the local inhabitants—to find out the precise line in their total experience between the things they detested and the things to which they gave their deepest love. Everyone possessed this line. With Jusek, Brady thought he knew where it was. With Halina, however, he was still completely unsure. In trying to get a perspective, he was like poor Dr. Rudnicka, squinting rather hopelessly at the world through a pair of broken glasses.

Halina dealt with all the letters and personal callers who arrived at the department. That morning Brady met a middle-aged couple descending the stairs. Both of them shot glances at him, which mingled fear and dislike to an extent that startled him. Obviously they were parents of one of the candidates, but when he asked Halina about them, she shrugged her shoulders and blew out more smoke. He did not pursue the matter; there were always undercurrents, confidential arrangements, secret understandings, about which she kept him in the dark.

Sometimes Halina said: "George, I really hate these people," and then, as though ashamed, would avoid his eye and look out of the window. But she never explained. From her point of view, all these goings on were part of a primitive ritual which implied social backwardness and was therefore to be concealed from foreigners. At times Brady was inclined to believe these private relationships to be more subtle and humane than the curricula and contracts that people worked by in the West. The university examinations were an exception: it was better that Halina and Jusek kept all the maneuvers from him.

All the same, they couldn't prevent other people from approaching him, and later that morning he was waylaid in the public gardens.

As though marking its significance in his memory, the encounter took place on the asphalt path between the statue of Copernicus and the building in which Joseph Conrad had gone to school. Very small and brittle-looking, the former Princess R— emerged suddenly among the syringa bushes. She wore an aged fur coat, canvas slippers from the State Department Store, and her forehead was crossed by an improbable fringe of russet-colored curls.

"Good morning. This is very lucky. I have just been visiting the convent where I take an interest. The little nuns are all praying for one of your candidates. They know her well, her mother is a cripple and her father disappeared in the War. They are so anxious that she should go to the University, they have been lighting candles and praying for her."

Brady felt as usual that the old lady was addressing him in a lofty fashion, as the occupant of his job: she could not be bothered with one as an individual. He had always admired her detachment. Other people had a calculus of misfortune, a hierarchy of griefs: she had risen above it.

"Do you think she has a chance?"

Brady, who felt that personal calamity in itself was no recommendation for a place, asked: "How good is her English?"

She shrugged. "How should I know?"

"I thought she might be a student of yours." He knew that she lived by giving private lessons. There had been an aged Irish governess in the R— family until 1939, and they spoke English perfectly.

"Unfortunately not, poor child. She could not afford it." The old lady chuckled. "I have one student who is a candidate, though. Clever as a monkey."

She paused, and he waited for her to say something.

"They are Jews." She wrinkled her nose. "They were over there—in the East—and came back after the War. They have everything they want, of course. No, no, you must please remember the nuns' little friend. Krystyna Nowalek." She repeated the name carefully, so that he would not forget. "Thank you, good morning."

She hurried off, terminating the conversation with the unlingering abruptness of her class. Brady was left wondering about Krystyna Nowalek, who now seemed to be backed by the support of the Party and the prayers of the Church.

The candidates were wearing their best clothes, the men in dark suits and the girls mostly in white blouses. Desks had been labeled for all of them, but the examination room was far too small and they were packed tightly together.

"I think they will cheat," Jusek Nowrot said, with the little laugh he reserved for things going wrong.

Both Halina and Jusek had already made up their minds about this. The department only offered twenty places, but the hundred or so candidates would help each other without hesitation, as though with some group instinct of survival. They would be united, too, by the tradition of hostility to the academic staff, whatever their politics. And it all seemed to be true: with a few exceptions—young men who already stared about them with unconvincing bravado—the candidates appeared to belong to a tribe ready to sabotage any attempt to discriminate between them.

In the corridor outside, various supporters and petitioners still lingered. Dr. Rudnicka, her glasses repaired, beckoned to Jusek: he went out and she whispered to him urgently. Then the examining commission, led by Dr. Karcz, walked up the aisle between the desks. Dean Karpinski had not yet arrived, and it was decided not to wait for him. Dr. Karcz delivered a short dry speech, pointing his words so that everyone laughed. Gloom, however, settled down again as Brady and Halina walked around handing out the question papers. Moving between the rows, Brady was conscious of the wave of anxiety that his presence caused. Some of the girls crossed themselves. A few of them, still white-faced after the long winter months, looked frail and ill. As they bowed over their desks, their necks seemed pitifully exposed: he thought of Lady Jane Grey. There was only a scattering of men among the candidates. A little soldier in uniform wore nailed boots which gritted on the stone floor and raised impatient looks from his neighbors. When the papers had been handed out, a buzz of whispering arose. It was quelled by Halina.

Karpinski, the head of the commission, arrived ten minutes later. He insisted on shaking hands with each of the examiners and, while their attention was distracted, the whispering started again. In his turn he addressed the candidates. His huge size and good-humored appearance created a strong impression, whether or not they knew of his Party connections. But they took advantage of the confusion caused by his arrival and departure to flick notes to each other between the rows.

Four hours later, after two girls had fainted, possibly from hunger, and three more had been escorted out, the whole operation dwindled to its end. The last to leave was the little soldier. You could hear his boots echoing away down the corridor as he escaped into the summer evening.

Halina said: "You see, I am afraid it is no use trying to make the examination work. They go against you the whole time."

Brady looked at the stack of papers covered with English words in foreign handwritings. Many of them were like spoiled voting papers, the only protest against a rigged election. Halina brooded over them in silence for a time. Then she lit a cigarette, and started to go to work with a red pencil.

"There's always the oral examination," Brady said. "Nobody can cheat on that."

When the oral examinations were taking place, however, he discovered that there was at least one exception: himself. Halina's chair creaked beside his, and sometimes she sighed. He did not look at her but he could sense her disappointment growing with his unreliability in judgment.

The thirty-second candidate had double-jointed hands; while he flushed and stammered down into silence, his hands led an active life of their own, tumbling over each other and twisting free. He was a boy of about eighteen with a placid, almost oriental face, but he seemed to give off a smell of fear, like a show jumper under the whip. Trying to get him started again with an easier question, Brady caught his gaze. For a moment they stared at each other in desperation, the candidate pilloried in his fear, the examiner shaken out of all capacity for judgment. For Brady now there was no way of escape out of this confrontation. He couldn't retreat into amateur status or foreigner's detachment; he had been too lazy to form an ideology to support his notion of the just. Like the candidate, he was locked into his role, which would have to work out the solution for both of them. It was a ritual, important and yet incredible, like the encounter of judge and criminal.

A few minutes before, Karpinski had made one of his periodic appearances. He pulled up a chair on the other side of Halina. When the boy had gone, they whispered together and began leafing through his dossier: identification photograph, teachers' report (excellent), parents' social status (agricultural worker), remarks. Pages were scrawled in round hand.

"Poor boy," Halina said.

"Where does he come from?"

"Some hole near the Russian frontier. Probably he is as good as the teachers in his school."

Karpinski shook his big Beethoven-like head sadly, but said nothing. For him schools and universities were the agents of social hope. Discouragement for him was a much more serious personal affair, like the failure of a marriage hung on to beyond the very last chance, until a whole life has been wasted.

Waiting for the next candidate, Brady stood up and walked over to the window. Soft rain was falling on to some old blackened houses held up by scaffolding, and a garden of lilacs. There was a low murmur from the Russian examination which was taking place in the next room. There, he felt sure, would be a few problems. The answers would be by rote, and there were always enough places for any candidate who wished to apply.

A girl came in. Black hair, the face of an intelligent marmoset. Brady looked down at the next name on the typed list. Nowalek Krystyna. Krystyna Nowalek! This, then, was why Dean Karpinski had made a point of being present. Probably Dr. Rudnicka was lurking somewhere offstage. An attentive ear, even, might have heard the wing beats of angels overhead, summoned by the nuns.

Brady braced himself to ask the questions with clarity and precision; there must be no shadow of doubt, no cause for complaint.

The girl surprised him by answering brightly and efficiently, with a good accent. He had seen from the list that she had come in twenty-third in the written paper, but under the circumstances this had hardly been a reliable gauge. When the last questions had been asked and she had left the room, her neat heels clicking on the stone floor, he felt he could relax. He dared to peer around at Halina, who nodded. Karpinski was looking pleased. When the candidate opened to the door to leave, there was Dr. Rudnicka, in her mustard-colored tweeds, waiting outside. Now that his own conscience was appeased, Brady experienced a small vision, with the Ursuline nuns clapping their hands and dancing for joy in their walled garden, the Party beaming benevolently, reconciliation all around and the millennium on its way.

Naumann Gabriela, the last candidate of the day, was like fifty others. A stolid, dull-looking girl, she read out a passage of English in an unrecognizable accent. At the first question she pouted a little as though at an impertinence, frowned, remained silent, and then shrugged her shoulders with an attempt at indifference. Halina asked a question and the same reaction followed. In the end, the easiest question: Had she ever read a book by an English or American writer? A vatic look came over the girl's face. She screwed up her eyes and began to chant in a high-pitched voice: "Charles Dickens was the greatest of the English writers, dealing with the lives of oppressed peoples." A deep breath. "Thackeray and Oscar Wilde have attacked the decadent aristocracy." Silence and another breath. "In our days we have the opportunity to read great masterpieces by Jack Lindsay and James Aldridge . . ."

"Thank you. That's all."

Sentences like these had turned up many times during the examination: they were quoted by heart, from a manual for schools written by a boring woman in the Ministry of Education. This was the last and worst candidate of the day. Karpinski sighed, and Halina pushed together the stack of dossiers. It was time for the daily reckoning.

Five of this afternoon's candidates were accepted, and the agricultural worker's son regretfully dismissed. "He is young, he may try again," Karpinski said. There was a silence, as though they all thought how unlikely this would be.

"Nowalek Krystyna."

Karpinski tapped the cardboard cover with a thick forefinger. "Excellent. Very promising."

Brady looked inside the file. Krystyna Nowalek turned out to have had poor marks in school, though this might mean an unsatisfactory teacher. Social report, good. Karpinski nodded, pushed back his chair and stood up. As the last candidate had been an obvious failure, he was ready to leave.

Brady turned to the front of the dossier, and the identity photograph. The dull stolid face of the last candidate.

"What happens now?" he whispered to Halina. "There's been a mixup."

She looked quickly at the photograph and hurried out of the room. Karpinski sat down again. Brady avoided his gaze. He was afraid that either he or Halina might be responsible for the confusion. Instead, he opened the folder marked Naumann Gabriela, and the small monkey face smiled confidently up at him. Born Magnitogorsk 1942. Father Naumann Jakub, engineer. Clearly this was the private pupil old Princess R—— had been telling him about.

Halina came back. "It's true," she said. "They changed places because one of them wanted a rest after doing the Russian exam. They thought it didn't matter."

A few days later Brady was sitting in the office, drinking tea with Halina and Jusek. They had just heard on the telephone that Dean Karpinski had emphatically rejected Dr. Rudnicka's request for another examination for Krystyna Nowalek.

Karpinski had been furious when the mistake was discovered. He pulled on his raincoat and stumped out of the room without speaking. He had undergone much pressure from Krystyna Nowalek's supporters, but he also believed that she was the sort of student that the University should do its best to help.

"It is very good of Dr. Karpinski, I think," Jusek said.

"There was nothing else he could do. She couldn't possibly have passed."

Jusek laughed. "George liked Naumann better. She is prettier, I think."

Brady appealed to Halina. As was her way, she preferred merely to brood over the situation. She stared out of the window and said: "Naumann would have got in, anyway. We know her father has influence with the Minister of Higher Education. They always help each other."

Brady knew which way the conversation was steering. "She was much better, that's all. You know that."

"She has been in America," Halina said. "And her parents can afford private lessons. I think she won't bother to turn up for classes."

Afterward he would realize that in choosing students there were not only personal and political influences; there were historical pressures as well. "Those to whom evil is done," he thought, "do evil in return." It was a quotation that often occurred to him at that period of his life. Though of course in Eastern Europe it usually meant that evil was not returned but handed on to the innocent. Thanks to his presence, Gabriela Naumann might get her place at the University, but in a few years' time she, with her family, would go into exile again.

"Why didn't you say all this before?" he asked Halina.

She snuffed out her cigarette and looked at him. "What could I say, George? I knew you wanted to pass her."

# *In the Hotel*

My brother and I arrived at this hotel last night. We drove through several small towns on the way, but these, although they had looked charming from a distance, turned out to be just the usual collection of general stores, petrol stations, and council estates that you find on this edge of Europe.

Why have we come here? My brother mumbled something about a holiday, but he did not explain further. He seems to be keeping a secret. So much has changed since the last time we were by ourselves together.

Now he is lying on the other bed, smoking and reading the London newspaper. He has taken his shoes off. His hair is ruffled, he is wearing a white shirt and tan trousers, and his socks are gray. He grunts occasionally. He has given up talking to me—what would he have to say? Already there is a faint smell of both of us here in this room. Outside in the darkness there is the sound of a watermill or a salmon weir. Before the light disappeared altogether, it was possible to make out the outlines of a rain-sodden garden. There were paths of gravel and some Portugal laurels. An air of neglect, too, but this may only be due to the season. Perhaps these people still look after their gardens. Perhaps the English used to like gardening so much because their gardens decayed so utterly, became so completely forlorn for long stretches of the year. Everything remains in abeyance, and then the hidden opportunities uncover themselves, and later the whole vegetable world takes off, parachuting into summer.

When I was an adolescent, I used to go for huge walks alone, setting out after lunch perhaps and trying to see how far I could get. The ploughed fields and the hedges and the discrete coppices of the shires were tedious with winter. The thing was to walk out, away from home as far as one could go, knowing the obligation of getting home again. After a while one would forget the boredom, the rhythm of walking would alter one's sense of time. On and on. Trying to hurt oneself, and also trying to be missed. Adolescence was full of so many great separations, of going to boarding schools, or to the Army or overseas, that to be missed was the evidence of being loved. At the same time the absent person, merely by being absent, gives himself the chance of being worried about, remembered again and again and in the end hated. And so, as I walked those long muddy pathways by the bare hedges jarred and thrummed by the wind, I used to hate the people I was expecting to see at home, who I hoped were missing me. Yet, while hating them, I hoped they would understand the dislike was because I was testing them by absence. Then I would not only be welcomed but humored, like somebody who has been ill.

I would wait till the dusk was dying and the lights were on in the cottages. At those moments, of course, my beast was in attendance, waiting just beyond the flooded stream in the valley, or behind the broken sheds that nobody visited. If I could have confronted it then, what else might have happened? But I didn't, and I went home and nothing was said: the walls closed in and there was a smell of frying food.

For some reason this hotel reminds me of that time. We have come a very long way. We are now on the edge of Wales and I have tried to believe that it is the edge of something else. The beast would know: surely it always does? I imagine it sometimes as one of those guardian beasts outside Chinese temples. Curly and snarling, like a rampant cat or a heraldic dog, but much, much larger, hard and gleaming. Sometimes it seems to be wet with rain. It is never inside anywhere, it is outside always, the guardian beast.

My brother stubs out his cigarette. He gets up from the bed, goes to the washbasin, and with his long nicotine-stained forefinger he pulls down the lower lid of his right eye. Probably he wants to see if his eyes are bloodshot. He has been driving westward into the sunlight for much of the day, and later the headlights have tired him. He repeats this action with the other eye and I imagine that I can hear the popping sound as the lid flips back into its place. He is now satisfied. He does his teeth and spits into the basin and lets the water run. The sound of water in the pipes alongside the room blots out the sound of the river which is outside. So that at one time I am listening to the sounds of plumbing while outside the water flickers and slops over the giant stones and the beast is listening to it, alone.

Always outside, can you imagine that? When did it begin to realize that nothing was going to change? It will be there this evening, while we are dining in the timbered dining room of the hotel. Perhaps it doesn't realize what is going on. I have often thought its faithfulness due to a sort of stupidity, a deficiency in the brain. Can it see, hear or smell? Can it do anything but just exist?

My brother says: "What about dinner?"

"Yes?"

"Why don't we go and have it?"

"Why not?"

I follow him down the staircase which is ill-lit and quaintly dangerous with beams. He won't, of course, let me have a drink beforehand. I am being dealt with; powers of attorney have been taken out: he has volunteered to look after me for this bit. We emerge into an area of tapestry-covered armchairs and parchment lampshades, where some old women in knitwear are looking at television.

Poor beast, I think of you at the moment when I walk into the dining room among the napery and the Malayan waiters. Why have I come as far as this? It is only to give myself additional evidence, to prove to myself that I can still live in the contingent world, the world from which you must always be excluded. But the world never used to be like this—everything has been reconstructed, becoming a parody of what I used to know.

My brother watches me cautiously while the waiter hands me a menu. But I'm all right, I shan't let anyone down. I don't need any guardians except you. The world invades me with offers to love it.

"The grapefruit juice, the fish, the chicken."

I can hardly eat for thinking about you. These last years, there has always been such a lot going on, time passing faster and faster. Besides, there has been nowhere much for you to live. You have been very patient and have waited for me in all sorts of dark corners, on soils sour with the urine of cats, where only privet bushes can grow. And once you spent months on the black slate roof of a Victorian crescent, up there among the soot and dead pigeons, looking over the city while it rained for a whole summer. At such times, even though my thoughts were completely occupied with other problems, I had only to remember you and it was like a stiletto touching the heart.

I am still sitting opposite my brother in the dining room of this well-known hotel. He has ordered half a bottle of wine—the third cheapest—and we are drinking it. The room is warm and glistening, and couples at other tables are conversing in quiet voices while they crumble their bread. If you looked through the window (but can you look anywhere, do you even possess eyes?) you would see us in fire-lit amity. If we looked outside, surely we would see you crouching, imploring, impotent, alone.

They bring us coffee. My brother and I as usual are silent. Then immediately through that silence I feel the ache which is your summons. The river, with its crying over the stones, all the scuffling movements of the night—these are drawing nearer and nearer. The walls of the hotel are ready to crack, as though an enormous weight was leaning on them.

"Let's go."

"You haven't finished your coffee," my brother says.

"I must go."

"No. Come and have a drink."

"I don't want a drink."

"Whisky," my brother says.

"No, really."

"A large one," he says.

Tamed, after three whiskies, I sit with my brother in the bar, until the crying dwindles and dies away. The rain continues, and the sound of the water over the weir. I hate to think of the mountains, which are not far off. One day, for certain, they will fall.

Will nobody bless me? Why don't they let me touch money any more? Where am I, anyway? The beast walks into the hallway and I can hear its stone claws clicking on the floorboards. It comes in and curls up in front of the fireplace, and suddenly it goes to sleep.

# The White Stick

A platform on the District line outside London, in the fine-drawn drizzle of a January morning. No place for the infirm of purpose. Unless you have effective prayers to mutter, it is better to be sure of your destination. Few of those waiting look as if they enjoyed this certainty.

An exception, though, is Nigel Griffin, aged about thirty, with longish hair, wearing a sheepskin coat and carrying a leather briefcase. From his untidy yet somehow expensive appearance, one might conclude that he does not live in London, and also that he is not competing in the ordinary worlds of commerce or administration. Both these conclusions are correct. Griffin's wife has money; they live in an old rectory in the west country and have two children. The previous day he has signed a contract for a new book and has visited the London Library. He has just been spending the night at his sister's house in Richmond. In three-quarters of an hour, his train will leave Paddington. Camilla will be waiting for him in the car, with their younger son strapped, moist and slithery, into his harnessed seat behind her. For the Griffins the world is often inconvenient and mismanaged (*au pair* girls hate to live in the country, workmen fail to turn up after all their promises to Camilla, Griffin's books sell fewer copies than anybody admits), but they are comfortable, worried, and happy.

Griffin stares across the railway line at an advertisement for men's toiletries. Some people, whose anxieties have almost dissevered them from the corporeal world, stare straight through billboards as though into an invisible gulf beyond. When the train arrives, you expect them to fall in front of it. Yet somehow they step into it all the same. Griffin is quite different: he sees the world around him for what it is.

For example, and purely for the purpose of checking, here is a girl approaching along the platform. Griffin would notice her in any case, because her face is a surprise, being very pale and almost beautiful, and her dark chestnut hair is unfurled down to her shoulders. Vulgarity, in the tall hairdos and prancing bottoms of working-class girls, never attracts him. But he finds this romantic, pre-Raphaelite look sharply moving, perhaps because its frame is so unexpected. Why should a girl like this be wearing, even though in a slovenly, uncommitted fashion, the uniform and peaked cap of a London Transport employee?

An old man is holding on to her arm. He is swinging a white stick from side to side. The girl keeps up an animated conversation with him while they proceed up the platform. The blind man answers briefly, impatiently. He is accustomed to making use of people's kindness. Of course, he is receiving an additional benefit he is quite unaware of—he cannot see how pretty the girl is.

Griffin is standing by himself. With dismay he observes the girl's questing look. She is propelling her companion directly toward him. Griffin would like to take evasive action, but immediately he tells himself that this is impermissible. Unflinching, he holds his ground.

"Do you mind, Sir, helping him into the second carriage from the front? It's a smoker and he likes to smoke."

She smiles at him charmingly. Her menial situation is at once explained by her voice. She is Irish. Griffin, though partly Irish himself, is reminded of the fact that we increasingly depend on a population of *Untermensch*. After a century or so of industrial progress, he wonders, do we all hate too much to be able to look after one another? It could bear looking into.

"You'll be all right with this gentleman, my dear."

"Thank you."

Griffin emerges from his argument with himself and begins exchanging remarks which concern the weather. From these he learns that the blind man, too, is from outside. Probably East European, Polish or Jewish.

Griffin tries not to think that this knowledge can affect their encounter in any way. But it does. He begins to have the surely justifiable feeling that, by agreeing to help, he is correcting an imbalance in the world. Perhaps he is even compensating for some innate meanness of spirit he finds in himself and his friends. For people of his own comfortable circumstances, Griffin thinks, being English has always meant that we never took part unless we were giving the orders. Even then we chose to be voluntary spectators who could get out whenever we wanted. Griffin is standing beside someone who has never given the orders; who, at a guess, has suffered because he did not get out in time.

"You see, I am not used to make this trip. I was one time living at Edgware. Now I am coming down here. The changing at Earl's Court is difficult to me."

"I can help you, then," Griffin commits himself further by continuing: "I change at Earl's Court too. I'm going to Paddington."

"That is good, then. We are taking the same train both times."

The pupils of the blind man's eyes are just visible under the half-closed lids, and he turns towards Griffin as he speaks. This may show that his affliction is recent, or that some sight persists. It lends him humanity; he is not merely a voice speaking out of a wall of darkness.

The train rumbles to a halt in front of them. Griffin secures his bag in his left hand and takes hold of his companion, gently steering him toward the opened doors. The ferrule of the white stick, a rod for divining the solidity of the world, taps up and down, jumps excitedly and lands on the sill of the train.

"There's a seat on the left," Griffin says.

All the other passengers are solitaries, morose in their inactivity. Now Griffin is grateful for the old man's presence. He is giving him a chance to act, to be useful, to be good.

"I want smoke. You have light?"

"No, I'm afraid I don't smoke."

Griffin appeals to one of the other passengers. This man hands over a cheap lighter which Griffin is unable to activate. There is a fussy moment or two before he can steer the flame against the cigarette which juts from the blind man's mouth.

Embarrassed by his incompetence, Griffin restores the lighter to its owner.

He has the odd impression that the other passengers ought somehow to be cooperating in his good action, or at least in some way commending him for it. A sudden fantasy grips him, in which their stares are cynical and contemptuous. They all know the old man is a fraud, not blind at all, and that this stiff-necked outsider is being made a fool of. Whenever Griffin comes up to London he gets ideas like this. Without minding about it too much, he realizes that he has become unfitted for metropolitan life. The smallest incidents upset him and he exists in anguish until the time comes to return to the Old Rectory, to Camilla and the children.

The blind man has begun talking again. He is commending Griffin for not smoking. There is a girl in his office, he says, lovely girl, only twenty-eight, yet she smokes three packs a day. Often she says she would not go out to work at all, only she needs the money for smokes. Just imagine it!

Griffin is aware of having heard of this girl before. She seems to have been employed in half the offices in London. The old man's voice betrays the peculiar shocked avidness with which the girl is usually mentioned; it is as though she were guilty of accommodating the whole board of directors during her lunch hour.

For himself, though, the blind man tells Griffin, smoking is one of his few pleasures. That, and the radio. Classical music, of course.

While he is talking, the ash of his cigarette falls and crumbles on the front of his overcoat. Griffin wonders whether it is part of his job to dust him down. Suddenly, however, a withered hand comes up and shakes the front of the coat clean. The awareness that this suggests is a bit disconcerting. It indicates in the blind man an insistent will, pushing at the borders of darkness.

In addition, he recites the name of each station as the train stops. He is always correct. At Earl's Court, he announces, the other train will be waiting. And, without a doubt, there it is.

This sort of thing never happens to Griffin. The working intelligentsia, the class in which he mockingly includes himself, can never give the material world its proper meed of attention. It keeps taking its revenge on them for this. The blind man can conjure up trains, whereas Griffin himself has the greatest difficulty in catching one.

Then, as though to throw doubt on all this, the train opposite stirs a little, threatening to leave without them. But it merely seems to be easing itself into a more comfortable position. Griffin has moved into action, again gripping his bag in his left hand and steering the old man with his right. Again the white stick ticks away, as though it had discovered precious metal in the black concrete under their feet, and in a moment they are across the platform and installed in the new train. They sit side by side, panting a little. Thanks to Griffin, all is well.

Then abruptly the whole pleasant picture disintegrates.

The blind man clutches his sides with his hands and shouts out: "My briefcase!"

"Briefcase?"

"It is on the other train. Hurry!"

Griffin steps back on to the platform to see the first train sliding away.

He returns to find his companion in a state of shock.

"Oh dear! Oh dear!" These hopelessly weak words of protest show that the old man is unused to employing English in situations of chagrin or despair. Soon he is muttering in another language, Polish or Yiddish.

Griffin watches him with apprehension. He is fairly sure that in a moment or two the blind man will start accusing him. For him, it would be the natural thing to do. He remembers the pretty Irish girl at Richmond. She would not have let the blind man down. Nor would Camilla. Women excel at such small responsibilities.

"What train was it? Where was it going?"

"Tower Hill."

"Oh dear, oh dear. Many stations for stopping. Somebody will take my briefcase."

Griffin can think of nothing helpful to say. He is dumbfounded by his inadequacy.

The old man mutters a little and goes on: "Already I lost one umbrella on this train. I telephone and telephone again, and after one week they are still saying, 'No, it has not arrived yet.' A new umbrella, mind you. And now, my briefcase."

"Were there important papers in it?"

"Papers? What papers? It was good leather, I tell you, not so new, but good."

"Perhaps they will find out who it belongs to, from the papers in it."

The blind man is not listening. "Aie, aie. The same thing was happening with one pair of gloves, quite new."

This list is beginning to preclude sympathy. To warm his feelings up again, Griffin tries to imagine the distance between Richmond and Bayswater where the old man is getting off, as a dark corridor full of angles. But warmth of feeling is no use now. In a few moments the train will arrive at Bayswater. How can Griffin recover his good action in time?

It is impossible. The old man has fallen into the hands of a false Samaritan. What he needed was one of those types whom Nature designed to take charge at awkward moments: men who organize streams of traffic after a mishap on the road; who guide articulated trucks into the narrowest of turnings; who, ambulant in dressing-gowns, assume control in the public wards of hospitals.

Bayswater station. For the last time (the encounter seems to have been going on for hours) Griffin helps the old man to his feet. He does this with a little less care, perhaps, for his assistance is now completely devalued. To recover anything, Griffin would have to lead the blind man up the stairs and out into the street. This would mean losing his own train at Paddington, Camilla would be kept waiting another hour, and Marcus would miss his afternoon sleep. One should be careful before embarking upon good actions. Egoism is better; at least you do no damage.

And now Griffin is launching the blind man into emptiness, like a little blank-faced owl which cannot fly. They shake hands.

They cannot say they are pleased to have met each other, because it is not true.

On the Bayswater platform, the blind man stands alone. But only for about ten seconds. The tapping of the white stick immediately attracts the attention of a man who has got off the same train. Wearing a blue anorak, with glasses and a cruel hair cut, he looks like a schoolmaster. Obviously this is the right guide to take charge of the blind man and lead him wherever it is he wants to go. Griffin slinks back into the carriage. He remains standing until the train reaches Paddington.

He is feeling a bit battered by the whole business. Yet his mind still makes retrospective efforts to help or atone. He tries to imagine the lost briefcase, to conjure it into existence again. First of all he summons up the pretty Irish girl approaching down the platform toward him. He can see the girl's pale skin and her uncoiled hair. And there is the old man, with his white stick held in his right hand, searching to and fro. His left arm is linked to the girl. How can he be carrying a briefcase? Quite clearly, he has left it at home.

Griffin tries peering more closely at this image that he has resurrected. Can't he just make out the briefcase, wedged in some fashion under the arm that is holding the white stick? No, he cannot. At least, he is not going to attempt it. Or is the girl perhaps holding it in her free hand, ready to give it back to the old man? Griffin's imagination fails to get beyond the girl's face, and he is content to let it fail. The exercise is over. He has given his imagination sufficient leash for it to retrieve his honor. What it has brought back in its slack jaws is not much, but it is something. It will have to be enough.

While thinking in this way, Griffin has proceeded, without noticing, right across Paddington Station, through the ticket barrier and onto the platform, where the train for the west is waiting. He has already bought the weekly reviews. He easily secures a corner seat in a first-class carriage. He has only to sit back now, to be delivered to his family. London lies behind him, the city of confusion, where the billboards hide gulfs, where one walks untrusting and untrustworthy among visible realities, like a blind man down a dark corridor without an end.

# *Love to Patsy*

She approached him with such a kind humorous sparkle in her eye that he thought for a moment that they had already met somewhere, that he knew and had forgotten her, and ought to be concerned about it.

Here he was in someone's house in the country; his sister, who had brought him here, had told him the name of his host and hostess, but it had escaped him. Those two fine children, owl-eyed and with bright fox-colored hair, obviously belonged to them. There were about a dozen people in the drawing room, which was pleasantly warm. Outside were bare trees, a glimpse of lawns blackened by winter, and cars parked down the drive.

One of the children came around with a plate of little things like owl pellets to eat. He took one nervously. It was extremely good minced meat, strongly spiced, rather Greek in taste. He tried to grab another, but the fox-child had already gone.

"Your sister told me who you were," she said. "I must introduce myself."

Her eyes were gray, large, very bright. Everyone in the room seemed to know her, and to want to talk to her. She wanted to talk to him, and what could be better, on a winter Sunday morning, with cars parked in the drive, and rooks blown about the sky? He supposed her to be in the late thirties; not really attractive, but happy, unsubdued. Yes, attractive. She would be the one to bring him, however temporarily, into the tone of the gathering. (But in the long run this would be created by sherry and gin and tonic, and later you'd hear cars started with violence, brakes squealing, and there'd be the tenseness of wives trying hard not to offer to drive home. But not yet, not yet—the time was only half past twelve.)

"I felt I simply had to talk to you," she went on, "because I know you know the Wickershams."

"Yes, of course I do."

He eased himself more comfortably against the chimney-piece. He felt that with this nice woman it would be easy to carry on a conversation about acquaintances. He hadn't caught her name, either, He wondered, without really bothering, which of the large booming husbands on the other side of the room belonged to her.

"Do tell me, how are they?"

"Flourishing as always."

When he thought about the Wickershams, who lived in London, he was reminded of the hymn that ends: "There beside my Father's throne, I shall know as I am known." The Wickershams were known, but they didn't know. People mentioned the Wickershams but they didn't, on the whole, mention people. They were a tall rather lank couple, distracted and elegant. When you were with them, they talked about you, because you were what they were dealing with then. And they always ended the conversation first, put down the telephone first; they never rang you, you rang them. They were remote and, since he had known them for some time, he knew that they had reasons for remoteness. It was strange that this nice friendly woman should know them as well.

"I haven't seen them for ages," she went on.

And suddenly he lost most of his equanimity. He saw danger ahead, fences, water jumps, elephant traps.

She had lost touch with the Wickershams, she told him, when her husband had been stationed abroad for five years. Abroad was a new subject, and he tried to deflect her on to it. However, it turned out to be some middle section of Africa he knew nothing about. In any case she was intent on getting back to the Wickershams.

"We all used to go to Positano, quite early, before everyone went there. We had marvelous times because John knows everything about Italy."

"He's written two books about it."

"We've got them at home somewhere."

"You're lucky. There are extremely few copies around."

She laughed at this. "Patsy was a great, great friend. She was quite lovely. I expect she still is. The boy was the same age as our eldest."

This was the first hurdle. John Wickersham's wife was called Victoria and had been for several years.

"Do they still live in Fulham?"

"It's Campden Hill Square now."

She nodded, appreciating this as part of John Wickersham's merited progress. In fact, of course, it was his second wife's money.

He accepted another drink. By his silence, he had suppressed the truth, and he was not going to be able to go back on it. It had been an instinctive choice, timorous and wrong. Yet otherwise their conversation, all right according to the not very high standards of before lunch on Sundays, would have become awful. Everyone else was talking about central heating or rosebushes. He had absolutely no luck.

"Does Patsy still paint?"

"Patsy?" he said, looking hard into his glass. "I haven't heard."

"You haven't heard?"

"I mean, not any exhibitions or anything."

"She never used to exhibit. She always sold privately."

She watched him intently and he could feel her beginning to have doubts about him.

Damn it, couldn't she accept that she was in a category of protected people? No shooting on Sundays, not in this part of the world, in commuting distance of London. It was not Renaissance

Florence, but in its own way it was not uncivilized: it could probably cope with much more human pain than one gave it credit for. But not before lunch on Sundays. After all, she probably had to go back and cook. Or at any rate go down on her nicely rounded haunches and fish the food out of the oven.

"We have one of her early things at home. A small landscape."

They had been in Africa when it happened, of course, and knew nothing. In any case, these things are easy to miss, and probably it hadn't even been in the newspapers. He wondered how she would react if he told her. There was the image of the dead child, the death of children being pretty much the absolute for human frightfulness.

"Ross-on-Wye," he said aloud, not thinking.

"What was that?" She observed him with a marked detachment. Perhaps she thought he was drunk.

"Nothing. I was trying to remember something about John."

"The Wickershams are a Suffolk family," she told him in a precise, distant way. "It was the Suffolk churches that started him off on Art History."

"I didn't know."

"He studied at the Courtauld Institute, of course."

"I knew that."

She relented. "You know I'd really love to see them all again. Edmund must be eleven now. He is the same age as Amanda. Have they any more?"

"No more."

She looked puzzled at this. She won't ask for their address, he thought. She realizes it has been too long, far too long. She thinks of John and Patsy as continuing elsewhere, step by step, as she and her husband have been continuing. Whereas Patsy has come to the end. When all the business about Victoria started, Patsy took Edmund to a hotel in Ross-on-Wye, or perhaps it was Hereford, and killed him with sleeping pills, and tried to kill herself. Luckily she died in the hospital. People said that she was mad. Absolutely nothing can be gained from anyone knowing this now.

"Please give my love to them when you see them."

"Of course I will."

"I know you probably think we're all suburban down here, and Patsy will not want to hear. But she will. So please tell her."

"Of course."

As she left him, she gave a funny little grimace. Either she didn't believe in him at all, or she thought he was being difficult and pretentious.

Oh, nice Mrs. Er—what was her name?—he addressed her retreating back, you will never realize how I have been protecting you from unhappiness. Because of me, you'll be able to eat a good lunch, with your nice booming husband, and the children too, if you haven't packed them off to boarding schools. I'm presenting you with this afternoon, for leafing through the *Sunday Express* and tidying in the garden and taking the spaniels for a run. All this has been in my gift, and I've bestowed it upon you with all the grace I could manage, which admittedly wasn't a great deal. Yet you're offended with me—you think I'm unfriendly and superior.

Then his sister came up and told him they were leaving.

He said good-bye to half the people in the room, the ones he had spoken to, and this involved saying "hullo" to the other half, the ones he hadn't spoken to before. Nearly at the door, he caught up with her again. She was talking to his sister.

She frowned and said to him quite crossly: "Now please don't forget, my best love to Patsy."

"Yes, of course," he said. "Of course."

# A Ghost Garden

The biographer Bamford Chetwynd immediately chose the best room in the house as a study and work room. Its window overlooked the entire garden, as far as a stream lined with water flags and alder trees and the white wooden bridge that led to the village. The room was apart, but it was not isolated. Susan Vincent, the biographer's lifelong friend, was a dedicated gardener, and as she bent over newly planted pentstemons or encouraged *Clematis tangutica* to ascend a stone wall, she would be able to hear the tapping of the typewriter. In the stone-flagged kitchen, she would hear the heavy tread of the biographer in the room overhead, the footsteps pacing to and fro in search of the phrases that would bring months of research to an ordered conclusion.

In fact, Midsomer Cottage was Susan Vincent's property. Bamford Chetwynd had published a string of books, all excellently reviewed in the "quality" Sunday newspapers. These were devoted to the lives of redoubtable French ladies, Madame de Maintenon, Madame de Sévigné and Madame de Staël—"Enough madams," their New York publisher remarked, "to run a whole street in New Orleans." Even with American sales, however, the total royalties were hardly sufficient to keep the author in cigars and brandy. It was Susan Vincent, sole daughter of a successful brickmaker, who had provided the financial background for all this creative effort. Throughout the years she had listened for the typewriter and, hearing it, had been content, knowing that dear "Bam" was at work again.

When Susan Vincent told people that she had bought the Wiltshire house because she longed to create a garden of her own, her friends guessed that this was only one reason. In recent years Bam had become increasingly addicted to the more accessible forms of London society, putting in regular appearances at publishers' parties, meetings of the PEN club, Arts Council receptions and lectures at the Royal Society of Literature. Wearing a cloak, a velvet suit, and a fedora hat, the biographer was a conspicuous figure. Oldish, much-educated young men, many of whom were called Simon, had come to regard Bamford Chetwynd as something between a joke and a cult object. "Life-enhancing," they said. "Bam's so life-enhancing." Just keeping life enhanced had cost Susan Vincent a good deal of money, and the strain had even begun to tell on Bamford Chetwynd: more and more, the dashing Regency Buck of past years had come to suggest a retired jockey too fond of the bottle. The force of the biographer's attack had always been mitigated by shortness of stature. A devoted friend, an Oxford don, had once compared Bam to "a bust of Radclyffe Hall, walking."

Susan Vincent was a gentle creature, tall and stooping, with large strong hands and an odd, wild glint in her eyes. Looking after Bam no longer gave her sufficient purpose in life, and seeing the garden at Midsomer Cottage for the first time, she had felt a lift of the heart. The countryside around was fertile, the trees in the parkland grew tall and the stream had deposited centuries of rich dark soil. The local people were great gardeners, and from early summer their herbaceous borders shocked the retina with a violent clash of colors. Miss Vincent's plans were for something very different. She held Gertrude Jekyll in high esteem, and Mrs. Fish, the goddess of "ground cover." But most of all she invoked Victoria Sackville-West of Sissinghurst.

By autumn, house and garden were hers. Still in the London flat, she started ordering plants from the best nurseries. A stroke of fortune took Bam to Paris for research. Rejoicing in her solitude, Miss Vincent got into her sports car and headed westward. She put up at the King's Arms in the nearest country town. When her purchases arrived, she went to work in the garden, planting according to a plan she had drawn up on squared paper. The days were sunny, the work went well, and she was happy, laughing and talking to herself as she encouraged the tangled roots into the black loam. "Vita, Vita," she murmured to herself, "I honor you in my breaches and my observances." And she began to have visions of opening the garden to the public, in a year or two's time, in aid of the District Nurses.

From the house during these still October days there emerged the constant sound of transistor radios. Two workmen were busy building fitted cupboards and putting up shelves. Soon they would start papering and painting. Miss Vincent, who got on well with men and liked their presence, took to making innumerable cups of Indian tea. During the next weeks she learned a great deal about the lives of Sydney and Kevin. Kevin was a golden-haired young man whose body had been burnt dark by the summer sun. But his physical beauty was accompanied by a marked unease, and Miss Vincent found him frustrated and confessional. It turned out that Charlene his wife suffered from gynecological complications which the village doctor refused to explain, considering the young couple too ignorant to understand.

But it was Sydney Woods who won Miss Vincent's heart. Sydney was forty, smaller than Kevin, and there was something compact and controlled about him that reminded Miss Vincent of her father the brickmaker. The physical world obeyed Sydney; while the radio shrilled to the Top Twenty, she watched his paintbrush move silkily across doors and wainscoting. He seemed to know everything she needed to know at this time. After a little she began to rejoice in Sydney, as she rejoiced in the new house and the future garden.

There remained two problems to worry her.

The first was that Sydney, too, was a great gardener. Whenever a new consignment of plants arrived, he stood beside her while she unpacked them.

"They'll never answer," he said. "Not in our soil."

And to compensate for what he saw as her inevitable failure, he kept offering great clumps of delphinium and goldenrod or the bulbs of dahlias, like the dry feces of dogs. "They'll give you a proper show," he said. It was quite useless telling him about the white garden at Sissinghurst. The same thing happened with vegetables: his cabbages, the size of footballs, and his scarlet runners, as sinewy as his own arms, won prizes at the Flower Show every year. How could she explain to him that she and Bam, travelers in France and Italy, considered such prodigies to be entirely inedible?

Miss Vincent's second problem was that all this warmth and complicity must come to an end. Soon the house would be ready, soon there would be the delivery of the furniture and pictures, and after that the advent of Bam. Long ago Bam's friend Simon had helped them to find amusing nonsenses at the London auctions, and some of these had turned out to be of value. They had bought gilded furniture, some Victoriana, and pictures by young painters who were now either dead or famous.

On the day when the moving men had come and gone, Sydney and Kevin dropped in to help Miss Vincent tidy up. Sydney inspected everything in a bristling silence. He kept looking at her and his look was very odd and disquieting. It seemed to involve pity, though she could not be sure of this. There was nothing she could say.

Kevin, on the other hand, was entirely fascinated, and she offered to give him a guided tour of the house. "Only for Charlene," he said, "I'd have liked to go in for this sort of line." As he was leaving, he talked more about Charlene, whose operation was to take place the following week. Miss Vincent felt a sudden sympathetic throb in her own barren tubes. Unwillingly she revived a childhood memory of Florry, an adored golden retriever whom Father had ordered spayed, and who had died at the hands of a drunken vet.

Bam arrived the following Saturday, brought down by Simon and his new friend, who were spending the weekend at a very grand house some thirty miles farther west. Simon and his friend approved of Midsomer Cottage; they planned parties, *fêtes champêtres*, for the new garden in the summer.

That evening, while she was cooking Spanish omelettes, Miss Vincent found herself praying that Sydney would not choose this moment to put in an appearance. Of course, he would be certain to confront Bam sooner or later, but she wanted something of the pleasure of these past weeks to be prolonged for yet another day.

Sydney never set eyes on Bam. That night he was killed on his motorbike at the corner where the lane from the village joined the main road. Mrs. Weller, the daily whom Miss Vincent had just found, arrived on Monday morning with her features set in dramatic gloom. Momentarily discomfited by the fact that Miss Vincent had already heard the news, Mrs. Weller looked around for something disobliging to say about Sydney; a newcomer to the village mustn't be allowed to get the upper hand.

"They say," she remarked loftily, "they say he was drunk. He and Mrs. Woods wasn't getting along too well."

Miss Vincent turned around from the sink in tears. "Oh Mrs. Weller," she said, "he was such a nice man."

She kept remembering Sydney through the idle days of winter, when there was little to do in the garden. The earth was quiet, full of promises for the spring. Though she trusted her own skills, there was always some doubt as to what would flourish, what would need cherishing, and what would die out without trace. In the upper room overlooking the garden, Bamford Chetwynd's biography of Madame Dudevant, otherwise known as George Sand, was proceeding well. Parcels of books arrived from the London Library, and the postman brought letters and photostats from distant collections. Meanwhile, the stream overflowed into the water garden and some of the new *Iris Kaempferi* were lost.

One day Kevin turned up. He was dying to tell Miss Vincent that Charlene and he had been accepted as adoptive parents of a little girl. Unfortunately that morning she was out shopping in the county town.

She returned to find Bam stumping up and down in fury. "I told him to go about his business, whatever that might be." A cigar butt flew through the window into the sleeping garden. "We're not interested in having squalling brats around. Not content with spawning their own, the lower orders now take in other people's bastards."

Susan Vincent was quite horrified. What would the whole village think? Then she reflected that, except for herself, no one, not even the Simons, had ever taken Bam seriously. The monocle, the fedora, the cloak had by now given way to National Health spectacles and jeans and sweaters from a local menswear department, yet the total impression remained gently ludicrous.

Spring came at last. Color returned first to the willows along the stream. New shoots appeared in the flower beds under the windows.

"I see you got a nice lot of daffs around." Mrs. Weller remarked. "They'll make a lovely show later on."

"No, no, they're not daffodils. At least, they're the same family, but special ones. I saw them first at Wisley."

Since Bamford Chetwynd had been around, people had begun to look at Miss Vincent with kindly pity. "They seem just like ordinary daffs to me, dear, but you know best."

A few weeks later, Miss Vincent asked Mrs. Weller: "Were there daffodils here last year?"

"Not a thing. You remember I told you, those lot never planted a thing. Everyone passed comments."

Miss Vincent wrote to the bulb merchants, who denied the possibility of a mistake. By this time the garden was as full of bright yellow as the others in the village.

Bamford Chetwynd was scathing. "Daffodils always remind me of urine."

The other kept her temper. "You mean dandelions."

Bam snorted and returned to Madame Dudevant's affairs.

By midsummer the garden was a total disaster; it looked like something off a cheap calendar, or a picture to be cross-stiched on a tea cosy. No sooner had puce aubretia and yellow alyssum done their worst than pillar-box red poppies hurt the eyes, clashing with the hard orange of marigolds. Delphiniums and dahlias were on the way. Among the vegetables, the carefully selected variety of French beans turned out to be scarlet runners, the courgettes swelled into vegetable marrows fit only for harvest festivals or ginger jam. Purple kohlrabi produced a comment from Mrs. Weller: "You've a nice row of swedes there. Should see you right through the winter."

Susan Vincent resigned herself and tended these monstrosities diligently. She knew there was some disorder, some primal fault in the makeup of things, but she did not protest. Like herself, the garden was a prey to forces that she flinched from trying to understand. Sydney Woods had won her heart and was proclaiming his triumph; everything was just as he would have wanted it.

Simon, passing through with a new friend, said: "It's quite wonderful, Vince. It's all so marvelously—" He stopped short, since the word he was about to utter was no longer at all fashionable. His friend Rodney, a hairdresser from Mitcham, was less inhibited.

"It's so camp, Vince," he said. "You've got the first camp garden!"

A year had passed since her first meeting with Sydney, and he seemed to be always closer to her. It seemed as though the house had been blessed: dripping taps had righted themselves; a window, found to be stuck, opened easily the following morning. Then he came nearer still. Sometimes in the garden she smelled smoke. It was neither a bonfire nor the unmistakable whiff of Bamford Chetwynd's cigars; she recognized the Player's Weights that Sydney always used. And other smells followed: the tweed of his old jacket, the sweat of his buttoned undershirt—unlike Kevin, he had never stripped down to work.

Miss Vincent knew well that odors are among the most frequent of hallucinations. But now to them were added snatches of pop music from unseen radios and the brisk whine of a Black & Decker drill. She would dart from room to room in search of him, and then rest, with her eyes closed, her forehead against the doorjamb.

She wondered whether she should consult a doctor. This meant going outside the village, and she was fearful of arousing Bam's suspicions. As it happened, the biographer was in a creative fury: Madame Dudevant had the unfortunate habit of falling for young men; in each case, new evidence had to be found to show that the affair might possibly have remained unconsummated.

Miss Vincent met Kevin in the village, in great excitement because he and his wife had just been to bring home their adopted daughter. He offered to bring the baby for her to see, and that evening he and Charlene came across the bridge pushing a glittering new pram. Pulling off her gardening gloves, she went across to meet them, but always at her back she felt the baleful gaze of Bam at the window of the workroom.

Charlene, a thin-faced girl with dragonfly glasses, handed over the small sour-smelling bundle. Miss Vincent was surprised to discover an instinctive skill at holding babies. She felt full of love for the baby, and for Kevin and Charlene. When she compared them with Bam and the Simons, she was shaken by a sense of the incompleteness of her world.

Kevin asked if Charlene might see around the house.

"Of course. Come along."

As she took them upstairs, the sound of the typewriter suddenly ceased. Silence oozed under the workroom door: it was almost, she thought, as though one were harboring something like the Glamis monster.

When Kevin and Charlene left, Susan Vincent sat in an armchair with her eyes closed. She had a vision of herself free and alone at Midsomer Cottage, a gruff, gardening spinster perhaps, but on friendly terms with all the village. There must be further Kevins and Charlenes to confide in here, more and more damp babies for her to hold, even perhaps other Sydneys for her to know. He was very close to her now; she even felt that, somehow, he was watching her.

She opened her eyes. It was Bam, furious and drunk.

"How dare you! How dare you bring those appalling louts trampling around the house! It's as though you deliberately wished to destroy my work."

"Kevin wanted his wife to see it, that's all."

"*Kevin!* I can't make out what's come over you. Are you ill? You seem besotted with these peasants."

"No, I'm not ill. They're a nice young couple. I like them."

"It's him, isn't it? You fancy him, don't you? You'd like him to fuck you. After all we've stood for. That's how it's ended."

"Nothing has ended."

"You've shown not the slightest interest in this new book I'm doing. You've made no effort to understand my work. You've changed all right, and you think I don't know why." Bam emitted a sudden, rasping sniff. "You never even call me Bambino anymore."

Miss Vincent did not answer, but she gave an odd wild laugh, like a tropical bird.

A frequent desire after such incidents is to stare at one's own face, to make sure that one is still the same person that one was before.

In the downstairs lavatory the smell of cigarettes was overpowering. The seat was up, the water in the bowl bright orange, with bubbles still breaking at the edge, and a cigarette end lazily unfurling at the center.

Miss Vincent closed her eyes. Her hand felt for the plug and pulled. A rush of waters put an end to the vision.

"Sydney," she whispered. "Sydney, where are you?"

Two days later she drove Bamford Chetwynd to London Airport. The biographer was silent, still sniffish, in spite of Vince's fat check to cover the expenses of a prolonged stay in Paris.

"You've been overworking," Miss Vincent had said firmly, thus throwing the ball into Bam's court.

At the airport, no deep embraces were exchanged, only the dry pecks of custom. She watched the biographer stump off down the ramp, a small, stout, offended figure.

And then she drove home down the old road, so that she passed Stonehenge just as the afternoon light was shining in long rays through the standing stones. Then Silbury Hill, across Salisbury Plain, and down the long slope of England toward Midsomer Cottage. She passed park gates and long stone walls; she drove wildly among falling leaves and rocketing pheasants.

Ahead of her lay Eden, with the serpent banished. The garden waited: what had he prepared for her for the coming year? The cottage had been exorcised; the unquiet being had departed, the benevolent spirit remained.

She unlocked the door. A radio was playing one of last year's pop tunes. For the first time, she heard footsteps.

She lay down on the sofa. "Sydney," she whispered. "Sydney."

# *Live Bait*

I

You travel southward toward the channel shore: there are petrol stations at intervals, council estates, a builder's yard, a used-tire depot, industrialized farmland. In patches of woodland, sign-posts at the ends of drives point to special schools, private nursing homes. Some show the headquarters of dubious-sounding companies or institutes: the large ugly mansions resound with the rattle of typewriters and the slow scythe-like rhythms of photocopying machines.

Long ago a house like this would shelter a different life, a life which was undergone in heavily furnished drawing rooms, bathrooms where taps poured out scalding niagaras, kitchens where food was fiercely boiled on enormous ranges. In the dining room, the mahogany sideboard smelled of pepper and Harvey's sauce, and contained a blue-glass bottle of indigestion mixture: "The Hon. Mrs. Peverill, to be taken as required."

Even then, families were getting smaller, visitors from outside were fewer. Daughters and sons-in-law were likely to be in India, in Bermuda, in Hong Kong. Grandchildren appeared for school holidays, but for them there were fewer suitable friendships available—the wrong sort of child might quite easily get invited to a children's party.

Of two boys bicycling one morning to Braxby Place, one belonged to this category. Andrew, small for his age, which was thirteen, was snub-nosed, crooked, and guilty. Jeremy, his companion, was altogether easier to commend, a handsome boy with blond hair and a milky complexion. The Peverills were distant connections of his mother; this was sufficient to allow him to approach the house without apprehension.

The drive was nearly half a mile long. For the first part the boys rode between cliffs of rhododendrons and conifers, where it was still damp and chill in the early morning. Then they came out into parkland. Oaks and horse chestnuts stood at intervals, and between them there was the flash of water.

The lake, which must long ago have been a stone quarry, was hidden among woods and outcrops of rock. They lost sight of it again as the drive went uphill. Neither of the boys liked to be the first to get off and walk. Andrew's bike was a woman's, which belonged to his mother. He was careful to mount and dismount in the masculine fashion, even though this sometimes hurt. Standing upright on the pedals, he zigzagged to and fro, dodging away from the trimmed edges, until he got to the top of the slope. There he waited for Jeremy who, in spite of his low-curved handlebars and three-speed gear, was usually first to start walking. They saw pergolas covered with climbing roses, clumps of pampas grass, a monkey-puzzle tree, and then the house, of glazed brick, turreted, and with mullioned windows. There was a line of plate-glass windows to a winter garden, where blinds were already pulled down against the morning sunlight.

"Shouldn't we go around to the back?" Andrew asked.

"Of course not." Jeremy pulled the bell handle. They were still a bit winded by the ascent, and against the noise of their breathing they could hear the bell ringing far away and then the muffled opening and closing of doors, the slow approach of heavy feet.

"I've come about fishing in the lake."

"Mr. Jeremy Cathcart is it, sir? Yes, we're expecting you." The butler turned a large, purplish face toward the other.

"I'm his friend."

The butler switched back to Jeremy: "Mrs. Peverill asked you to come up for tea at half past four, sir."

"Please thank her and say I'll come. By the way, which is the best way to the lake?"

The butler pointed out the path. "You can leave your bicycle in the stables."

"Thank you." Jeremy's voice to people like that was taut and high-pitched.

While Andrew listened he realized that, against the excitement of fishing in the lake, there would be the dull anxiety about what he should do at teatime. Should he bicycle home by himself, or slope off into the shrubbery and wait for Jeremy to emerge? He knew he was saddled with some intangible burden that people like Jeremy did not possess.

In the stable yard, the boys leaned their bicycles against a wall and unstrapped the rods and fishing bags. A man who had been hammering something came to a doorway and pointed the way down to the lake.

"Good luck," he said. "There's a big jack down there."

"How big?" Andrew asked.

"Must be all of twenty pounds."

Jeremy thanked the man in the same high voice he had used to the butler. He led the way down a cart track.

Andrew followed him. He felt deaf. Twenty pounds: the man's words had caused a sort of minor explosion in his head. Suddenly the sky was lower and the air had grown darker. The smell of crushed vegetation was strong and heavy, and some gilded flies were buzzing upward from a dead bird. The track went downhill sharply and under some beech trees it opened out at the shore of the lake. The big pike was waiting like something in time rather than place: it was a sort of dread, like the anticipation of being swished at school, or the holidays approaching their end, only there was wild pleasure in it as well.

A wooden jetty projected a few yards out, surrounded by water lily leaves. A moorhen took off suddenly, skittering over the leaves, and settled fretfully among some undergrowth.

Andrew put down his rod and bag and walked out along the

jetty. Halfway along some of the boards were missing; he knelt down and could make out some small fish circling slowly in the shafts of light going down into deep water. He went on to the end of the jetty. The lake stretched for about two hundred yards, the surface mostly packed with water lily leaves. On the opposite side birch trees grew on a rocky outcrop; from a cave underneath you could just distinguish the prow of a rowboat sticking out. Nearer, a shoal of small fish flipped through the surface, followed by a broad gulping swirl of water. A pike was feeding, probably a small one. To get out there you would need stronger tackle than any they had with them; live bait and hooks with wire traces; and, most of all perhaps, the boat which lay in the cave across the lake.

A rattling sound distracted him: Jeremy was peeing into some dock leaves beside the path. Andrew went and unbuttoned beside him. He watched his steam rising off the leaves.

Jeremy shuddered and stopped. "We'll both have to fish off the jetty," he said.

"It looks jolly good," Andrew said. Impatience made him button up too quickly, so that the last drops trickled warm and sore on the inside of his thigh.

The gardener's news of the big pike forced him to keep a check on his eagerness. He would not be allowed to come here without Jeremy, and Jeremy could very easily get bored with him and with fishing in the lake. Later in the holidays, Jeremy would go to relations who lived in Ireland, where there'd be trout and salmon, and perhaps some rough shooting. The number of claims Andrew could make was limited; he was not even Jeremy's best friend at school.

When the hook was baited with a worm and the float sitting upright beyond the lily leaves, Andrew felt at ease in the continual mild excitement that came from fishing and from being alive. Of course there would always be a gulf of apprehension ahead. If he avoided thinking about what he would do this afternoon, while Jeremy was having tea at the house, then there was next term to think about, when he would sit the entrance scholarship to his Public School. It had been implied that, if he failed, he would be cast into some sort of outer darkness, and his mother would be disappointed and weep. Nobody had ever explained why this had to happen; why it was that Jeremy, for instance, should proceed to Harrow without trouble, having been put down for the school at his birth.

By mid-afternoon, he knew Jeremy was growing restive. They had caught four perch, and had eaten the sandwiches and fruit they had brought with them. The sun was straight ahead of them. A wood pigeon dived and soared in the empty air over the lake.

There was a splash nearby. "That was a pike," Jeremy said. "A monster pike."

Andrew opened his eyes and saw the core of Jeremy's apple floating in circles of water.

He was appalled at this breach of the conventions, but knew better than to protest.

"Let's explore around the other side," he suggested.

They fought their way through a thicket of rhododendrons, and emerged on to a path which led down to the boathouse. At the bottom of some steps, slippery with moss, there was an iron gate. The boat, with the oars shipped in it, could be seen just beyond it. The boys shook the gate, but it was locked.

"We need the key."

"I suppose I could ask them at the house," Jeremy said.

"Could you? That would be super."

Jeremy seemed less confident suddenly. "I could try."

The path went around the lake through two tunnels in the rock and ended up near the jetty. Coming back there was comforting, an arrival at a place already known.

"I must go up to tea," Jeremy said. "They'll be waiting for me."

## II

Andrew lurked under some elders near a potting shed, where lawn mowers had been emptied through the years. He was used to lurking: there was a lot of time to waste at school or in the holidays, and there were other times when it was better to keep out of people's sight. He had a great experience of damp corners by broken sheds, of hollows full of bedsprings and buckets without bottoms, and of streams littered with empty tins. In such places he pondered the possibility of hiding himself completely, of keeping absolutely still, blending with the background, taking on a protective coloration like a bird or an animal. He tried this now for a time, but got bored; the only person to find him would be the friendly gardener who had told them about the big pike.

He picked up a dry elder twig and began digging into the pile of rotten grass cuttings. It was full of worms, the active ones with brown and yellow rings which are best for fishing. However, he had left his bait tin with the bicycles. He was wondering whether to go for it, which would have meant coming into view of the windows of the house, when he received a blow on his left shoulder.

He yelped, and turned around. It was Jeremy Cathcart.

"I've been told to fetch you. You're expected too."

Andrew wiped his hands on his trousers. "Jesus."

"Yes, come on." Jeremy jerked his head and led the way. Andrew followed him at an undignified stumble.

Andrew had never seen anybody quite so old as the small old woman who was sitting in a basket chair in the winter garden. Her white hair was drawn tightly back, and her hands and forehead were deeply spotted like a seagull's egg. She wore a dark gray dress with a lace front, and a circular cairngorm brooch on a black ribbon around her neck.

"Let me see him," Mrs. Peverill said. "He'll have to come closer."

He was accustomed to soft, smiling old women who doted and said silly things. This one, however, looked at him without apparent friendliness.

"Yer Jeremy's friend?"

"Yes, that's right."

"What's yer father do?"

"He's in the Air Force. In Egypt."

"That used not to be well thought of, as a career."

The man standing beside her said: "That would hardly enter into it, Mother."

The man, who looked very nearly as old as Mrs. Peverill

herself, smiled broadly at Andrew, who smiled back with an attempt at confidence.

"They had better sit down," Mrs. Peverill said. "Get me a cup of tea," she added to her son.

Major Peverill walked across to the table. He was a tall old man, wearing a gray tweed knickerbocker suit, with ribbed stockings and garter-tabs. The back of his neck was wispy, with a smile of flesh above the collar.

"Tea for them too."

"What's happened to Burgess?"

"I told him to go and find Rowena. Nurse Partridge thought she might come down."

"Is this a—a wise departure?"

"What?"

"Rowena's descent among us."

Mrs. Peverill drank some tea and dabbed at her mouth with a handkerchief. "She knows Jeremy. From children's parties." She replaced her cup and stared at Andrew.

"The Air Force," she said with sudden scorn. "Times change, I suppose."

The cups rattled continuously in the saucers, as Major Peverill handed the boys their tea. Andrew tried hard to return his smile.

"The little wretch keeps grinning at me," Major Peverill muttered angrily.

Jeremy kicked Andrew under the table. Andrew sat with his eyes lowered. He felt his face heating up and a terrifying desire to giggle. Major Peverill had not been smiling at him at all; he suffered from a tightening of the facial muscles which gave him protruding eyes and this fixed grimace. Viewed from the side, the old man's head was like a bird's: an ostrich, an emu, or a cassowary. In a magazine his mother took, Andrew had seen an advertisement with a sketch of a bird's grinning head, which asked "Can you change my expression?" If you could, using the smallest number of lines, you were offered free tuition by world-famous, but unnamed, artists.

Major Peverill was like this bird; he should have been smiling cheerfully but he looked tense and ruffled with his feathery wisps of hair. Could he, or anyone, change his expression?

Mrs. Peverill spoke to Andrew in a clear voice as though he were deaf. "My granddaughter is staying with us. She has not been well."

He nodded stupidly. At his age, he felt panicky at the thought of girls not being well.

While she spoke, the girl had come out of the hall into the winter garden. Jeremy jumped to his feet. At school he was well known for good manners and so Andrew copied him.

Mrs. Peverill said: "Rowena, you remember Jeremy."

Jeremy greeted her with his foppish skill.

"This is one of Jeremy's school friends."

The girl looked at Andrew without smiling. She was a large girl with a round face and dark hair plaited into two pigtails. Though she was two or three years older, she did not scare him. There was a sadness in her eyes that reminded you of the oppressed look you saw in boys at Chalgrove Park. Boys at school looked like this after the master in charge of the Navy set had twisted the short hairs in front of their ears. Even if this girl ended up despising him—a condition he was completely accustomed to—Andrew felt himself enlisted on her side.

The girl pulled down her tweed skirt and straightened together large feet in brown regulation school shoes.

"Did they send up Nurse Partridge's tea?" Mrs. Peverill asked.

"I think so."

"What does that mean?"

"Yes they did. They did. They did."

The old lady's face seemed to slam shut, like a box. A silence, long, resonant, and uncoiling, followed.

"Jeremy has come to fish in our lake," Major Peverill said.

"I hope they haven't caught anything," Rowena said quickly.

Andrew broke out. "Yes, we did. Four perch."

She gave him an angry intense look, which pleased him more than anything that had happened so far.

"Well, I think you're jolly cruel. Don't tell me anything about it."

Major Peverill put down a rock cake he was munching. "They're just mud fish. No one minds about mud fish. The gardener's boy used to catch them."

"I made the gardener's boy put them back," Rowena said. "Please promise you will, too."

"We usually put most of them back." He felt he had to be the spokesman for fishing. Jeremy was an uncertain ally: his politeness made him agree with people easily and talk lightly of things that were enormously important. The boys might be argued out of returning to the lake, because of danger or inconvenience, and the holidays would be spoiled, and the big pike would go on swimming there forever.

The girl, however, soon changed the subject. She told him about India, where she had been until two years ago and where her parents still lived. While he talked to her Andrew realized that, for him too, it would be easy to agree with everything she said, in part because he liked her, in part because she seemed hurt and ill at ease. The grandmother was watching them all the time, while eating a rock cake, bits of which fell down from her mouth. Jeremy and Major Peverill were having a conversation about cricket.

In the end the girl leaned over to Andrew and whispered: "Look, I've got to go now. Nothing about you. I hope to see you another time."

She stood up and the grandmother said: "Is anything the matter, Rowena?"

"No, nothing. I'm going, that's all." She pushed back her chair and it fell over.

"Try not to be clumsy, Rowena."

Major Peverill had also got to his feet. "I'll ring for Nurse Partridge," he said.

The girl stared at him, and then averted her gaze with contempt. She walked away between the palm trees, and then they could hear her footsteps breaking into a run across the tiled floor of the hall.

There was another ear-splitting silence. In the end, Jeremy stood up.

"I'm afraid we ought to go," he said. "It takes about three quarters of an hour to get home."

He went over and kissed the old lady's withered cheek. Andrew thanked her. She nodded to him but did not say anything.

"Give them one chocolate each," she said to her son. "Outside. I don't like the sound of chewing."

The boys went out into the hall. While they waited for Major Peverill they were watched by dozens of glittering eyes: the walls were lined with cases of stuffed seabirds, hovering on wires or squatting on papier-mâché rocks which the taxidermist had left unwhitened by droppings.

There turned out to be few chocolates remaining in the large ornate box. While Andrew's fingers searched among the crisp empty frills, the old man said to him: "I hope you were properly grateful to Mrs. Peverill. It's a great privilege for a boy like you, a great privilege."

"I did say thank you."

"You mustn't expect to come here frequently. There will be no question of that. Jeremy understands. It is different for him."

Andrew nodded. He was used to the absolute oddity of grown-ups. Major Peverill, however, didn't seem to be quite the same as a grown-up: he reminded you of an enormous boy from another school.

Major Peverill put his hand down hard on Andrew's shoulder, kneading it, and said in a scoffing voice: "You're very lucky to be at Chalgrove Park. It used to be one of the best private schools in the country."

"Yes, it is."

"Well, we had better just say it used to be. People of your parents' class must find it rather expensive."

Andrew quoted the words he had often heard spoken hushed and meaningly above his head. "I'm there on special terms."

The old man cackled mirthlessly. "Good God, he admits it. The little brat admits it."

When the boys had escaped into the open air, Andrew asked: "What did he mean by that?"

Jeremy kicked a stone across the drive. "Oh, he's bats. At least, everybody says he's bats. We'd better eat our chocolates."

Andrew examined his chocolate, which had a sort of greenish bloom on it. He bit a piece off it, and a taste of sour mold spread through his mouth. He spat it out and started retching. Jeremy was doing the same thing. They glanced at each other and suddenly burst into loud moans, and ended up butting each other, falling about on the grass and whooping with laughter.

When they were tired of doing this, they looked up. Major Peverill was standing behind the plate-glass front of the winter garden, so close to the glass that his nose made a pale circle against it.

"Ought we to go back and apologize?"

"No, let's go home. He doesn't matter."

While they were getting their bicycles, Andrew asked: "Is he Rowena's uncle?"

"Sort of. Not really. She's adopted. They were too old to have children when they were married."

"Who were?"

"Her parents. I mean, they weren't her parents. Mrs. Peverill's daughter. You know."

Andrew was uncertain that he did know, but guessed it was something that older people found embarrassing, like the prolonged absence of his own father and the continual presence at home of his mother's friend, Group-Captain Weare.

"How do you know about Rowena?"

"The nannies all talked about it at children's parties."

They were both embarrassed by this conversation. They found it rather awful to admit they had ever been younger than they now were. At school people blushed and lied when it was discovered that they had younger brothers or, much worse, sisters. No one knew what exacting god laid down such conditions. But his judgment could follow you, Andrew had discovered, even into dreams.

## III

He free-wheeled down through the village and over the bridge that crossed the dull little river he had fished in since he was ten. Beyond the railway crossing there was a huge advertisement: BOVRIL—PREVENTS THAT SINKING FEELING.

His home was not far from the railway station, a red-brick villa which had "Braeside" painted on the fanlight above the front door. The adjoining houses were called "Ambleside" and "Glen Lomond." All three of the houses had upright pianos in the front rooms, but his mother was the only qualified pianist there and in the summer when the windows were open he could always recognize her playing as he drew near the three houses. He could also tell what was happening from what was being played: the thumping scales and chords when she was giving a lesson, or the stumbling of one of her pupils through a party piece; her own playing of Chopin or Schumann, and the casades of jazz which meant that Group-Captain Weare had come on one of his visits.

His mother was full of random enthusiasms and intensities, about a new friend or a letter from an old one, or about her new novel from the library, which lay with its suede bookmark on the brass-topped Indian table in the sitting room. To Andrew she was gentle-skinned and warm, and smelt of sweetish cake crumbs. Recently, though, he had begun to practice looking at her as though he had no idea who she was. Then he saw a small plump woman with reddish-blonde hair and a soft complexion, a cigarette in the corner of her mouth, her rings parked on the side of the piano, playing with marked expression, the backs of the small plump hands arched, poised and pouncing at the notes of a piece by her favorite Billy Mayerl, which fell in tinselly cascades, while Godfrey Weare sat on the settee trying to hook a dottle out of his pipe.

When she was playing the piano, she could not hear the ticking sound of the bicycle as he wheeled it along the cinder path to the back of the house. In the shed at the back where he kept his things, there were also two trunks; not the tin ones, which his father had taken to Egypt, but a traveling trunk of his mother's, and an old round-topped one, which was locked. This contained, among other objects, the sea-fishing tackle they had bought to fish for pollack in Devon about four years ago.

He would ask his mother to open the trunk after supper. It was full of his father's belongings and they had a sort of malign aura about them. Whenever he remembered them, he got the sinking feeling in the Bovril advertisement, and he remembered the time when his mother's sweet, woeful voice told him that his father had gone on leave to Cyprus with a Greek lady. After that, he had heard her crying once or twice, when he was in a different room.

He took his fishing bag into the kitchen. You could hear the piano thumping away, just beyond the thin wall. He opened the fishing bag and let out a sharp exciting gust of wet rubber and fish slime. He took out his two fish and then turned the bag inside out and left it under a running tap. The two perch looked less interesting in death, the prickly fins folded down and the dark stripes fading. He got out a rusty kitchen knife and ripped them open from the vent upwards and pulled out their insides. There was no sinking feeling anymore as he did this, which proved you could train yourself to do anything, like becoming a vet or a medical student. He washed out the cleaned fish, rubbed salt into them and put them on a white plate in the larder; he would have them for breakfast tomorrow.

When his mother had stopped playing, he went through to the sitting room.

"There he is! How long have you been in? Come and kiss Mummy."

Godfrey Weare was in uniform, but kept a somewhat odd appearance. His jacket stuck out over his large behind, and his hair stuck out where it had been sorely clipped.

"Hullo, Andrew old man."

"Hullo." He had no way of addressing Godfrey Weare at all. If he had been obliged to shout to him in the street, he would have had to shout "I say."

"Did you catch anything? He's been on the Peverills' estate, Braxby Park."

"It's a super lake. I caught three perch and I gave one to Jeremy, who caught one. We met a man who said there was a giant pike in the lake." He decided it would be embarrassing to admit having tea up at the house.

At supper he asked: "Can I open the big trunk in the shed?"

His mother looked agitated. "What do you want to do that for? They're not your things."

He spoke with his mouth full. "Sea tackle. It'd do for pike."

His mother said: "I think we had better discuss this another time. Some more ham, Godfrey?"

"I need it. I need it after supper."

"That's enough." She was trembling, obviously, enraged at him.

Godfrey Weare caught his eye and winked. It was an attempt at ingratiation; Andrew despised him for doing this when he could have no idea what the dispute was about.

## IV

On the second day, they caught nothing at all. The weather had grown much warmer; dragonflies hovered and made sudden turns above the water lilies. Halfway through the afternoon, Jeremy announced that he was returning home early because he had relations coming to tea. Andrew felt let down; he wondered if this excuse were true, or whether it marked the beginning of a desertion. He decided to stay on alone.

He fished with the lighter of his two rods off the jetty. The lake water was dark, reflecting the massed green leaves of summer. He watched two dragonflies in a mating dance settle on his float.

Then, among all the other sounds, he heard a long way off something approaching through the undergrowth: there was a crash of heavy footsteps, followed by sharp breathing. He wondered whether to hide and watch, but decided to hold his ground as the footsteps drew nearer, crashing on dry foliage and twigs.

The girl came out on to the path by the jetty. She was dark in the face, and there were bits of greenery stuck to her long plaits.

"I took a shortcut. I thought I wasn't going to make it."

"Are you running away?" he asked.

This seemed to him a feasible form of activity. From some boarding schools people did it all the time, though rarely from Chalgrove Park, which had a high reputation.

"No, not really. I just had to get away from them for a bit. Gosh, I'm thirsty. Have you got anything to drink? I could drink the lake."

"I've got some Tizer."

He fished out the bottle and undid it. She drank straight from the bottle without wiping it, and this impressed him a good deal. He noticed she was wearing the same blouse and herringbone tweed skirt as the first time they had met. He thought it was odd to wear school clothes in the summer holidays, especially for a girl.

She handed back the bottle. "That was fine. Where's Jeremy got to?"

"He had to go back. His aunts were coming to tea." He blushed. "I suppose I shouldn't be here alone, actually."

"Don't worry. Nobody ever comes here." She inspected him in silence for a moment. He thought she was going to attack him for fishing, which she had seemed to disapprove of. Instead she asked him: "Were you shy up at the house the other day?"

"Not really."

"You looked shy. You looked as though you'd never been anywhere like that before, or met anybody like them." He turned away to pull in his line and examine the bait. Nothing had touched it yet.

"Uncle Maurice is a bit peculiar. Did you notice?"

"Well, I suppose so."

"Suppose so? You don't know much, do you?"

He was silent, not knowing whether to like her or to hate her. The pigtails certainly fascinated him; they were secured at the ends with twisted rubber bands, and had been so tightly plaited that bits of hair seemed to have broken under protest. She tossed them around her shoulders with confidence, but somehow this seemed the only thing she was confident about. Liking her completely would be like succumbing to a bully at school—one of those bullies who tried to frighten you because they themselves were frightened. Outram, for instance, a big bland boy with smooth, almost concave, knees. Rowena had a distinct look of Outram.

"My grandmother's terribly rich, did you know?"

"No, I didn't."

"Well, she is. That's why she thinks she's perfect. Lots of rich old women get like that, you know. Even if their husbands leave them or shoot themselves in the gunroom or die of drink, they go on thinking themselves perfect. She's like that."

He did not know what to make of this, except to think that she must have heard it from somebody grown-up.

Quite close by, a musical voice shouted: "Cooee! Cooee!"

"Don't worry. It's only Nurse Partridge. I ran away from her."

"Why do you have to have a nurse?"

"She's been here since I got ill at school. She's Australian. My parents employ her," she added with some grandeur. "They can afford it, you see."

Without turning his head, he began to watch the girl cautiously. He had hoped to be alone when Jeremy left, and here she was extremely close to him, with her large tweed behind planted on the bank beside him and her regulation shoes staring at him with the bright eyeholes of the laces. She was as close as Outram was when he sneaked up behind you and pinched the chilblains on your ears with stamp tweezers. Andrew imagined pulling her pigtails until she would weaken and cry out and honor him.

"Cooee!"

The nurse's voice, raised in forced cheerfulness, re-echoed among the sandstone rocks: if she came any nearer, there was risk of frightening the fish. A silence followed. The nurse must have been approaching along one of the paths that twisted downhill through the rhododendrons.

"I'd better go," Rowena said. "Will you come here again?"

"I'd like to come every day but it depends on Jeremy."

"Honestly, no one ever comes down here. You can get in without going near the house. There's a gap in the wall on the main road. See you tomorrow, then."

## V

He was surprised that he missed her when she had gone. It was as though nothing would be quite as exciting and interesting as before. Then he saw that his float had moved a long way over towards the water lilies. He pulled in the line and found a small roach deeply hooked. He did not unhook it, but left it swimming in the clear water under the jetty. Back on the bank, he drew his father's sea rod out of its canvas case.

Dusk was approaching and small fish began to flip through the black surface of the lake. Andrew felt gloomy and guilty and treacherous at what he was doing. Yesterday he had stood by while his mother had unlocked the big trunk. There was a strong smell of mothballs and pipe tobacco. His father's remaining possessions included a winter overcoat, a porkpie hat with a salmon fly in it, a pair of brogues, some sports jackets and gray flannel bags. When she saw them, his mother made a little sharp sobbing noise, as though she had cut her finger. She pointed to three tin boxes at one end of the trunk.

"Those are the things you want, aren't they? Hurry up and get them out."

His mother held her face averted. When he had collected the boxes, she smoothed out the clothes again and slammed the lid of the trunk shut. He wanted to comfort her but she pulled herself away.

"No, don't touch me. You've no idea of what you're making me do."

He had an apprehensive feeling as he thought of the world of childhood closeness dying out, of there being nobody he could touch anymore. He already knew that he was physically unattractive, because people didn't much like him leaning on them at school. The naval master, who would often tickle Jeremy Cathcart to the verge of asphyxiation, usually pushed Andrew away. But his mother's coldness would be temporary; she was too changeable and excitable to stay in one mood for long. She would get up from the piano and dance him around the room, saying: "You haven't a spark of rhythm in your body. Watch me." He would trample on her feet and they'd collapse on the settee together, weak with laughter, until she'd suddenly stare closely at his face and say: "Why are you so ugly? I can't imagine where you came from."

He threaded the flax line through the four white porcelain rings on the sea rod, and knotted on the weighted wire trace with a single triangle hook. Then he pulled out the roach, unhooked it and laid it on the still-warm boards of the jetty. He slipped one barbed point of the triangle under the back fin and felt the slight crunch of the hook entering living flesh. The little fish wriggled and then lay still gasping, trying to recover. He let it swim around in the water and it seemed to accept its fate.

He pulled several yards of line off the reel and let them fall at his feet. Then he cast out, releasing the line as the live bait swung out in front of him, so that it hit the black water about fifteen yards out. The slack line whipped through into the fading rings of water until none of it was left and the reel began ticking, faster and faster. He was not sure what was happening, except that he could see the line cutting through the surface towards the water lilies and knew he had stop it. He put his hand on the reel and it was like having the whole lake moving. The reel jerked down and he held on in panic. The line snapped and sprang back in a tangle.

A great wave of loss rose up and hit him. He dropped the rod, and back on the bank he threw himself down with his hands on his crotch, moaning and jeering at himself and shouting all the bad words he knew.

It took him about five minutes to recover. He had no more live bait or tackle, it was growing dark and he knew he would have to go home. But he kept staring at the lake, the reed beds and the water lilies, as though by force of will he could bring the big pike out of the water. He packed up the rods and put the bag over his shoulder. Then, as he looked once more at the lake, a gray shape on the bank, which his eyes must have raced across again and again, turned into the figure of a man standing quite still, watching him.

His insides leaped upwards. Fear was confused with the sense that he had been watched making a fool of himself.

"Boy! Boy!" the figure called out to him. "Come here! Don't be frightened."

Andrew was already on the cart track that led up through the woods. He ran without stopping until he arrived at the bicycle in the stable yard. For the first time he looked back: nobody was following him.

He strapped the two rods to the bar of the bicycle. He was able to free-wheel most of the way down the long drive; between the big gate posts he stopped to look at his watch, which showed eight o'clock. He had promised to be home by half past six. He switched on the bicycle lamp, which threw an uneasy circle of light on the cow parsley at the road's edge, and seemed to make the surrounding darkness darker. When he set off, two cars approached him from behind: he thought he was being followed, but the cars roared off down the long straight road. Each time they passed his shadow leaped out and staggered down the long wall of the Braxby estate. By the lights from the second car, he saw the gap in the wall which Rowena had told him about. It had been roughly blocked off with a stack of dead thornbushes, but you could get through these fairly easily. Obviously the girl could be trusted about things like that.

A third car was slow in passing. It seemed to pause about thirty yards behind him. When he turned to look at it he got the full glare of the headlights in his eyes. Somehow he convinced himself that this time he was being pursued by the man, whoever he was, who had been watching by the lake. He pedaled as hard as he could but the road began to go uphill and he sensed the car drawing nearer until it was beside him.

Then suddenly, his mother's voice was shouting: "Stop at once, you little fool."

He recognized the car as Group-Captain Weare's Sunbeam. He swiveled the bicycle around so that the lamp shone in the car window at his mother's white furious face and Godfrey Weare's, concerned and keen. The moment he saw them he knew that no excuses would be worth making. For his own self-respect he had to sulk and say nothing.

His mother got out and stood beside him. "Get in," she said.

"What about the bike?"

There was a cottage not far off on the other side of the road. His mother wheeled the bicycle toward it. Andrew sat on the bench seat next to Group-Captain Weare, who fiddled around with his pipe and tobacco pouch. They were silent; his mother would be giving them the clue to how the scene was to be carried out.

"I told them one of us would fetch it tomorrow." She got in beside Andrew and when he brushed against her, she shrank away. "Don't touch me," she said. "You've upset me very much."

He moved closer to Godfrey Weare's massive gray-flannel thigh. Neither of them was likely to speak while his mother was in a bad temper.

However, she could not be silent for long. After about a mile she said: "I rang up Mrs. Carthcart and she told me Jeremy had been back since four o'clock. I felt such a fool."

They were approaching the village when she said: "She was most unfriendly, I thought." While they were getting out of the car, she took his arm: "I don't know why you want to chum up with that boy. They're a lot of snobs if you ask me."

He pulled himself away, although his heart sank with pity for her and her obtuseness. How could she know that he had to proceed with immense caution in order to have any friends at all? People at school were pretty good at estimating just how much you were worth in the popularity stakes. The fact that Jeremy lived nearby had been a piece of God-given good luck.

He refused anything to eat and went up to his bedroom.

After a time his mother started to play the piano, and later the wireless was switched on to dance music from Radio Luxembourg. He heard the Sunbeam drive off at about ten o'clock. He felt starved, but going downstairs would be a defeat, and his mother knew very well how to turn honorable defeat into abject surrender. He lay back determined to punish himself and her by keeping awake as long as he could.

He hoped his mother's telephone call hadn't spoiled things between him and Jeremy. Even though the girl had told him about the gap in the wall, he still needed Jeremy's help in getting the key to the boat. If you hooked the pike from the shore, it would always head straight for the water lilies and break the line; with the boat there was a chance of keeping it out in the open water. Jeremy had as good as promised to get hold of the key.

When the last train had gone through, the village was quiet. Beyond it, the sleeping fields stretched out towards Braxby Park, five miles away, a place cut off from the rest of the world. When he thought of it, he imagined a special darkness in the air overhead, like a sepia photograph. At the bottom of the lake the great pike lay with the hook stinging in its jaw; it had to keep fanning its pectoral fins, otherwise it would rise slowly upward through the water. Up at the house, the girl was fast asleep; perhaps the Australian nurse had administered some broken-up pill, so that Rowena slept with her mouth open, her plump arms outside the white sheets. When he thought about her, he knew he was frightened of her and that he enjoyed his fear. But now she was a captive, guarded by the nurse, the peculiar uncle, and the hard old lady. Who was the man at nightfall at the edge of the lake? He might have been a keeper, or the gardener, or the butler from the house. By the time Andrew had got around to this, the evidence of dreams indicated that the man was Godfrey Weare, and the girl and his mother kept changing identities, and he himself was running through the rhododendrons from the unseen Australian nurse, so that he wet himself and people stared at him and told him he was completely impossible.

## VI

Each taking one oar, they rowed out toward the open water. The sun was already high up, shining blurred through the treetops, and it would soon enter the empty patch of sky above the lake. Andrew knew that they had arrived too late and the expedition would probably fail. He had planned for today with passion but had forgotten to cross his fingers.

After the previous day at the lake, he had fallen asleep in his clothes. He woke early and changed into pajamas before his mother called him. She was still angry with him, but three children were arriving for piano lessons and she could not give him much attention.

The first part of his plan involved getting some money. A small girl was thumping out scales in the front room, and he saw his mother's handbag on a table in the narrow hallway. Almost without touching it, he fished out a ten shilling note. It was the first time he had ever done this, and he found that the action disturbed him a good deal. Probably his mother would have given him extra pocket money if he had asked for it: he stole from her because he wanted to be able not to love her.

He spent the ten shilling note on wire traces and triangle

hooks at the village tobacconist's shop. In the afternoon he went to collect the bicycle from the cottage near Braxby Park and later he fished for gudgeon in the stream near the village. He caught eight of them. Two were stiff and white next morning but the rest, for live bait, were now in a paint tin at the bottom of the boat.

They shipped the oars. There was no anchor but the boat stayed, held in the water lilies by the open water. It was Jeremy's fault that they had arrived so late. He had refused to come out until the middle of the morning; he had needed a good deal of persuasion before he would ask the butler for the key to the boathouse. Then he had pretended to be unable to unlock the iron gate at the top of the steps. Now the rods were out and nothing was happening. While they sat looking at the rays of sunlight fanning down into the deep water or watched the wood pigeons rocketing across the sky, Andrew could feel Jeremy getting bored again. It was like a weakening fever, he felt it infecting himself and breaking down his own will.

"Cooee! Cooee!"

This time it was the girl herself, who must have adopted from her nurse this Antipodean call sign. She was standing on the jetty on the other side of the lake, her pale face and blouse shining out against the shadow of the trees. They waved to her, hoping she would go away.

"Give me a ride."

"No, we can't. We're fishing."

"Come on, do. Please."

"You'll scare the fish," Andrew called.

"You'll sink the boat," Jeremy said. "You're too fat," he added more quietly.

"What was that?"

They both giggled, and whispered together: "Too fat, too fat."

"Please take me."

"No." Inside himself, Andrew was already twisted with shame and sorrow and ready to surrender. With Jeremy there, however, it was easy to fall back into shared silliness.

"I think you're both beastly," Rowena said. Then the tall navy-blue shape of the nurse appeared beside her. Some sort of heated discussion followed, which ended with both of them walking off together under the beech trees.

After the girl had gone, the boys avoided looking at each other for some time. Andrew felt saddened. Everything about her, even the ugly plaits and the fawn stockings which wrinkled over her round knees, struck him with a guilty and pleasurable melancholy, like singing "The Day Thou Gavest" at Sunday evening service.

A little later there was a splash near the boat, and a ginger-pop bottle surfaced among the weeds.

"That was a bloody silly thing to do."

"Wa-wa. Why don't you cry about it?" Jeremy wriggled around to face him. "Who are you to go about giving the orders, that's what I'd like to know."

He picked up one of the oars and slapped it up and down on the surface of the water. The sounds echoed from the rocks and startled a flight of pigeons.

"Why did you do that?"

Jeremy mumbled something under his breath.

"I didn't hear. Why did you do that?"

"Because you stink, that's why."

Andrew began to reel in his line. Jeremy had got into a terrific rage: obviously the girl's presence and the way they had both reacted to it had made him feel guilty and angry too.

"Why don't you just admit you stink and be done with it?"

"I don't."

"Of course you stink, it's famous. You fart worse than anyone else in Lower Changing Room. Only last term I heard someone say "I'm not going in there because that oik's farted."

"Let's go back."

"I'll say whether we go back or not, you little oik. This boat belongs to my friends, doesn't it? You haven't got any friends."

Andrew began to untwist the ferrules of his rod. His eyes were getting hot and blurred.

"You haven't got any friends because you are an oik. You live in a house in a row. Your mother's as common as muck. You remember when she rang us up the other day at home? Well, we all thought it must be one of the servants' friends."

By the conventions of Chalgrove Park, Jeremy's attack had gone through three stages. You could tell people they stank and be easily forgiven: it was a matter of style. Even being an oik could still be considered a temporary matter, arising out of one particular piece of behavior. But to attack somebody's "people" to his face was to break a tabu. Jeremy did it so that they would never be able to speak to each other again.

A few moments later they realized that this created difficulties. They were in the middle of the lake, aware to their fingertips of the black depth of water underneath them, and the hundred yards which lay between them and the boathouse.

Without speaking they rowed with quick, light strokes, shaking off the lily stems, and glided in under the rock. Together they slid the boat on to dry land. There were five live bait remaining. Andrew sank the tin in shallow water, which could enter the holes pierced in the lid. Jeremy had hurried ahead and did not see him do this. As he had done earlier, Jeremy found the lock too stiff to move; he handed Andrew the key again. Andrew stood in front of the iron gate and turned the key, but made sure that it did not click shut. He jammed a stone under the gate: it would appear to be locked but he could always get in when he wanted.

At the front of the house, Jeremy waited to return the key to the butler.

Andrew lingered for a little, and then called "Good-bye," when it seemed unlikely that the other could hear him. It was strange to be alone, bicycling home in the empty middle of the afternoon, as though he was entering on a newer harsher period of his life. Next term when he and Jeremy met at Chalgrove Park, they would not speak to each other anymore. This would not cause any problems, because they had always belonged to different gangs; in any case, the unwritten laws compelled a certain shame about knowing each other in the holidays.

Finding the front door of "Braeside" closed on the chain, he pushed it open as far as he could and shouted.

After some minutes, his mother came downstairs in her dressing-gown. "I wondered who on earth it was. I was resting. I thought you said you'd be out all day."

"It was no good. Too hot."

She opened the door in silence.

Trying to please her, he said: "I had a row with Jeremy Cathcart."

She did not respond to this but turned away, pulling the dressing-gown more tightly around her.

"Is there anything to eat?"

"Take some biscuits. You ought to be out in the open air."

"All right, I'm going. You won't catch me staying around this dump."

This remark, too, had no visible effect on her. He took a handful of gingersnaps from the kitchen. Her unusual silence retained him for a moment. Then he shuffled off, kicking a stone along down the path in front of him. But the silence persisted until he heard her close the door again.

He crossed the main road by the Bovril advertisement, and walked uphill until he reached the Recreation Ground. Stuck in the middle of the country, it was an odd, townish place with its park seats, sandpit and swings, and a cricket pavilion of dark-green corrugated iron. Everything here seemed much-handled and grimy, and Woodbine packets and sweet papers were trodden into the earth.

Some boys were playing cricket in the middle of the field. He sat on a bench and watched them while he ate the gingersnaps. On three sides of the Recreation Ground there were rows of young pine trees. The fourth side overlooked the village and the railway station. Four cars were parked in front of the station, one of them a Sunbeam, the same color as Godfrey Weare's. But it couldn't be Godfrey Weare's; why should he travel anywhere by train? With a telescope, he would be able to focus on the number plate and be sure.

A little later, though, he saw Godfrey Weare coming across the road near the Bovril advertisement, could not mistake the penguin walk, the large behind, and the bouncing cock's tail of hair. Godfrey Weare got into the Sunbeam. He reversed, went forward to pause by the main road, and then he drove across the level crossing toward London.

## VII

The pike was firmly hooked and it fought strongly. He could glimpse it down below, a dull gold bar flashing in the deep water. Then, apparently surrendering, it rose slowly upward, but when its long head broke the surface it shook with new violence, knocking against the side of the boat. The broad tail fin twisted out, thrashing the water with a noise that echoed across the lake.

He dropped the tip of the rod, and the fish lay captive alongside the boat, with the back fin just out of the water. It was not really large, probably about four pounds, and he had already decided to let it go. If you fished alone, you caught more but there was nobody to witness the result. At home his mother seemed too distracted to pretend any interest.

Nevertheless, he watched the fish with triumph and pleasure. He looked at his watch: it was half past eight in the morning. The sun had not yet risen above the trees and the water was black and dead-looking. He willed himself to remember this moment, its surroundings, and what he was feeling. Whatever lay ahead, like school examinations, he hoped such feelings would continue, although, whenever you looked at adults, it seemed unlikely that they should. He leaned over the side of the boat and the pike turned over showing one flat furious eye. He hauled it into the boat and stuck a piece of wood into its mouth. Talking to it, he tried to get the hook free past the rows of tiny teeth. The hook finally yielded and came out dragging a large piece of living gristle. Appalled by what he had done he heaved the fish back into the water. It sank and then surfaced again, lying on its side. It flapped for a time, righted itself and disappeared. At least he had tried to save it; perhaps it would survive after all.

He was covered with fish slime and he longed to pee. He had observed his bearings from the trees on the shore, and so he rowed without looking back until he saw the rock walls on either side of him. The boat gritted on the floor of the cave.

He jumped out and collided with a buttoned, tweed-covered mass, smelling of tobacco, that felt like an old armchair. In the reflected light from the water, he could just make out the face with the startled permanent grin, like a pike's.

Andrew put down his head and tried to get past to the steps that led to the open air.

Major Peverill put out large wrinkled hands to stop him. "Where are you off to? There's no hurry."

"I must go out. I—I want to be excused."

"What does that mean? Oh, I understand." The old man laughed. "You can do it here. We are all men here."

There was a long pause while Andrew faced the wall. Outside the sun had begun to strike the lake water. He wondered what had happened to the pike he had caught, and whether it would die.

"Well, aren't you going to?"

"I can't," he admitted. He buttoned up and turned around again.

"Where's the other boy?"

"He didn't—want to come today."

"So you're alone?" The old man observed him with a livelier interest. "The brat's alone. Do you mind me calling you 'brat'?"

Andrew stood on one leg and then the other. The immediate urgency seemed to have gone, but he was contorted with something which was like shyness but much stronger.

"After all, why shouldn't I call you 'brat'? You are a brat, aren't you? Come here."

"No, I don't want to."

"You don't know what you want, at your age. You have to be shown. How old are you, brat?"

"Twelve and three quarters." Andrew went quiet and respectful; Chalgrove Park had trained him to behave like this unthinkingly in front of adults. "Excuse me, I'll just get my things."

He took his rod and fishing bag out of the boat. He went in front up the steps, while the old man's fingers pinched his backside and tried to get up his shorts. When he reached the last step, he ran as hard as he could.

"Come here, damn you. Here."

Out of breath at the top of the slope, Andrew looked down through a gap in the rhododendrons. He saw Major Peverill standing there, calling for him like a dog. He was so accustomed to obeying schoolmasters that he still felt he was in some way breaking the rules by not going down again. Now, too, he noticed a droop of sadness and frustration about the old man which made him obscurely sorry.

He returned home to hear his mother giving a piano lesson.

She had reached the point in the proceedings when she would firmly displace the pupil from the stool and take over, letting loose a stampede of chords, arpeggios, and glissandi, twisting around, showing her teeth and saying "Lovely thing, isn't it?" All of this he took for showing-off and it embarrassed him deeply. Even the noise of it made him cringe going past the window. In the kitchen he poured out a big glass of orange Kia-Ora, which he took upstairs to his bedroom, together with one of his mother's library books, which he had just started to read.

He heard the front door open and close. His mother came upstairs and stood in his bedroom doorway, with an airy and mysterious look about her.

"Isn't that book too old for you?"

"No, it isn't. I like it."

"You'll tire your eyes." She turned over his hairbrush and dug his comb deeply into it. "What are you going to do with yourself all afternoon? Godfrey wants me to go out with him."

"Read. Can I have a bath? I stink of fish."

His mother affected an expression of amused tolerance. She went back dowstairs, where he heard her singing as she drifted from room to room.

The geyser flared up and subsided to a steady flame. In the bath, hot water pounded on to rusty stains where the taps had been weeping. When he came back from undressing, the bathroom window had steamed up. Wiping a patch clear, he looked out at the bright noon light over the neighboring gardens, yellow and green privet hedge and creosoted sheds. On one of the sheds a wooden airplane was spinning in a light breeze.

He waited till the bath was nearly full, before turning off the taps. While he looked at himself in the mirror his fingers explored the silky hair which had started growing in a line just above his cock. Now, with a pair of nail scissors, he trimmed the hairs off neatly, so that that part was quite bare again, as it had been a few weeks ago.

## VIII

For some time he did not visit Braxby Park, except when he dreamed about it at night, and then it appeared as though he hardly ever left it. In dreams there were several ways of arriving there. Once or twice it was through his preparatory school: toward the end of the holidays his dream life usually attempted to make bridges between the opposing worlds, and his school dream was of drifting without will from the bare classrooms and dormitories, along the corridors, through the swing doors into the Headmaster's part of the house. There, in carpeted rooms lit by roaring log fires, the Headmaster's wife would discover him and expel him with ignominy. Sometimes now, however, the school corridors led directly into Braxby Park, and he met Rowena, who told him: "We thought you would keep away and not cause trouble. No wonder we are disappointed."

But on other occasions it was through unvisited rooms upstairs at "Braeside." Once he had found them (you knew these rooms existed but somehow they escaped your memory) the lake and the jetty were easily visible from the windows. Later, though, he was running down the paths between the rhododendrons and, although Braxby Park was behind him, there was some bias in his footsteps which pulled him back to the front door where Major Peverill was waiting. He awoke full of of apprehension from these encounters, blinking their persistent sad twilight out of his eyes, which seemed unaccustomed to the ordinary light of morning.

On the last evening of the holidays, he was back at the lake with his fishing tackle. As he had expected, the boathouse was securely locked again; he followed the path around until he reached the jetty. Now, in September, the shadows were already long, and some of the trees had golden reflections in the still water.

He took a long time assembling his rods, paying elaborate attention to each knot, in order to avoid tomorrow in his thoughts.

His mother had told him that Godfrey Weare had very kindly offered to take him back to Chalgrove Park in the Sunbeam. It would mean leaving him at school a good deal earlier than usual, because Godfrey Weare and his mother would be driving on to Brighton, to dine together and see a show. She couldn't realize the sharp twinge she caused by announcing jolly plans for the time when he would be out of the way.

In some ways he was surprised to find himself here this evening, nearly a month after his last visit. In the village street he had run into Jeremy, returned from Ireland: with a single instinct they had cut each other dead. Then this morning he had discovered three frogs in some long grass at the end of the garden. He had read Izaak Walton's *Compleat Angler* and he remembered the instruction for using them as live bait: "Use him as though you love him, that he may live the longer." A frog would not only live longer but swim out into the clear water. Suddenly his passion was aroused all over again. Nevertheless, he was almost sure that this was the last time he would come here. The future was getting fuller and fuller of other things; part of his childhood was being crowded out, not because he wanted to let it go, but because there was nobody to share it with.

In spite of Izaak Walton, he had found the business of hooking on the frog rather appalling: you needed somebody else at hand to encourage you to do such things. He hoped to catch a small fish for live bait on the lighter of the two rods. By the time everything was ready, moths were starting to flutter clumsily and rooks were going home across the pale sky. His two floats lay far out on the pale water, the smaller one motionless, the larger one trembling, agitated by the desperately swimming frog.

Later, he heard footsteps approaching. He thought it better to disappear, in case it was Major Peverill. He climbed to the top of the rocks nearby and, hidden by a holly tree, looked down. It was the girl.

This time she was wearing a flowered dress, a shapeless effort with smocking and puffed sleeves. It was accompanied by the same crinkled stockings and sturdy shoes. The great difference was the hair, no longer in plaits but flowing loose on to her shoulders. It still framed her face but in a way that made it less round and doll-like. He scrambled down the slope toward her.

"I thought these must be your things. What's been happening to you?"

"Oh, I've been very busy," he said.

She laughed, as though he was too young to be eligible for this word. "When Uncle Maurice said he had found you down here, I came back several times."

"I'm sorry."

"In the end, I guessed that he had probably frightened you and you wouldn't come back. 'The poor boy's frightened,' I thought."

He blushed so hard his face was ready to explode. She was teasing him but, now that the pigtails had gone, you couldn't really tell what she mightn't know.

Now she went to the end of the jetty, pushing her hair back behind her ears and posing in profile against the water.

"It's nice that you've come back," she said.

"This is the last time."

"Why's that?"

"Because I've got to go back to school tomorrow."

"Have you caught the big fish yet?"

"Not yet." He felt embarrassed by something which two months ago had been the most important thing in the world.

"Not yet!"

She laughed. All at once, she pulled her long hair in a curtain over her eyes and, staring through it with a funny spooky face, she turned on him, waving her arms with the hands ready for clutching. He nearly fell off the jetty.

"Nervous, aren't you?"

To get a bit of his own back, he asked: "Where's that Australian person?"

Rowena stroked her hair into place behind her ears, and looked remote. "Oh, she left. Ages ago, actually. I'm going to school in Switzerland after Christmas."

While they were talking he had forgotten to keep watch on his two floats. The smaller one was still there, but the other had vanished. He picked up the sea rod and pulled hard. The float jerked back from where the water lilies had hidden it. He reeled the line in, and prepared to cast again.

"You've caught a little frog. Look, it's wriggling."

He tried not to let this display of female ignorance put him off his stroke. He cast out smoothly towards the middle of the lake.

"Didn't you see it?" she asked him in wonder.

"That was the bait. When you're fishing for pike, live frogs are good bait."

She stared as though she could not believe him. "But that's horrible. It must hurt it dreadfully. Do you know what you are? You're a sadist."

"What's that mean?"

"If you don't know, I'm certainly not going to tell you. Poor, poor little thing."

"They don't feel like we do."

"You little beast. You mean *you* don't feel."

He laughed. "No, they don't really."

He watched her doubtfully. No boy would ever make a fuss like this: at Chalgrove Park you could easily collect a crowd by burning a worm or an insect with a magnifying glass. He was quite shocked to see that she was crying in earnest.

"They all said you were horrible. They were quite right."

"Who said?"

Rowena did not answer, but turned around and fled, large and splay-footed, into the darkening woods.

"Who said? Tell me," he called after her.

He followed her to a point where the path forked, and the rhododendrons were too tall to allow him to see which way she had taken. Her tears had scattered his wits completely. Returning, still thinking about her last statement and not looking where he went, he tripped headlong over an elbow of tree-root sticking out of the path.

With the skin grazed off both his knees, he limped back to the jetty. There, a curious noise hung in the air. He could not identify it until he noticed that the big rod had fallen over and the noise came from the ratchet of the reel as the line was being dragged off it.

He grabbed the rod and held on. Whatever had seized the bait was now in the middle of the lake, fighting deep down. Though he was still sniveling with pain, the usual mixture of rage and glee took hold of him. Each time he started regaining some line, the fish headed off again, and he knew it must be deeply hooked because its strength was fighting directly against his own. This made him sure that it was the same pike he had hooked on the day Jeremy had gone home early.

After about ten minutes his arms began to ache. Hot water ran down his leg, though he hadn't felt himself peeing, and made the scraped knee sting. His eyes stung too, and he wiped the back of his hand against them. He couldn't see any better because it was getting dark, although a piece of the setting sun was still visible through the trees on the opposite shore.

By now he knew the battle was going his way: the fish had tired itself fighting out there in the open, and each failing effort gave him a little more slack line, so that he could steer it nearer the water lilies around the jetty. Suddenly he saw the rounded back fin, the one near the tail, break the surface: it was like a dark sail against the luminous water.

All his dreams came to a quiet conclusion as the pike slid gently towards him. To keep it from tangling among the lilies, he held the rod as high as he could. This brought the great head out of the water, the body looped and thrashed wildly, but the hook held. Gradually he eased the pike alongside the jetty, like a liner coming into dock, and into the shallow water. He dropped the rod and plunged in on top of the fish and manhandled it on to the bank. In the wild stink of mud and marsh gas it lay there, huge and terrible to him. While he watched it, a mounting sense of triumph began to break through all the webs of disbelief.

To stop the line from tangling, he cut the knot above the wire trace. The pike gave a number of violent heaves, and its scales became covered with dry leaves and earth. The two eyes that glared from the corners of the head belonged now to a monster of the woods more than the water. In the twilight, Andrew lay on the ground and worshipped it.

For a time, the only noise seemed to be of the blood pounding in his ears. This turned into the murmur of voices, not far off. He had just time to heave the big pike down the bank. By the faint shine that still came from the lake, he could see it indignantly right itself and then the furious swirl with which it regained the deep water.

When he had clambered once more on to the top of his rock, he was aware of several people approaching down the path between the rhododendrons. They carried electric torches, and soon you could see the long cylinders of light shifting to and fro, stopped by tree trunks and then reaching out again among the shadows.

He heard Major Peverill's voice, high-pitched like a well-bred sneeze. "The poor girl got back to the house in a terrible state."

Other voices answered, in the lower tones of country people accustomed to agreement.

"He should not have been allowed to come here in the first place." By now Major Peverill was standing about directly below. "It was a misunderstanding, which must be put right without more ado."

There was complete darkness under the holly tree on the rock. Andrew kept his head down, in case a beam of torchlight should sweep across to show his face as a pale patch among the bristling leaves. If you hated people enough, he thought, you could hold out as long as they could. In a short while they would find his gear lying where he had left it by the lake. It would hardly make much difference; they knew he was still here, but it was improbable that they would ever find him.

Soon after this, though, he saw other, different torches flash out on the far side of the lake. He heard his mother calling, and knew he would have to surrender.